Laura Navarre

Gemini Hunted

***My enemies say I'm the witching world's
most vicious and violent queen.
I say I'm the most hunted.***

A lethal new queen killer I can't see stalking me.

A seductive new ally I can never trust.

A wicked new twist in the diabolical Academy Dean's Challenge my warlock harem and I never saw coming.

I might be the celebrity bad girl and royal wild child of the whole witching world. A little unstable. A lot reckless. Supposedly a bit psychotic.

But I'm just a freshman at the dark witch academy, with a scary compendium of deadly new powers I can't control and irresistible superheats I can't suppress.

I never asked to be the rebel queen.

Or the final hope of the witching world resistance.

But I'll save the witching races before we all go extinct.

Or I'll die trying.

Gemini Hunted is a queer-friendly dark witch adult academy paranormal romance and the spicy sequel to *Gemini Wicked*. This fully completed series delivers a broody wolf shifter headmaster, a possessive alpha dragon shifter, a spicy-pretty punk rock warlock, a twisted Dark Fae King and his hunky bi boyfriend, one horribly moody demon, all swords crossed, and a confident queen who never needs to choose.

Chapter One
Zara

The shark comes at me out of nowhere.

Minutes ago, I was somersaulting backward off the *Filibuster*'s gunwale, with my dive mask and regulator held to my face so the choppy wind-whipped surf off Icarus Island wouldn't knock my mask loose or my mouthpiece off.

Despite the danger of this stunt we're about to pull, I was even enjoying the tropical warmth of the Med. I mean, the water's warm in comparison to the gale-force winds that buffeted our bodies in the dinghy.

Of course, we'd need to do this dive on the edge of the worst tropical cyclone this ocean has seen in decades.

Encased in a black wetsuit, Ronin's powerful frame knifed into the churn beside me, sleek and deadly as a barracuda, dark ponytail streaming in his wake. Holding his own mask in place with one hand and gripping his speargun with the other. Barely lit by the little lantern in the *Filibuster*'s prow, I curled my arms overhead in the diver's universal signal to the pilot to give the *all clear*.

As the rubber dinghy motored away under Neo's careful steer through the boulder-strewn surf, I ducked under the wavetops, switched on my flashlight to get my dive buddy and me both oriented, and used the fins strapped on my feet to propel myself deeper.

Ronin swam at my side, speargun tucked close to his streamlined body. Guarding my ass the same way he guards my heart.

For better or worse, all our words have been said.

Back on the yacht a nautical mile out, we left Vasili and Zephyr practically at each other's throats.

And not in a good way. (They're warlocks, not vampires.)

Ronin and me?

We agreed to get under this tropical storm, like, ASAP. Top priority. Under the violent churn of this storm-tossed sea, our prize is waiting.

God knows, these powerful currents haven't been making this deadly contest any easier. I'm a strong swimmer and a hella experienced diver. But this is red flag weather—and then some.

Plus I'm tiny.

These waves have been throwing around my little body, hindered by my gear and the heavy cylinder of compressed air strapped to my back. Making me bob along the dangerous tides that swirl around the rocky cliffs of Icarus Island at midnight like a buoy busted free from my anchor.

Until a whiplash of vicious undertow ripped Ronin from my side. In a blink, his powerful body was gone. Vanished.

I swept the beam of my flashlight through the inky depths and reached through our telepathic bond.

Ronin! You okay?

After an alarming silence, his reply bounced back like a sonar ping.

No worries, love. I've got this. Meet you in the grotto, yeah? Current's headed straight for it.

The worst of my tension eased its grip. Ronin's solid in the water, trained and certified in the choppy surf of the Irish Sea. Plus he's more than my dive buddy.

So I trust him.

Same way he trusts me.

Besides, it's not like we have a choice. That big fat zero currently sitting on our team's scoreboard for our witch academy finals isn't gonna correct itself.

Roger that, I shot back. *Stick to the plan—and watch yourself till I get there, for real. See you at the grotto.*

I thumbed the button to bleed air from the inflatable BCD zipped around my torso, shedding buoyancy and swimming deeper, looking to hitch a ride on the same current. Struggling to sink under the surge and get farther away from the highly visible orange dinghy having its own problems in this storm, even with Neo's capable hand on the tiller—

That's when I see the shark.

Arrowing straight up from the inky depths into the searching beam of my flashlight.

Like that fucker's just been waiting for us to stop dicking around and make our play for the enchanted artifact hidden in the Emerald Grotto that every witch and warlock at this Academy is hunting.

The steel-gray wedge of a sharky head, nightmare jaws grinning over a corpse-white belly the size of the Goodyear Blimp, explodes from the darkness like a shout.

A spurt of elemental terror plunges my body into an icy vat of fight-or-flight shock. Adrenaline floods every cell and synapse of my body like a bolt of lightning.

Except I can't summon lightning when I'm submerged.

Even though I am an actual lightning witch.

As the shark barrels toward me, a yell claws up my throat and bursts past my lips in a rush of bubbles.

I barely remember to keep my teeth clamped around my mouthpiece, so I don't lose my oxygen source and drown.

As I twist to snatch the serrated dive knife from my belt, flashlight playing wildly over the streamlined contours of the shark attack I'm about to experience, I have a split second to process that I'm gonna be the first dragon shifter queen in the history of the witching world to get eaten by a great white shark.

My inner dragon, who's afraid of the water and can't swim a stroke when I'm shifted, bugles in helpless rage.

Still caught in the wind-whipped currents near the surface, an errant riptide spins me away from the shark's grinning snout. Helpless in the cyclone's grip, I sweep my knife in a wicked slice. (Thankfully, it's a U.S. Navy combat blade and made for this shit.) I'm aiming for the carnivore's dead black eye. Too bad, as I go spinning past, I only manage to score the gunmetal-gray snout.

Despite my sucky aim, a random pass of my flashlight (which I'm clutching in a death grip) plays through the water over an inky swirl of blood.

I could swear that shark snarls at me.

Right before the monster's freight train momentum sweeps him out of sight with a powerful flick of his rear caudal fin.

My breath, amplified by the Darth Vader rasp of my regulator, scrapes loud and ragged in the undersea hush. My panicky heart hammers against my sternum in the dark, sending frantic electrical impulses that shout *here I am* for any shark in sensing distance. My skinny beam of light searches desperately (and fruitlessly) through the murk.

That's when the thought that's been tugging at my sleeve for attention finally penetrates the clamor of alarm bells ringing in my head.

A great white is a cold-water shark.

There *are* no great whites in the Med.

Which means the shark that almost swallowed me in a single gulp must be our resident great white shifter.

Malcolm Uranus.

Malky's a nasty piece of work, even nastier than his brother Lev. He's part of the House Tiberius clique of bullies that supports my vicious bitch of a rival for the witching world throne. Those bullies are taking their finals as a team, just like me with my house.

And with one prize, there can only be one winner.

I can't see him anywhere. But I know he's out there.

Ronin! I broadcast in all directions and hope like hell my guy's still in receiving range (because he's the strongest telepath at Icarus, but even he has his limits). *Shark! I think it's Uranus.*

I wait for the powerful ping of Ronin's callback…

And wait.

Hey, Adam? That's my nickname for my guy, who's a literal doppelgänger for Kylo Ren from *Star Wars. You still with me?*

Nada.

Cheese on toast.

Not good.

Has that shark swallowed him in a single bite? Or has the riptide swept me way beyond my mate's impressive psychic range?

I sneak a peek at the illuminated dial of my dive watch. Check out the compass and depth gauge on the dial to orient myself and steady my jittery vitals. Already forty feet down, so swimming for the surface would put the shark under me, which any kinda *Jaws* fan could tell you is a bad idea. Besides, what the hell would I do up there on the surface? By now, Neo and the *Filibuster* are long gone.

Steady there, showgirl, I tell myself (and my fretful dragon). *We got a job to finish down here. Then we can vamoose.*

Grimly I swing my flashlight east toward shore. That's where I'll find the Emerald Grotto. That's where I need to go.

Plus, the entrance to that undersea cave is too snug to accommodate Malky's big ass shark.

My searching beam sweeps across a thick stub of stalagmite—one of the frequent rocky pinnacles that litter this coast and make it so treacherous. (That's why the yacht's moored so far out.) I put my fins to use and swim for cover, working crosswise to the current's strong pull.

When I reach the rocky crag, crusted with coral and thick with fronds of seaweed that sway hypnotically with the tide, I tuck in against the thing, putting its reassuringly solid bulwark squarely at my back. I need to be careful not to get tangled up in the foliage.

But if I do, that's why I have the knife.

Besides, I really wanna lose that shark before I cross the open stretch of cove to the grotto.

Floating in a kelp forest with my O2 tank scraping the rock behind me, I clutch my knife and flashlight and wage a brief inner battle. Chilled to the bone by the unforgiving knowledge of the next thing I need to do.

Then I suck in a breath, pull up my big girl panties, and switch off my light.

This far down, impenetrable darkness descends like a blanket. The harsh mechanical rasp of my breath fills my ears. I work on slowing my respiration, so my frantic heartbeat isn't ringing the dinner bell for every shark in the neighborhood. (Not that the possibility of multiple sharks in my immediate neighborhood is a thought I wanna dwell on).

Shit.

I can't feel Ronin in our bond, like, anyfuckingwhere.

Neo, who's my fated mate and thus also linked to me, is way outta range.

With any luck, Neo's back at the yacht with the rest of my unhappy harem, talking down Zephyr (a non-diver) from his testosterone-fueled threat to hightail it after me. All of them weathering these worsening seas till we rendezvous at the extraction point—with the artifact.

With any luck, Ronin's at the grotto already.

With any luck, Ronin's got the Horn of Ceres snatched and securely squirreled away in his game bag right now.

Fuck. We're never that lucky.

Or maybe Ronin's much closer. Searching for me. And I just can't feel him because there's a nullifying object in play. Possible, because the bad guys at House Tiberius have one of those. Yeah, like a magical artifact that blocks the telepathic bonds between me and my warlocks.

This alarming mental calculus, which I'm doing to stay sane and not piss myself in a shark-fueled panic, ticks along to the inevitable outcome.

If Malcolm Uranus is in the water *and* there's a nullifying object in play, that must mean *she's* close.

My ex-bestie, ex-partner-in-crime, ex-lover. Ex-everything. My vicious rival for the witching world crown.

The mortal world knows her as celebrity supermodel Cleo Ferrari. To the witching world, she's the current queen's chosen heir.

Cleopatra Aquarius.

To me, she's always just been Cleo.

My entire body prickles with a thrill of alertness, like a smack of jellyfish stinging my skin in the dark. My survival sense is already going haywire (because shark). But the cold finger of nerves sliding down my spine magnifies that creepy sense of watching eyes tenfold.

I literally can't stand it.

Just waiting in the dark for the steel vise of carnassial jaws to close around my torso—from above or below—and bite me in two.

I'm breathing too hard, sucking down precious oxygen. Close to hyperventilating, judging by the swirly sense of vertigo that's overtaking me. If not for the solid presence of the big rock at my back, I'd be totally disoriented in this floaty darkness.

That sense of being watched by hostile eyes deepens. The floating tendrils of my ponytail tickle my face like ghostly fingers. Ropes of slimy seaweed slither against my limbs like snakes. Cold seeps through my shortie, my naked legs are icy, and my chest is tight.

No matter how deeply I breathe, I can't seem to pull enough air into my lungs. Maybe my O2 is already running low. Maybe my valve is leaking. But I can't see the gauge (which is on the tank behind me).

Straight up, I can't see fuck-all down here without my flashlight.

I'm a goddamn sitting duck.

This is bullshit.

I'm Zara Gemini. Royal wild child. Badass general of the witching world rebellion.

I can't stay here forever, cowering against this rock like a clingfish. People up there are counting on me.

Plus, what if Ronin's in trouble? What if my dive buddy needs me?

The best thing I can do right now—the only thing, TBH—is to follow the plan and head for the grotto.

Shark or no shark.

Overcome by the drive to take some action, *any* action, even if only to reorient myself and banish the bogeyman of my runaway imagination, I swing up my flashlight and switch on the light.

To my fully dilated pupils, the narrow beam is blinding.

As my pupils constrict to pinpricks, something takes shape in my little light.

A wicked wedge of head, sheathed in crimson scales and crowned with a crest of scarlet tentacles that float like Medusa snakes in the current. Two malignant golden eyes, slit by narrow vertical pupils like a goat's, glare into mine from barely six feet away. A deadly muzzle parts to reveal a mouthful of needle-sharp teeth.

That head alone is the size of my whole self. Sensed more than seen, the vast weight of a massive body hovers in the twilight behind.

An electric jolt of recognition spikes my vitals, because this is a monster I've seen before.

Just never this close.

I'm staring straight into the clever eyes of a sea dragon.

The only sea dragon that exists in the whole witching world, because they're supposed to be extinct.

Specifically, I'm floating—alone and helpless forty feet down, armed only with a knife—within killing reach of the sea dragon shifter who's my most vicious enemy.

I'm staring at Cleo.

Here in her element, I'm pretty much at her mercy.

Chapter Two
Neo

By the time I fight my way back through these heavy seas to the *Queen's Veto* and tie up the dinghy behind my dad's yacht, my hands are shaking with adrenaline and fatigue.

Despite how long I've been gone, the guys are still fighting.

Great.

Over the shrill moan of a rising wind, I can hear the clash of voices—harsh with anger—ringing all the way from the main deck.

While I've been away, the fight's moved up from the bedroom to the salon, I guess.

Honestly speaking, that fight sounds like it's getting worse.

Just like the weather.

As I trudge across the exposed platform of the afterdeck through muggy air that's thick as soup, the lowering skies finally open. Preceded by the tinny tang of ozone, a sheet of rain hisses across the open water behind me, drums against the deck, and drenches me to the skin in like five seconds.

The jagged silhouette of the tiny islet, whose craggy cliffs protect and hide the little pocket cove where we're moored, vanishes in an eyeblink behind a gray curtain of rain.

At least the thunder of torrential rain against the hull muffles the whiplash snap of Zephyr's raised voice—electric with frustration and wrath—crackling from the salon. The jab and slice of Vasili's cutting retort (because that snake never raises his voice, even when he's furious) is almost blunted by the rain.

Almost.

"…because if you're not singing to Zara's tune in perfect fucking pitch with the rest of us, darling," Vasili hisses, sharp as a hornet, "you and that flying Godzilla of yours are welcome to exit this harem stage left. Straight back through that portal to the Avalon hell that spawned you…"

Before I can hear any more of this upsetting argument, I duck into the covered companionway, fumble off my glasses, and make a futile attempt to dry my lenses on the soaked hem of my polo shirt. In the blurry dark, while rain thunders against the roof, I slick a hand over my face to swipe the water out of my eyes. Then I park my still rain-streaked glasses resolutely on my nose.

For whatever limited good that does.

I still can't see.

But at least I can't hear any more fighting either.

I hunch my shoulders miserably (because the stairs are narrow, the ceiling's low, and my shoulders are broad) and trudge up the steep ladder to the quarterdeck.

My steps are slow for obvious reasons.

Zara and Ronin won't need pickup at the extraction point for a while. We agreed in advance to give them extra time. And honestly, I'm fed up with my guys fighting like this. Our polycule's whole dynamic right now is exhausting, for real. Vasili's been riding Zephyr's ass (and not in the way we'd all like) since way before we all zipped through the portal to Icarus this morning to join the Dean's Challenge.

Two days late.

We're late to join the Challenge due to Zara and Vasili getting suspended for fighting with Cleo and her sidekicks in the student commons. Even Lucius got suspended by the Dean from his headmaster duties—just for being in the room when it happened, I guess.

Never mind the fact that Vasili's terrifying father (who's on Cleo's side and not ours) was literally holding Lucius hostage at knifepoint the whole time.

Anyway, that disciplinary call the Dean made was so unfair. I'm still indignant. Cleo started that fight with Zara and got off scot free. Now our team is days behind everyone else in the whole Academy in our hunt for the Horn of Ceres.

At least we have a hidden advantage, thanks to Zara's secret new superpowers, that *should* help us close the gap—

"You just gonna stand there all night drippin' on the deck, kid?" A rumbly drawl from the captain's cabin, practically on top of me, almost makes me jump out of my skin. "C'mon up here and lemme getcha dried off."

I rub my chest to quiet my pounding heart (which is racing now for multiple reasons, yay) and peer through my glasses up the ladder at the captain's cabin.

Framed in the open door with the blue glow of the navigation console behind him, the familiar form of a massive male fills the space, crowned with a spiky head of pewter hair. Cool electric light outlines the naked bulge of muscled shoulders, bare biceps thick enough to sink your teeth into, and the tight ripple of abs that won't quit, knifing down to a pair of distressed jeans that ride low on his hips and cling to his thick quads.

With his naked feet spread comfortably to command the space and a steaming mug gripped in one big hand, my new boyfriend looks more like a vagabond sailor—or a pirate—than the Prince of the Light Born Fae.

"Ash!" I squeak, like a mouse or something. "Gosh, you scared the heck out of me."

"Sorry." Ash braces one powerful arm against the doorframe, biceps flexing under the inky tat of bloody thorns wound around the muscle in a way that's practically hypnotic. "Kid, you look like a wet puppy. Lemme get you a towel and some hot coffee before you catch a cold or something."

"Okay." I heave out a breath. "Thanks."

While rain hammers against the roof like hail, I hustle across the quarterdeck and swarm up the ladder.

Ash steps back to let me in.

As I duck past, I catch the patient drone of Lucius' voice drifting from the salon, worn thin and ragged around the edges. "My dears, it's pointless to prolong this wrenching debate. Zara has, all too clearly, made her choice. We don't even know if the demon followed us through the portal—"

Ash casually nudges the door closed behind me to shut us both in.

That action blocks out the vicious volley of argument and counterargument still ping-ponging back and forth on the main deck.

Which I don't think is a coincidence.

Ash passes me a thick towel, monogrammed with the name of my dad's vacation yacht, then turns away toward the coffeepot. I figure he's giving me my space, because he's really good like that.

"Thanks," I repeat on a sigh, fumbling off my glasses again to blot my face.

After a little hesitation, I peel out of my wet shirt and give my back a vigorous scrub with the towel too. My chinos stay firmly in place. They're really just damp, and I have no intention of dropping trou right in front of Ash.

I mean, they're boat shorts. They'll dry.

I know. I know.

It's ridiculous to feel so shy and self-conscious about stripping down in front of a guy I just fucked into a sex coma (even if only for the first time) last night, right?

But, after all, me fucking him was Zara's idea and not Ash's.

Maybe he was only, you know, being polite?

I bend over to towel my legs and breathe in deeply, letting the acrid scent of coffee fill my lungs. I'm weirdly soothed by the soft chink of the silver spoon against heavy china as Ash swirls sugar and heavy cream into my coffee.

Just the way he knows I like it.

I'm not really used to being taken care of like this. In our polycule—with all these alphas and all this testosterone, plus a really strong queen—I'm usually the guy who does the babying. That means it's normally me taking care of everyone else, and it makes me so happy to do it. Taking care of my cherished one Zara and all our guys, that's my love language.

But I have to admit, I'm not totally hating the way Ash is taking care of me right now.

It's actually… kind of… sweet.

Especially since he's the first guy I've ever topped.

Still, when the big guy comes up behind me to rest a warm callused hand on my bare waist, I jump like a nervous cat.

"Take it easy, kid." Gently he fishes the damp towel out of my worried fist, tosses it aside, then folds my fingers around the mug's solid warmth. "Not gonna expect ya to jump my bones while you're dripping and shivering in your dad's own digs, you feel me?" He huffs out a wry chuckle. "Especially since I'm old enough to be your dad myself."

"Uh, thanks." Hastily, I bury my blushing face in the steaming mug (which also carries the ship's monogram). I mumble into the cup, "And you're not old. You're just right. For all of us."

"Aw, shucks." Ash gives a soft chuckle. "You're good for an old guy's ego."

He ruffles my curly hair with a friendly hand, then leaves me to wrestle my blushes (the curse of a fair complexion) into submission and relocate my lost composure. Meanwhile, he moves quietly around the dim-lit cabin with its polished wood and gleaming brass, hanging my wet shirt and towel neatly over a heated drying rack on the wall.

Because the *Queen's Veto* really is that luxe.

She's an oceangoing yacht, and Dad has hosted the Queen and a bunch of his fellow senators and A-list witching world glitterati on board. So Theo Mercury's spared no expense, especially in here. The adjacent captain's bedroom has the only bed on board that's big enough (barely) to sleep all eight of us.

Not that we've done any actual sleeping in it.

I mean… yet.

As I sip the sweet creamy bliss of fresh-brewed java, a comforting warmth seeps through me. Gradually, my fluttery pulse and jittery heartbeat settle.

Finding my dad's yacht bobbing at anchor, just waiting for us in Icarus Harbor when we showed up for the Dean's Challenge—along with my dad's note, neatly typed on Arcane Senate letterhead, proclaiming his fealty to Zara as the rightful Gemini queen—was a really nice surprise.

Dad is a major bigshot in the Arcane Senate. He's never met a bill he can't pass or an election he can't win. With his pompadour hair, easy charm, and megawatt smile, he's like the Ted Kennedy of the witching world.

That makes him a good ally for Zara to have.

Still cradling my mug, I finally get my head together and turn toward Ash. "So, uh, speaking of my dad… his plane's probably landed in DC by now. With any luck, he's already wrangling the Senate to reject Cleo's claim and stand behind Zara."

"Like they should." Now standing with his back to me at the helm, Ash shrugs his big shoulders.

I'm one hundred percent loyal to Zara. So, obviously, I agree. But the words I'm about to say float right out of my head and evaporate like ether.

That's because the shattering full-on visual of Ash viewed from behind, with that stunning black-and-pewter angel's wing tattoo inked across his broad shoulders and plunging down his corded back, is really distracting.

Not to mention the way those faded jeans hug his bubble butt.

If he's feeling tender back there from the way I reamed him last night (while he simultaneously fucked Zara and made her come so hard she summoned lightning), he isn't showing it.

I wonder how long he might need before he could take my dick, bottoming out inside his tight heat, again.

I mean, assuming he ever wants that, without Zara urging us on.

And, gosh, I *really* need to stop thinking about his ass and reaming him like I'm obsessed with the guy or something.

I mean, he's the Light Fae Prince.

And the visiting Potions prof at the Icarus Academy.

I'm First Boy on the Dean's List. Ash is, like, faculty.

Not my own personal fuckboy.

I'm already blushing and breathless and tingly and, gosh, now I'm getting hard. So hard my dick is shoving against my zipper and visibly tenting my chinos. Thank goodness Ash isn't a telepath and can't know what I'm thinking.

Neo Mercury, I tell myself sternly. *Now is not the time to pop a chubbie, with Zara and Ronin night-diving for the Horn right now and probably in all kinds of danger.*

First Boy, you need to keep your dick in your pants.

"They voted her in, didn't they?" Ash murmurs. "Before the Aquarius chick showed up? Our princess is supposed to be the lawful queen in waiting."

I clear my throat and stroll casually over to stand next to Ash. I'm really grateful for the solid comfort of his quiet company, but I'm super careful not to crowd him.

Through the rain-washed glass, the red cedar expanse of the main deck spreads below us.

"Sure." I dredge up my mental study notes from our Witching World Law class. "The Senate voted in Zara as Messalina's lawful heir after Messy's daughter died. But now Messalina wants a do-over, to call a new vote for Cleo—who's like this long-lost other daughter we all just learned about. Calling a vote is within Messalina's royal prerogative, as the current Queen, under the lore. Still, the Senate needs to consent. We're a constitutional monarchy and not a dictatorship."

Against the dim golden glow of the salon window below, a slim taut figure is pacing with a feral grace. By the crackling energy that sparks from his restless frame, plus the spill of moss-green hair falling down his back, I recognize Zephyr with no problem.

He's the Dark Fae King, and he's really hard to miss.

"That's why Zara acing her finals is so important," Ash says with an easy nod, but he too is watching Zephyr. "Our gal needs to win, and Cleo needs to lose. Once Zara wins the Dean's Challenge—if she wins—that'll help your dad keep the Senate in line."

"And she has to do it with just her student team," I remind him. "Faculty like you and Lucius and Zephyr can't help—at least, not directly, or we'll forfeit the contest and fail our finals. Even Vasili can't help, despite being a graduating senior, because he's also an adjunct prof this semester."

"And none of those guys are used to sittin' on the sidelines, huh?" Ash grunts. "That's why we got trouble. Why we're ass-deep in alligators on the Love Boat."

"Yeah, pretty much," I agree glumly.

When he falls silent, I sneak a peek at Ash's craggy profile. He's all square jaw and Roman nose and furrowed brow. But his thoughtful silver gaze stays fixed on Zephyr—the guy he affectionately calls Sparrow— because Ash is the King's acknowledged consort back in Avalon.

Those two are like the Fae equivalent of Romeo and Juliet. The Unseelie King and his Seelie Prince. Star-crossed lovers from two warring races. (Only hopefully, you know, with a better ending.)

Normally, those two are really cute together.

Which makes me wonder what Ash is doing alone up here, instead of down in the salon keeping Vasili from burying one (or more) of his hidden cache of knives hilt-deep in Zephyr's back.

I guess leading this whole witching world rebellion has thrown us all off balance.

"Once Zara and Ronin are back," I say slowly, "either with the Horn or without it, we really need to get home to the *domus*. Not only so we can sync up with Racetrack and Dez and Mallory and her guys. But also so I can reach my dad on our house landline. Before this storm blows the phone line down."

"Yeah, I've been canoodling with the comms on this dreamboat." Ash runs an appreciative hand over the gleaming wood of the console. "Looks like the storm—or maybe your witch academy hocus pocus—is messing with the radio and the WiFi. Heck, even the satellite phone. Can't get that gizmo to work either."

"It's not the storm." I sigh. "The magical wards around Icarus Island extend for miles, and they mess with our electronics. Now that we've entered the contest, we can't pass the wards without breaking the rules and failing our finals. So the only ways to connect with the outside world are the post… which takes weeks… and the landline."

Ash is starting to reply when the salon door below flies open.

Zephyr bursts into view, wearing the sleek green dragonscale armor he dons when he means business, double swords crossed over his slim back. By now, it's raining cats and dogs, so the rain just sheets over him and plasters his long hair to his head in seconds, until the tips of his pointy ears peek through. The green eyepatch he wears over his ruined socket and feral face is a dark slash against his olive skin.

Totally undaunted by the downpour, the guy sprints down the companionway toward the foredeck, light footed and fleet on the rain-slick planks.

Suddenly a wickedly tall figure, rocking his usual punked-out version of the Academy uniform and a frosted shag of punk-rock hair, appears in the doorway behind Zephyr. Pale eyes, rimmed in smoky liner, flash like warning lights in a cold face.

My gaze zooms right in on Vasili.

Not only because he's one of my alphas and by far the most difficult to handle. But also because he's the most dangerous warlock on this ship.

Not to mention the least stable.

As he stares intently after Zephyr, V's pretty face is chiseled ice. At his side, his lethal casting hand twitches.

Beside me, Ash sucks in a sharp breath. His big shoulders bristle and spread in instinctive threat.

Before either V or Ash can act on their various threats, Lucius too appears in the doorway and slips an imploring arm around V's waist. Our wolf shifter headmaster definitely looks the part tonight, rangy but restrained in the Old World elegance of his seersucker suit and ascot, with his scholarly features all somber under his goatee and his dark Renaissance curls tied back respectably at his nape.

Whatever Lucius murmurs in Vasili's ear seems to do the trick. Or maybe it's the way Lucius rubs his jaw affectionately against V's cheek to scent him and nuzzles V's diamond-pierced ear.

Either way, Vasili's casting hand relaxes. His malignant stare shifts away. Without saying a word, he uncoils and slithers back into his den like the pit viper he is.

Leaving Zephyr ambulatory and breathing.

At least for tonight.

Frowning, Lucius glances up at the captain's cabin. His worried eyes, glowing red with restrained violence like Gary Oldman's in *Bram Stoker's Dracula*, pass over Ash and me in the window.

I raise my hand in a hopeful wave and mouth *Hi, Lucius*!

Lucius' jaw unclenches. His stern mouth softens in a tender smile that's just for me.

Between one crisis and another, the two of us haven't had much together time lately, and I really miss him. But I can see from the affectionate way he gazes at me that he still loves me. Even if he refuses to bite me and be one of my alphas. (Do *not* get me started, but I'm determined to get that bite.)

While I glow with wistful love for my headmaster, Lucius nods at Ash gravely, then dips back inside after V and gently closes the door.

A flicker of movement snaps my gaze to the prow. Zephyr bursts into view, scrambles down the bowsprit that juts over the churning sea at a dead run, then hurls himself from the bow in a lithe twisting leap.

I let out a yelp of alarm.

I mean, there's a cyclone brewing. That sea is not swimmable right now, for real.

Especially for a guy wearing boots and dragonscale armor, with two swords strapped to his back, for cripes' sake.

"Easy," Ash murmurs. "He's got this."

"How?" I bleat. "Can he even swim?"

Before I can have an actual heart attack, a vast green shadow sweeps from the cliff and swoops under Zephyr's falling form. Then Zephyr's big green dragon Xhevith soars for the clouds, letting loose with a skull-splitting nails-on-chalkboard *screeeeech!* and the Dark Fae King clinging nimbly to his fighting harness.

Phew.

I've been so worried I forgot, just for a sec, that he's a dragonrider.

"Guess that's one way to finish a fight, huh?" Ash mutters. Together we watch as Zephyr and his dragon climb swiftly to vanish in the threatening clouds.

"Hopefully he's gonna do like Zara asked?" I offer. "Flying decoy, like Max, on the other side of Icarus?"

Those two guys—Max and Zephyr—are two of the most visible

warlocks in Zara's harem, at least when they're on the wing. So their job is to draw Cleo and her gang of hunters away from the Emerald Grotto, where Zara's new powers tell her the Horn of Ceres is hidden. Max left, grumbling and suspicious, to do his part hours ago, like Zara told him (even if under extreme protest, due to the fact that Max is in the middle of a mating rut and really broody).

But Zephyr balked and wouldn't go at all. Just flatly refused to leave his bride unprotected.

That exact phrasing is what set Vasili off.

Like our queen is Zephyr's and not ours.

Like the rest of us aren't strong enough to protect our cherished one without Zephyr.

"Hope so," Ash mutters. "With him, it's kinda hard to say. Sparrow's all up in his head about that demon." Neatly he collects my empty mug, rinses it out, then parks it next to his in the galley sink. "He's been pretty twitchy since Mordred showed up outta the blue like that for Zara, then skedaddled before the rest of us could nab him like we planned."

"Half incubus, half kraken," I agree morosely, because Mordred the demon shifter has been on all our minds. "Definitely doesn't help that Zara still won't tell us what he said—or did—when he materialized last night. Plus Zephyr already hates that demon's guts for trying to usurp the Dark Fae throne. Just what we *didn't* need following us from Avalon."

"Truth." Ash slings a brawny arm around my neck (which is contact I have to remind myself firmly isn't meant to be sexual) and steers me toward the door. "Guess it's safe for you and me to come out now. Anyway, you gotta hop back in that dinghy soon for the pickup. Maybe you can take poor Lucius with ya. Figure the guy could probably use a little breather from all that Vasili drama."

"That's a safe bet." My wry grin dissolves into a worried frown. "I just wish we knew where Cleo's hiding. We really need to find her, Ash. Before *she* finds Zara."

Chapter Three
Zara

I've never been this close to Cleo in her sea dragon form.

I mean, until a few days ago, I didn't even know my ex-bestie *has* a sea dragon form.

I know her favorite champagne and the type of oyster she pairs it with. I know the cons that always work best for her when she grifts and how to use her shady skills to my advantage whenever we'd run a heist. I know how to massage her aching feet after those endless hours she spent walking the runways during Paris Fashion week, while I burgled high-end hotel safes to finance our living-on-the-edge lifestyle. I know how to make her laugh and I know how to make her moan.

What I don't know is what happens next.

With my heart jackhammering against my sternum and my mechanical breath rasping fast and noisy in my ears, I stare through my visor straight into oblong golden eyes the size of serving platters. In the blinding glare of my flashlight, as a school of tiny purple fish darts between us, the protective membrane drops over her orbs. Her pupils constrict to menacing vertical slits.

My throat closes in dread. I angle the flashlight out of her eyes and let it play warily over the rest of her.

Sweet Jesus. She's massive.

She's a monster.

Nostrils pinch closed over a wicked muzzle split by rows of needle-sharp teeth. Snaky tendrils of crimson sea dragon crest undulate like eels in the tide. The slow rhythmic flare of gills opens and closes behind her vast jaws. The sinuous coil of her body glimmers—merlot with glints of copper—in my wavering light.

My hand is so unsteady, with the adrenaline rush flooding every synapse, I can barely hold the flashlight.

My own inner dragon has never confronted another queen, except those scrawny ferals on Avalon who always cringe and defer to her. In any population, my dragon has always been the dominant queen.

If not the only queen.

Now she's snout to snout with a rival who's older, bigger, possibly stronger than she is.

And she *really* doesn't like it.

While my agitated dragon trumpets and batters her wings against the fragile shell of my human skin, I'm holding off my shift by my fingernails.

You can't breathe underwater, showgirl, I remind my inner queen, teeth clenched around the mouthpiece of my respirator so hard my jaws ache. *And you can't swim either, remember? If we shift down here, we're shark meat.*

My dragon emits a frustrated whine. But she eases back (a little) on that forced shift bullshit. Of course, like any diva, she resists and resents the hell outta every inconvenient shred of logic.

But it's still the truth.

With my flashlight angled considerately away from her eyes, Cleo's pupils dilate. But her optical membrane stays down—for protection. A trickle of tiny bubbles leaks through her razor teeth. Suddenly the water flowing past my icy limbs heats like an eddy of shower spray.

All dragons have breath weapons. Mine is lightning. Max's is flame. Zephyr's green dragon (who doesn't shift) breathes acid.

And Cleo, very clearly, breathes a scalding steam.

My ex-bestie is capable of melting the flesh from my bones like soup stock with a single pissed-off breath.

My dragon thrashes against the bars of her mortal cage, both frantic and enraged. My human vitals are going haywire, pulse rabbiting, skin prickling, the pit of my belly shrinking to an ice cube of elemental terror.

Yet I'm also… powerfully… intrigued.

Cleo + Zara.

Once upon a time, my ex-BFF tattooed our names in tiny letters on her inner forearm—right down the vein—in Sanskrit.

We were lovers and roomies and partners in crime for over a year. What kind of strength and guile and sheer stubborn grit did it demand from her to hide this monumental secret?

Slowly, so slowly, my free hand drifts out and up. Cleo's sea dragon pupils squeeze to slits. A warning trickle of superheated bubbles squirts between her scimitar teeth.

Barely even breathing, I hold her gaze with mine.

I'm too terrified to blink.

Yet, somehow, I muster the resolve to graze the very tips of my fingers along Cleo's muzzle, just above those ferocious teeth. Under my careful fingertips, her wine-colored scales are sleek as suede. She's not cold like a fish. Like the hide of an air-breathing dragon, she's banked heat.

Her yellow irises pulse and shimmer like a furnace.

But she doesn't bite my hand off.

Not even when my open palm settles gently against her cheek.

A slow shuddery exhale hisses through my respirator. The fist of terror clenching my guts, very slightly, eases its grip.

I don't know if she's a telepath—because, clearly, nothing I thought I knew about her was true. But I'm a telepath myself, a good one, and Ronin has been honing my skills.

I gaze into the glowing lanterns of her eyes and breathe *Ciao, bella.*

A resonant rumble rises from the vast coil of her body. To mortal ears, that rumble sounds like a menacing growl.

But I'm no mere mortal. I know dragons.

This one… Cleo…

She's…

Purring.

A lightning bolt of new ideas dances through my cerebral cortex and lights up neural pathways that have been clotted with betrayal and grief for months over her bitter treachery. What was it she said to me, the night of my birthday bash, when we met and clashed on the royal yacht?

You do not wish to be queen, no? Cleo's perfect teeth sank into the violet matte of her lower lip. *But I—don't you see—I was given no choice.*

I can hardly wrap my head around the fucked-up electric insight that's sparking and crackling through my stunned brain. Obviously, I wasn't given much choice myself. Lucius and Ronin kidnapped my ass in mid-heist from a Singapore penthouse and dragged me through the wards to the Icarus Academy by force.

It took me months, but I finally accepted this whole ball-and-chain queen gig.

I had to.

Had to accept.

Had to *act* to save the witching world and reverse our slow extinction.

Is it so hard to believe another witch, blessed (or cursed) with powerful recessives and a pedigree as royal as mine, could also feel… compelled?

I'm trying to wrestle my chaotic thoughts into some kinda order, with one hand resting on the sea dragon's muzzle and the other limp around my flashlight, when a shadow flickers across my peripheral vision.

Suddenly I remember the shark.

Fuck.

Alarmed, I swing my flashlight up. It's not the shark, but a sleek black diver who darts into view. For a sec, I think it's Ronin. But rather than sporting a long ribbon of sable ponytail, this guy's head is encased in a hood. He's narrower through the shoulders and hips than Ronin's powerful frame. This diver, he's rapier slim. He's speed and stealth instead of muscle. He darts through the sea like a barracuda.

His fist drives forward with a flash of serrated dive knife.

I barely have time to suck in a breath of precious oxygen before that knife slices through my breathing tube. A last wisp of air slips between my lips. Followed by a sudden flood of seawater, salty and bitter as brine.

I spit out the useless mouthpiece and clamp my mouth shut to preserve that last precious lungful of air.

Last time I checked, I was forty feet down.

I need to surface.

Fast.

But the flashlight I'm still clutching plays over the game bag fastened to the diver's weight belt. Through the cloudy mesh, I make out a gleaming crescent of gold.

My clairvoyance—that new gene that got switched on when I became Zephyr's queen—sparks to life. The flaring curve of a cornucopia, swirling with arcane glyphs for fertility and abundance, encrusted with the jeweled symbols of the twelve witching houses, dances in my mind's eye.

The Horn of Ceres.

That's the magical artifact that'll win the Dean's Challenge. Another diver—one of Cleo's, damn it—has clearly gotten there before me.

Fuck.

Me.

Sideways.

Through the shield of our visors, my eyes lock with his. The rival diver. A jolt of recognition steals half my oxygen. Those eyes are hauntingly familiar, almond-shaped and tilted like Vasili's—but chocolate gold instead of arctic blue, divided by the narrow bridge of an aristocratic nose.

I'm staring at Nikolai Romanov.

Vasili's Russian oligarch dickwad of a dad.

Nikolai's been Team Cleo since Day One.

Behind him, the sea erupts in a violent explosion of bubbles. Water churns under the powerful convulsion of a massive merlot body. As my beam dances wildly over the scene, the sea darkens with a sudden cloud of green dragon ichor. Cleo writhes in a spasm of agony.

The slender shaft of a barbed fishing spear sprouts from her long throat.

At her anguished periphery, I glimpse the broad-shouldered frame of another diver, still gripping his speargun at the ready. An inky swirl of ponytail floats around his head.

Ronin.

Nikolai spins to combat this new threat. As he does, my hand drops to the sheath at my belt. A heartbeat later, my dive knife slices through the fragile mesh of Nikolai's game bag.

The torn fabric floats aside. Gently, the Horn of Ceres tumbles into my hand.

A bubble of elation swells my chest like a mushroom cloud.

I have the Horn.

It's way more than a contest prize. This ancient thing is an enchanted object. It's powerfully bespelled for fertility.

This is the magic I need to save my fellow witches, whose bloodlines are so diluted we're practically sterile. This Horn will help the whole witching world make babies to restore our dying races.

But this is no time to rest on my laurels.

The aching pressure in my lungs demands relief. I need to surface.

Like, *now.*

Clutching the Horn under my arm like a football, I swing my flashlight over the chaos to find an escape route.

Ronin and Nikolai are fighting, knife to knife, both expert divers and master killers. It'd be a thing of beauty to watch them go at it—if I weren't so terrified for Ronin. Looming over their struggling bodies and dangerously close, Cleo thrashes in a blind agony that tears at my own stupid heart.

That spear still bristles from her throat.

Damn it. Don't be a moron, showgirl. That's me, giving myself a lecture. *She betrayed you, remember?*

Before I can decide whether to try and intervene, a violent spasm of her thick forked tail slams into the two human combatants—Ronin and Nikolai—and sends them spinning apart.

Propelled by the powerful impact, Nikolai tumbles end over end.

Right into me.

The heavy cylinder of his tank knocks the Horn from my grip. The glittering crescent spins into the darkness, then drops under my light into the murky deep.

Fuck. Fuck. Fuck!

I have to surface. Have to.

Ronin! I shout blindly through our bond, shoving the image into my mate's head by brute force. *I'm outta air. Get the Horn!*

But I can already tell by the muddy feeling in our bond that a nullifying object is still in play. Even as Vasili's dad fins away, struggling with his battered gear, I'm guessing Nikolai has the nullifying object tucked under his wetsuit.

Ronin can't hear me.

The pit of my belly drops in despair.

But Ronin can still see.

Suddenly, my mate's floating before me. Through the visor, his urgent amber eyes lock on mine.

Roughly Ronin pulls the respirator from his mouth and presses it to my lips. I grip his wrist to stabilize both of us and suck in a desperate breath of delicious air, easing the crushing ache in my starved lungs with sweet oxygen. I pull in two more greedy gulps to replenish my empty lungs, then pass the respirator back to him.

We're buddy breathing.

Over his shoulder, I catch a flashing glimpse of something new emerging from the deep. A thick tangle of tentacles, purple as eggplant, speckled with sinister black. A cruel beak gapes wide under an indigo eye, cold and remorseless as death.

Cheese on toast.

Another monster.

I've never seen one in the flesh before, but I've done my witch academy homework.

That's a kraken.

A fucking *kraken*.

And since they're not any more native to the Med than great white sharks, I'm pretty fucking certain that kraken is Mordred the demon. Who's clearly followed us from Avalon. Just like he threatened.

Never mind the fact that I never asked for his help. Or the fact that I explicitly ordered him *not* to follow us back, for *reasons*.

He's a complication I don't want.

An ally I don't trust.

At least twenty kinds of trouble I don't need.

Clearly disregarding every single word I ever said to him, Mordred's kraken and Cleo's sea dragon collide in vicious combat. Now Malky the great white joins the fray with a pale flash of belly and a gunmetal thrash of fin. The shark twists away with a bloody hunk of Mordred's tentacle dangling from his jaws.

Oh my God, gross.

It's *Clash of the Titans* down here, for real.

A hasty sweep of my beam in all directions confirms what I already know. Nikolai Romanov is nowhere to be found.

The sonic boom that splits my brain is either the impact of Cleo's agonized body colliding with the big stalagmite…

Or the sound of my strategy to win the Dean's Challenge getting blown to smithereens.

Nikolai might be twice my age (and then some), but he's clever and he's quick. No way to know if he saw the Horn fall and dove after it… or if the damage to his own gear after that violent collision drove him to the surface.

Same way that need is driving me.

Buddy breathing is an emergency measure. Ronin and me, we can't search like this. And we definitely can't fight.

But the Horn… it could be right under me…

I'm breathing in another hit of Ronin's dwindling air supply, panning the bottomless depths repeatedly with my flashlight, when Ronin makes the tough call for me.

With a single decisive twist, he unbuckles his weight belt—the gear that gives a diver ballast so we can stay submerged at depth—and lets it drop. Then, winding one leg around mine to keep us joined, he deftly unbuckles mine. As the heavy belt falls into the endless night, I wrestle the now useless oxygen tank off my shoulders and let it fall too. Then I throw my arms around Ronin's neck.

Below us as we start to rise, the panorama of that deep-sea battle unfolds. Cleo is writhing in a sea of purple tentacles, spraying superheated steam in all directions, bleeding freely from the gaping tear in her neck where Ronin's spear has been violently wrenched free.

But, damn, that girl's holding her own.

Especially with Malcolm Uranus' great white tearing savagely at the giant squid-like kraken from behind. The churning water around their writhing bodies is black with blood.

I don't even know if demons can die. But Mordred is half Fae. And he's losing a lotta blood—

The violent spectacle falls away beneath us. Now Ronin and I are racing for the surface. When Ronin gooses his regulator to inflate the buoyancy control device buckled around his torso, our natural buoyancy gets turbocharged.

Even though I can't inflate mine without oxygen, we're shooting from the depths like a submarine-launched ballistic missile. His fins and mine churn in tandem, both of us pushing out the expanding air from our throats in a steady yell to protect our fragile lungs from rupturing under the pressure of our too-rapid ascent.

Because we don't have time to pause every ten feet to decompress and acclimate to the changing pressure, the way you're supposed to do in a sitch like this, you feel me?

Still locked together, we burst to the surface.

A literal deluge of rain batters our heads and shoulders like pellets. God, that tropical storm is right on top of us.

The heavy seas throw us around like air-blown balls in a lottery draw. But Ronin's inflated BCD functions as a life jacket to keep us both afloat. My flashlight picks out the rocky crags that thrust above the surface—deadly dangers that need to be avoided. Clinging tightly together in the vicious seas, while the wind howls around us and the rain lashes our limbs and streaks our visors, our situation is too chaotic and uncomfortable for speech.

I don't even have the energy to spare for telepathy.

In grim silence, we ride the powerful surface current that sweeps us swiftly along the jagged coast of Icarus Island toward the extraction point.

Just like we planned.

Only we don't have the Horn.

And maybe Cleo's team does.

I'm starting to lose my grip, heavy fatigue clouding my thoughts and weighing down every limb, when I glimpse the warm glow of a lantern bobbing on an inflatable orange dinghy.

That's Neo and the *Filibuster*, moored to the rocky outcrop that marks the end of this drift dive for Ronin and me.

I use the last of my fading strength to help Ronin propel us through the churn toward the dinghy. The dark figure at the prow tosses out an orange life jacket on a rope to meet us halfway. I wrap a chilled but thankful arm around the flotation device and Neo hauls us swiftly the last few feet through the furious seas.

Dimly I'm aware there are two of my warlocks—Neo and Lucius, both zipped into life jackets and drenched to the skin—dragging Ronin and me over the gunwale into the boat. Concerned hands lift the visor from my face and settle me into the stern. Beneath me, the dinghy pitches and rolls.

By now, my teeth are chattering with shock and exposure. Even when I clench my molars to suppress that shit.

"L-L-Lucius." I unlock my jaws long enough to chatter into my headmaster's pale face. He crouches protectively over me, dark hair plastered to his head, eyes glowing a wicked red in the darkness. "W-we n-n-n-need to go back d-d-down."

"Don't even think of it, my dear." Firmly Lucius wraps me in an oversized mackintosh to shelter me from the lashing rain. Gently he closes my fingers around an insulated thermos that emanates the blissful acrid smell of coffee. "This tropical storm is turning into a full-blown cyclone. Staying on the water at all, much less diving in it, would be a suicide mission."

I pause only long enough to slurp a bracing gulp of scalding coffee, laced with the bite of Irish whiskey. My eyes drift closed in momentary bliss. Like a magic potion, the hot java moistens my dry mouth, coats my parched throat, and seeds my cold tummy with a kernel of precious warmth.

Ambrosia.

Doggedly, I force my eyes open and push up to sit.

"We have to, Lucius," I project my hoarse voice above the hiss and patter of rain so I can also reach Neo, who's busy in the prow, taking care of Ronin. "We have to go back. We don't have the Horn."

Chapter Four
Lucius

To my profound relief, Zara has finally stopped shivering.

My precious mate is buried in the velvet depths of the sectional sofa, her tiny body wrapped in yoga pants and Neo's oversized Academy sweatshirt, knees drawn tight to her chest and a steaming mug of peppermint cocoa (blazoned with this yacht's lofty name) gripped in her small hands. The salon's subdued lighting, dimmed for comfort as the vessel rocks violently on these sloppy seas, plays over the damp teal ponytail that spills down her shoulder.

I'm relieved beyond measure to see color steal back to her pale cheeks.

And wary beyond measure to see her soft mouth regain its familiar stubborn tilt.

As for myself, I struggle unsuccessfully not to hover—although it's a cosseting behavior she tolerates from me tonight. For once, she's letting me express the alpha instinct flooding my overprotective body. Allowing herself to lean into my strength. Still, I don't want to press my luck.

Merciful Christ.

My queen. My student. My mate.

She's mine to protect.

Mine.

She nearly *died.*

The mere notion plunges my sharp shifter incisors from my palate to fill my mouth. I slaver like a mad dog with the rabid need to tear out Nikolai Romanov's throat.

Of course, Zara downplays the severity of the incident. But I plucked the truth from Ronin's mind while Neo and I bundled our exhausted mates back to the yacht.

Zara's clutching that mug I brought her like a talisman, but she isn't drinking. She's clearly exhausted, but she isn't sleeping.

Incandescent with resolve and the eerie glow of psi fire, her turquoise eyes are fixed on the dark rain-washed glass. As though she can peer straight through the storm to wherever that wretched Horn is hiding.

Over the howl of wind around the hull and the hammer of rain against the deck, my keen wolfish senses can barely discern the comforting hiss of the shower from the head below, where Ronin is soaking the chill from his storm-battered bones.

I swallow down my bloodlust. Force my fangs to retract.

I am man, not beast. I am man. I am man.

Trapped in the cage of my human skin, my agitated wolf paces and growls.

Both our mates are safe, I reassure my beast and myself, for at least the dozenth time since we hustled the pair of them—drenched and shivering— from the half-drowned dinghy to the kingly comfort of Senator Mercury's yacht. *Zara and Ronin both. They're safe.*

We will slaughter the sea dragon, my wolf vows darkly. *And the human. Him, we will kill slowly.*

Now he's speaking of Nikolai Romanov, who presents his own damnable tangle of problems. Not only is he the complicated father who abandoned his own son for the so-called sin of being queer—the father Vasili both loathes and loves, whether he cares to admit it or not. Nikolai is also a damned trustee on the Academy board.

We will eat that human's entrails, my wolf proclaims, untroubled by my academic scruples, *while he screams for mercy.*

Suffice it to say, my brain is battered by powerful surges of adrenaline and rage.

I'm far too well aware that I won't be able to keep my intrepid queen—or my dear one, my Ronin, the only other certified diver in our polycule—safely out of the shark and monster-infested seas around Icarus Island for long.

As the silence stretches, a warning frown gathers between Zara's teal brows.

"Soon as it's light out, I'm going back in," she announces firmly, setting her cocoa aside. Clearly, as a highly acute telepath, she's following my thoughts. Thanks to that mating bite she demanded—a forbidden bite, administered to my own student the day of our first fuck, a scandalous indiscretion my wolf and I proved woefully unable to resist—Zara and I are deeply bonded.

"Not if I have anything to say about it," Vasili says shortly, appearing at the head of the companionway without warning. "Certainly not until this wretched storm blows itself out. Then we'll see."

Until just now, my co-alpha has been below, brooding over Ronin while I hovered over Zara, the two of us dividing our protective strength between our mates without need for discussion. Over the months we've been together—the original four who first joined with Zara to form the nucleus of her harem—we've all more or less settled into our roles.

Vasili. Ronin. Neo. Myself.

Once scattered atoms, now we're locked in place, drawn and soldered irrevocably to Zara's magnetic pull. We've even made room to accommodate Maxim's disruptive force, the dragon shifter belatedly joining Vasili and myself as Zara's possessive third alpha.

Zephyr and Ash, in contrast, are free radicals.

The obsessed and twisted Dark Fae King, in particular, is an unstable electron whose erratic orbit has unsettled the balance of power in this harem all over again—

"Yeah, well, you *don't* have anything to say about it," Zara tells Vasili dryly, still a bit hoarse from her prolonged exposure to the elements. "I need to go back down—this time with nitrox, so I can stay down longer and come up faster—if we're gonna win this thing. Except for Ronin and me, no one else in this polycule is a diver."

Vasili doesn't even hum in acknowledgment.

Yet his sharp-edged silence speaks louder than the throb of this vessel's nine thousand horsepower diesel engines.

Zara's wary eyes follow Vasili's graceful progress (graceful despite the yacht's slow heave and tilt, because he's always graceful) across the expanse of cream carpet to the shining Art Deco splendor of the liquor cabinet.

Still clad in the black trousers and white shirt of his Academy uniform, collar unbuttoned to expose his slim throat and cuffs rolled back to bare his sinewy forearms, the warlock is tall as a cypress, slender as a whip, and vicious as a spitting cobra.

Deftly Vasili splashes vodka and dry vermouth into the silver cocktail shaker—a procedure which makes it impossible to read his hooded gaze.

"I mean it, Goblin King," Zara says with a frown. Of course she senses his malevolent fury over her misadventures, just as I do, tightly contained behind his facade of icy calm. "It's my ass and my call."

"Is it?" He closes the shaker with a single cruel twist.

Eyes sparking with irritation, she leans forward. "For fuck's sake, you aren't even allowed to intervene. These are finals, and you're faculty. You don't have a say—"

"Don't I?" Under a fallen ribbon of silver punk-rock hair, damp from "helping" Ronin in the shower, he slices Zara a vicious glance, crackling with an electric flash of blue ice. "Try leaving this wretched boat without my complete consent, darling, and we'll see precisely how much 'say' I have. Faculty or no."

From my wary post near the bow window, straining for any glimpse of Neo or Ash through the deluge, I turn alertly to defuse the impending argument.

"My dears," I remind the room as gently as I can manage, with my wolf snapping and growling in my ear, "as faculty, neither Vasili nor I are permitted to interfere in the exam. Our role is merely to observe and—*very* discreetly—to advise. I'm a test proctor, for pity's sake. I beg that we not be rash—"

"Lucius, pet, we've gone well beyond *rash* into sheer stubborn stupidity." Violently agitating the cocktail shaker like he's snapping someone's neck, Vasili impales me with a glare. "Look, I'm hardly that smothery dragon or that fucking tyrannical Fae, both determined to swathe Zara in bubble wrap like she's a vase that will shatter if she's dropped."

Zara chuffs out a breath that speaks eloquently of her frustration with our possessive alpha drama.

Her frustration is understandable, genetically speaking, since she herself is an alpha. In this way and many others, our polycule is rare—virtually unknown among the arcane races—boasting four strong alphas instead of the typical one.

Our collective strength, and the bond of trust and love that binds us so tightly together, is our greatest advantage.

But if you heed the gossip, that very uniqueness is also our greatest weakness.

According to Zara's enemies and the witching world airwaves they dominate, our queen and her harem are dangerously unstable.

As for Zara herself? They claim she's violent.

Vicious.

Even psychotic.

I watched the latest *Zara Gemini: Unstable Rebel* documentary today on WNN (the Witching News Network) in appalled dismay.

That propaganda piece was a hatchet job.

Admittedly, with witchcraft like hers, Zara certainly can be dangerous—yes, even deadly. But never to anyone she loves. Behind her tabloid notoriety, the terrifying power of her lightning voice, and all that mouthy rebel sass, she's alarmingly vulnerable.

Even now, my beast longs to fling himself across her lap and smother her in wolf. This is a deeply primal instinct I'm barely holding at bay. Vasili is managing somewhat better…

But not by much.

Very clearly, he's hiding something.

Of course, he's always hiding something. He's Vasili.

Still, now that I think upon it, his demeanor all day has been deeply suspicious. At the very least, he's more abrasive than usual, by turns malignant and gloating.

Now Vasili slices Zara's impatient face a narrow look. Subtly, the serrated edge of his tone softens.

"Believe me," he says to her quietly, "I know what you're capable of. While everyone else in this harem was wringing their hands and fussing over your daredevil plan to retrieve that Horn, I was the first to agree you needed to make that dive. I was the one who persuaded Max— *and* that Dark Fae tyrant—to fly decoy patrols and throw Cleo's odious little clique off the scent, while you and Ronin conducted your risky offshore excursion."

"Yeah." Her grim mouth softens in a smile. "That was a good idea, Goblin King."

"He's right to be cautious, my dear." Firmly ordering my wolf to behave, I gather a fleece throw and cross to Zara's side to tuck it gently around her cold legs. "For all the good those decoys seem to have done."

She gives me a grateful smile and reaches for my hand, tugging me down for a sweet kiss with a lick of tongue that melts my mouth with mint and chocolate.

My wolf rumbles his approval.

With some difficulty, I force myself to relinquish the warm press of my mate's lush lips. Still clasping her hand, I lower myself to the sofa at her side.

It's not hovering when we hold hands.

Or so I tell myself.

With the clatter of ice against metal, Vasili upends the shaker harshly into the inverted pyramid of his martini glass. "That was *before* the fucking kraken showed up. Not to mention my fucking father—who, as an outsider, is supposedly forbidden to interfere."

"Much less try to murder you," I growl at Zara, tone thick and distorted with wolf.

Damnation.

My fangs have dropped at the threat.

Again.

"Exactly. They're not even following the rules. The time to play it safe is in the rearview mirror. That's obvi. I mean, it's not like we have a choice, do we?" Now Zara divides her frustration between both of us. "Not if we wanna pass our finals and keep Cleo's ass outta my throne. We have to be smart."

Firmly recalling my duty as proctor and headmaster of our residential college, I tighten my protective grip on her restless hand and force my fangs to retract.

As calmly as possible, I state, "The rules of the Dean's Challenge forbid outside involvement. Rest assured I intend to take up Nikolai's interference with the Dean—"

"Yeah, but we have to do more than file a complaint. We have to *win*." Zara's voice drops to a cautious murmur. Her eyes dart to the windows, as though the legion of paparazzi who routinely stalk our celebrity wild child have their arsenal of telephoto lenses plastered to the glass.

Her capable hand tightens around mine, then slips from my protective clasp.

"Cleo's already cheating," she whispers, "and with Vasili's dad in the game, the school board itself is compromised. If we bend the rules, we just can't get caught."

It's times like these that remind me Zara Gemini began her notorious life, before she became the rebel queen of the witching world, as a cat burglar.

With highly flexible morals.

"Hmmm." Vasili's hum is noncommittal as he sips his martini, but his thoughts in our bond are guarded. (Even more so than usual, I can't help noting.) "Are we so certain your charming ex-lover survived the kraken?"

"I dunno." Tightly, Zara hugs her knees to her chest and looks haunted. "If she didn't, I just feel like… I'd know."

"An interesting assumption," Vasili says softly, eyes hidden behind his smoky lids.

I do wonder what he's thinking—what he's clearly hiding. But I know too well this particular warlock (who is not only my lover, but also my professional associate *and* my student, at least until he passes his qualifying examinations and graduates next month… assuming he survives the process).

I know him far too well to ask.

The yacht's anchor chain groans in protest, like a damned soul, holding us moored against the pull of the heavy seas. Even in this sheltered harbor, the cyclone has swollen the tide. Now the currents are truly deadly.

The rules be damned.

Then and there, I make an irrevocable choice.

I shan't—I won't—I *can't*—simply sit by and passively observe while my prize pupil, my cherished queen, the precious mate I yearn to bear and nurse my pups—the mate who may already have conceived our offspring, God willing—hurls herself recklessly into danger.

Here is my bottom line.

Maxim and Zephyr were right to balk over this mad scheme. Damnation. They were *right*.

My mate is diving back into that lethal sea over my dead and decomposing body.

Bad enough that sweet Neo is out there on deck, exposed to the wicked elements, even as we speak. Doing… something or other… with the storm anchor, with Ash's strong back and watchful eye to assist. Watching those two circle each other all day—bashful Neo in an agony of blushes, Ash clearly besotted with the boy, but biding his time with an older man's patience—has lent a rare grace note of sweetness to an otherwise intolerable ordeal.

"Here's the thing." Zara releases her knees and uncurls her legs. Spurred by instinct, I rise and move subtly to place myself between my determined mate and the door. "That Horn of Ceres isn't gonna recover itself. And Neo's dad needs *something* to help him keep the Arcane Senate in line."

Abruptly (and inevitably), she flings the blanket aside and shoots to her feet. "Lucius, get the nitrox. I'm going back down. Right now. We need that Horn."

The hackles rise down the back of my neck. Every hair on my body bristles in elemental resistance.

"Darling, there's no point appealing to Lucius," Vasili says, soft and silken with menace, without even looking at me. "When *I'm* the one stopping you."

Zara's head tilts to study him. Her aqua eyes narrow. Purple sparks of irritation dance and crackle along her fingers. The curly ends of her ponytail start floating in the psychic charge she generates when her temper rises.

"Is that so?" she says softly.

God help us all.

In this moment, our queen looks every bit as deadly as that slanderous documentary alleged.

Vasili sips his martini and looks bored with the entire tedious affair, but I know better. He's an adder, poised to strike.

Abruptly, the distant hiss of the shower cuts short. Clearly, Ronin's keen telepathic antennae are picking up the amperage our queen and our alpha are generating.

As well as the electric current of Vasili's wrathful resolve.

"What about you, Lucius?" Zara's considering gaze shifts to find me, idling casually near the bookcase of battered paperbacks near the door. Theo Mercury's shipboard library gives me a plausible pretense to obstruct the exit.

Faced with my silence, her soft mouth tightens. "Whose side are *you* on?"

We are on your side, my mate, my wolf growls in my ear. *We are your wolf king, the sire of your pups, and we will slaughter—*

"It isn't so much about being on a side," I begin carefully, speaking over my wolf's bloodthirsty promises, gut spiraling in a sinking sense of dread at the prospect of yet another wrenching quarrel. "My dear, we're all on the same side together. I'm simply saying that plunging back into the sea, with only Ronin for backup, in the midst of a tropical cyclone—

even if the sea dragon and the shark and Vasili's homicidal parent were *not* in play—would be… ill advised."

"And unnecessary." Vasili lowers his martini glass to examine his black-painted nails. Despite the urgency of this moment, his cruel mouth curls in a sly smile that's wicked with anticipation. "*Quite.* Unnecessary."

Zara plants her hands on her hips and scowls. "What, are you thinking Cleo already has the Horn? We can't make that assumption. We can't just… give up! Whenever I do that whole clairvoyance thing, it's all muddy, it's a power I still don't really know how to wield. But I do know that Horn's still at sea—"

"Oh, indeed it is." Grim with purpose, Vasili turns toward the dark window, grips the sill to anchor himself against the vessel's pitch and yaw, and murmurs, "This seems to be your curtain call, darling."

I'm frowning at his slender back when a thin yell rises outside. Christ, that's Neo's voice, pitched high in astonishment, coupled with Ash's low curse.

My wolf bristles under my skin. As I pivot toward the hatch, I'm already shedding my ascot and preparing to drop to all fours.

But I'm still human (if barely) when the outer door flies open.

The hatch fills with a swarthy shirtless body, powerful shoulders and broad pecs rippling and packed with muscle in an impressive male physique. A tattooed sleeve of indigo scales sheathes one brawny arm from shoulder to wrist. Under the six-pack flex of abdominal muscle, a sort of sleek black armor (like fish scales) clings to narrow hips and bulging quads. Bare feet with webbed toes grip the carpet to complete the effect.

"Yo," this apparition says casually in a baritone rumble, shaking back a dripping mane of midnight blue hair to reveal his pointed ears. "Pretty gnarly weather you got this side of the portal, baby queen. Doesn't hold a candle to the demon realm, natch."

Every synapse in my body fires with agitation and aggression.

Saints defend us, it's the demon.

Zephyr's mortal enemy.

Half Unseelie.

Half incubus.

All trouble.

"*Mordred?*" Zara recovers from our collective shock far more swiftly than I. She closes her open mouth and crosses her arms across her chest. "Dude. We talked about this in Avalon. You are *not* welcome here. Seriously. You need to vamoose, like, now. Before Zephyr gets back."

"My good ole second cousin once removed," the new arrival drawls. Above his sleek blue goatee, two mischievous dimples appear in his cheeks. "Kissing cousin too. Bet Cousin Z never told you *that*, did he?"

Casually this creature prowls into the salon, abs flexing and hips shifting like a walking sex show. Given his incubus magic, he exudes a potent sexual spell that thickens the indoor air like incense.

Neo and Ash crowd into the doorway behind him. Neo is wide-eyed and staring, green eyes enormous behind his glasses under a windblown mop of magenta curls.

Ash bristles with watchful menace beside him—craggy face hard under his spiky pewter hair, massive shoulders bunching, legs spread for balance on the rocking deck.

Vasili lounges gracefully against the window, martini glass in hand. Making no move whatsoever to oppose our infernal intruder.

All too clearly, the demon's surprise appearance comes as no surprise to Vasili.

Sudden comprehension zooms all my dark suspicions into knife-sharp focus. Of course, Vasili's not surprised. He knew Mordred was near. He's probably known all day. A moment ago, Vasili practically summoned the vile creature.

Zara's assessing gaze flickers briefly to Vasili and narrows.

Judging by the indignation and outrage crackling through our bond, she's drawing the same unpalatable conclusion as I.

Then her turquoise glare locks on the demon and her tone turns steely. "That's far enough, Aquaman. You can kiss the ring—and my aerobicized ass—from over there."

"Shit, I just got here, and already gettin' hit on." The demon's clever purple eyes crease in an easy grin. Playful as an imp, his rumbly pitch feels intimate, like a lover's hand wrapping around my cock.

God knows, I've never been one for his type.

Cocky. Swaggering. Flippant. Flirty.

But he's a sex demon, and every tingling molecule of my body knows it. An inconvenient heat rushes to my groin and tightens my testicles until they tingle.

If the lore is to be believed, he's the most powerful arcane creature on this yacht. All too clearly, that's something the demon too knows.

Because he still hasn't stopped coming.

"Yeah, no, that wasn't a come-on," Zara says curtly, sparkly toes tapping on the carpet in restless alert. The potent cream-and-roses scent of her own arousal—entirely involuntary, I realize—perfumes the air. "That's far enough, Mordred. I mean it. Till you say what you're doing here."

She doesn't bother asking how he arrived here. A kraken shifter can handle cyclone seas.

Although I do wonder powerfully who summoned him.

"Yeah, what she said." Ash peels away from Neo and saunters toward the sofa, barefooted, stealthy, and moving with deceptive speed. His giant body quickly flanks the more compact demon.

Neo is more tentative, clean cut and earnest in his chinos and windbreaker, hanging back, always alert to Zara's mood and taking his cues from her. But Vasili loops a casual hand in Neo's belt and tugs him close—simultaneously making our First Boy part of our group and pointedly claiming him in this sex demon's seductive presence.

As for myself, I've managed to fend off my shift, choosing human speech over mindless violence. Now I place myself squarely between the demon and my mate. Still, my claws sprout from my fingers, and I know my eyes glow red.

The physical barrier of my placement finally halts the intruder's advance.

"How's it hangin', wolf man," the demon says easily. His violet eyes slide over my rather unruly head of chestnut curls, windblown but twisted into a knot at my nape. Then that insolent gaze wanders over my orderly frame, properly clad in the seersucker slacks and button-down shirt of my professorial attire. Finally, his interested stare comes to rest on my groin.

I find this unsubtle attention… unsettling.

Particularly given the fact I'm still hard as tungsten.

I clear my throat and say gruffly, "I'm properly addressed at this Academy as Master Aries. You may do the same."

"I *may*," Mordred drawls, with a playful wink. "You gonna bend me over your desk if I don't? Or maybe you'll bend for me instead, Teach. I'm real versatile that way, you feel me?"

Behind me, Zara utters a rude snort.

While I silently curse the discomfiting heat that's rising in my face, I sense Ash's watchful presence at Zara's side and draw an obscure comfort from the Seelie Prince's stalwart strength. He knows this demon better than any of us, except the absent Zephyr.

Looming behind our uninvited guest and observing closely while he pretends to ignore the entire exchange, Vasili rolls his scornful eyes and sips his martini.

"I'm rather less so, I'm afraid," I say stiffly to the demon. "Less… versatile. This is a committed polycule, your infernal charms notwithstanding."

"Yeah, Aquaman, that goes for all of us," Zara says behind me, her tone hard with challenge. "So stop trying to sex the place up."

The insolent creature greets these proclamations with another lazy grin that brings out his dimples.

This close to him, I'm suddenly distracted by the perfect double puncture of what appears to be a fresh mating bite, sunk into the smooth amber skin where his corded shoulder meets his neck. My own mating bites are messy affairs, thanks to my wolf's brutal bicuspids. That bite I gave Ronin, savage with forbidden lust for my own student I'd suppressed far too long, nearly killed him.

But I'd recognize anywhere the delicate double puncture, administered with savage precision by needle-sharp teeth, adorning this demon's brawny neck.

After all, that bite is identical to the mating scars I wear myself.

My uneasy observations end abruptly when the demon hoists a sleek pouch that looks like sealskin, which until now I've rather overlooked (given his overall effect) dangling from his fist.

Mordred's sly stare swerves past me to find Zara.

Somehow, the powerful physical impact of his sex magic intensifies. Under my trousers, my knot swells to an aching bulge.

"Word on the street is you been lookin' for this, baby queen, amiright?" he drawls, swinging the pouch. "Goddamn shark shifter bit a big hunk outta my ass, I just about lost a tentacle, but worth it. To bring you this beauty."

Zara sucks in an audible breath and steps swiftly to my side. Her gorgeous Hollywood face is alight with anticipation, eyes glowing ultraviolet like the powerful witch she is.

Since claiming the Dark Fae crown when she mated Zephyr, Zara is now clairvoyant (another of her potent recessive genes switched on). Which is how we knew where to search for the artifact in the first place.

Clearly, she senses what's in the pouch.

Even before the demon carelessly tugs open the drawstring, tilts the heavy gleaming crescent into his waiting palm, and lifts the object for our inspection with a cocky grin.

Neo blurts out a startled sound and cranes to peer around Mordred's obstructive body, face flushed with excitement and eyes shining. "Oh my gosh. Is that…?"

His question trails off with a hopeful hitch. The sweet lad is afraid even to voice what we all scarcely dare to hope.

"Oh, good boy," Vasili breathes on a slow hiss into the spellbound silence. "Good demon. I knew you'd make a decent ally if you tried."

"Truth," the demon says with a wink.

Together, my mates and I stare in shocked fascination at the Horn of Ceres.

Chapter Five
Zara

"Oh, bloody fucking *hell*."

That astonished voice is Ronin's.

Pretty much voicing my own thoughts.

He's standing at the head of the stairs, barely wearing a pair of Max's ripped jeans dragged hastily over his narrow hips. The zipper's still gaping to expose the sinewy vee of his Adonis belt. His naked torso is dripping, black hair streaming water over his tawny skin and dragon tattoo belching inky flames across his chest.

His eyes are riveted on the gleaming golden horn resting oh so casually in that sex demon's cocky hand.

"Blimey." Ronin shoulders into the salon, zipping his jeans as he advances. "I could feel that blooming thing calling all the way from the loo."

Mordred cocks his head to get a good look at Ronin. No surprise. That mate of mine is practically a sex demon himself. The kraken's sly purple eyes acquire an appreciative gleam.

"Ronin, right?" Mordred gives him a slow once-over. "Whassup? Heard all about you from my cuz. You're the guy who popped Cousin Z's cherry. No lie, I kinda hate you for that." One eyelid drops in a playful wink. "But can't say I blame you."

Wow.

Way to make friends with Ronin right off the bat.

Ronin and Zephyr literally *just* got back together after years of misunderstanding and wrenching heartbreak.

And those two getting back together is a *really* touchy subject for Vasili.

"What the fuck's that to you, mate?" Ronin stalks toward the demon with a scowl and ranges himself squarely at Vasili's side, with Neo. I can tell when Ronin gets a whiff of the sex magic clogging the air, because his golden eyes get all smoldery. Discreetly, he adjusts himself behind his zipper.

"My dears, I beg that we not get distracted," Lucius murmurs. Even though my headmaster's looking kinda distracted himself with his thick dick bulging like a cola can behind his own zipper.

I swallow and try hard not to fixate on the slick heat building under my yoga pants.

Right now, it's really important that *I* not get distracted.

"Guess that's the thingamajig, huh?" Ash says grimly beside me. He's watching my face instead of the Horn. Plus his own face hardened the second Ronin showed up. Square jaw knotting, furrow digging between his brows, Ash's eyes flash liquid metal with caution—because he and Ronin also have major baggage they're working through.

Let's just say V's not the only warlock in my harem who isn't thrilled about Zephyr and Ronin hooking back up.

Ash is protective of Zephyr.

And Vasili's over-the-top possessive of Ronin.

But for me and the two most directly affected—Ronin and Zephyr— their reconciliation means everything. Those two are in love, they have been for years, and they're so beautiful together.

Anyway.

Everyone in this room is waiting for my answer.

"Yeah," I say softly, eyeing the Horn. "That's it."

To my enhanced senses, especially this new clairvoyance I've barely started to channel, the ancient artifact hums and throbs with power. It's an enchanted object—a fertility talisman—and the potency of its siren song is magnified tenfold by the sex demon who's holding it.

A sigh slips past my breathless lips. "That's the Horn of Ceres all right. The question is… what's this demon planning to do with it?"

"Tell you true, that depends on you." Mordred's smoky stare lingers on my mouth in a speculative way that makes me suddenly warm and breathless.

Shit.

I have to actively resist the impulse to lick my lips.

The demon tilts the talisman so we can all admire the jeweled glyphs that sparkle in all that gold. The ancient sigils of the zodiac, a fortune in priceless gems, that signify the twelve witching world houses. Runes for fertility and abundance spiral around the golden crescent.

"Me?" Fighting like hell the sex magic this guy's pumping out by the gallon, I plant a hand on my waist and pop my hip like Cleo on the runway. "Okay, Aquaman. I'll bite. What do you want from me?"

The demon's violet gaze slides slowly over my body, curves disguised by Neo's Academy sweatshirt, legs showcased by my yoga pants. Under the heat of his stare, my sparkly toes curl in the carpet.

His slow grin widens till his white teeth gleam.

He has pointed incisors like Zephyr and all the Dark Fae, pointed ears peeking through that wet spill of midnight blue hair dripping seawater halfway down his back. Those ear tips are erogenous zones for a Fae—

But I don't know why I'm thinking about erogenous zones at this exact moment.

No, really. I don't.

"Told you last night in Avalon." The demon's muscled shoulders flex in an easy shrug. "I want in. Wanna hop on board the harem train and ride, baby, ride."

Neo sucks in a shocked gasp, loud in the startled silence.

"Aw, crap," Ash mutters.

"Bloomin' hell." Ronin chuffs out a mean chuckle that makes me suddenly recall he used to be one of my bullies. "Keep dreaming, mate."

But Vasili—who's by far the most territorial alpha in this room (because Max is thankfully not present) and who should therefore be losing his everloving shit—only smirks.

What the fuck?

For a fraction of a second, V's icy blue stare connects with Mordred's. Something sneaky passes between those two that rouses all my suspicions to tingling alert.

That's when my gaze lands on the delicate twin punctures where Mordred's neck meets his shoulder.

We don't have vampires in the witching world (I mean, that I know about. Until this week, I didn't know demons were a thing either.)

But I do know that's a fresh mating bite.

And it's a bite I fucking recognize.

In complete outrage, my glare crackles across the salon, past the grinning demon, to electrocute Vasili. I mean, metaphorically speaking. Believe me, if I could hurl bolts of lightning with my eyes, that snake would be a smoking crater in Neo's dad's carpet right now.

"Wait a sec. You fucking *bit* him?"

That outraged question is mine, it literally flew out of my mouth on its own the second I got a look at that demon's neck.

"Well, darling, I needed to communicate with him over a distance *somehow*, didn't I?" Vasili waves a slender hand, glittering with chunky punk-rock rings, in casual dismissal of my mounting fury. "Besides, it's hardly a mating bite. It's a *disciplinary* bite, simply to reinforce my authority over the creature. The exchange was entirely non-sexual, believe me."

"Speak for yourself, babydoll." The demon pivots to address him, every heavy shift of that potent male body screaming sex. "I'm an incubus, true? When you're me, everything's sexual. Including discipline, in case you're curious."

Vasili surveys his posturing with the look of supercilious disdain my entire harem has dubbed the Romanov eyebrow.

"You have cisgender hetero male written all over every inch of your ridiculous half-naked body," Vasili says loftily. "I certainly assumed you're straight."

"I'm pan. And you're drippy, for real. It all works for me. Works for me fiiiine." Mordred lifts the Horn of Ceres to his mouth to cover his grin and eyes V over the gleaming crescent like he's the fucking Cheshire Cat. "If you didn't wanna get me off, guess you shoulda asked before you summoned me and then bit me."

Vasili eyes him coldly over his cocktail. That snake looks like he already regrets whatever fuckery he secretly got up to with Mordred.

But not as much as he's gonna regret it by the time I'm finished.

"You *summoned* him?" I plant my hands on my hips and scowl at V. "So *that's* how he got over here from Avalon to this side of the portal? Jesus. How do you even know how to summon demons?"

Because I'm pretty sure they don't teach that shit at the Icarus Academy. Not even in Senior Seminar, which V just finished.

I mean, Neo's already devoured that whole textbook (even though he's only a junior) and *he's* not summoning demons.

"That pointy-eared Unseelie tyrant you're currently fucking possesses an adequate library of arcane texts in Avalon. I merely... borrowed one." Vasili takes a delicate nibble of his cocktail olive. His cruel mouth curls in a secretive smirk. "Oh, darling, don't look so worried. I intend to return it... and the demon. Eventually."

Ronin mutters a foul curse under his breath. Neo snuggles up against Ronin for comfort and looks dubious.

Mordred just chuckles under his breath like he's an imp instead of an incubus.

I glare straight at my dominant alpha. "Cheese on toast, Goblin King. Like we don't have enough problems around here with this contest and Cleo and your dad and my superheat? Now we got this piece of work—" I gesture toward the demon "—who wants to overthrow Zephyr and steal his throne right out from under him? How could you possibly bite him… any kind of bite, even if it wasn't supposed to be sexual… without telling us? What the fuck were you think—?"

"Now that's where you're wrong, baby queen." Casually, like he's lobbing a sandwich wrapper in the trash, Mordred dumps the priceless artifact he's holding back into his sealskin pouch. "My brother Lothian— you know, the guy whose head got lopped off? *He* wanted the Dark Fae throne, for real. Kinda fixation for that cat."

Involuntarily my mind's eye zooms in on the severed Fae head Zephyr left in my bedroom at the *domus*. He called it a bridal gift… then seemed genuinely perplexed when I wasn't delighted.

The last I knew, he buried that head in our *domus* garden. To fertilize Dez's roses.

I mighta mentioned that Dark Fae King I just mated is kinda feral?

"If memory serves," Lucius says mildly, cupping his chin and surveying the demon with interest, "the late Lothian was a bit more than your brother. He was your twin, wasn't he?"

"Yeah. Fraternal. But that don't mean shit in the demon world. Me?" Mordred grimaces in the first display of (possibly) genuine emotion I've seen from him. "I went after Cousin Z's throne because I was bound to it. Under a summoning spell."

Keenly interested, Lucius leans forward. "Bound to it by whom?"

"By the Unseelie chick who summoned me outta the demon realm to Avalon. That dame was old school aristocrat, real cozy with old Queen Maeve. Zephyr was his mom's rival for the throne, true? So my summoner, Maeve's ally, she wanted Z gone. Condition of my release, you feel me?"

"What, never fancied that throne for yourself?" Ronin wraps a protective arm around Neo, who nestles trustingly against him, and chuffs out a skeptical breath. "Who's this bloke trying to fool? Three pence short of a shilling, he is."

Suddenly I find myself wondering if Mordred *can* lie.

The pureblooded Dark Fae, like Zephyr, can't.

But this guy's half demon.

"Sure, hot stuff." The incubus in our salon swings his sealskin pouch and smiles. "Ain't saying I didn't enjoy it. Got under Cousin Z's skin, for real, so it was kinda trippy. But when babydoll here summoned me through the portal—" He gives Vasili an easy nod "—your dude broke my previous summoning bond. That's how it works. Now I'm bound to him. He's my new summoner. I gotta do what he asked when he summoned me into his circle."

I give him my most suspicious and skeptical look. "So you didn't have a choice?"

The demon shrugs one burly shoulder. "I mean, I coulda said no, but then your dude would have banished me, and I woulda gone straight back to the demonical realm. Which is one place I don't wanna go. Once I agreed to do his task, kinda like a genie in a bottle, your guy broke my summoning circle and let me run loose."

Eyes dancing like this whole thing's one big joke, Mordred swings back around to grin at me. "And his thing was, I needed to find the Horn of Ceres and give it to *you*."

Then he extends his tattooed arm, encased in an inky sleeve of scales, and offers the pouch—and the Horn—to me.

Startled by the sudden plot twist, I fall back a step. Then I stare at that pouch like it's a sack full of rattlesnakes.

There's probably some arcane rule about not accepting gifts from demons. There's definitely one about not accepting gifts from the Dark Fae. And this dude's half Fae.

But, sweet Jesus, I need that Horn.

If I don't take it, Cleo or one of the other teams in the contest definitely will.

Pushing past my weird hesitation, suppressing the clamor of warning bells in my head, I lift my chin and reach for it—

"Actually, I'd advise you *not* to take it just yet." Whiplash-sharp, Vasili's warning freezes me in my tracks. My gaze flies to his—intent and glittering like ice behind a veil of cobalt lashes.

I scrunch up my brow and tap my toes on the carpet. "Um, isn't the whole point of you summoning him for me to take the Horn?"

"My power over this creature," he says precisely, "only remains intact until you do. Once his task is complete, his summoning bond shatters, and the demon is free."

"Well, dayum," I say softly into the sudden silence.

Naturally, we all look at Mordred.

Who's suddenly inscrutable, the way only a Dark Fae royal can be. His indigo eyes lock on mine without blinking. He's still holding the pouch extended. Even hidden from sight, the Horn hums and murmurs in a way I suspect only I can hear.

In that one way, this artifact is like the Dark Fae crown I have locked in the yacht's safe. A crown I can still hear crooning my name through the hull.

Zaaaarrraa. That's the crown right now, whispering in my fucked-up head. *Claim my power.*

Now here's the Horn of Ceres.

Sounding, like, similar.

Maybe I'm fated to have it. I mean, if it's gonna help me save the witching world. Until now, I've wondered, but I couldn't be sure.

Now, feeling the powerful tug of the thing's magnetic pull, I know.

That Horn is meant to be mine.

Without looking away from the demon, I ask V, "If I don't take it now, what are we supposed to do we do with it?"

"To complete the Dean's Challenge," Vasili says calmly, "the artifact must be returned to the Vault. Until then, we keep this creature— and his prize—securely at our side."

My gaze swerves back to my alpha. My mouth falls open in protest.

"So, what, now we're adding demon trafficking-slash-kidnapping… I mean, since the demon doesn't really have a choice about coming with… to our list of legally questionable actions?" I fold my arms across my chest. "This is no way to run a queendom, V."

Vasili's own mouth, slick with the pale pink gloss he favors, turns down in a moue of distaste. "Well, darling, I'd like to get rid of him too, believe me. For now, I'll simply command the demon to guard the Horn in that unfashionable man purse—"

"Hey now, don't be mean," Mordred teases, but his cocky grin has slipped. "It's a messenger bag."

"—and he'll remain bound to my will," Vasili wraps up with a sigh. "Zara, *do* stop glaring at me and hating me for biting him. Simply imagine what this means! An actual demon at our beck and call. A kraken to give your sea dragon ex the fate she deserves in the briny deep. That's the only reason I bit him. *Obviously*."

"Easy as pie, right, beautiful?" Ash says to V grimly. The Seelie Prince hasn't budged from my side since he planted himself there when that sex demon sauntered in. "This hootenanny ends when the thingy's returned to the Academy Vault. Is that right, Lucius?"

"Indeed." Lucius sounds like I feel, which is kinda dazed.

"So that's where we all need to get." Ash heaves a sigh of resignation and turns to me. "Once we're through the shit and in the Vault, this demonical joe hands over the Horn to you, princess. You toss it inside, win the contest, pass your finals, and flip Cleo the bird in one bold stroke. Easy-peasey."

This glib portrayal makes my headmaster frown. "Except that the Horn must be placed precisely where it belongs in the Vault, not merely tossed inside like a banana peel in the rubbish. That's the final task of the Challenge."

"Groovy." I sigh. "Let's hope that'll be obvi once we get inside."

We all fall silent to ponder both the obvious advantages and the obvious risks of this crazy scheme, swaying in unison as the yacht rocks and groans in the heavy seas. Rain scours the windows and wind howls around the hull.

Grimly, I wonder how I'm supposed to convince the absent Max, and *especially* the absent Zephyr (both due back anytime), to accept this temporary addition to our merry band.

Particularly since Mordred has now helpfully informed the entire ship (the same way he told me privately in Avalon) that he wants to join my harem.

Which would make him… not so temporary.

Not for the first time, I wonder *why* he wants to join. Maybe that's another of my newly manifested Dark Fae powers—the power of attraction, which is super inconvenient, I'm like a Siren right now to all genders, apparently—busy at work.

If so, there has to be some way to turn that shit off.

It's finally Neo who breaks the pensive silence.

My bookworm clears his throat and pushes his glasses up his earnest nose. "So, wow, that's a lot. But aren't we all forgetting something major? Mordred isn't a student, so he isn't allowed to help. With any of this. Or, gosh, we'll all fail our finals and probably the whole semester—"

"Take a chill pill, Einstein. Got that covered," Mordred says casually, his composure regained. "Enrolled this morning, just like babydoll here told me."

Mordred jerks his chin at Vasili and grins, white teeth flashing in his blue goatee. "I'm the first Avalon exchange student to be admitted to the Icarus Academy. Lucky me."

Okay, I gotta admit, that snake of an alpha I've mated really has put that ruthless, diabolical, snaky, scheming brain of his to impressive use. Obviously I don't like that he sneakily did this whole thing on his own—especially biting Mordred, even if it's supposed to be platonic for disciplinary and communications purposes and not a mating bite—without saying one fucking work to anyone.

But, you know, that's Vasili.

"The storm's moving pretty fast," Neo offers hesitantly, because he senses my mood and he knows how *not* crazy I am about this entire half-baked plan. "The weather'll get better. So we should be able to weigh anchor in a few hours. I mean, once it's light out. Max and Zephyr should be back by then too."

Ronin releases Neo with a final squeeze and folds his arms across his tattooed chest with a dark scowl. "Then we haul arse for Icarus Island—all fucking nine of us—like we've got a brace of hunting hounds breathing down our bloody necks."

"And return the Horn to the Academy Vault in the crypt." Lucius gives a thoughtful nod, but he looks and feels troubled in our mating bond. "Which is where it belongs, of course."

Lucius isn't the only one who feels troubled.

I chuff out a grim breath. "Yeah, but there's another big ass problem. I mean, aside from Cleo and Nikolai and this demon and *one* of us fucking biting him without talking to the rest of us about it first."

I give the Goblin King a narrow look that tells him we're not finished with that little convo, like, *at all*. Our come-to-Jesus moment is only postponed.

"Precisely," V murmurs, following *all* my thoughts without any problem whatsoever. But he deftly sidesteps the consequences of his fuckery by spotlighting the most immediate problem we have. "Reaching the Vault alive—*with* the artifact—will not be easily achieved. Every witch and warlock on that island will be hunting us."

Chapter Six
Vasili

"Despicable me," I say lightly into the prickly silence. "All too clearly, I'm in horrible disgrace."

I'm posing on the cushioned bench before the vanity in the master cabin, peering critically at my pouting reflection (framed in Hollywood lighting, as it should be) while I dab silky pink facial cream under my wary eyes.

"You behaving horribly is, like, a daily occurrence. But, yeah, this is a whole other level." Zara's sharing the bench and the mirror *and* my facial cream, the same way we always do. Sharing this bedtime ritual is typically an enjoyable prelude to sharing other nocturnal pleasures.

Tonight, however, her aqua eyes are glowing with psi fire and annoyance like ultraviolet pinwheels on American Independence Day. This effect is alluring but unsettling—and not at all typical.

In fact, the little darling is still so annoyed with yours truly for biting that demon that I'm surprised she's not hurling lightning.

Fortunately, Lucius has taught her to channel that lethal energy in ways that are more, shall we say, satisfying?

Thankfully Neo, her fated mate, is a soothing presence. He hovers close behind her tonight, brushing the thick teal mane that falls to her waist in the slow hypnotic rhythm that typically soothes all of us.

Still, Zara's mermaid curls discharge tiny sparks with every stroke.

In the glass, her gorgeous pinup girl face is flushed with temper and mating heat. It's far too soon for certainty, but all her alphas—myself (very secretly) included—are hoping she might soon be pregnant.

Whether she is or isn't, my girl's tiny body is so delicious in her lingerie—lush sun-kissed curves spilling from the tangerine lace bra and boy-cut briefs I had shipped in our last box from Paris—that I'm prepared to use all my little tricks (even the sneaky ones) to coax her past her pissy mood.

Now I pluck one of the sneakier tricks from my bag of mischief…
Honesty.

I stop dabbing rosewater goop beneath my eyes, carefully assess the result, and fluff the punk-rock shag of silver hair that grazes my shoulders for a sassy boost of volume.

Then I meet Zara's angry gaze in the glass. "Surely you realize I never meant to give that ridiculous demon a mating bite."

She rolls her pretty eyes at her own reflection and abandons my facial goop in favor of a tiny pot of honey lip balm. She swipes the balm along the pert bow of her Betty Boop lips with an agitated finger.

"You should have asked first," she says tartly. "Like Lucius said, we're all committed, Goblin King. Even you. All of us have a say in a mating bite."

"I'd like to reiterate, in my own defense, that it *wasn't* a mating bite." My discontented gaze shifts to Ronin, also visible in the glass. My boyfriend is sprawled shirtless across Theo Mercury's surprisingly massive bed (what *does* that senator get up to in here?) with his head resting on Lucius' thigh, his sleek black hair spilling over Lucius' legs, and Lucius' absentminded hand stroking him like a cat.

Simultaneously, our frowning headmaster—propped against a tidy stack of pillows and primly buttoned into what Zara calls his *Downton Abbey* pajamas—is poring diligently over that demonic tome I filched from Zephyr.

The dim golden light of the bedside lamp lends the entire scene an air of deceptively cozy intimacy.

Believe me, I intend to take full advantage.

Keep trying, love, Ronin murmurs wryly through our mating bond. *Our girl's not having any, is she? And neither am I. Fancy we can all feel the bloke next door lusting.*

Regrettably, this appears to be true. For the moment, I've ordered our amorous demon to take up residence in the adjacent cabin and stay put. Safely out of the way, but close enough for me to keep a wary eye on him (and the artifact) through our fledgling bond.

Now I suspect that demon may be a great deal *too* close to assist my argument.

Waves of potent sexual arousal emanate from the wicked creature, right through the wall between us, like heat from a fiery coal.

Consequently, under the flimsy camouflage of my black silk

kimono, I'm doing my best to ignore a raging cockstand. I suspect the sustained sensual assault from being this close to a horny sex demon is making us all irritable.

Especially Zara.

Twisting toward me on the bench, she props her pointed chin on one fist. "Are you even going to take care of that bite you gave him? Since you're now—apparently—his alpha?"

I heave an inward sigh.

During the deed itself, I gave the initial bite a few obligatory licks to stop the bleeding, of course, with the shifter biochemicals in my saliva. I've certainly been hoping that demon wouldn't require much more from me in the way of tending. They're fast healers, like shifters, according to that grisly volume I borrowed (oh, very well, *stole*) from Zephyr.

"I suppose," I mutter, sounding sulky even to myself, since Zara's plainly waiting for my answer. "I'll tend the wretched creature and his wretched bite. Eventually."

Lucius, fueled by his own powerful alpha instincts, raises his lovely sherry-colored gaze from the demonic text he's perusing to give me a piercing look. "Best not delay too long, Mr. Romanov. Or we'll have a raging case of mating fever on our hands. Surely you considered that risk before you mated him."

These days, with Lucius and me so intimate, that formal mode of address is strictly reserved for those occasions when I disappoint him.

Irritably I rise to my feet, giving my kimono a dramatic swirl for effect. "For fuck's sake, Lucius. I'm running out of ways to say this. Try to hear me this time, pet, *do*. I. Did not. Mate him. That bite was meant to be platonic. I said so *explicitly* before I bit him."

Zara snorts and leans into Neo, which interrupts the rhythm of their sweet bedtime grooming ritual. "Did you wait for him to agree?"

She knows me so well.

I pout down at her skeptical face.

"He certainly didn't protest." Searching for allies, my gaze shifts to Neo, who promptly abandons the hairbrush to crowd into my vacant spot, straddle the bench, and nestle Zara's back against his front.

So much for being on my side.

Neo is, as always, on Zara's side.

Unexpectedly, his wide leaf-green gaze lifts to mine.

I'm not on anyone's side. I mean, we're all on the same side, he says meekly through our mating bond, which takes me aback. Despite being one of his alphas, neither of us are natural telepaths, so I must be projecting.

Dear me. How gauche.

"That demon," I say grimly to the room at large, "presented himself to me this morning as *very* straight. My typically excellent gaydar was simply not pinging. How on earth was I to know the fucking kraken is pansexual?"

Neo gives me a sympathetic grimace.

Our First Boy is both looking and feeling a bit flustered himself, given his proximity to Zara's lingering heat, not to mention his susceptibility to the sex magic emanating from the neighboring cabin— to say nothing of his susceptibility to *me*, his horrible alpha. The poor boy is flushed and his glasses are steamy.

Hmmm.

I might just have to do something about that.

No point letting Ash have *all* the fun with this one.

"Yeah, well, he probably wasn't trying to sex you up from inside his summoning circle," Zara says, *very* dryly, still fixated on the demon. "He wanted out—free rein to wreak havoc on a whole new plane of existence—and that's exactly what you gave him."

Reluctantly I stop eye-fucking Neo and indulge in a bit of pacing between the Alaskan king bed and the wall of rain-scoured glass that overlooks the cabin's private deck.

"The Horn was in the sea," I say curtly. "Your charming ex-BFF is a sea dragon shifter. We needed an aquatic ally. A powerful one. And that's precisely what we've obtained. Now our team holds the prize—*and* a demonic watchdog. As usual, my horrid little plan is working perfectly."

"So far," Zara says softly, leaning into Neo for comfort. He gives her an affectionate murmur and nuzzles the side of her neck.

Indeed. Everything I've said is the truth.

So far.

Of course, needless to say, I've kept a little something to myself.

Namely, the highly motivating fact that Mordred is still Zephyr's mortal enemy. The kraken is the primary threat to that pointy-eared tyrant and his Dark Fae throne.

Zephyr is my rival in this harem.

The enemy of my enemy is, as they say, my friend.

Better yet, my minion.

While the vessel rocks beneath me and rain drums against the roof, I stare at our polycule's collective reflection, wavering in the rain-washed glass. Of course, Maxim is missing. Ash too is briefly absent, having nobly volunteered to take first watch above at the helm.

Probably because we're expecting Zephyr back at any moment, and Ash wants a chance to warn him about our dangerous new ally.

Lucius is still frowning over that ghastly Unseelie grimoire (which I'm fairly certain is bound in human skin and inked in human blood, probably some poor unfortunate who pissed off the wrong Unseelie centuries ago) and doggedly trying to read. But Ronin is clearly succumbing to the powerful pulse of demon sex magic. Rolling lazily onto hands and knees, Ronin straddles our headmaster's hips and starts unbuttoning our wolf's lord-of-the-manor pajama shirt.

Lucius glances up in surprise. His whiskey eyes acquire a reddish tinge.

"Ronin, my dear one, I'm trying to locate—"

"Put that thing away, love," my horny boyfriend says huskily. "You'll give yourself a migraine poring over that faded text in this pissy light. Besides, your boner's been poking me in the ear all night."

Ronin punctuates this revelation by curling a hand over the prominent bulge between Lucius' legs and kneading. "This your knot then, is it?"

Our headmaster growls and closes the grimoire without even marking his place with the tattered silk ribbon. "You know it is, Mr. Pendragon. Are you offering to take it?"

Still watching through the glass with my back to the room, I swallow past a sudden dryness in my throat. Lucius' knot, which made its first appearance when Zara stopped taking her birth control, is a recent addition to our harem. I fuck Lucius, but I don't bend for him, so my direct experience with that portion of his anatomy is still limited.

However, whenever that knot makes an appearance, Zara and Ronin (and Neo, who hasn't yet been knotted, but is clearly curious) are *quite* enamored.

"Oh, I dunno. Bit much to handle, isn't it?" With a mischievous upward look, Ronin finishes slipping Lucius' buttons and pushes open the monogrammed shirt to lick a slow swipe up our wolf's hard belly over his hairy chest. "Why don't you *make* me take it?"

With a sudden growl, our headmaster tosses the book aside, then rolls to pin Ronin beneath him.

"Oppositional defiance," Lucius informs the room grimly. "Which, as you're all well aware, I never care to tolerate."

Our wolf's fangs drop and his elegant scholar's hands sprout talons.

Of course Ronin is laughing, like the maniacal imp he is. Lucius dives in to shut him up with a hard claiming kiss.

Neo gives a rather adorable squeak of mingled surprise and excitement. Zara's inner dragon purrs like a cat as she wiggles around and wraps herself around Neo, so she's straddling his lap on the bench.

Our bookworm spans her waist with his big hands and buries his face in her gorgeous breasts, pushed up so delectably by her tangerine lace. Her face softens and her eyes grow heavy with pleasure.

Over Neo's magenta mop of curls, Zara's gaze finds me, standing in solitary splendor with my back to the room.

Holding my stare in the glass, she reaches deftly behind to pop the clasp of her brassiere, then lets the lacy scrap drop. The tiny pale triangles of her bikini tan lines leap into view, framing the globes of her full breasts.

Neo's moan, coupled with the sight of my girl's aureolae and pierced nipples, swells my boner nearly to the breaking point. Especially when Zara pulls our First Boy's tee shirt over his head to bare the pale skin and muscled shoulders we all love to mark. The pearly crescent of Zara's mating bite gleams beside the pinpoint pricks of my precise double punctures, like a sickle moon and stars, along the side of his neck.

Beyond the pair of them, locked together on the vanity bench while Zara winds her arms around Neo's neck and wiggles the crotch of her boy-cut briefs against his chinos, Ronin and Lucius are tussling violently on the bed. Ronin fists Lucius' hair and, with a rough pull, frees the unruly chestnut curls from their confinement to tumble over Lucius' shoulders.

My co-alpha is already half shifted (because it turns out Ronin likes that quite a bit). Now he snarls and wrestles Ronin's jeans down his thighs.

"Come on then," Ronin mutters, egging him on, even while he puts up a bruising struggle, because he knows Lucius (secretly) likes a little non-con with his role play. "You fancy making me take your knot? You going to rail me till I beg you to stop?"

"You'll beg, but I won't listen," Lucius says gruffly, practically beyond human speech at this point. His pelt is spreading across his rangy back, the brutish snarl of primal instinct overwhelming his orderly thoughts in our mating bond.

Oh, he'll remain firmly bipedal, out of deference to our collective sensibilities. But he certainly looks and feels primed to fuck Ronin senseless.

Admittedly, I'm feeling a trifle overheated myself.

Zara is still watching me, standing with my back to the room, even while Neo suckles and kneads her pretty tits and nuzzles the punctures of my mating scars on her breast.

The first night we mated, I bit the little queen like the Egyptian asp biting Cleopatra in Shakespeare's play. A few weeks ago, I bit her again for good measure. And I've never for a moment regretted it.

Bite or no bite, given my latest misdemeanor, I haven't been certain Zara will want anything to do with me tonight.

To be honest, I'm still wondering.

Holding her gaze in the glass, I tug loose the sash at my waist so my kimono falls open.

I haven't bothered with PJ's tonight. Most of my lingerie collection is back at the *domus*.

Thus, my cock juts before me like an inquisitive antenna. (Darling, don't laugh. I'd never be so *cliché* as to call it a sword or a battering ram or, God forbid, a trouser snake.) Besides, the analogy works, because I'm actively searching for a signal.

I know from experience that Lucius needs his space while he and that knot of his are wolfing out over Ronin. Until my co-alpha has soundly subdued and knotted our mischievous mate, I won't challenge Lucius by moving in on Ronin.

But Neo, sweet Neo, is always more than happy to share.

The real question is whether Zara will let me anywhere near her tonight.

One way to find out, Goblin King, she whispers through our bond. Her tone is mocking, hard to read, and I don't entirely trust her in this mood.

But, through the link between us, her dragon purrs a welcome.

Still holding my queen's challenging stare, I trail a hand down the sleek plane of my chest, feeling my nipples stiffen under my own teasing touch. My palm flattens along my abs, twitching with restless heat.

I'm still standing with my back to the room. But I'm the dominant alpha in this polycule.

By the time my fingertips trail along the exquisitely sensitive length of my cock in a slow stroke from base to tip, all my lovers are very much aware of what I'm doing.

Even the demon's watchful presence next door sharpens to a sudden edge. He too is keenly aware of me, in a way I hadn't anticipated, since my plan was never to mate him.

Well, let him watch. I rarely mind an audience.

When my own slick oozes from my swollen cockhead, I swipe my index finger through the mess, then bring it to my lips for a playful suck.

"Oh, fuuuuck," Zara breathes on a moan.

I smirk around my finger at the naked craving in her face. Simultaneously, my free hand wraps around my aching dick in a long slow pull.

Dear fuck. I'm so hard I'm nearly bursting.

But I'm not moving an inch closer to my queen until I'm utterly certain I won't be rebuffed, so she's simply going to have to ask—

The soft thud of boots against the rain-hammered deck jerks my gaze from Zara's lamplit reflection to the view through the glass. Directly before me, a lithe body, clad in green dragonscale, rises swiftly from a crouch. A feral Fae face, divided by the slash of a green eyepatch, lifts alertly to find my startled features. Beyond, I catch a flash of pale belly as his massive dragon wings away.

Apparently, this reckless Fae leaped from dragonback—buffeted by gale-force winds—to the miniscule moving target of the master cabin's private deck.

So much for loyal Ash, waiting patiently above at the helm like a faithful hound for his consort's return.

Hand still wrapped around my throbbing cock, I huff out a wry breath.

Our new arrival's jade eye sweeps over me and narrows on my length. His lips part to reveal his tiny Unseelie fangs. Then, more slowly, his gaze retraces the terrain of my body—inch by tingling inch—until he locks on my face. As torrents of rain plaster his green hair to his head and shoulders, his eyelid lowers in a slow blink.

Well, what else can I do? I deploy the lifted Romanov eyebrow with a sneer.

His jaw hardens and his lips press together. With an eerie burst of inhuman speed, the Dark Fae King fires into motion, opens the sliding door, and darts into the sanctum of our shared bedroom.

"I trust I don't intrude at an awkward moment." He spares a smirk at my prominent boner, sweeps the room with a keen stare that takes in Zara and Ronin—both his lovers, as the rest of us are not—then drops his wadded cloak onto a chair with a soft exhale that speaks (very subtly) of relief.

A gust of cool rain blows in with him to spatter my overheated body.

Irritably, I release my dick and slide the door shut behind Zephyr, His Moon-Dazzled Radiance, the *lah-dee-dah* Dark Fae King…

And my deadly rival.

"Mmmm, just in time, Your Radiance," Zara murmurs, still wrapped around Neo on the vanity bench. "We missed you, for real."

"Not all of us," I mutter, *sotto voce*, turning irritably to watch as Zephyr bends to toe out of his wet boots. I take a vicious pleasure in noting that Unseelie is dripping all over Theo Mercury's Aubusson carpet.

The Dark Fae King, whose pointed ears possess extremely acute hearing, glances up with a mocking twist. "Pray don't allow me to interrupt what you were just doing, Vasili Nikolayevich Romanov. Your need appears to be most… pressing."

That single scornful look—encompassing my aching erection and dismissing my need with a shrug—makes me hum with rage. A vicious spike of temper, honed by arousal to a deadly point, spurs me swiftly across the carpet to loom over him.

Seemingly unconcerned by my proximity, the fool sheds one boot and shifts his attention to the other.

I glare down at his bent head, delicate ears exposed in a spill of wet green hair, the nape of his neck a sleek handspan of bare olive skin. The crossed swords strapped to his armored back form an X over his shoulders like a warning sign that reads *Do Not Touch*. His spicy-sweet scent of burnt amber and nutmeg invades my brain.

Invading his space in return, I rear over him like the pit viper they all call me.

"Why should I tend to the matter myself?" Deliberately, I shrug out of my kimono and let it fall. Fully naked and hard as fuck, I angle one hip and pose before him with a smirk. "You might as well make your radiant self useful… while you're down there."

Chapter Seven
Zara

Cheese on toast.

I'm more than aware—we're all aware—of the unsettled state of play between Zephyr and Vasili.

My snake doesn't trust easily (like, *at all*) and he's always viewed Zephyr as a rival. The problem started with Ronin brooding over his Dark Fae ex and V getting jealous. When Zephyr ghosted me and the polycule for months to put down the insurrection (caused by Mordred, so you're tracking) on Avalon—an explanation Zephyr never deigned to communicate until much later—Vasili's native distrust of the Unseelie in my harem sharpened to acute aggression.

The fact that he and Zephyr have enough gigajoules of unconsummated sexual tension crackling between them to electrify this superyacht—just in case we lose both engines in the storm—only makes their prickly dynamic more complicated.

And that dynamic doesn't even take into account the latest complication. Namely, that sex demon sporting V's mating bite who's bunked down in our guest room.

Obviously, Zephyr doesn't know.

Clearly, we gotta tell him.

But just as clearly, now is not the time.

I'm still holding my breath over that inflammatory challenge the Goblin King threw down when Zephyr, very precisely, sets his wet boots aside. Still crouching in his form-fitting dragonscale like an Avenger on our designer carpet, he looks slowly over the naked warlock looming over him.

An arc of electric silence leaps between them. Potent enough to ignite the atmosphere in here like it's pyrophoric.

As Lucius wrestles out of his *Downton Abbey* PJ's, Ronin's wary head pops up to check out the sitch. Peering over Lucius' shoulder, Ronin's topaz eyes are all smoldery with arousal, but he looks (understandably) concerned. Lucius, who's at least half wolf by now, gives an irritable snarl over his other shoulder, eyes glowing red as embers.

"I vow, Vasili Nikolayevich Romanov. Is that an order thou art giving?" the Dark Fae King says softly into the humming silence. "One does not issue orders to a king."

Shit.

It's always a bad sign when Zephyr goes all ancient Fae formal. And it's worse (like, an actual threat, given he's also a warlock) when he uses someone's full name.

Now the entire bedroom holds its breath.

Ronin tries to sit up. Lucius pins him flat (where he's safe) with a wolfish growl of warning.

Slowly Zephyr sleeks back a spill of wet hair. His single eye narrows and his face kindles. "I do not abide being *ordered*. You may, however, extend an invitation."

"Call it whatever you like." Vasili's nostrils flare wide in disdain. V sneers down at his rival in that obnoxious way that always makes me want to slap him. I know my snake is feeling uncertain about where he stands with me tonight, thanks to that whole Mordred mating bite situation.

Any hint of his own normal human vulnerability triggers V's hidden fear of rejection.

That fear always brings out the absolute worst in Vasili.

But he hides his uncertainty by wrapping a hand around his long slim shaft, painted fingernails gleaming like black ink in the lamplight. He strokes his hard cock, base to head, in a slow pull that stokes the warmth pulsing between my thighs to a lick of fire.

I moan at the sight.

Helpless to resist, I rock my cunt, sheathed in damp lace, against the impressive bulge of Neo's boner.

Neo cradles my hips between his strong hands to fit his thick dick against my slit. Holding me steady while I writhe in his lap, he twists around to watch the drama.

One look, and our bookworm huffs out an exasperated breath. "Gosh, V, that Fae is soaking wet. At least give the guy a chance to stop shivering before you start bullying him, will you?"

Vasili blinks and his gaze narrows.

My stare swerves abruptly from the electrifying visual of my masturbating alpha to the tensile figure of the Dark Fae King crouched warily at his feet. Under Zephyr's sleek green armor, still dripping with rain, a slight but visible tremor ripples through his supple form.

"Oh, shit," I say softly, rising to my knees in concern. "Zephyr. God. You're freezing."

"It is no matter." A little of the tension cracks as Zephyr pulls off his gauntlets, tosses them onto the chair, then twists his long swath of hair into a thick coil and squeezes.

A thin trickle of rainwater drips onto Neo's dad's carpet.

"Bloody hell, love. It matters." Ronin's dismay pings through our bond. He snatches the climate control console from the nightstand to dial back the A/C. Then he pushes against Lucius' unyielding frame, but our wolf has him pinned. "You need a proper shower, Zeph, and a bowl of that goulash Lucius whipped up to set you to rights. Haven't eaten yet, have you?"

"Xhevith took a goat while we were out." Casually, Zephyr shakes the mass of wet green hair down his back and out of his way. "I ate."

We all take a sec to process that disturbing factoid.

His dragon Xhevith, who isn't a firedrake, devours his meat raw and bloody. Xhev's rider, raised like an alley cat in a hardship sitch where food and fire were both scarce, generally prefers his meat cooked.

But that dragonrider isn't what you'd call overly discerning.

Like I said before, he's feral.

"Um…" I give a hard swallow. "Think we can do better than that, Your Radiance. You need an actual hot meal."

Zephyr shrugs an irritable shoulder and looks indifferent at the concept.

But with him, it's hard to tell.

He could be fucking starving, and he'd never let on.

It upsets me that he flew off—exposed to the brutal elements for *hours*—without a bowl of Lucius' heartening and heavily spiced Hungarian stew warming his belly, for real. Just another sign that Zephyr still doesn't feel enough at home in our harem to ask for what he needs.

My distress radiates through my mating bonds. Still crouched over Ronin like the predator he is, Lucius rumbles a thick growl and looks menacing.

Gently but firmly, Neo swings me off his lap, settles me safely on the bed with Lucius and Ronin, then trots into the master bath. It's big enough to get lost in there, but my fated mate pops out a breath later, clutching a pile of thick towels I know he's pulled right off the heating rack.

That's what we all love about this guy.

He's always willing—sometimes *too* willing—to put his own needs on the back burner and place the rest of us first.

Neo hurries across the cabin, gives the silent V a stern look that warns him to behave, then drops a thick warm towel over Zephyr's shoulders.

That's finally the Unseelie's cue to uncoil to his feet, slip out of the sheathed swords strapped across his back, and prop his deadly weapons against the wall. Now safely disarmed, Zephyr engulfs his dripping head in the warm towel and indulges in a vigorous scrubbing.

I dip a hand into the nightstand drawer, find the lube we stowed in there earlier when we unpacked, and drop the tube discreetly into Lucius' hand. His wolf might not be thinking about lube right now, but Ronin's gonna need it tonight to take that knot.

Then I scramble off the bed, naked except for my panties, and hurry across the cabin to see how Zephyr's doing up close.

Neo is unzipping Zephyr's dragonscale and wrestling the gear off the Dark Fae King's knotted shoulders. Zephyr doesn't wear anything underneath, he's all sleek olive skin and the twisting flex of muscle, honed to a keen edge by the brute strength required for reining a three-ton dragon. While Neo peels the supple armor down the dragonrider's torso, Zephyr dries off carelessly with the towel.

Up close, I can see the goosebumps stippling his skin.

"Shit, Zephyr." I sigh and fold myself around his icy body from behind, wrapping my arms around his taut waist and snuggling my warm front against his cold back. "You shouldn't have stayed out so long."

"My bride." Zephyr thaws enough to turn his head and nuzzle my ear with his rain-chilled lips, because he's no taller than I am. "You supported me to win my crown. Now I intend to support you to win yours. Of that, you may be certain."

"I am," I assure him. "I believe you."

Of course, we all know he can't lie. Twist his words like pretzels, yeah. But outright lie? Nope. It's an Unseelie thing.

Honesty.

He sighs into my ear. "Tell me. Did you succeed in your quest? Did you acquire the artifact?"

I lean into the hot suck of his mouth. His deft tongue teases the piercings along the curve of my upper ear. The sting of a tiny fang pricks my earlobe. A tingly warmth races down my neck to make me shiver. Ears are foreplay for him, and I'm more than willing to go where he's leading.

Still, I hesitate to answer that question about the Horn—and exactly how we nabbed it. "Uh, yeah, we got it. But…"

"Worth it then." Zephyr eases back and drops the damp towel carelessly to the floor. He surrenders to Neo's anxious ministrations with a bone-deep sigh that breathes fatigue, accepting the attention with the innate ease of a male born and bred to be king. "By the moon, Neo Mercury, I swear you are Goddess-sent."

"Gosh, no, it's nothing." Neo is pulling Zephyr's armor down his legs and helping him slither out of it, while I simultaneously share body heat and lend a hand from behind. So I can't see our bookworm's face.

But I know he's blushing with happiness.

"You are indeed something. Both of you," Zephyr says softly, turning to nuzzle the side of my neck. "Sweet boy. And my sweet bride."

I quiver under the brush of his cool mouth against my hot skin. My pulse kicks up and my nipples tingle. I breathe out a moan and lean into him. My fingers graze his flat belly to brush his wiry lick of pubic hair.

Like the rest of his hair, it's green.

I never meant to marry the guy legally (according to Unseelie lore) the night he and I broke the curse that was killing his people back on Avalon. Because I fully intend to marry my whole polycule together, officially, over here.

I mean, when I'm crowned.

Still, at some point, I've stopped protesting when Zephyr calls me his bride.

Firmly I clear my head and fortify my resolve so I can kinda, you know, warn my Dark Fae about that incubus—his mortal enemy—who's shacking up next door.

"I can heat you some goulash in the galley?" Neo offers hopefully, rising with his arms full of dripping dragonscale. "Just let me hang this in the bathroom to dry—"

"I am not hungry," Zephyr says softly. "For food."

A fresh jolt of tension hums and crackles through the still air.

In unison, we all glance toward Vasili.

While Neo and I fuss over his rival, the Goblin King has withdrawn to sulk near the window, eyes shuttered and face in shadow, with the deck lights glowing through his silver hair like a halo. His tall silhouette lurks, lean and sinewy, against the glass.

Still naked, still hard, still wicked.

I love him. I always will. He's my snake.

But, when it comes to him and Zephyr, I don't trust my own alpha.

Sure, V might've made the tactical choice to ease back (temporarily) on the bullying. But that sexual command he gave the Dark Fae King still echoes in the air between them like an incantation.

"Am I correct in deducing, Vasili Romanov," Zephyr murmurs, "that you'd relish my imperial tongue wrapped around your pretty cock?"

Still leaning into Zephyr's lean back with my arms wrapped around his waist and my chin perched on his shoulder, my mouth falls open on a gasp.

Even Lucius rolls over and props himself on one elbow, his half-shifted features intense with interest, to hear the answer to that one. Ronin shoots up to sit, clutching Lucius' shoulder with barely contained anticipation.

No doubt about it. It'd be way easier for Ronin—and me, and all of us—if V and Zephyr stopped fighting and started fucking.

But, considering the two guys hate each other, that outcome's been hard to finagle.

"What I'd 'relish' is for you to suck me off until I unload down your imperial throat," Vasili snaps. "Now you can tell me a *lah-dee-dah* Unseelie royal doesn't sully his royal mouth by giving head."

"I am not opposed," Zephyr says mildly—to my complete fucking shock (because he's dommy as hell, and I've definitely been assuming the same thing as V). "So long as you're prepared to return the favor… Goblin King."

That's the first time Zephyr's ever used Vasili's nickname.

"Oh, hell to the yeah," I whisper.

Jesus.

I'm so into this whole idea of those two finally getting together, I'm surprised I don't burst into flames on the spot.

Neo's jaw falls open. In fact, he's so startled by Zephyr's totally unexpected concession that he drops the armful of wet towels he just gathered. Ignoring the mess at his feet, he gropes blindly to adjust his glasses, like that's gonna help him hear better.

"Oh, fuck me." Ronin surges to his knees and grips Lucius' shoulder till his knuckles whiten. "Am I hearing this shit?"

"A king for a king," Zephyr breathes into the spellbound stillness. "That seems only fitting, does it not?"

Abruptly I decide the whole tricky subject of the incubus in our guest bedroom can definitely wait. The next few minutes are gonna be way too good to interrupt.

Because I'm still hugging Zephyr to warm him all the way up, I can feel the tension running through his lithe naked frame. The tight flex of his ass presses into my hips. The ripply twist of his abs twitches under my palms.

"However, I won't come at your call like a dog," the Dark Fae states. "If I am indeed the lover you wish to pleasure tonight, Romanov, then you'll come to me. That token of your respect, I do require."

The air floods with the sudden scent of my own pheromones—sharp and sweet, like creamy peaches. That biochemical hit of my arousal affects all my guys. There isn't a limp dick within smelling distance, so that extra dash of hormones ratchets the tension in here to the breaking point.

I swallow hard and bite my lip.

Shit, shit, shit. I want this for these two. I want it so bad I can taste it.

But V… he's… unpredictable.

He'll never admit it, but he feels threatened by Zephyr.

That makes him even more dangerous.

Vasili shifts into motion and saunters forward. The deck lights limn his supple frame and gilded mane, but cast his face into shadow. When he glides into the cone of light from the bedside lamp, the illumination lends his pale skin a warmth he usually lacks. Without the smoky eyeliner and shimmery lip gloss that play up his '80s punk rock glam, his sharp chiseled features are naked.

Exposed.

But he's still so dangerous.

As he looms over Zephyr, his ice-blue eyes glitter like that glacier must've done with the *Titanic*'s floodlights bearing down. A deadly warning—received too late.

Graceful as a Siren, regal as a king, Vasili sinks slowly to his knees.

Still wrapped in my arms from behind, Zephyr is wary and tight as a coiled spring. Not unwisely, he's poised for one of Vasili's nasty tricks.

Even violence.

Behave yourself, Goblin King, I whisper through our bond. *He's one of us now. He really is. Be nice to him for me.*

Vasili's diamond eyes flash, sharp with spite. His vicious stare never leaves our Unseelie. Those two are locked together, eyeball to eyeball, like cobra and mongoose in a fighting pit. But Vasili's head inclines, very slightly, to acknowledge he's heard me.

"You'd better make this… accommodation… worth my while, Your Radiance," V says on a savage hiss. "Or I fucking swear to you, I'll bite off your imperial cock and swallow it."

Guess that's Vasili's version of being nice.

Chapter Eight
Zephyr

By the moon.

There's certainly something in the air tonight.

I've been hard as granite since the moment I entered this sex-drenched room. I've been straining for control since well before this sweet Mercury boy stripped me naked and my luscious bride pressed her soft breasts against my back.

By now, I'm a smoking volcano of sexual need.

The silken slide of my horrible rival's fingers up my thighs is nearly sufficient, all on its own, to make me erupt.

Vasili Romanov.

With every caress, his lacquered nails—black as pitch—spark tectonic shocks of alarm and arousal down the backs of my thighs. Against the terrain of my skin, the dark gleam of a square ruby graces his middle finger like a *fuck you.* From his opposing hand, a silver skull leers at me, with icy diamond chips for eyes.

An accursed object, that ring, or I am no Unseelie.

Suffice it to say, this deadly creature's proximity to my exposed and furiously erect manhood is threatening enough to spill goosebumps down my spine.

Zara's soft but lethal hand glides down the quivering jut of my hip bone to close over his. Abruptly, the leering skull on his knuckle is hidden.

My bride is warning him—this most complicated and dangerous of all her mates.

She is warning him to behave.

But she is also… coaxing him.

"Be nice to him for me, Goblin King," she whispers to him, this dreadful alpha she inexplicably adores. Her petal-soft lips graze my shoulder. "And I'll be nice to you."

"My, my, little queen. Is that *absolution* you're offering?" Cobra-quick, the warlock's gilded head rears up. His wicked eyes, glittering like frost in the moonlight, flick toward me. "For my… *many sins*?"

Dryly, I wonder what the latest of those might be.

I'm no Catholic, which is how my bride was raised (to the extent anyone gave a damn) by her Irish mob boss father. Obviously, I'm not even Christian. But I've read their quaint lore.

Christian superstition, it transpires, can be quite useful for banishing demons.

Hearing Vasili seek absolution for his mysterious sins, Zara's breath hitches. My bride nestles her lush breasts into my back, nipples ripe as grapes teasing my skin. Her hot cunt, barely covered by a scrap of lace, tucks against my buttocks.

"Yeah," she says huskily. "I forgive you. But if this is your Act of Contrition, you snake, then you better make it good for Zephyr. I mean it."

"Oh, well, in that case." Vasili's cruel mouth curls from a pout to an evil grin that simultaneously hardens my cock and makes my blood run cold. *"Deus meus, ex toto corde poenitet me…"*

He's still whispering the words of a Catholic prayer like an incantation when his gilded head dips. Delicate as a butterfly alighting on a blade of grass, his lips graze the sensitive sac of my balls. My testicles tighten and clench. Molten heat races down my thighs and swells my shaft, punctuated by a ragged gasp.

Fuck the moon. That desperate, needy, starved sound was *mine*.

My tormentor pauses his prayers long enough to spare me a coy upward look. Through his slip of a smile, one razor-sharp fang peeks out.

What *is* it with this yacht tonight? The air in this intimate, dim-lit boudoir veritably pulses with sex.

The snake is my rival. One I never dare trust. At the moment, I hardly care.

I burn to touch him.

Still, I must be wary.

I don't have Ash here to guard my back. My reliable consort, who should surely be appearing to welcome me home any moment, is oddly absent. That sweet Mercury boy, who's rushed off with my dripping armor like a helpful house elf and is now rushing back—flushed and earnest, so worried yet so excited for everything he believes may shortly occur—is not the ally I'll need if I trigger one of Romanov's killing rages.

Instead, I clench my fists at my sides. *"Vasili."*

Romanov smirks at my response, then leans in to lick my quivering bollocks like a cat licks cream.

Speaking of which…

My gaze darts toward the fur-lined riding cloak I've left wadded on the chair, the protective garment no dragonrider ever ascends into the frigid skies without. For moon's sake, I've nearly forgotten—

"Are you paying attention, Your Radiance?" Vasili's silken lips drop a tiny kiss among the wiry green curls at the base of my cock.

It's the first kiss he's ever given me… there.

Every drop of blood in my body rushes straight to my shaft. Every thought in my head dissolves into smoke. My rival licks a slow hot stripe up the underside of my straining cock like a streak of lava.

Goddess save me.

The moment he reaches my tip and starts suckling, I'll empty my load in this vile creature's mouth.

Barely in time, my hands shoot out and lock around Romanov's head. My fingers lace through his tousled shag of hair. His pale eyes, glittering with arousal and malice in equal measure, veer to mine.

"Vasili," I groan, fingers grazing the rims of his ears, even though he's no Fae and they're not pointed. If I don't establish the pecking order between us tonight, this warlock will challenge and threaten me forever. "You heard our queen. Be good for me, beautiful one."

That is Ash's name for him. *Beautiful.* I have already seen how well the snake likes it. The surest way to this one's narcissistic heart is by pampering his vanity.

He rewards me for it now with a sultry wink.

"Ideo firmiter propono," he whispers, a hot lick of breath against the swollen and twitching head of my cock, *"adiuvante gratia Tua—"*

Unless I'm greatly mistaken, this dreadful warlock is uttering the Roman Catholic Act of Contrition.

In Latin.

He is playing with me.

The narrow band of my eyepatch cuts into my perspiring brow. I long to tear the thing off, but I don't care to expose my deformity before this exquisite and vicious man. Instead, I narrow my eye at the top of his head and tighten my fingers in his hair.

"Be warned, fellow monarch," I rasp. "I do not intend to become one more of your casual conquests."

"Hmmmm. You don't say?" He pauses to circle the engorged head of my cock with his tongue and taste my weeping slit, while I close my eyes and pray for fortitude. "What precisely do you mean?"

"I mean," I groan through gritted teeth, "that I see you. I *see* you—wielding your charms like a witch and your body like a Siren to lure men to their doom. I've watched you do it with the dragon. Maxim. He's a cunning and vicious killer, but he's mindless clay in your hands—"

He acknowledges the truth of my words (because, after all, I cannot lie) with a self-satisfied smirk. Simultaneously, he cups and fondles my swollen balls in a wicked hand. I break off on a ragged groan.

Eruption is imminent.

Neo gasps and falls to his own knees to watch. At some point, the bookworm has quietly shed his own remaining garments—anticipating my needs without waiting for my command—like the good compliant boy he is.

Ah, Neo.

He is my bride's fated mate, and Ash's lover. The first of her mates to welcome Ash and me into the harem. The sight of his buff body kneeling at my feet (precisely where I've burned to order him), with his bitable buttocks resting on his heels and his big hands spread over those bulging quads, innocent eyes wide and soft lips parted…

The sight of Neo Theodophilus Mercury kneeling at my feet nearly finishes the job and unmans me on the spot.

The other one—Vasili—is still fondling my balls and blowing on my wet cock. By sheer force of will, I grit my teeth and finish what I intend to say to that one.

"Vasili Nikolayevich Romanov. Every warlock in this harem dances to your tune like rats trailing the moon-fucked Piper. Without Zara to stay your malice, they'd happily follow you to their doom. But I am the Unseelie King. Dip into your cauldron of tricks to manipulate me, and you will find me… unreceptive."

The perverse creature doesn't even bother with a denial.

Instead, he hums and encases my quivering cockhead in the wet silk of his mouth.

Blind with pleasure, my eye nearly rolls back in my head.

"Uh-oh. Looks like he sees you, Goblin King." Zara's hot little body undulates against my back. Her fingers dance over mine, then smooth the hair from his face so we can all watch him suck.

Inch by inch, Romanov swallows me down, sharp eyes lifted to mine to observe his effect. Zara moans softly and nuzzles my ear. I clench my jaw and tremble with the urge to seat myself balls deep in his alluring suck.

"An Unseelie," I pant, "perceives… what mere mortals… cannot."

Ronin's husky chuckle rises from the bed. "Best be careful with that Dark Fae, love. Looks like he's got your number, dead to rights."

Since the moment I returned to this sex-drunk ship, I've been intensely aware of Ronin. The way I'm always intensely aware of him—my lost love, my first love, the savage mortal boy I loved to despair, now grown to a man most formidable—crouching on the edge of the senator's obscenely large bed to savor my undoing.

While I clutch Vasili's head and rock into his divine mouth, my gaze slews toward Ronin. Black hair swirling in a cloud of ink around him, he falls forward on hands and knees to accommodate the wolf—Lucius Aries—who looms behind, lubing his own thick girth and the ruddy knot swelling at the base of his shaft.

Vasili hums around my cock in a way that's so intensely pleasurable he makes my vision blur. He backs off a little, then sucks me in deeper, his skilled tongue lapping the tender underside of my cock. His finger steals behind my balls to tickle the vulnerable nerve-packed span of my perineum.

My rear passage—which is certainly off limits to this creature, just as his hole is off limits to me—flutters and clenches in protective instinct.

"You're being so nice to him, Goblin King," Zara whispers. Her small hand glides down my abdomen and wraps around the base of my cock. Her fingers stroke and knead me in a building rhythm.

Under Neo's fascinated gaze, she's holding my cock for Vasili to suck.

Neo gasps and leans closer to watch. I vow, the poor boy's glasses are steaming.

Goddess save me.

This witch and her warlocks will be my absolute ruin.

Vasili closes a slender hand over hers. Fuck the moon, now they're both kneading me. His silken mouth bobs along my straining length like he knows his business. Well, he's certainly watched closely enough while Zara and Ash and Ronin get me off. He knows how I like it. Hard and fast and ruthless the first time, then languid and lingering as the night lengthens.

How I wish I could fuck him. I'd risk my own crown for that rare pleasure. But he guards that precious hole of his like a sacred talisman.

As matters now stand, I cannot fuck him.

Failing that, I wish I could trust him.

But I am no such fool.

He has my vulnerable cock fully seated in his fanged mouth. If I press him before he's ready, Vasili Romanov is eminently capable of following through on his threat of castration.

"Mmmm, that's so nice," Zara encourages both of us. "Look what the two of you are doing to Neo… and Ronin."

In the senator's big bed, Lucius and Ronin are fucking. The headmaster has a fist wrapped in Ronin's long hair and Ronin's face shoved brutally into a pillow. But Ronin has twisted so he can still watch, amber eyes gone glassy and pupils blown wide with pleasure. As Lucius pounds into him from behind, powerful body flexing, chestnut curls flying around his shoulders, the wolf shifter bares his fangs at me in a savage grin.

As for Neo, he's hovering so close that he's practically pressed his nose to my thigh. Now he glances up at me for permission, which I grant with a lordly nod, then lays a timid hand on my hip. He's holding me steady, like Zara herself. But his other hand hovers near his own prodigious length. Through his steamy glasses, his beseeching stare lifts again to mine.

He's aching to touch himself. But he's waiting for permission.

"You're a very good boy, sweeting," I tell him, my own voice slurred with pleasure. "Show me how you touch yourself."

His throat moves as he swallows. A blush washes over his strong cheekbones to warm his fair skin.

"Go on, baby," Zara encourages him, voice soft with love. "You're allowed."

She's still holding my dick for Vasili to suckle, but she ruffles Neo's magenta curls with a gentle hand. She's his alpha as well as his queen, so that's all the consent he requires.

In an agony of blushes, Neo bows his head and presses his brow to my thigh. But his hand sneaks down to palm his own thick shaft.

"My, my," Vasili backs off my cock to murmur. "Someone has big eyes for our First Boy. But I'm his alpha too, Your Radiance. You should also be asking *my* permission—"

"*You* are otherwise occupied." Heartless, I clench my fists in Vasili's gilded hair to pin him in place and thrust into his wicked mouth until my cock bumps the back of his throat. "No more sulking and mouthing off. Show me how much of my cock you can take. King to king."

No doubt, this is a calculated risk.

But this infuriating warlock has been teasing me with nibbles at the apple all night, and I'm mindless with hunger for a proper bite.

The air is swimming with the citrus sweetness of Zara's mating scent and the dark musk of Vasili's—both Mogadon, exuding pheromones that are genetically designed for seduction. The gamy scent of wolf, wafting from the aroused shifter, delivers an added kick.

With all these biochemicals swirling through the room, 'tis no wonder we're all drunk.

Yet surely, there's something more in the air tonight than the familiar scents of my bride and her harem. The very air we breathe is thick, a plush fabric of primal sex that strokes my skin like a tangible brush of velvet. At the same time, Ash's absence chafes me like an ill-fitting boot. Even the dragon, Maxim, has surely been away too long.

Then the snake stops teasing my perineum to circle my pucker with an insinuating finger. My half-formed worries eddy through my brain and swirl into ether.

For the first time in many hours, I'm no longer chilled to the bone.

I'm burning up.

Consumed and devoured by a raging inferno of need.

Maddened with craving, I rip off the eyepatch that's cutting into my brow and cast the detestable thing wildly aside. Then I thrust deep into the divine suck of my enemy's delectable mouth.

"*Mine,*" I snarl, pumping into Vasili in a frenzy, as though I'm nothing more than the frothing, feral, half-wild beast he believes me to be. "Your wicked, naughty tease of a mouth. You can guard your precious hole like the Crown Jewels. This mouth of yours is *mine*."

His pale eyes flash with spiteful malice. I imagine he'd like to hiss at me like a rattlesnake.

But his mouth is full.

His eyes narrow in vengeful promise of the unpleasantries that are certain to come. But his throat tightens and ripples around my shaft as he swallows me down, then eases off and does it again. His throat kneads every inch of my throbbing length like a fist.

Even as his finger rims my defenseless hole.

Oh, my Goddess. I can no longer refrain.

My back arches, my hips flex, my balls clench. With a savage shout that rips loose from deep in my chest, I erupt and unload endless months of hostility and aggression and enmity down my rival's accommodating throat.

My entire world goes red with an obliterating pleasure that roars and pulses and jets through my veins like lava.

Dimly, I feel the hot spurt of another man's spend spattering my thigh. Not Vasili, because the warlock is far too self-contained for that. Denying me the pleasure of his climax is Vasili's way of maintaining what he imagines to be his dominance in this harem.

No. The warlock spilling his lavish seed down my legs with a whine of relief is the sweet one.

Neo.

Eye still closed, I fumble blindly to find the boy's muscled shoulder, then give him a clumsy squeeze to convey my praise. He moans and rubs his cheek against my knuckles.

An eternity later, my spent and twitching dick slips from Vasili's mouth. The snake swallows down the last of my seed, then releases me with a lazy lick that wrings out of me a rather pathetic whimper.

My whimper gives rise to his satisfied chuckle. My dazed eye struggles to focus. Vasili licks a final creamy droplet of my seed from the corner of his mouth with a hum.

Well, let the prideful creature preen. I am well past caring.

My knees are buckling.

My body is swaying.

Zara's strength alone holds me on my feet.

"Mmmmm, that's my snake. You've been so nice to him, Vasili. Look what you've done to him." My bride nuzzles the back of my drooping neck, then lets me sag gently into Neo's waiting arms.

The boy accepts the burden of my boneless weight with a shy smile, then settles back comfortably to his haunches with me cradled to his chest. I throw an affectionate arm around his neck. Both of us are messy with his release, but I'm of no mind to complain.

My bride gives the cum-spattered tableau of Neo and me, wrapped clumsily in each other's arms, an approving grin.

Next, she spares an assessing glance at a groaning Ronin, who is fisting the sheets and biting the pillow as the wolf works the ruddy bulge of his knot ruthlessly into Ronin's tight hole.

For the moment, very clearly, those two mates on the bed are consumed by each other.

Zara sighs with contentment, then cocks her sexy hip. She gifts Vasili, poised alertly on his knees on the senator's expensive carpet, with her sultry smile. "Looks like it's my turn to be nice to you. Come and get me, bad boy."

"Oh, wow," Neo whispers. "This is gonna be good."

I lift my sagging head from Neo's accommodating shoulder just in time to see the snake pounce.

Chapter Nine
Zara

"You've been positively *wicked*, little queen." Vasili's vengeful hiss strokes my skin like dragonscale. "Making me wait to ruin that pretty pussy."

Indignant as fuck, my mouth pops open. "Well, it's my pussy, isn't it? Besides, after that shit you pulled today with Mor—"

"Silence." His long pale body springs like a striking cobra. He drives me three reeling steps back. The words splinter in my mouth. I'm a cat burglar, not easy to unbalance (or silence). But I have zero chance against a warlock like him.

Not with the mood he's in.

Still, I recover my balance, stand my ground, pop a hip for attitude, and give it the old college try. "Look, Goblin King—"

"First you make me beg. Then you make me *wait*. How dare you. Now of all times!" He means, now when we're trying to get pregnant.

And he's fucking psychotic about it.

I open my mouth to say so. But he runs right over my conversational opening.

"I'm going to ruin you. I'm going to fuck that naughty, needy, greedy little pussy until you're a drippy, squishy, filthy *mess*." He crowds into me, my tits crushed against his chest, his rigid cock pressed into my tummy and smearing precum over my skin. His potent mating scent of caramel and vetiver hits me like a freight train. That scent—laced with his powerful pheromones—makes my heart pound and my head swim. Plus there's a yummy note of birchwood lurking underneath all that sexy that's new.

Which is… interesting.

His scent's changing.

Just like mine did when I nixed the BC and got serious about making baby witches.

Breathless with all this excitement, I reach up to grip his sinewy shoulders, lean and corded like a ballet dancer at the Cirque du Soleil, for leverage. As I stagger back under the weight of his much taller body, my face level with the sleek lickable plane of his chest, I breathe him in deep (mistake) and try to reason with him (also a mistake).

"Okay, V. In my own defense. You were the last warlock in this whole harem I thought would give a single shit about knocking me up—"

"I don't! Of course I don't. This isn't about that!" Viciously, he shoves me backward, herding me toward the bed, and just keeps coming. His jutting dick precedes his relentless advance like a battering ram.

Sweet Jesus.

Sucking Zephyr off has made this snake of mine *so* hard. Just looking at the long curving length of V's furious boner makes my mouth water.

I bite my lip and slide a hand down his lean body. He catches my arm neatly and twists it behind my back. My shoulder heats, poised on the edge of pain like a gymnast on the balance beam.

I could still break free (because black belt, I'm one and he isn't) but I don't. I let my enraged alpha have his little moment of dominance. My excited pulse throbs, hot and heavy, between my legs.

Of course, being me, I've still gotta yank his chain.

Vasili Romanov can bully everyone else in this entire Academy like the sociopathic asshole he is.

But I'm not gonna let him bully me.

Or anyone else in this harem.

"I don't believe you, bad boy." Bent backward over his unforgiving arm while he pins my wrist, I trail my free hand down his sinewy torso, cool skin quivering under my touch, and lock onto his basilisk stare. "Here's your issue. You wanna make me pregnant so bad, you can't think straight."

A furious flush of color races across the elegant slant of his cheekbones.

"For fuck's sake! You know I despise infants!" My dominant alpha tightens his grip and looms over me, venomous with wrath.

"Yeah. So you keep saying." I snort. "All *I'm* saying is, that's a lotta exclamation marks for a guy who doesn't give a shit."

That genderfluid dragon he shifts into (who apparently carries eggs that could potentially get fertilized, which is a totally new discovery, who knew?) Anyway. Vasili carrying fertilizable eggs in dragon form is an off-limits topic.

Still, even if we're not talking about it, he and Max *have* started fucking while they're both shifted.

Which is pretty sus, if you ask me.

I shift my hand from V's slim waist to the taut plane of his cheek, glittering with the icy dust of late-night stubble.

It's a novel sensation, having him all raspy like that.

He's been so unsettled tonight, with a horny demon lurking next door and me all pissy right here, that he hasn't even shaved the way he normally does, persecuting any follicle of hair that dares to sprout anywhere on his body with fanatical zeal.

"If it's not about me, is this about you—I mean, uh, your dragon getting pregnant?" I say carefully. "Because, like, the witching world needs witches. We'd all be totally into that, I would too, if you and Max wanted—"

"Silence!" Incandescent with fury, he twists my arm like a licorice stick, grips my waist in a ruthless hand, and drives me backward across the carpet. Clearly, he's not even gonna let me finish.

With a sigh, I let my free hand drop from his intriguingly raspy cheek.

"Still a sore subject then," I say tartly. "Clearly. But I definitely wanna talk about you and Max at some point."

"What a pity." His cold eyes gleam like stars as his body presses into me. "There's nothing about me and Max that I particularly care to discuss."

Annoyance sizzles in my chest like heartburn. "Yeah, well, you're not the only one in this relationship. I don't want Max hurt."

"He won't be." To shut me up, he gives me a good shove. (Like somehow that's gonna prove his whole point.)

Under V's twisting weight, the backs of my knees hit the back of the bed. Then I'm toppling backward onto the mattress, arms and hair flying around me, almost clobbering Lucius—who ducks with a startled snarl, but never stops driving that knot of his into Ronin in a frenzy.

Vasili uncoils and lands on top of me, catching his weight on his arms to pin me beneath him. His eager cock nudges my closed thighs till I squirm.

"Alright, loves?" Ronin stops moaning and writhing long enough to check.

Braced on hands and knees with his muscular ass in the air and his golden skin sheened with sweat while our wild half-shifted headmaster pounds into him from behind, Ronin Pendragon is a thing of beauty and power.

Sweet fuck.

Lucius is wrecking his hole with that knot.

"We should be asking you that." I turn my head fully to Ronin. That warlock of mine is a wicked telepath and he's clearly okay—more than okay—with getting dicked and knotted by our prof.

But actual consent is always good to get. And Vasili in particular could use a role model.

"You shitting me? With V and Zeph finally hooking up like that?" Ronin's face lights up with his savage grin. "I'm right as rain, love."

With a growl, Lucius fists Ronin's hair and shoves his face roughly into the pillow.

Yowsa.

Looks like both my alphas in this bed are losing their shit.

Especially when Vasili twists up to sit, pins me to the bed with a brutal hand around my throat, straddles my thighs, then darts a hand under the pillow. He emerges with a knife from his hidden stash.

Despite his punishing grip on my throat, I give a good yell. Damn it, I know where he's going with this.

"Wait, you snake! Don't you fucking dare. I like these panties—"

"Too bad." His knife slashes down. "No more waiting."

I howl in protest as he slices through my panties and ruins yet another set of my lingerie from Paris. The slashed scrap of tangerine lace falls away.

Which I guess is better than him slitting someone's throat while he's this sexed up.

"You asshole," I grumble. "We barely packed for this boating trip. I'm gonna run outta undies. One more fuck with you and your knives, and I'll be down to my granny panties."

"Good." V's cruel mouth curls in a grin that exposes the razor-sharp tips of his pretty fangs. "I vastly prefer you naked."

That heated look in his cold eyes makes me shiver… all over.

Like all my alphas, Vasili's been worked up since I noped out on my birth control. Me being pissed at him tonight hasn't helped. He really doesn't handle any kind of rejection well, *at all*.

This is the result.

With a single vicious strike, he buries his knife to the hilt in the mattress—gouging a good slash in the poofy silver duvet Neo's dad probably ordered special for this Alaskan king bed. Somewhere in the room, Neo gives a squeak of dismay.

Undaunted, V spreads my thighs wide under his hands and gazes down at my splayed body with his diamond stare.

I sprawl beneath his weight, wild hair flung across the bed and trapped under me, tits heaving as I work to fill my lungs. The mattress jolts beneath me under Lucius' fierce thrusts. Neo's interested face appears over Vasili's shoulder, glasses sliding down his nose, as he gently decants a satisfied-looking Zephyr into our bed.

With a lazy grin, Zephyr reaches for Neo's hand and tugs him into bed alongside him.

Oh, hell to the yeah.

Every night I manage to get Zephyr into the same bed with any of my alphas is, like, a major victory.

We're finally making progress knitting this crazy quilt of generally hostile and headstrong individuals into one beautiful polycule.

I mean, you know, *slowly*.

Without looking away from my sprawled and naked body, Vasili curls his lip to show Zephyr a little fang. Then V nudges my thighs wider, spreads my pussy with his thumbs, and leans in to take a long slow sniff. His pupils blow wide and black with need.

Wow.

My snatch has been soaked ever since V went down on Zephyr and pretty much destroyed the guy with his wicked Goblin King mouth. Now, when I'm so exposed to V's heated stare, when he's openly breathing in the scent of my cunt, I'm totally dripping with my own slick.

I swear, he's got me spreadeagled and pinned to this bed like a butterfly in a display case.

Poised over my pussy like Gollum with the Ring of Power, V is mesmerized. Totally mesmerized. Absolutely silent and still, except for the rhythmic sway we're all experiencing due to Lucius fucking Ronin into the mattress.

Zephyr crawls up for a better view and sits, propped against the headboard, like the Unseelie King he is, then gathers Neo possessively against his side. That feral Dark Fae face looks naked without his eyepatch, the empty socket soft and defenseless under his scarred eyelid, tousled green hair scattered over his knotted shoulders. His single keen eye darts between Ronin and me—both his mates—in this bed.

Both of us getting fucked by other guys.

Still relaxed and sated from his own recent O, with a contented Neo snuggled into his side and our bookworm's trusting head resting on Zephyr's shoulder, my royal Unseelie mate is tolerating the sitch going down in this bed better than I feared.

So far.

Staring down at my splayed and dripping pussy, Vasili's throat ripples in a hard swallow.

I lick my lips and say huskily, "What happens next, bad boy?"

V's eyes flash up to meet mine and narrow. "Am I… forgiven? For all my nasty little sins?"

For a sec, it's a literal struggle to remember what sins I'm even supposed to be forgiving him for. Then in a rush, I recall him summoning and then biting the sex demon in our guest room. A demon who just so happens to be Zephyr's mortal enemy. An enemy whose proximity Zephyr still doesn't even know about. (Yeah, I know. But it still seems like an awkward moment to tell him.)

Right now, I'm focused on Vasili.

My snake is a complicated creature.

Sure, he should've talked it through with us before he bit, like I said. But nursing a grudge and withholding sex from him?

Just not my style.

Anyway, that shit would only make him worse.

I suck in a breath that makes my boobs rise, which draws his stare like a magnet. Low and throaty with need, I say, "Let's talk about it while we're fucking."

Despite the intensity of the moment, V breaks into a riff of surprised laughter. He doesn't laugh often, so that makes me smile too. I'm still smiling when he purrs, "I do love the way you think."

I wonder if that's his Goblin King way of saying he loves *me*.

With a hum, he fits the engorged head of his pretty cock against my slick hole. Pulse hammering in my ears and throbbing in my cunt, I bend my knees and tilt my hips in welcome.

His narrow hips flex and he surges inside, well lubed by my own abundant cream. My aching core clenches and ripples around all that length and more-than-welcome hardness. His head falls back and his spine arches. His lips part to reveal the sharp incisors he normally wants to hide.

With a long breathy *"Aaaahhh!"* he fills me up, inch by inch, till he nudges my cervix.

I'm so fucking fertile I can feel myself unfurl like a flower, sucking the first droplets of his jizz deep into my womb.

I draw up my knees till they graze my biceps, wrap my feet around his thrusting hips, and angle my pelvis to let him press deeper. He snarls and falls forward on his elbows, locks his mouth against Lucius' mating scars on my throat, and fucks into me like he's punishing both of us with pleasure.

The first pulse of climax catches me by surprise and clenches my pussy around his cock. The sensation is so intense my eyes practically cross. By now, my alpha is buried so deep inside me, I swear I can taste him in the back of my throat.

"Cheese on toast," I say on a long moan. "Fuck, V, you're so hard."

"And you're so wet for me, darling." Vasili withdraws till I whimper, the bastard, then slides back into me with the sinuous undulation of a sidewinder writhing across the sand. "You're so tight and needy for my alpha cock inside you tonight, aren't you?"

My words are gone. By now, given the way he's fucking me, all I can do is moan.

"Hmmmm." He hums with satisfaction and presses his deadly mouth to my ear so I can feel the prick of his fangs. "I do believe I'm going to destroy you."

I'd be more concerned by that threat if he wasn't literally shaking with the force of his own need. He yearns to seed my uterus with his own baby witch or warlock so bad, I fucking know it.

No matter what he says.

He grips behind my knees to deepen the angle and spread me wider, lining up his cock with my cervix like a pilot landing a 747. Then he throttles for my runway and pistons into me, pace quickening, voicing a hiss on every downstroke.

Experiencing the force of manhood that's him in a mating rut still blows my mind.

Every. Goddamn. Time.

I mean, this is a guy who never even thought he liked girls till he met me.

He literally identified as gay.

Even now, he's barely bi.

We've all figured out I'm the only girl who's ever gonna do it for him. Even if he won't admit how psychotically obsessed he is to be the one who knocks me up.

"You do realize, of course, I can hear you," he mutters into my boob, mouthing the twin mating scars he left just over my nipple. "Psychotic, am I?"

Delicious little shocks of pleasure ripple through me, knifing straight from my tit to my clit.

"Yeah, I know, Goblin King. And you're not denying a word of it. Are you?" I dig my heels into his flexing ass, bury one hand in his tousled shag of hair, and stretch the other to catch Ronin's outflung hand.

As Lucius snarls and pistons into his mate, my fingers lace with Ronin's hot Leo grip.

Lucius' reddish gaze fixes on V—his co-alpha—reaming the queen they share. His wolf voices a growl of approval. Then Lucius bends over Ronin's back, wraps an arm around Ronin's waist and a hand around Ronin's straining dick, and starts pumping.

"Oh, fuck me," Ronin groans. "Fuck. *Lucius.* Keep that up and I'll—make a bloody mess—all over the senator's bed."

"That's the general idea, my dear one," Lucius says, gruff with tenderness, in his guttural wolf voice. "I live to make you messy."

"Sign me up for that too," I gasp and tighten my grip on Ronin, just to add my two cents. I love those two guys together.

Then I gasp again, because V latches onto my nipple in a hard sucking pull, tugging and twisting my nipple ring just the way I love it. Simultaneously, his hand burrows between us to tease the mating scars next to my pussy. Those scars are from his newest bite, and they're extra sensitive.

I'm already tingling like I stuck a fork in a socket, and hoping like hell I don't accidentally summon lightning, when he starts teasing my swollen clit.

He wants my full attention.

Like I need to be concentrating on just him so he can win the fertility race of little spermatozoon swimmers going down in my uterus.

Obligingly, I scrape my nails down the graceful sweep of V's spine and burrow a finger between the perky swells of his ass. I'm kinda jealous of all the ass play my guys get, for real. I myself would enjoy having a cock for one night so I could ream *them* for once.

Hmmm, now that would *be entertaining.* V's thoughts twine around mine as his clever finger circles my clit. *But I'd still be your dominant alpha.*

Maybe, I parry, just to tease him, even while I rock my clit into his touch. *You let Max fuck you. Bet you'd let me do it too, wouldn't you?*

I barely let Max… oh, wicked hell… Zara…

Grazing the tight rim of V's pucker with my index finger makes him speechless. He shivers and moans and his arms break out in goosebumps. All of which just spurs him to fuck into me harder and faster and deeper.

He's losing his heartless Goblin King mind inside me and I fucking love it.

In fact, I love it so much I'm gonna come.

Again.

This time, I'm not doing that shit alone. I probe Vasili's puckered hole, while he shudders and whimpers behind his teeth. Moaning, he mouths his way up my sweating neck. When I wiggle my finger past the tight ring of muscle and penetrate him barely an inch, he loses it.

His ass squeezes my finger like a vise. His cock swells and spasms, then spurts hot jets of warlock jizz against the rippling walls of my pussy. I can practically visualize, against my currently closed eyelids, the milky kick of his seed shooting into my uterus.

My bent knees dig into my shoulders, my hips strain and pump into him, and my head falls back in a primal scream of triumph.

The bedside lamp flickers under the force of my witchcraft, but the bulb doesn't burst.

Jesus, he's still coming.

He's still fucking *coming*, he's drenching my inner walls and filling every nook and crevice of my uterus with ribbons of potent goblin spunk.

That's when he sinks his vicious fangs into the side of my neck.

I wail from the heart, in a vibrato of mingled protest and intense pleasure. His deep groan of satisfaction is muffled in my flesh.

While I swear at V like a breathless sailor, Ronin clutches my hand and bellows his own climax to the rafters and basically makes a cum-splattered mess out of the senatorial splendor of Neo's dad's bed. Lucius barely manages to stay bipedal while he fucks himself into a howling shuddering frenzy of a finish deep in Ronin's receptive ass.

Those two are knotted together, so they topple sideways in unison and spoon into each other (with Lucius's hairy body functioning as the big spoon), falling across Zephyr's unresisting legs.

The Dark Fae King strokes Ronin's tangled hair tenderly out of his glassy eyes, then holds out a tentative hand to Lucius. Our headmaster rubs his whiskered jaw roughly into Zephyr's palm.

Aaawwww. Lucius is scenting him.

That sign of Lucius' acceptance makes Zephyr's wary face soften into a slight but definite smile.

Still half-hard inside me and pumping his hips lazily into mine, Vasili hums with contentment and laps at my bite to stop the thin double drip of bleeding with the biochemicals in his shifty saliva. I submit to this familiar tending with a sigh of resignation.

He's supposed to ask before he bites. But by now, we've pretty much established that he never does what he's supposed to.

Literally. Never.

"Pot, kettle." Following my disgruntled thoughts through our mating bond without effort, my snake chuckles like the Devil against my skin.

Yeah, he's maybe got a point about that. V and I are well matched for a whole lotta reasons.

Neo roots around the headboard for the thickest, softest pillow he can find, then nudges it gently under my head.

"Such a good boy," Zephyr praises him warmly. My Fae's definitely got a thing for our bookworm, and I am here for it.

"Hey," Neo grumbles good-naturedly, snuggling back into his place against Zephyr's side. "I'm not actually a boy. I'm older than Ronin. I'm twenty-one, and he's only nineteen."

"Ronin was a man at fifteen. You'll still be a boy at fifty." Zephyr's sleepy voice goes silky. "There's no shame in it, sweeting. I intend to take exceeding good care of you. You'll always be my special boy."

Whoa.

Zephyr truly is finding his place in our polycule. The incredible sweetness of this moment seeps through me like a sugar rush.

Of course, being us, that moment of peaceful sweetness doesn't last.

It ends at the exact moment the sliding glass door to the balcony whizzes open to admit a gust of windblown rain. Immediately followed by a naked and violently disturbed dragon shifter.

Soaked to the skin and growling like a bear, Maxim gives his head a ferocious shake to fling dripping ribbons of drenched blond hair out of his flaming eyes. Rainwater flies in all directions.

"I smell a strange male!" my newly arrived alpha announces with a roar. "Who threatens my mates!"

"Oh, dear fuck." Vasili gives my latest bite a final lick, slides lazily out of my drenched and sated pussy, and rolls onto his back. "Don't burst a blood vessel, darling. Or a testicle, with all that testosterone you're pumping out. Truly, I can explain."

That seems highly doubtful.

Ever since we agreed to let that demon bunk down next door, I've known Maxim—the most fiercely territorial and violent of all my alphas—is gonna be hard to handle.

I grimace and struggle onto my elbows, limbs limp and heavy as overcooked spaghetti. A trickle of V's cum spills out of me, which makes Vasili tut with real annoyance.

Sweet Jesus. I'm so saturated with warlock spunk I practically squish.

Before I can muster the brainpower inside my sluggish noggin to settle Max down and form actual words to defuse this looming crisis, the door to the adjacent guest room flies open.

Oh, groovy.

"Yo." That deep demonish rumble rolls from Mordred, whose brawny and still-shirtless frame now fills the doorway. "Guess that's me you're smelling, homeboy. My deodorant musta washed off while I was rocking my kraken and getting your chick her trophy Horn, you feel me? My bad."

With a shocked exclamation that explodes from the depths of the duvet, Zephyr shakes off the multiple warlocks lying across his legs and shoots to his feet.

"You!" Maxim roars at the newly arrived Mordred, definitely using his outdoor voice.

My alpha dragon shifter charges across the bedroom to hurl himself between us—all his mates, but especially the two (counting V when he's shifted) that Max is trying to get pregnant—and this new danger.

"Yup. That'd be me." Unfazed by all this commotion he's clearly causing, Mordred props a hip comfortably against the door jamb, winds a long ribbon of midnight-blue hair around his finger, and grins at us till his dimples pop.

"By the moon," Zephyr hisses, naked and literally trembling with fury. "What is this vile treachery?"

"Hiya, cuz. We can all fight this thing out if that's what you want, true?" the demon drawls in that voice like maple syrup drizzled over hotcakes. "But wouldn't you rather we all fuck it out instead?"

Chapter Ten
Maxim

"No, I will not sit down," I say fiercely to my mates, all of them, for at least the fifth time. "I will not stop pacing and I will not be calm. I will not welcome another male into our harem no matter who my reckless mate has now bitten!"

Barefoot and vengeful in the ripped jeans and tee shirt I have dragged over my body to cover the shame of my hideously scarred back from the alarming intruder in our bedroom, I keep one eye on the demon at all times.

But I underscore my promise with a ferocious glare at Vasili.

Wrapped tightly in his black silk kimono, tall and silent as a pillar of granite lurking near the window, Vasili gives my pacing and agitated body a cold blue stare. One perfectly groomed eyebrow lifts in disdain. This is the look Zara calls the Romanov eyebrow.

Tonight, I am in no mood for it.

I bare my teeth at him—always my most infuriating and difficult mate—in a snarl.

"For once," Zephyr grates out, "that dragon and I are in perfect accord."

If I am agitated, Zephyr is furious. While I lunged for a shirt to cover my scars, he reacted to the demon's appearance—his mortal enemy, of whose nearness he was clearly ignorant—by lunging for his eyepatch to cover his own deformity. (For so he perceives it, his missing eye, the only flaw in his deadly Dark Fae beauty.)

Now he lunges for his swords.

"Don't you dare draw a sword in this bedroom, Your Transcendence," Zara says to him, for at least the third time. That is the name she gives him when she is irritated. "I mean it. No bloodshed. Talk first."

"Talk." Naked and quivering with barely contained rage, the Unseelie grips his crossed swords (which are still sheathed, but barely) and sneers at the enemy demon. His nostrils flare wide with scorn. "The

only words I intend to speak are the banishing spell that will send this treacherous creature back to the hell that spawned him."

The kraken—Mordred, he whose webbed feet and bronze skin and ink-blue hair exude the decadent scent of rum spice and molasses that perfumes the air in this bedroom like the reek of sex—shifts his thickly muscled frame. His clever purple eyes narrow at Zephyr.

The creature looks crafty. I do not trust him.

If that kraken moves against any of my mates—even Zephyr, who is (temporarily) Zara's but not mine—I will destroy him!

A dragonish growl rumbles from my chest. The kraken's gaze shifts to me. Casually, he reaches into the room behind him and produces a trident, taller than he is, capped with three wicked prongs capable of disemboweling a shark.

Or a dragon.

I drop into a defensive crouch and measure the weapon's range with a wary eye. I wonder how far he can hurl it.

"Oh, dear." Naked, Lucius leaps from the bed.

"Yeah, no. Let's not be hasty. That goes for you too, Max." Hastily, my queen scrambles to her feet, then pulls her Academy bathrobe around her lush and fertile nakedness. "Aquaman, you put that thing away. I mean, where did that trident even come from?"

"Happens I was holding it when my new master over there summoned me through the veil. That's how a summoning spell works." Mordred gives my Vasili (who is still inscrutable) a cheeky grin and a wink that infuriates me all over again.

How dare this kraken leer and grin at my mate with those dimples?

At least, in obedience to my queen's command, the kraken leans that menacing trident casually against the wall. Still, I notice that he keeps it well within reach.

I resume my pacing, careful to keep my body solidly between my Zara and this strange sex demon lounging in our doorway.

Meanwhile, Zephyr has positioned himself near the wall so that none of us (including Vasili) lurk in his blind spot.

It is a telling choice.

Whatever tentative bonds of trust might have been woven between him and my mates in this bedroom before I arrived, those bonds did not survive being ambushed by his enemy. The very air we breathe is thick and the silence frayed with broken trust.

"Neo, baby," Zara says with a sigh, "go find Ash for me, okay? We really need him."

Already buttoned into his chinos, Neo nods and pulls a polo shirt over his broad shoulders.

Instead of leaving at once to do her bidding as I expect, he hurries to me. He interrupts my pacing by the simple act of planting his warm hands on my tense shoulders and gazing into my scowling face with his worried eyes.

"Hey, Max," he says softly. "Take a breath, okay?"

He is my Neo. He must never be made to worry.

For his sake, I breathe.

My mate's reassuring scent of sage and lavender and hand-milled soap seeps through me. As always with him, the gentlest of all my mates, my raging dragon is soothed.

My beast greets Neo with an affectionate grumble.

I cannot resist running my hands over Neo's solid and reassuring warmth to ensure he is well. Finding no injury on any part of him, I growl in relief. I rub my cheek against his, to scent him and claim him, especially before this intruder.

Knowing shifters as he does (for we are a tactile race), my mate kneads my tense shoulders with his steady hands and tolerates these possessive claimings with patience.

"That's good, Max. You're doing great. Just keep breathing, low in your belly, like when Zara does her yoga. I'm gonna go find Ash. Don't kill anyone while I'm gone, okay?" Neo says earnestly. "You'll really upset Zara if you do."

Without waiting for me to agree, because I have not and will not— I must keep my mates safe!—Neo gives me a quick warm hug, then trots purposefully toward the door.

It is not so easy to remain angry after being hugged.

Still wrathful and damp with rain, my long hair dripping on Neo's father's carpet, I sneak my queen a concerned look. Truly, all this excitement cannot be good for her. Or Vasili.

Especially if (as I suspect) they are both pregnant.

Surely, at least one of them (or, in Vasili's case, his dragon) is clutching. That is what you call a dragon who is carrying a clutch of dragonets.

A warm flood of tenderness for both of them—Zara and Vasili, both mine in every way, and for our coming offspring—swells my heart to overflowing. My love is chased by a surge of protective worry. We must manage this business of the Dean's Challenge and kill the rival queen quickly, quickly. Only then can I rush my mates to my dragon lair, hidden deep in the Siberian tundra, and tend them and spoil them and cosset them, and protect them both while they are breeding—

A sudden exclamation of disgust from Vasili, who is now sneering at me in a horrible way, reminds me sharply to guard my thoughts.

Very quickly, I have learned to guard my thoughts on this entire matter from Vasili.

He does not yet know his own mind.

For once in his fiendishly clever life, he does not know what I know.

"Yeah, what Neo said." Zara gives the belt of her robe a firm tug to knot it, then divides a warning look between me and Zephyr. "No killing. And you put pants on, Your Radiance."

Ronin, who has no modesty and is indifferent to his own nudity (a condition which normally pleases all of us), grunts and tosses his own leather pants at Zephyr.

The garment falls unheeded to the floor at Zephyr's feet.

Lucius exhales a sigh of disappointment. Our headmaster's intelligent sherry-gold eyes plead with Zephyr for restraint.

Unmoved, the naked Unseelie grips the complicated harness that holds his crossed swords in both hands and glares furiously at the demon. Vasili says that Zephyr is our enemy. All the same, a naked Zephyr is a splendid sight, every muscle and sinew tight and quivering under olive skin, pubic hair a vivid lick of green between his thighs. His jade eye burns, incandescent with hatred.

"Fuck's sake," Ronin mutters. "Best hurry right back with Ash, will you, love?"

Neo gives us all a worried look, locks onto my scowling face and mouths *Easy,* then ducks into the hallway and vanishes.

At least, that one of my mates is safe.

I give a satisfied snarl and resume my pacing. I am marking my territory. Establishing a clear perimeter between my precious mates and that demon.

If Mordred dares to cross it by a toenail, I will slay him without mercy.

Lucius, who is quickly buttoning himself into his linen pajamas, gives the entire scene (including my pacing, Vasili's lurking, Zephyr's silent fulminating, and Mordred's lazy smirking) a keen look. Then Lucius murmurs in Ronin's ear.

Still wearing nothing but his own golden skin and a lush mane of midnight hair that is tousled from the rough sex he has clearly been having, Ronin grunts and saunters across the bedroom to Zephyr under the demon's interested eye.

"Right." Ronin scoops up his fallen leathers with an agile foot and offers them to Zephyr. "These'll look wicked on you, Zeph. Good to wear in a scuffle too. Go on, then. I'll mind your swords for a tick."

I find it highly unlikely the Unseelie will yield those swords for any amount of time in his enemy's presence. But Ronin's powers of persuasion are potent.

Especially when he is naked.

Zephyr drills the demon lounging in our doorway with a hard look, then jerks his chin in a short nod and snatches the pants. While he shoves his legs into the leathers and wrestles the garment over his hips in a silent fury, Zara hurries to fill the charged silence with a few jumbled sentences of hasty explanation for the demon's presence in our bedroom… a summoning ritual, the magical artifact retrieved, then the biting… that I am barely able to absorb.

When I do, I jolt to a halt and whirl toward Vasili. His graceful frame skulks against the glass doors, face cast fully into shadow, beyond the circle of light from the bedside lamp.

"*You.*" I scowl ferociously at my foolish mate. "You dared to summon this infernal creature out of Avalon into our world without consulting or warning any of us… and then you bit him?"

"I'm running out of ways to say this." Vasili's tone drips with acid. "But let us try once more, *do.*"

"Indeed." Zephyr buttons his leather trousers with aggravated motions and glares under his spill of green hair at Vasili. "*Let's.*"

"*That.*" V jabs a finger precisely toward the demon's love-bitten neck. "Is not. A mating bite. He isn't joining the harem, he's hired help. For fuck's sake, he's brought us the Horn of Ceres! Snatched the prize of the whole contest right out from under Cleo's nose. If he hadn't, both this contest and this delightful little rebellion we're leading would be over. They'd be crowning Cleo queen of the witching world as we speak."

Zara taps her sparkly toes on the carpet and looks thoughtful. Of course, this is presumably not the first time she has heard this argument. She does not feel angry in our mating bond.

She is listening to Vasili.

And she is thinking.

Hard.

"For moon's sake. I should have known." With a look of abject disgust, Zephyr snatches his swords back from Ronin and swings the harness across his bare shoulders. As his single eye drills into Vasili, his tone shifts from wrath to bitterness. "Another of your twisted plots to punish me for the so-called misdeeds of my past with Ronin. With any luck, you must've fancied my demonic cousin would slay me and spare you the trouble. I knew 'twas too much to hope you might finally have begun to tolerate my presence."

"Well, since you mention it…" Vasili murmurs, his face still in shadow. "You have a cock that won't quit, I'll give you that. You fuck like a porn star. But there's still no place for you in this harem."

Zara's dragon voices a chirp of annoyance.

This is one of the evocative bird-like sounds my queen has begun vocalizing since she has grown accustomed to her dragon. Her turquoise eyes narrow and her sparkly toes tap.

Her annoyance with Vasili crackles through our mating bond like static.

"Bloody hell." Ronin too swings around to give Vasili an irate look. His tawny face ignites with wrath. "You still feeling threatened by Zephyr then? Better not be for my sake, mate. Because him and me, we're solid. We've worked it all out. He's forgiven me for knifing him in the eye. And I… I've forgiven him. For all of it."

"Until the next time he ghosts you for four years and lets you believe he's dead." Vasili sneers. "Have you also *forgiven* the role that guilt over his supposed death played in your sister's suicide?"

Dragging the late Gwendolyn Pendragon into this mess is a very low blow. Even for Vasili.

Ronin's shoulders hunch and his face goes tight in a rictus of old grief.

Even I stop glaring at the demon long enough to glare at Vasili.

How could he ever hurt Ronin?

As for the Dark Fae King, he bristles with barely contained fury. "Serpent, hold thy wicked tongue. The state of affairs between Ronin and myself is naught of your concern, Vasili Nikolayevich Romanov."

Now Zephyr is lapsing into ancient Fae. And he is threatening Vasili. Neither is a good sign.

"The devil it isn't," Vasili says shortly.

Ronin crosses his muscled arms over his chest and scowls at Vasili. "You know what, mate? I don't bloody need your protection. Not against Zeph. So you can drop this angel of vengeance bullshit and piss off."

Saints of the northern steppes.

By this point, no one (except myself) is even watching the demon. As for that spawn of Satan, now leaning comfortably against the wall, Mordred appears ready to settle in with a bowl of popcorn (assuming he eats popcorn, because krakens typically consume raw fish) and enjoy the show.

"Sweet Jesus. What. A. *Mess*." Zara voices an unhappy groan and gives our feuding mates a pensive look. Her big aqua eyes are clouded with concern.

My precious queen. In our mating bond, she feels so sad.

My dragon growls in protest. Exerting all my will, I cease my pointless pacing, range myself close beside Zara, and wrap a protective arm around her tiny waist. She slips her arm around me and tucks into my side with a sigh of relief. Very discreetly, I spread a sheltering palm over her lower belly.

Beneath my hand, surely, she is clutching our dragonets.

The rich musk of caramel and vetiver and birchwood fills my head. Christ, she is drenched in Vasili's mating scent. Under her bathrobe, I sense, her thighs are slick with Vasili's seed. The fresh mating bite decorating her neck, too, is Vasili's.

My Vasili.

But he is also her Vasili.

And he is Ronin's Vasili.

This time, our vengeful, spiteful, secretly insecure Vasili has truly caused a mess.

As furious and alarmed as I remain to find a strange male lurking about our harem while both Zara and Vasili are (hopefully) breeding—as difficult as I find it to think clearly with this truckload of testosterone flooding every cell and synapse in my mating rut—I am slowly grasping the reality that my outraged sentiments are not the current focus of anyone's concern.

No.

The biggest danger by far to the integrity of my queen's cobbled-together harem—as always—is the gaping rupture of distrust and suspicion the sex demon's presence has not only exposed, but widened, between Vasili and Zephyr.

Lucius too takes his place beside Zara and addresses this crisis with his resolute voice. "My dears, let's all be as practical as we can. What's done is done. The demon is here. And he is, for the moment, our ally. The question now becomes, where do we all go next?"

Well.

As to that, after my midnight flight over Icarus Island, after what I saw from the air and learned on the ground, I have something to say.

"If we are speaking of battle tactics—" I begin.

The bedroom door flies open, and Neo drags Ash inside. Warily, I fall silent.

Asher Apollo Aurelius.

Prince of the Light Born Fae.

The Seelie Prince is Zephyr's ally and thus Vasili's rival (and, I suppose, mine), so I do not know him well. Wearing naught but a pair of faded jeans that cling to his thick thighs, with rainwater dripping down the broad slabs of his chest and trickling down his chiseled six-pack abs, the Seelie fills the doorframe with his wide shoulders. A circlet of black ivy, spiked with thorns and daubed with crimson blood, is inked around his bulging biceps. His spiky head of pewter hair nearly bumps the ceiling.

Ash drags a big hand down the craggy planes of his face, pushes rain out of his eyes, and blinks at the impasse. His keen silver stare shoots straight to Zephyr, bristling in the harness of his crossed swords, then to the lounging demon with his trident.

"Ash," Zephyr breathes, low and lethal. "Did you know of this… this calumny?"

English is not my first language and that is not a word I know.

But I presume he means the demon.

"Hiya, Sparrow. Good to see ya, kid. For real." Ash slings a towel carelessly around his wet shoulders and saunters right over my defensive perimeter, pausing to press a tender kiss on Zara's worried forehead. She rises on tiptoe and leans into his touch.

My possessive dragon rumbles a growl of warning.

"You too, Max." Ash gives an easy nod to me and my growling dragon as he ambles past.

But he knows better than to touch me.

He knows I am Vasili's ally (because I have sworn to be, and a dragon honors his word) and not his.

Clearly, Ash's goal is to reach the fulminating Zephyr before the Dark Fae King combusts. As Ash closes the distance between them, I see the immediate effect of his nearness on his consort. The deep furrow smooths between Zephyr's green brows. The worst of the deadly tension eases its grip on his lithe body.

Ash sweeps the armed Unseelie into a rough embrace, then swings around to face the room. The smooth maneuver places his own formidable frame between his lover and the demon.

"Dramamine," Ash announces to the room with a grimace. "Been a while since I did the whole boat thing. I was turning green up there. So I popped a few of those little pills."

"A few?" In the midst of fetching clothes from his own suitcase for Ronin, Lucius creases his brow in a worried frown. "I believe the prescribed dose is a single tablet."

Ash hitches his massive shoulders in a wry shrug. "Yeah, well, like I said. Knocked me out cold. Didn't move a muscle, even though Xhevith musta flew right over me bringing Sparrow in. If not for Neo coming to wake my ass up, I'd still be lights out."

"I checked the storm anchor while I was out there," Neo pipes up helpfully. "I was worried it might be dragging again, but it's holding. The weather might be clearing up. It's mostly just heavy rain now. I'm gonna see if I can maybe get a weather report on the VHF."

Without waiting for a reply, Neo ducks back out into the storm.

"Ash," Zephyr says tightly. "Did. You. Know."

"About the squid over there?" Ash looks resigned. "Yeah, sure. I knew. He brought us the thingamajig, didn't he? Says he caused all that ruckus with the insurrection back on Avalon cuz he was bound to it by his last summoner. Sounds like your great aunt Blossom."

"Blossom?" Zephyr scoffs. "Don't be absurd. She must be two hundred years old."

"Whoa. Did you just say *two hundred*?" Still tucked protectively against my side, Zara looks dazed and a little horrified.

"Yep." Ash gives an easy nod. "Unseelie witchcraft extends a Fae's life. Mad old Maeve was way up there in the triple digits herself. But Great Aunt Blossom's kinda feeble. That's what Sparrow's getting at."

"Auntie Blossom can't piss without a bedpan and a nurse, but she inherited your mom's old spell books, cuz," Mordred says to Zephyr. "Besides, good old Uncle Puck egged her on. With those two holding my summoning leash, what's a demon to do?"

"Puck." Zephyr's nostrils flare. I can nearly see his pointed ears twitch. *"Fuck."*

We all wait for more, but Zephyr is not forthcoming.

Whoever good old Uncle Puck may be, apparently his nephew considers him eminently capable of treason, demon-summoning, and regicide.

"Your cuz says he's not jonesing for your throne anymore. Now that Beautiful over there's calling the shots." Ash jerks his chin at Vasili, still skulking near the window. "Guess this demon is ours now. Kinda like a genie in a lamp."

"Ours?" Zephyr's head tilts. "By the moon, 'tis more accurate to say the demon is *his*. Is that not so, Vasili Romanov?"

Vasili speaks at last, in a voice like silk. "Purely a matter of semantics, darling. I'm Zara's alpha, aren't I?"

"Yeah, you are." Zara detaches gently from my side and plants a hand on her hip. "Let's keep that in mind, okay, Goblin King?"

"Unless I'm greatly mistaken, little queen, those are *my* mating bites you're wearing. All three of them. I believe that fact cements my already certain status as your dominant alpha. I'm yours. And he's mine." Vasili's cruel mouth curls in a smug smile. "By that logic, my adorable pet demon also belongs to you."

I know my Vasili very well.

When he sounds like that, he is not to be trusted.

Zara's eyes narrow in suspicion.

This is because she also knows him very well.

"Bingo. Now we're getting somewhere. I ain't here to pinch Cousin Z's crown, am I?" Sounding deeply satisfied (which is also suspicious), the demon oozes into our bedroom and swanks across the floor toward Zara. Lean hips swaying, indigo hair swirling, those damnable dimples digging into his swarthy cheeks above his blue goatee. White teeth flash in a lazy grin.

If he fucks like he walks, I swear, he will make any woman (and many men) scream with pleasure.

And he is still coming.

"For whatever reason you are here, if you wish to keep breathing, kraken, you will come no closer," I snarl, pushing Zara behind me into Lucius' waiting arms.

Alphas in a royal harem are traditional rivals, but the alphas in this harem are all lovers. To protect our sovereign, we cooperate. (Even Vasili, who does not have a cooperative bone in his entire lethal body.)

Just beyond the defensive perimeter I have established and thickly scented with my brimstone mating scent, Mordred stops.

"Told you straight up, baby queen. Wanna hop on board the harem train and ride." The demon eyes my bristling frame, looming threateningly in his path, and winks. "You too, blondie."

"*What* about me?" I growl. I distrust that wink of his.

"You're that dragon of theirs, true? You look good enough to lick like a popsicle." The maddening demon actually licks his lips. The toothsome scent of rum spice and saltwater taffy fills the air. "Any chance that scaly critter of yours is maybe amphibious? Cuz if you are? Your dragon? My kraken? Dude. We can make that work."

"I am not a frog," I say stiffly. I am deeply affronted.

Even if the thought of stuffing this creature's impudent mouth with my forked dragon dick does hold a certain (secret) appeal.

At least, in that case, the imp would finally be silent.

"As you may recall I mentioned, Mordred," Lucius says mildly, coming up in his supportive way beside me, "ours is a committed polycule. Kindly refrain from sexually propositioning our dragon. I'd advise that we focus instead on hearing what Maxim learned on his patrol. Next, we should establish the strategy we intend to deploy, once this storm finally breaks, to complete the Dean's Challenge and secure Zara's reign."

"All I'm saying is, it'd be fun to try, wolf daddy." The demon's purple eyes dance with mischief. "Anyway, even if I'm not officially in the harem... *yet*... I'm a friendly. You got my word."

Never one to hide in the rear of any conflict, Zara pushes forward to stand between Lucius and me. "This demon's half Unseelie, right, Zephyr? Can he lie?"

"He cannot," Zephyr says shortly. "At least, not without causing himself immense discomfort. But he rarely reveals everything he knows—only the truths that serve him. Never make the mistake of trusting him."

"Thanks for the warning, love." Ronin has been hovering near Zephyr and keeping his back to Vasili. But he also keeps a wary distance between himself and Ash. This is another unsolved problem in our harem. But it is only a problem if Vasili cannot finally rid us of these two Fae, as he surely intends. (Zephyr is right to be suspicious of my snake and his motives.)

At least Mordred is keeping his distance—for the moment—from Zara. I give him a narrow look, then turn eagerly toward her.

"Here is what I have been trying to tell you. The entirety of House Tiberius is now massed around the church," I report to my queen, speaking of the gothic cathedral where all our classes are held. The Academy Vault lies, warded and deadly, in the crypt beneath. "I spied their formation from the air. This is how I knew you must have claimed the artifact, my sovereign. Now Cleo and her allies will kill to keep you—and the Horn of Ceres—from entering the Vault to return it."

"Shit," Zara says grimly. "Guess Cleo must've sussed out that we have the Horn. Just our luck that House Tiberius is the biggest residential college at Icarus. That means she's got a lotta allies."

"Then it is fortunate we have allies of our own," I announce proudly. This is the other news I was rushing back to tell her when I smelled a strange male and became distracted. "Allies who know another way—a secret way—to sneak beneath the wards into the Academy Vault… from underneath."

Curiosity sparks in Zara's gaze.

But she too is distracted by the kraken.

Mordred has been strolling casually along the edge of my defensive perimeter. Now he has reached our bed. He launches himself onto the mattress in a powerful belly flop that makes the bed frame groan, crosses his ankles, and swings his bare feet (which are very webbed) in the air. "Sounds like a gnarly ally to have. Assuming you can trust him."

"Her," I say shortly, disliking his presence in our bed intensely. "And, for your information, we can."

"*Her?* Oh, hell to the yeah." Zara spins toward me and gives an excited little hop. Her big eyes glow ultraviolet. The teal curls lift from her shoulders in a crackle of static charge.

Seeing my sovereign so excited and so hopeful makes me proud to have served her so well. I lean into Lucius, whom I have not yet greeted properly, and rub my chin into his tumbled chestnut mane to scent him as well.

"Hello, Maxim." Lucius wraps his steady arm around my hips, below my scarred back where I do not like to be touched, and gives me a reassuring squeeze that draws me close against his rangy strength. "You've done so very well tonight, dear boy."

My dragon rumbles happily at him.

I do not know why my dragon (who is an extremely strong alpha) submits to Lucius' wolf. But I am deeply thankful for it, because that dynamic allows me to submit to Lucius myself, and he is such a worthy male.

"Your ally's a chick?" Mordred tents his hands under his chin and bats his eyes at Zara playfully. "Will I like her?"

"I assume you mean woman, not small bird." Wryly Zara eyes the incubus sexing up our bed with his demonic presence. Then she shakes her head and moves decisively toward the dressing table to finish her bedtime ritual, which her recent sexual encounter with Vasili apparently interrupted.

"Yeah, you'll like her all right," she says over her shoulder to Mordred. "Almost everyone does. She's a Hufflepuff."

"For real?" Mordred scrambles up to sit in a twist of blankets, cross legged and wide-eyed with excitement, like a boy on Christmas morning. "You mean she goes to Hogwarts? I always figured that was a made-up place."

Vasili gives Ronin's pointedly averted back a narrow look, then unbends enough to stroll toward the vanity himself, because he and Zara like to primp together. "Oh, don't be so literal. It's called a metaphor."

"You don't say," the demon says with a wink, clearly having his fun at V's expense.

"Nonetheless, the ally in question is certainly real. She's one of my brightest and most resourceful students, as well as Zara's loyal friend." Lucius too looks concerned about the sex demon in our bed, and he is also taking careful note of the tension between V and Ronin.

Still, Lucius never misses an opportunity to offer instruction. "Her name is Mallory McSnicker."

All this time, Ash has quietly been murmuring to Zephyr near the window, weaving his own personal tapestry of magic around the highly strung Dark Fae, and generally making patient and incremental progress toward persuading a reluctant Zephyr to relinquish his swords without bloodshed.

Now the Seelie Prince starts like someone pricked that impressive tattooed hide of his with a blow dart.

My suspicious gaze veers immediately to the demon. The infernal creature is crawling happily under the duvet and energetically plumping the pillows. In fact, he is giving every appearance of settling in to sleep in my sovereign's bed.

For the moment, at least, he is not deviling Zephyr—or Ash.

I am replaying the last few moments in my mind when the realization surfaces.

For some reason, the normally calm and unflappable Ash started like a bee-stung stallion the moment he heard Mallory's name.

Nor is he the only one who is behaving strangely.

For the past several minutes, Vasili has been staring suspiciously at Zephyr's discarded riding cloak, which is wadded on the chair near the balcony. At first I was not certain why, but my dragonish senses are keen.

Clearly, Vasili too has spotted a small shape inside Zephyr's cloak… Squirming.

Now, with an impatient huff, V shifts suddenly into motion, glides forward, and gives the wadded cloak an irritable twitch.

A small feline head, tufted ears quivering over a furry white brow, pokes into view.

"What is that?!" Vasili leaps straight into the air like a cat himself and levitates near the ceiling (a power which is part of his terrible witchcraft) in bristling alarm.

"Oh, Goddess. With all this havoc, I nearly forgot." Zephyr sighs. He eyes V's levitating form. One corner of the Unseelie's mouth twitches. "I found this soaked little scrap cowering in the church belfry. Apparently she's the last of her litter. Half-starved and soaked to the skin, the poor wretch."

Zephyr glances toward Zara, that covert half-smile still lurking. "I seem to recall you once mentioned, my bride, that you wished for a kitten? Consider this a bridal gift."

"Oh my God, a *kitten*!" Zara rushes forward, her face transformed, to crouch beside the white kitten. Eagerly she frees the bedraggled creature and gathers it into her careful arms. "Oh, Zephyr, she's so sweet! And so tiny. I think we should definitely feed her right away. Maybe she can manage a little of that fresh tuna from the galley…"

It is very true that, for many months, Zara has been longing for a kitten. The rest of us, well, we have all been willing—

Except for Vasili.

Now Lucius hurries off to the galley to fetch the tuna and Ronin rushes to bring Zara a warm dry towel, while Ash offers helpful advice and agrees, in his amiable way, with every cooing endearment and compliment Zara lavishes upon the blinking kitten. The tiny creature stares bashfully up at Zara—who is clearly her new mother—through wide green eyes shining with trust.

The Unseelie King watches the entire commotion unfold with a small satisfied smile lurking on his feral face.

"Well," I say to the room with a shrug of resignation, "at least his gifts to her are improving, no? This one is better than the severed head of his enemy, which he gave to her last week."

"Yo, that was a brother of mine," Mordred reminds the room lazily, buried to the chin in the comfortable nest of pillows and blankets he has created in our bed. "Total dickhead, though. Deserved to lose his head if you ask me. So I ain't holding a grudge, just in case anyone's wondering."

Vasili, who has been vocal about despising all felines, floats warily down from the ceiling. The full focus of his suspicious gaze is now riveted on the kitten, which Zara is carefully drying and wrapping in the warm towel for a cuddle.

Already, our queen's face is soft with love. In contrast, V's pretty face is etched and eloquent with horror.

The kitten mews.

Our sovereign croons.

White to the lips, Vasili mutters, "Oh, *fuck*."

Chapter Eleven
Zara

"Eeek!" Mordred giggles. "Is that a haunted house?"

"Quiet." Max levels a repressive look at the giggling demon we're reluctantly dragging with us through the forest toward Villa Caligula. That's the *domus* for House Hadrian, which isn't our residential college at all. It's Mallory's.

That's where Mal and her guys are (secretly) meeting us.

We motored in this morning from the yacht on the reliable *Filibuster,* then dragged the dinghy ashore and hid it in a sea cave they used to stow bootleg liquor, like a hundred years ago, in the Academy's Prohibition era.

As we sneak through the creepy forest that huddles against the villa's flanks, we catch glimpses of the tumbledown structure through gaps in the bristly vault of evergreen branches hanging over us. Dark and spooky in the pearly gray mist of a rainy morning, the college's crooked walls and twisted turrets lean over the sea cliff like a suicide getting ready to jump.

Villa Caligula, my ass. That place is straight outta *The Addams Family.*

Despite the ominous vibe their *domus* gives off, Mal and her menage are friendlies. That was still Max's read when Mallory signaled him down from the skies with a flashlight for a huddled consult on the sea cliff last night.

Those three (Mal and her guys) were the first to join the revolution and side with us when Cleo stole my crown. Her guys weird me out, but I do trust Mal.

Still, the Dean's Challenge is in full swing.

Only one team can win.

So we're all twitchy as fuck.

Except for Mordred, who's still giggling. With Neo's preppy raincoat hanging open around the sex demon's bare bronze chest and Aquaman pants, his webbed feet laced into a pair of V's chunky combat boots, and the messenger bag holding the Horn of Ceres bumping against his hip, that incubus oughta look ridiculous.

Even though he left his big trident on the boat.

Instead, that naked expanse of flexing chest and sculpted abs makes me wanna lick him all over like an ice cream cone. Starting at the top of his corded neck and just working my way down. All the way to that thick bulge between his thighs.

I give a hard swallow and remind myself of a few difficult truths.

Sex demon. This shit isn't real. He's sexing you up.

Plus it's pretty obvi Mordred's having a similar effect on Vasili. I mean, my snake did bite the guy, so of course V's pheromones are going alpha batshit crazy. I saw it this morning when he loaned the demon his footwear.

(By *loaned*, I mean V dropped the shoes at Mordred's feet and basically forced the demon to wear them.)

"Awwww," Mordred teased at the time, with one of his trademark winks. "Master has given Dobby a sock."

Without missing a beat, V fired back, "It places the boots on its feet or else it gets the hose again."

The chilling effect of Vasili Romanov going all Hannibal Lector would be a lot to handle for the average demon.

But not this one.

Mordred only flashed his dimples and whispered to me, "I think he likes me. Do you think he likes me?"

Like I said.

Sex magic.

His is some potent shit.

Adding to the spooky atmosphere in this shadowy forest, with mist winding through the trunks and cool rain plopping through the branches, a bat flutters into view and nearly gets tangled in the demon's blue hair.

"Eeee!" Mordred squeals like a girl, then giggles again.

At least one of us is enjoying himself.

Like, *thoroughly*.

"Ssshhh," I remind him, settling the duffel bag we've converted to a breathable cat carrier more securely over my shoulder. Despite our current circumstances, just thinking about that fluffy white kitten asleep inside on a thick soft towel, her little tummy distended with a good tuna breakfast, makes my whole chest flood with warmth.

Zephyr did himself a solid with that kitten.

I really hope he and V can work their shit out.

Mordred lowers his rumbly baritone approximately one decibel to a piercing whisper that's practically a roar. "*Is* it a haunted house though? Sure looks like one."

"Why don't you bloody bellow that shit through a police bullhorn, mate?" Ronin hisses.

Clad head to toe in assassin black like the trained killer he is, Ronin creeps through the trees at the head of our huddled group without snapping a single twig. He's tracking Lucius' shifted paw prints (which I can't even see) through the detritus of evergreen needles and pinecones and rotted wood that carpets the forest.

I know, I know. Evergreen isn't the right kinda flora for the Med.

But this is an enchanted island, so the magical wards that hide us from the normals also mess with the climate.

"For fuck's sake. Should've left you on the blooming boat," Ronin mutters as Mordred capers along happily beside us.

"You need me on this gig," Mordred says comfortably. "Besides, imma grow on you. Always do."

Ronin scoffs and rolls his fiery topaz eyes. "Just mind that fucking Horn and keep your gob shut, mate. That's all we need from you."

If only that were true.

I'm just coming out of a big superheat, so everything about this incubus who's taken up residence in my harem is extra distracting. The way his scaly pants cling to his thick thighs and sinewy calves and the hard globes of his bitable ass is disturbing, for real. He's like Quadzilla forging through the trees ahead of me, with that tangle of ink-blue hair spilling down his back. I wanna sit him down with a hairbrush and tidy him up.

Then mess him back up again.

Shit.

"I'll be quiet, hot stuff." The demon leers at Ronin's own ass, which could fucking stop traffic in his fighting leathers. "Long as I get me a reward later."

"*Later*, I suspect," Vasili murmurs with poisonous spite as he winds through the trees like a rattlesnake beside me, "you'll be roasting that tight demon ass of yours in hellfire. The moment we return that Horn, your Unseelie tyrant of a cousin intends to banish you back to the demonical realm that spawned you."

"Does he now." Mordred turns around to walk backward and winks.

When his gaze lands on me, that demon's purple eyes turn crafty in a way I find worrying.

Vasili stalks through the woods at my side, looking wicked as fuck in his punk-rock twist on the Academy uni, glittery violet combat boots thudding into the earth. With his moussed-up hair and smoky eyes and black-lacquered nails and pissed-off pout, my dominant alpha is rocking his Duran Duran today.

With Lucius and his keen wolfish senses in the lead, though not currently visible as he scouts ahead, Ash and Zephyr guard our rear. That way, my Dark Fae can keep his eye on all of us… especially Mordred… *and* Vasili, who is (very subtly) staying as far from the kitten as possible. (And how could I not have known my snake is afraid of cats?)

Long story short? We've barely managed to cobble my distrustful polycule together enough to run this heist.

It kills me to admit this.

But we're only together on the surface.

Ronin, who's blatantly been a card-carrying member of Team Zephyr in the Vasili-Zephyr throwdown since the exact moment V summoned that demon, hasn't spoken a syllable to Vasili all day. Plus Zephyr won't speak to *any* of my guys except Ash, Ronin, and an extremely contrite Neo, who's just too endearing to ignore.

Guess we're back to Square One on integrating Zephyr (and therefore Ash, since those two are a package deal) into my harem.

When I swing my makeshift cat carrier to my other side to give my shoulder a break, Vasili edges away from the cat.

But he does it in a way that's too subtle for anyone else to notice.

You really shoulda told me, Goblin King, I tell my dominant alpha softly through our mating bond. Because this isn't the kinda shit you say out loud to a snake like him. *It's called ailurophobia. I looked it up. Fear of cats.*

Vasili's glacial eyes flash like danger beacons. *I'm not afraid! I simply don't care for the detestable creatures.*

"She's just a kitten, bad boy," I whisper, clutching the strap of my duffel. "And she needs us. She really does."

Our bond fills up with his silence. A silence that's more raw than lurky. With Ronin still so pissed and broody, plus all V's insecurities about Zephyr and now his secret fear of cats exposed, my Goblin King's morning really has been kinda sucky.

"Isn't anyone *ever* gonna answer my question?" Mordred asks at an alarming volume. "I *said*—"

"Hush!" I whisper in a rush, sensing both Ronin and Max about to launch into orbit. "It is, okay? Villa Caligula actually is a haunted house. I mean, kinda. It's really old and falling down, the basement's condemned, it used to be the Academy dungeon in medieval times. They used to torture the students in detention, and rumor says a bunch of them died down there—"

"And *that's* where we're going?" Mordred asks, wide-eyed.

At speaking volume, natch.

"Way to sell the place, love. But yeah, that's where Mal wants to meet." Ronin glances sharply at Neo. "Mind you don't step in that trap, Red."

That's what Ronin calls Neo.

Red.

On account of our bookworm's constant blushing.

"Is that a *bear* trap?" Neo gasps, giving the horrible rusty-jawed thing—yawning wide and half hidden in the fallen foliage—a very wide berth.

"Mantrap," Ronin says grimly. "They've got a new sheriff in town at Mal's *domus*. Forced retirement for Mistress Aggie. She's been back-benched to make way for a proper headmaster. Not sure I fancy the new bloke, considering."

"Yeah, me neither." I frown at the mantrap. "New sheriff or not, what's that thing even doing out here? We're literally on school grounds."

I'm indignant, for real.

I don't need any help spotting and avoiding hidden mantraps, because cat burglar, I'm trained for that shit.

But that doesn't mean I like it.

Or Mal's new headmaster.

Anyone who even grazes that rusty thing's jagged steel jaws is gonna need like five tetanus shots. I suppress a shiver and edge warily around the barbaric device.

"Oh my gosh," Neo moans. "*Lucius.* I really hope his wolf watches where he's stepping."

"Lucius Aries is far too canny to step into a mantrap," Max says stoutly. "We will find him ahead at the *domus*, just as we arranged."

I sure hope so. Because what if we don't? I think but don't say.

Although thinking is basically the same as speaking in a telepathic harem, unless I deliberately guard my thoughts. Which I don't like doing from my guys. We've had enough secrets, including this latest one with V summoning Mordred, to do real damage to the trust factor in this harem.

I mean, not that Mordred's *in* the harem.

He definitely isn't.

Mordred is just a temporary thing.

Even if he ended up sleeping at the foot of our bed last night—basically lying across everyone's feet (minus his trident) because he *really* wanted to stay with us and I didn't have the heart to send him away—while Zephyr and Ash pointedly slept on deck.

Which was as far from the demon—and V—as Zephyr could physically get without actually leaving the boat.

So, yeah, we've got a few trust holes to patch up.

Over the patter of rain against the canopy, my sharp shifter ears catch the tiny *krich!* of a snapped twig.

Ronin's fist shoots up in the silent signal to freeze.

We all go rigid.

Max places himself between me and V and drops to a defensive crouch. Lean and lethal in his battered leather biker jacket, blond hair twisted into a braid that bares his ruthless Russian face, he's gone full alpha guarding both V and me.

Electricity crackles through my body and sends violet sparks dancing down my fingers.

I lower the cat carrier gently to the ground and palm the stiletto that's strapped to my thigh, because you better believe I'm wearing my catsuit and not my schoolgirl uni for this heist.

Feeling way better with cold steel in my grip, I breathe in deep, trying to sift through the sharp piney scent of evergreen, the damp green smell of moss, and the heady cocktail of pheromones from my various mates.

Beside me, Vasili lets out a low hiss.

Whatever it is that's coming, clearly, he's getting a whiff before I do. His feet lift from the ground as he levitates, shooting fifteen feet into the air. There he hovers in silent threat.

For him, that's an intimidation display, like a cobra rearing to spread its hood.

Ronin leaps lithely to catch a low-hanging branch and swings himself into a tree with catlike grace. In a blink, he's hidden from view.

Zephyr's crossed swords flash free in his grip. The silver-feathered splendor of Ash's wings sprouts from his shoulders, around the doeskin vest that's cut to accommodate his wingspan. The two Fae pivot back to back, in the easy rhythm of two guys who've been guarding each other's backs forever.

And Mordred? That demon holds out a hand like Thor calling his hammer in an Avengers film. His three-pronged trident literally materializes in his fist.

As for Neo, my fated mate stands protectively over the kitten in my duffel.

For the longest ten seconds of my entire fucking life, we all wait in prickly silence.

Then a lean shadow slinks from the trees.

It's bipedal, I mean the thing walks like a man and it's wearing pants. But its head is a long wolfish snout filled with wicked fangs. Curling black talons sprout from twisted hands and velociraptor feet. Bristly black fur covers its wiry torso. Inky dreads, threaded with colorful beads and juju, part around wolfish ears and swing around its slinking frame.

That wolf is… not Lucius.

"By the moon," Zephyr breathes. "What manner of foul creature…?"

Neo pushes his glasses up his nose, then unexpectedly steps forward. "It's a *loup-garou*. Cajun werewolf. I think that's Mallory's boyfriend. Hey, Jae Labête, is that you?"

The werewolf grins at him, long tongue sweeping over slavering fangs. Its eyes burn and pulse a wicked emerald green.

Fearless, our bookworm eases toward it, one cautious hand extended for the wolf to sniff.

"Neo Mercury, you be careful," Max mutters.

A hum gathers in my throat. That's the lightning voice. It's how I summon. But I don't wanna do that shit and start hurling lightning, especially in these close quarters, unless I gotta.

The werewolf studies the approaching bookworm with its monstrous head tilted. Saliva drips from its terrifying jaws.

I glance up to find Vasili's casting hand twitching as he hovers overhead. He's Neo's alpha as well as mine, and super protective. I know if that werewolf makes one wrong move, V will hurl the thing fifty feet through the air or crush the wolf like a beer can with his telekinesis.

I guess we're all feeling a little twitchy.

"It's okay, Jae." Low and soothing, Neo weaves his bookworm magic and sidles toward the wolf, step by step. "Nobody hurt him, okay? He's only half-sentient in this form. I mean, according to what I read in Zoology of Magical Creatures class."

"The kiddo's right," Ash murmurs. "There's no reasoning with 'em. When a *loup-garou* attacks, you gotta put him down like a mad dog. We sure that's the *loup-garou* you know?"

"Precisely how many Cajun werewolves do you imagine this island contains?" Vasili says tartly. "They're a critically endangered species."

But my dominant alpha's still levitating, which means he isn't sure.

With alarming suddenness, the werewolf leaps. Mordred's shoulder bunches and his brawny arm cocks. I barely grab the demon's wrist in time to keep the wolf from getting a trident through its throat.

It's the first time I've ever touched him.

Mordred.

He's hot to the touch like any shifter, like placing your hand on a warm stove, barely far enough from the flame not to burn. His skin is smooth as sin and his pulse leaps against my fingers. My palm tingles with a rush of heat. A sound fills my head, like the ocean's muted roar when you cup a seashell to your ear. In the back of my mind, I register that Mordred's ready to kill for one of my guys, even without a command from his summoner.

And that my silent command stops him in his tracks.

The werewolf bounds to a halt right in front of Neo and lowers its scary head to give my fated mate's extended hand a good sniff.

"That's a good boy, Jae." Neo stands very still and repeats softly, "Nobody hurt him."

Slowly I let my hand fall from Mordred's wrist. I can't look away from Neo, but I can feel the demon watching me.

"Your call, baby queen," Mordred whispers. "You're the head honcho. I'm just the hired help."

That's what V calls him. But it feels wrong.

The werewolf sniffs all along Neo's hand, then gives his fingers a tentative lick. For all I know, that wolf could be trying a taste before he tucks in for dinner. Neo gives the wolf's ears a cautious scratch, exactly the way he does with Lucius. The werewolf grins at him, then spins away and bounds off the path we've been following to the edge of a sinister-looking thicket of untamed forest.

There he pauses to look back with his head tilted.

"He wants us to follow him off the trail," Neo says happily. "Come on."

"Oh, *hells* yeah. We're gonna crush this contest." Mordred's trident vanishes in a blink. The demon forges ahead with Neo, blue hair swinging down his back and messenger bag thumping against his hip.

I guess he's pretty eager to get rid of that Horn of Ceres and break the spell that binds him to his summoner.

When he does, that'll be the end of this playful demon's fleeting stay in our harem. Which I tell myself is totally a good thing, considering all the trouble he's caused.

Right?

With a sigh, I sheath my stiletto and reclaim my cat carrier.

"The notion of blindly following that moon-fucked werewolf to his hidden den seems to me the very pinnacle of foolishness." Zephyr sheathes his swords over his back, then grimaces as a dollop of rain from the water-laden branches smacks him in the forehead. "But at least, I suppose, we'll be out of the rain."

"Gotta say I won't complain, Sparrow." Ash retracts his wings, which fold across his shoulders and melt into the gorgeous pewter angel's wing tattoo that spreads across his muscular back. "I'm too old to be running around in the woods."

Sharp-faced and suspicious, Vasili floats after Neo like Tinkerbell flitting after Peter Pan, without bothering to descend. The glittery soles of V's combat boots add to the general effect.

Clearly, my snake is still on edge.

Neo and the werewolf have nearly vanished in the trees when Ronin drops from his branch with a suddenness that makes the werewolf spin and snarl.

"Blooming hell, Red." Ronin twists his inky ponytail into the careless man-bun thing he prefers when he fights, then strides toward the growly wolf and the dark thicket beyond with a grim expression. "Best let me lead this cock-up, love. If anything sentient comes within a click, I'll fucking sense it."

"What? Do we not trust the werewolf?" Mordred blinks back at me innocently.

I grimace and lift my shoulders in a *kinda?* that makes the demon cluck his tongue and make a reproachful face. "Whoa there. I feel like we maybe got ourselves a little bit of a trust issue around here. For real."

Great.

Now even the demon can see it.

Chapter Twelve
Ronin

The axe hurtles at me out of bloody nowhere.

One tick I'm tracking that slinky Cajun werewolf through a brambly thicket into a hidden tunnel that sneaks into his *domus* the back way, straight to the condemned dungeon basement of Villa Caligula. But the shifty fuck's too fast for me and I don't have a torch, so I lose Jae Labête in the shadowy maze inside.

I fucking lose him.

The next tick, barely visible in the dim gray light leaking through a narrow slit of skylight, there's a medieval battle axe tumbling end over end straight at my noggin.

I swear and leap aside, diving into a somersault that softens my bruising collision with the bone-breaking stone floor. The axe clangs into the wall where I was literally just standing, then clatters to the flagstones at my heels.

Rolling to my feet and sprinting along the wall so I'm harder to target, I summon up a pulsing ball of orange psi fire and hurl that shit at the threat.

My fireball lights up the space like a flaming comet.

In a flash, I register the vast underground cavern of the *domus*'s rainwater cistern, built in Roman times but still somehow functional. Under the skylight, a long rectangle of spooky ink-black water recedes into the distance between a double row of pillars.

Dripping gobbets of liquid fire like lava, my fireball sears toward a lurking shape—broad shoulders bristling in a spiked leather jacket, skull sporting a military buzzcut of white-blond hair, eyes glowing the wintry gray-blue of whitecaps in the Celtic Sea.

The bloke curses in Icelandic and dives behind a pillar as my fireball crackles past.

"Whoa!" A nearby flashlight winks on. Above the light, I spy the pale oval of a concerned female face. That's Mallory McSnicker.

The girl peeks out from behind another pillar and frowns sternly at my assailant. "Geez, we totally talked about this, remember? Talk first, violence last—as in, literally the last option. Draco, you could've killed Ronin."

"Good *fokking* riddance, you ask me," my attacker grumbles from behind his own pillar.

"Draco Mars? That you?" My indignant glare ping-pongs between Mal and the pillar that hides her warlock. "Blooming hell, mate."

"Yeah." His chiseled, square-jawed face emerges warily into view. "You done lobbing fireballs at my head, Pendragon?"

"Depends," I say dryly. "You done hurling axes at mine?"

"*Helvitis*. Been a body count already this Dean's Challenge, you feel me? When it comes to keeping my girl safe, I don't apologize for shit."

Hearing that intel, at least I can respect his motive.

Draco emerges cautiously from behind his pillar. He's a grumpy fuck and he's never much fancied me, probably because Mal used to crush on me, and he remembers my one-and-done days and thinks I shagged her or wanted to (which I didn't).

Too innocent to suit my fancy.

Then and now.

"Thanks, Draco, that's really sweet. But I'm one hundred percent safe with Ronin." Now Mal comes fully out of hiding, looking all First Girl proper in her plaid schoolgirl skirt and neatly buttoned blouse, socks pulled up to her bony knees, wild mane of copper curls tamed into pigtails with scraps of green plaid ribbon. The knapsack buckled to her back is bulging with textbooks, a hall monitor's first aid kit's strapped to her waist, and she's toting the electric torch that provides the only practical source of light down here.

In other words, typical McSnicker.

Like a Girl Scout, she's always prepared.

I'm eyeballing the shadows her torch doesn't penetrate and wondering what happened to the werewolf (not to mention my own wolf, because Lucius is definitely supposed to be here) when the rapid echo of running feet fills the space. The brimstone whiff of rutting dragon hits my nose a beat before Max bursts in, golden eyes flaming and face fierce with rage.

Our dragon gives a good roar that makes the walls tremble. "Who threatens my mate!"

"Easy, love. Just a miscommunication between Mars and me, that was." I downplay the whole murder attempt just to placate him. He's excitable, Max is. If he shifts in here, he'll bring the roof down.

Not so easy on my mates, is it, being bonded to the strongest telepath on this island? Especially now, when Max has his alpha dialed all the way up, because mating rut. Thank gods he's not smothering me to death the way he does V and Zara.

He's protective enough as is.

Now Max catches sight of the fallen axe and his nostrils flare. He eyes Draco with open suspicion. "What kind of *miscommunication* involves a medieval weapon… and my mate!?"

"Forget about it. We're over it," Draco says gruffly, clumping up in his shitkickers to retrieve the axe. "You two bring Zara with you like Mallory told you?"

"Like I'd let them leave me behind?" Zara snorts and saunters in like the badass she is, looking good enough to lick in her catsuit, tiny and curvy and formidable, with her teal braid coiled tight round her head like Princess Leia in *The Empire Strikes Back*. "Hey, Mal."

Mordred, Vasili, and Neo crowd in behind her. V's still levitating, and his sharp gaze shoots straight to me, scanning every centimeter of my body for the slightest injury. You'd not know it to look at his aloof and wintry face, but he caught my telepathic broadside of battle adrenaline full on.

Bollocks, he'll never admit it.

But he's worried about me.

I'm a literal sucker for Vasili Romanov, always have been, and my stupid heart gives a ping at the sight of him. But I tamp that shit down, give him a curt nod to let him know I'm not bleeding out, and force myself to turn away.

He's got to get over his pissing match with Zeph. Got to. They're making me mental. Those two were bloody made for each other.

If they'd just stop trying to kill each other.

"Ohmygosh, Zara!" Mal's freckled face lights up in a smile that makes her gray eyes glow like stars. The two girls rush together for a hug and a hurried jumble of words, while Mordred leers and jokes about wanting to be the bacon in a schoolgirl sandwich.

The whole time, Draco glowers at the sex demon and me like he'd fancy setting us both on fire.

Me, I'm left wondering where Zeph and Ash have gotten to, and whether Lucius has pitched up here at all.

We've three warlocks in our polycule gone missing. And I don't bloody like it.

The lovey-dovey Zara-Mallory reunion breaks up when Mal's Cajun slinks out of the darkness and announces in his singsong cadence, "Coast is clear, *chere*, but it won't stay that way. Looks like Zara has the Horn just the way you said, you. We should all go now if we're going."

Clearly, Jean-Emilien Labête's got his wolf back under proper wraps. Fangs, fur, snout, claws all tucked away behind his sinewy human frame. The wicked green glow of his monster stare submerged under his sultry honey-gold human peepers. While he ties his long dreadlocks into a messy ponytail and buttons a crisp Academy uniform shirt over his naked torso, I give the bloke a friendly wink.

Because he's one of the multitudes I *did* shag (once) back in the day.

Come to think of it, that's probably another reason Draco hates me.

Red doesn't bother with flirting. He blinks at the werewolf through his bookworm glasses. "Wait, how'd you know Zara has the Horn?"

"And where is it you imagine we are all going?" Max's slitted dragon pupils narrow in suspicion.

Mallory gives us all a serious look, then swings her flashlight toward the cavern's shadowy rear. The narrow beam, reflected in the smooth water like a moonbeam on a river of ink, dwindles into the distance without finding the far wall.

"There's a secret passage back there. I found it while I was researching a term paper for Master Aries' History of Witchcraft class." Mal's studious voice bounces off the walls. "The passage leads to the church crypt—or at least, it used to. We need to use it. Because Cleo has every witch and warlock in House Tiberius standing between you, that Horn, and the Academy Vault. But I don't think she knows about the passage. I mean, nobody does. Except us."

"Hmmm." Still levitating, Vasili zips down the reservoir's length to examine the rear. Blimey, it's dark as the Devil's arsehole back there.

But V's part shifter, he can see in the dark.

His hollow voice echoes faintly from the walls and the distant ceiling like he's trapped at the bottom of a deep dark well. "I presume we're supposed to conclude, McSnicker, that you intend to help Zara win the Dean's Challenge from the goodness of your First Girl heart? We're meant to trust the monster, the mafioso, and the conscientious Goody Two Shoes hall monitor who's never met a rule she'll break, even in the most minuscule way?"

"Jae isn't a monster," Mallory says flatly. "And Draco's not your average Mars. Plus we wouldn't be breaking any rules, not the way I'm proposing. And finally, we're not just doing this to be nice."

"Time to bend over, loves," I mutter to my mates. "Here it bloody comes."

"And not in a good way." Max gives Zara a look that's meant to warn her to be careful.

Yeah, good luck with that, mate.

Of course he's all broody, he wants her clutching dragon eggs in his Siberian lair, not mucking about with secret passages down here. Not that I eavesdrop on what goes down in his noggin, that's bad manners for a telepath without an invite. But he broadcasts that shit on all psychic channels.

While Jae twists his uniform tie into a careless knot at his throat, Draco leans against a pillar and crosses his brawny arms over his chest. His handsome puss darkens in a scowl. "*Hel*, Romanov. Stop flitting around like a bat back there."

"A *bat*?" I can't even see Vasili, but I know he's pouting. "Really. There's no need to be offensive."

"Mal's the only witch on this island who's smart enough to know how to open that passage." Draco forges on. "And she won't. Not unless you agree to our terms."

Zara's booted toe starts tapping the stone floor.

"We're willing to play fair," my girl says, but her pretty turquoise eyes linger on the door we came through. Through our bond, I sense her growing worry for our missing mates.

"Good. So are we." Mallory gives a decisive nod, straightens Jae's tie for him, then tucks her hand into his and leads him over to join Draco. "Our plan isn't complicated. It's a fair exchange. Let us join your team, and we'll help you win the contest."

"*That's* supposed to be uncomplicated?" Zara tilts her head and looks quizzical. Her turquoise gaze moves over Mal and her menage, measuring them one by one, taking her good sweet time about it.

"You can't join our team because you're not part of our *domus*. It's against the rules," Neo says, earnest as fuck, though I'm pretty sure Mallory McSnicker already knows this. "You're part of House Hadrian. We're Villa Augustus."

"Well, yeah, that's obvi." Mal leans into Draco, who engulfs her narrow waist with his possessive arm. "We can only join your team if we join your harem."

Vasili zips back over the water before the echo's faded. His startled gaze rivets mine, then darts to Zara, who's staring at her bestie with her lush lips parted.

But it's Max who's first to find his tongue.

Planting himself firmly at Zara's side, our dragon snarls, "This harem is closed! No others are allowed. Especially other males."

"We'd only be joining temporarily," Mallory says patiently. "No offense or anything, Maxim, but you are totally not my type. You scare the heck out of me when you're shifted. And Lucius is my prof, so he'd be completely against the rules. Plus I'm straight and not questioning, so Zara's not my type either. No offense."

"None taken," Zara murmurs. She cocks a hip, shifts her duffel, and looks thoughtful.

Jae rubs his face affectionately into Mal's neck to scent her, then hitches one shoulder in a fatalistic shrug. His amber eyes gleam at me. "I'm not straight, me, but I'm with my *bébé*. On everything she said."

"Same," Draco mutters. "*Fokk.* And you didn't mention Pendragon, either of you, but you both fucking shoulda."

I can't be certain in the eerie light, but I think Mal might be awkward-blushing. We were never a thing, she and I, but I'm used to this sort of reaction.

What's a chap to do? Like Zara says, my hotness is my superpower.

Taking pity on Mallory's embarrassment, I mutter, "Put a sock in it, Mars. My one-and-done days are history. I'm committed to this lot, aren't I? All bloody seven of them."

"He means eight," Mordred pipes up. "There's eight of us. Right, hot stuff?"

Yeah, no. I'm not including Mordred in the headcount, not with the way Zeph feels about him. But I've been with Zara long enough to recognize the signs. Our girl falls in love like a skydiver jumping out of a plane.

She's curious about that demon. Attracted to him. Whether she wants to be or not.

And he's curious as hell about her. In fact, he acts like he's drawn to all of us.

Fucking pansexual sex demon.

"Guess that's legit." Draco dips his chin at me in a grudging nod. "Just don't get me started on Romanov."

"Or whatever kind of *terifyan* creature that is, *oui*?" Jae jabs a finger at Mordred, who's knelt to peer curiously into the black water, with his own dark look. "Even so, queen, the offer stands. We wish to join your harem. Temporarily."

No one has expressed any sort of reservation about Neo, natch, because any polycule would gladly make room for him. Now our book-worm pushes his glasses up his nose and asks what we're all wondering.

"So, just to be clear, this wouldn't be a harem with benefits?"

"There will be zero fucking benefits," Draco growls, glaring straight at me for some bloody reason. "We clear, Pendragon?"

Annoyed as fuck by this point, I snap back, "Crystal. Already had your boyfriend anyway, haven't I?"

"You have?" Zara dips a hand into the carrier to stroke her kitten and gives me an interested look.

"Just another of my one-and-dones. Freshman year." I shrug. "He's a right proper shag, if you're asking."

Zara giggles like the vixen she is. "I wasn't. But thanks for sharing."

"Glad you enjoyed him," Draco growls. "Because now he's off limits. Touch Jean-Emilien *once* and I'll rip your arm off."

"Bon bagay." Jae rolls his amber eyes at both of us. "You're not helping, you."

Draco and I are still scowling at each other when Ash sidles into the room. He's a big guy and I haven't heard him coming, so I'm guessing he's been lurking out there in the tunnel and having himself a proper nosey.

"Could be a lil' bit of a hiccup with that whole 'join the harem' plan." For once, the Seelie Prince—who's typically chill, the mellowest and most laid-back guy in any group—looks awkward and apologetic.

From Mallory's general vicinity, a stricken gasp rushes out. But my eyes stay locked on Ash, who's filling the doorway and shifting from foot to foot.

"Color me curious, big man." Zara, too, is staring wide-eyed at this totally new version of Ash. "What's the hiccup?"

Ash scuffs a booted toe against the flagstone floor.

"With benefits or without 'em, you're not legally allowed to be in a harem with your own sister." Ash rubs a sheepish hand over his face, then smiles right at Mallory and finishes softly, "Hiya, kiddo."

Her silver eyes wide and round as vintage CDs, Mal takes in a long speechless look at the Seelie Prince who's just invaded her *domus*.

Suddenly, her eyes flood with tears.

Jae Labête snarls and drops into a defensive crouch between Mal and the rest of us. Black talons, wicked long like box cutters, sprout from his curled fingers.

"Hjartfólgin." Draco's powerful body bunches and swells. He looms over his girl protectively. "Who is this bastard to you?"

Still speechless, Mallory shakes her head.

"Give her some space," Ash says softly. "Been a minute since she's seen me. But she's still my kid sis. The only one I got."

Without warning, Mal's freckled face lights up in a grin that makes her whole body glow.

Blooming hell. All of a sudden, the rule-following First Girl looks a bit more than human.

"Oh my gosh, *Ash!*" Our normally quiet and well-mannered Mallory squeals like a piglet, then scrambles past a snarling Jae and launches herself across the room like she's airborne.

Straight into Ash's welcoming arms.

She's a tall girl, but Ash catches her like she's a kid, swinging her into the air, all long legs and pigtails and flying plaid skirts. Her face burrows into his shoulder and her skinny back heaves with emotion, but *his* face is a blooming study. Normally the reliable steady eddie, somehow he manages to look simultaneously guilty, sheepish, and pleased as punch.

"The fuck?" I stare blankly at this bizarro spectacle.

Mal is literally crying happy tears. Ash lowers her gently to the ground, then pats her back and kisses her forehead and looks pretty close to tears himself.

"Dear God. She's his *sister*?" V murmurs. He's standing beside me, and he's way too bloody close considering I'm supposed to be pissed as hell at him.

But we've bigger troubles than my mixed-up feelings to contend with, haven't we, at the mo?

"Truly, I never even suspected she's Seelie." Vasili lifts one perfectly groomed eyebrow. "How could she be? She's McSnicker."

I grunt in agreement, because I grasp what he's getting at. Mal has to be the most unmagical, unpedigreed, unremarkable witch in the whole Academy. She gets by on wicked smarts and solid study skills, always has. Plus she's handy at hiding from the bullies.

Not to mention she's so clumsy she can barely walk without tripping over her own big feet.

Not very Faelike, that.

Looking thoughtful, V taps a black-lacquered finger against his pursed lips. "Mallory McSnicker is secretly the sister of the Seelie Prince?"

"Looks that way to me, love." My casual endearment ignites a flame of fierce emotion that melts my boyfriend's pissy facade in a heartbeat.

V lowers his hand and smolders at me like he's ready to shove me facedown over the nearest bed and ruin me.

I look away from him fast, before my foolish heart gets all mushy, and say the first non-sexual thing that pops into my noggin. "Since Ash is the Prince, and the royal Light Fae line's matrilineal, that would make McSnicker…"

"She's the next Seelie Queen." Draco scowls ferociously at all of us. "After her mom. And *no one* can fucking know. Especially the Dark Fae King. Or that sick twisted fuck will kidnap her just like he did her brother. Then he'll kill her."

"So, yeah." Ash shifts his big body and manages to look even more sheepish. "About that whole kidnapping yarn…"

Right on cue, the gray silk voice of my Unseelie lover twines through the dense silence like a ribbon.

"'Tis rather late in the game to conceal this dangerous secret from me." Zephyr slips into the cavern behind Ash, jade eye burning with purpose in his feral face. His crossed swords jut over his armored shoulders like skeletal wings. "Since I am, unfortunately, the twisted fuck in question. Even so, I fear I'm the least of your current troubles."

That's the precise moment in this monumental cock-up of a day when all bloody hell breaks loose.

Chapter Thirteen
Zara

I've been standing with my back to Draco Mars while I take in Ash's reunion with my friend who turns out to be, apparently, his long-lost sister. (Like, seriously, who knew? Shy, smart, unassuming Mallory is the future Seelie Queen? She definitely kept that shit quiet.)

Anyway.

I never even see the attack coming.

Barely a heartbeat after Zephyr shows up and proclaims his identity to the whole room like the royal Unseelie prick he can sometimes be, Draco growls and thunders past me in a murderous rush.

I catch a single horrific glimpse of the Icelander's brutal face, full lips curling in a snarl, strong features blazing with the ruthless light of a Viking berserker in a killing rage. Then that medieval battle axe he's clutching descends in a glittering sweep toward Zephyr's unprotected green head.

The hum of the lightning voice buzzes into my throat. The duffel falls from my grip a beat before all that deadly voltage crackles through my body, so I don't zap my kitten. I'm a human lightning rod.

But even I need time to summon and cast.

More time than Zephyr has.

Ash functions as Zephyr's bodyguard as well as his consort. But Ash's arms are full of Mallory and, for once, the vigilant protector is distracted. Time stretches like taffy as Draco closes on Zephyr's bad side—his blind spot. Draco is taller than Vasili with greater reach. He's twice Zephyr's size and fueled by an incinerating fury.

My Dark Fae doesn't even have time to draw his swords.

As the axe cleaves down, Draco bellows, *"You will not touch her!"* at a volume that turns every head in the room.

Too late, Zephyr's head snaps toward the threat. His face fires with alarm. He twists and leaps straight back like a cat, arms sweeping up to summon his own elemental Fae magic.

A sloppy curl of Fae-summoned wind, thick with rain, howls through the skylight.

But Zephyr's greatest defense has always been his dragon. Xhevith is halfway across the island (since we're trying to be subtle) and way too big anyway to squeeze into this *domus*. By the same token, there's not enough room in here for me to shift.

Not without knocking out a bunch of those supportive pillars and bringing the roof down.

I have a split second to roar in the lightning voice. It's a cry of frustration and rage. My bellow lights up the drippy gray sky beyond the skylight with a jagged fork of ultraviolet lightning that's way too dangerous to hurl.

Not in these close quarters.

Not with my mates in the way.

I can only watch, in a paralysis of terror, as Draco's axe descends.

Then the pale sweep of V's casting hand summons an invisible telekinetic wallop that sucks all the air out of the room. His telekinesis catches that awful axe in mid-swing. V's witchcraft wrenches the weapon from Draco's fist and sends it tumbling end over end. Right over Mordred's startled blue head, where the demon's crouched by the water with his tattooed hand dangling in the inky depths.

The axe sails into the rainwater reservoir and vanishes with a splash.

Under the vicious lash of his will, V's power coils and snaps like a bullwhip. Every electrically charged hair on my body is already standing on end. Now my skin tingles under the lethal brush of all that magic, filling the air like a swarm of bees.

But I'm not Vasili's target.

Draco's broad-shouldered body soars high and flies backward, shitkicker boots churning the air. He slams into a pillar with crushing force.

The Icelander hits so hard I expect to see him crushed to a bloody smear on the marble.

But my Goblin King has wicked control.

The walls ring with the guttural *oof!* of impact. That's Draco getting his wind knocked out. The back of his white-blond head thuds into the pillar. But, miraculously, his skull doesn't shatter like a dropped egg.

Pinned to the pillar and suspended ten feet in the air, Draco shakes his stunned head and looks groggy.

I can practically see cartoon sparrows circling the guy's cranium.

The rest of the room is riveted.

Mallory frozen and white-faced, clutching her equally shocked brother for comfort, matching pairs of gray eyes wide with fear for their respective mates.

Ronin crouched and battle-ready, ashen with shock.

Neo with his glasses sliding down his startled nose.

Max growling and hovering protectively over me, like I was ever the one in danger.

Vasili stands, alone and rigid, with his casting hand outflung. He glares at Draco's suspended frame in venomous menace. The dark vetiver scent of V's aggression floods the dank air.

If he closes that fist and means it, he'll crush Draco's vital organs to a pulp and pulverize Draco's bones to powder.

"Sweet Jesus," I gasp. Sparks crackle in my hair and dance along my fingers. "What the *fuck*—?"

I'm still swearing when Zephyr recovers his balance, coils to his full height (which isn't much, since he's no taller than I am), and seizes the lapels of Vasili's Academy blazer in both fists. V's startled head swivels around and his face snaps toward him. Then Zephyr's mouth slams into his.

It's a kiss.

A hard claiming kiss.

A kiss that's more like a bite than an actual kiss.

Still—cheese on toast!—my Dark Fae King is *kissing* my snake.

Vasili is so startled that he drops Draco. The Icelander slides down the pillar, tries and fails to get his legs under him, and lands heavily at its base in a crumpled heap.

"Fokk," Draco groans, raspy with shock.

Jae snarls in concern and rushes over to help him.

V's gilded head angles down to Zephyr's to let the kiss deepen. His casting hand floats up to rest on Zephyr's shoulder. While Zephyr feeds ravenously from that kiss like he's determined to devour Vasili from the inside out, V's black-nailed fingers tighten and dig into Zephyr's dragonscale.

I keep a sharp eye on that deadly hand of his, but the Goblin King appears to be behaving.

For once.

After a long breathless moment when no one moves or speaks, those two surface gently from their kiss. In unison, they release the long-drawn breath they've both been holding.

My own held breath rushes out in parallel.

"Thank you," Zephyr says softly.

Behind the green slash of his eyepatch, the Unseelie King's face is open, unguarded, soft with a fragile moment of wonder.

Like he's thanking his rival both for saving his life and sharing his kiss.

Of course, being V, my snake has to go and ruin the moment. He releases Zephyr's shoulder and steps back abruptly, breaking Zephyr's grip on his lapels.

"I did it for Ronin and not you," Vasili says, every word stinging like a wasp. "He's suffered enough trauma on your account."

Zephyr's face shutters and closes. His eye narrows and his mouth hardens. Quietly he says, "Even so. I owe you a debt, beautiful one. A life for a life. You may be certain I will repay it."

Then, without waiting for the acknowledgement he probably knows he won't be getting, the Dark Fae King pivots on his booted heel and stalks toward the pillar where Draco lies sprawled, trying to clear his head.

The Cajun twists around and bares his werewolf fangs—newly emerged, but fully descended—at Zephyr with a rumble of warning.

"*Jae.* Whoa. Hold up.*" Mallory extracts herself from her brother's arms and hurries over to her guys. But I notice she gives Zephyr a really wide berth. "I honestly think we've had enough violence in this *domus* for one morning."

"I'm not the one you should be telling, *chere*." Jae crouches and angles his body to stay between Draco and Zephyr. The Cajun's amber eyes are getting wolfy, a spark of green fire glowing in each pupil.

Of course Zephyr, being Zephyr, just keeps coming. His lithe green-armored body slows to a prowl.

But that only makes him look more menacing.

"Everybody take it easy, okay?" Ash moseys over there himself, his long legs eating up the distance. "If this is about Sparrow nabbing me way back when, Freckles, you're blaming the wrong joe."

It takes me a sec to realize he's talking to Mallory, who is indeed very freckled.

"You mean he *didn't* kidnap you?" By now, Mal has reached Draco's side. She swings off her heavy backpack and huddles beside her guy, but her worried eyes track Zephyr's every move.

Behind that pale golden sprinkle of nutmeg freckles, her face is white with fear.

"You may be certain I did," Zephyr says loftily. "I covet your brother relentlessly. Whatsoever a Dark Fae covets, he steals. 'Tis been our custom for millennia."

"Not helping, Your Transcendence." I snort and head that way myself, with a protective Max dogging my every step. "Let's focus on why Draco swung that axe at your head."

"Yeah, what she said." Ash sidles up alongside Zephyr and slings an affectionate arm over his shoulders, which manages to halt his advance about two seconds before that werewolf would've lunged for Zephyr's throat. "Been in love with this guy for a good long time, ain't I, Sparrow?"

"There were witnesses to the kidnapping," Mal reminds Ash in a tight voice. "Including *Mom.* The whole thing happened right outside the council room. They all said you fought like heck."

Huh.

Maybe that's why Draco just tried to kill him.

"Let's just say I didn't fight all that hard." Ash tucks Zephyr against his side and basically makes clear to the whole room that they're together.

"*Fokking* Stockholm syndrome." Draco gathers his big frame in a gingerly way and clambers to his feet with a wince. "*Hel.* Your brother thinks he's in love with his *fokking* kidnapper."

Mal shakes her head like she can't cope with her brother and his love life right now (understandable) and rootles around in the first aid kit belted to her waist. With a small sound of triumph, she extracts a plastic vial of acetaminophen and scrambles up. We all watch in bemusement while she slips a bottle of water from her well-stocked backpack, shakes out a couple of tablets, and firmly instructs Draco to take them.

He grumbles at her, then swallows the pills dry, like the grumpy Neanderthal he clearly is.

Mal tugs Jae gently to her side as well and holds his hand tightly, which seems to help with his wolf. Watching the three of them interact, I'm starting to realize shy Mallory McSnicker is every bit as much the queen of her small harem as I am the queen of mine.

Maybe it's not so hard after all to imagine her as the Seelie Queen.

Under her pale face, her color is rising as she watches her brother cuddle the Dark Fae King.

"Then there's the part about you being gone *four years*." For the first time I can ever recall, Mallory's meek and mannerly First Girl voice is rising. "Without a single word to anyone. God, I read a poem at your funeral. We all thought you were *dead*, Ash."

"Bit of a dick move, that," Ronin mutters, with a chiding look at Ash, who meets it with his own level stare.

Ugh.

I was honestly hoping Ash and Ronin were maybe getting past that stage.

But those two still swipe at each other (which is something like Problem 912 in our harem's growing list). While Vasili blames Zephyr for Zephyr's agonizing estrangement from Ronin, Ash has always blamed Ronin.

By now, we're all gathered around the looming shitstorm near Draco's pillar. Neo scoops the kitten gently from her carrier and trots over with her creamy innocence curled, alert and blinking, in the crook of his arm.

V eyes the kitten and edges away.

Meanwhile, under Mal's accusing stare, Ash is starting to look kinda hounded.

Zephyr gives the room a sidelong smirk and steps in. "For his long silence, I will take the blame. Ash couldn't pass beyond the Avalon portal. After all, your prince was my captive… and my concubine. I largely kept him chained to my bed."

"Whoa." Draco rolls his shoulders and kneads the back of his neck with a wince. "TMI. Mal's his kid sister. She doesn't need to know that shit."

Hopefully Mal thinks Zephyr's being facetious.

Since I happen to know Zephyr does have chains in his bedroom and uses them, and since everyone in our polycule knows Ash is a born submissive and consensually submits to Zephyr, I'm pretty sure Zephyr is being literal.

At this point, I figure I better step in before that grouchy mafia bully of Mal's gets annoyed enough to take another swing at Zephyr.

Because next time, I'm not gonna be as forgiving.

"Lemme see if I got this straight." I plant myself between the two parties to keep everyone civil. Max growls and bristles at my shoulder like a hostile watchdog. "Draco attacked Zephyr out of some effed-up impulse to protect Mal. Draco must've figured all that bad blood between the Dark and the Light Fae, like the genocidal history and all, was playing out. The way Mal thought it was, back when Zephyr took Ash."

"Can you blame her?" Draco grumbles. "If that shit was voluntary, dude shoulda sent an email or something, for real."

"You think we got internet bennies in Avalon?" Ash exchanges a fond look with Zephyr. "Heck, that joint isn't even electrified."

"The thing is," I say firmly, before we all get off track again, "Ash is, like, a prisoner of love. He's with Zephyr—with *all* of us—totally willingly. He's part of my harem. That means he'll be one of my kings."

Then I play my trump card. "He's even gonna be a visiting prof here next semester."

Confronted with this academic newsflash, First Girl Mallory looks torn between disbelief and delight. She tucks a stray copper curl behind her ear and darts her brother an intent look. "Is that true? What subject are you teaching?"

"Yeah, sure. Potions prof. I hear the school needs one." Ash hitches his big shoulders in a shrug that flexes the biceps under the bloody vine-and-thorns tattoo—Zephyr's tat—which twines around Ash's upper arm. "Plus I'll teach a new elective. Healing Arts for Witches 101. We'll see how it goes."

What he means is, we'll see how it works having him and Zephyr sharing a roof and a bed with the rest of my harem on a full-time basis.

Needless to say, I'm all in on this plan. I'm grateful as fuck to him and Lucius for coming up with it.

And determined as hell to make the plan succeed.

"Look. We finally finished trying to kill each other or what?" Ronin shoves his hands in his pockets and looks darkly at Draco. In turn, the Icelander aims a wary glance at Vasili (who lingers, silent but terrifying, near Ronin).

Finally, Draco jerks his chin in a surly nod.

"Brilliant." Ronin sounds less than thrilled, but we're linked, he knows what I've just decided we need, and he's going with it. "You lot still want to be our allies in the Dean's Challenge or not?"

Jae, who's fully human again with Mallory holding his hand, hisses in a breath. Mal leans into him, exchanges a speaking look with Draco, then opens her mouth.

Before she can get a word out, the rapid patter of galloping paws on stone spins us all toward the door. A massive timber wolf, shaggy with gray and chestnut fur, explodes through the doorway at a dead run. Instantly, Jae Labête lunges forward with a bark of challenge.

But this is a wolf I know.

Even if Jae (who's running purely on werewolf instinct) apparently doesn't.

Before we can plunge into yet another mortal combat sitch, the galloping wolf rises on his hind legs. In mid-stride, his fur dwindles, his muzzle flattens, and his torso lengthens. A blinding flash of light makes us all squint.

When my vision clears, a fully human Lucius is running toward us. Naked.

Mallory has two seconds to look startled and scandalized at the sight of my naked headmaster before Draco covers her eyes with a muttered curse. Jae pulls up in mid-lunge and retracts his fangs with a grimace.

Normally, Lucius does not parade around naked in front of his students (I mean, the ones who aren't in our polycule and whom he's therefore not fucking). He's really modest for a shifter, and very conscious of things like decorum and propriety that the rest of us mostly ignore.

Which is why the sight of our headmaster loping toward us, mother naked with dick dangling, fires me with a spurt of instant alarm.

"Was it truly necessary," he gasps, coming to a halt directly before me and hunching over to catch his breath, "for you to summon lightning?"

"Yeah, I know." I heave a sigh. "Might as well hire a blimp to tell the whole island *Zara is here*. Sorry about that, Lucius."

Ronin tucks up behind Max and rummages through the pack our dragon is carrying for Lucius' spare clothes. With an abashed look at Mal and her guys, Lucius plucks his trousers out of Ronin's hand, exchanges a quick scenting rub with Max to calm our excited dragon, then turns away modestly to button himself into his pants.

Zephyr's single eye narrows on the door Lucius just ran through. "Lucius Aries. Are you pursued?"

"I don't believe anyone has spotted me specifically. But the entire island witnessed Zara's lightning." Lucius sweeps his wild mane of chestnut curls into a decorous ponytail and turns to face us. Before my eyes, he's morphing from savage wolf to the sober headmaster who keeps us all safe.

"And now," Lucius finishes grimly, "they're coming."

Max growls and plants himself squarely between me and the door, even as Draco does the same with Mallory. As soon as Lucius zipped his fly, the Icelander stopped trying to cover her eyes.

"Who is coming?" my dragon says fiercely.

Lucius closes his starched shirt over his hairy chest and buttons himself swiftly to the chin. Bemused, I wonder if he's going to don a tie.

"Either we were seen sailing into the harbor," Lucius frowns, "or the others picked up your scent in the woods. Either way, the pack was already in the vicinity when Zara summoned lightning."

"Pack?" My skin prickles with alarm. My voice thickens and goes resonant with electricity.

Lucius locks onto my wide eyes. He'd normally hug me for reassurance, but he's more reserved in front of other students.

Stiffly, he inclines his head. "I fear a sizable pack of shifters is headed straight for this *domus*, Ms. Gemini."

"Like, *multiple* shifters?" Neo pushes his glasses up his nose and frowns. "Would Cleo and her team leave the Vault unguarded?"

"No way." I'm already shaking my head. "She set that trap and she knows we gotta walk into it. She wouldn't have any problem waiting to spring it. She's not the impatient type."

"Not like some," Ronin mutters with a sidelong grin at me.

Despite whatever's headed toward us, the smolder in his amber eyes makes me warm. He's not one of the guys who's particularly trying to knock me up. But he was the very first of my warlocks, and we have our own special thing.

I lace a hand through his hot fingers (because, very appropriately, he's a fire sign) and tug him to my side. Ronin wraps a possessive arm around my waist, claims my mouth with a scorching kiss that tastes like sin and whiskey, and gives me the lick of contact I crave.

Meanwhile, Mallory snatches up her backpack and reactivates her flashlight. The slender cylinder snicks on in a businesslike way.

When my head clears from Ronin's kiss, my gaze veers back to Lucius. "We don't have that many shifters on this island, Teach. If that, uh, pack isn't Cleo's, then whose are they?"

"Rather unfortunately, your pursuers don't appear to be students at all." Lucius does indeed pluck a burgundy silk tie from Max's pack and deftly knots it around his neck. I guess he wants to be properly attired when we have to fight. (I mean, until he shifts. Then, once again, he'll be nakey.)

"Not students?" Vasili closes in to straighten Lucius' tie for him, but his eyes are sharp with what, on anyone else, I would label alarm. "This island's sole population consists of students and faculty. Plus the occasional random Fae." He exchanges a wry look with Zephyr.

"That's right." Mallory gives an earnest nod. "No one else is allowed inside the wards, especially during the Dean's Challenge. That would be against the rules. Right, Master Aries?"

"Be that as it may." Lucius hastens into his blazer. "We're currently tracked and hunted by a sizable pack of hyena shifters."

V's wary face fires with recognition. His diamond eyes glitter like ice. "Sweet fuck. That's an AIB kill squad. Undoubtedly deployed by my father."

Right on cue, a low chuckle floats through the open door. A chorus of distant chortles chases it, rising to a hail of inhuman whoops.

That demented chortling makes my scalp crawl. My chest squeezes in a fist of dread. Unlike my dragon, hyenas are just the right size to maneuver in the confines of this dungeon. Their jaws are strong enough to snap bones. They're cunning.

And they're nasty.

In the wild, hyena shifters do more than attack humans.

What they kill, they also eat.

"Geez, how is that even allowed?" Neo exclaims, cuddling the kitten for mutual reassurance. "It's outside interference. Totally against the Academy Codex. Right, Lucius?"

"Zara has been accused of inciting a rebellion against the lawful queen. Now all of us collectively—except the Fae, who have no legal standing in the witching world—are alleged accomplices to the crime. That's high treason, which is a felony offense," Lucius murmurs. "In this case, intervention by the Arcane Investigative Bureau may be classified as a legal action. Which is permitted under the Codex."

While Ronin swears and Max paces, I fight to clear my head and come up with some kinda plan. I can't help feeling it's my fault they're all in danger. Both my friends and my mates.

The least I can do is protect them.

"Nobody panic," Mallory announces firmly, before we all lose our shit. "I know what to do. Follow me."

Bemused, I turn and stare at her. The First Girl swings her loaded backpack over her skinny shoulder with a grunt and heads purposefully for the cavern's shadowy rear.

Unfortunately, she's unbalanced by her heavy pack. When she trips over her own big feet in her schoolgirl saddle shoes, Jae leaps forward to catch her.

With a growl, Draco slings her pack over his own big shoulder.

"*Helvitis,*" the Icelander grumbles. "Do you have to carry every textbook you own in this thing?"

"Just the ones we need to survive. Including the grimoire that'll open the passage… I hope." Mal hesitates. "I'll need a little time to invoke the spell. It might take me a minute to untangle—I mean, without triggering the booby trap."

"What booby trap?" Vasili's eyes narrow.

"Hold that thought, beautiful," Ash says to him, then turns toward his kid sister with a degree of respect and trust I find reassuring. "Freckles needs a diversion to buy her some time. Let's give the gal what she needs."

"Right. That'll be me then. Who's with me?" Ronin springs into action, swiftly organizing our gang into two squads. One to protect the passage and provide magical backup while Mal does her thing, the other to play offense and meet that pack of hyenas out in the woods before they're expecting it.

Needless to say, I wanna be right out front.

Playing offense.

My inner dragon is chafing and fretting about protecting our dragonets and saving our mates in a way that's increasingly distracting and hard to handle.

Long story short, she's more than ready to rumble.

But I run up hard against the solid refusal of all three of my alphas—and their out-of-control mating ruts—to tolerate even the idea of me deliberately putting myself in danger.

After a short but intense convo that's moderated by a very firm Lucius, I end up (frustrated and begrudging, but not actively resisting, because there's no time for that shit) relegated safely to the rear. Along with V, Lucius, Mal, Jae, and Neo (plus the kitten). At least I can join Vasili and Jae on defense. Lucius and Neo are already huddled over the grimoire with Mallory against the rear wall. Neo is lighting a ring of candles and Lucius is holding the flashlight and murmuring the spell notes, while Mal inscribes a big pentacle on the flagstones with a piece of chalk.

Meanwhile, our attack squad—Max, Draco, Zephyr, Ash, and Ronin—move out right away. Their immediate goal is to avoid getting trapped in the *domus* by those hyenas. If Max can get outside and airborne fast enough, he'll *flambé* the whole pack.

With any luck, he'll also fricassee V's asshole father.

In case Max needs help, Zephyr's calling in his own airborne backup. His green dragon Xhevith should be here within minutes.

Which only leaves Mordred unaccounted for.

My gaze shoots to the sex demon, who's risen to his feet to lounge against a pillar and eavesdrop on the spell. But his clever eyes are fixed on me.

He's V's demon and not mine.

Still, he's clearly waiting for my orders.

"You're kinda the ace up our sleeve, Aquaman," I tell him. "Because Nikolai Romanov might not even know we have a half incubus, half kraken shifter on our team. You're our last line of defense. You gotta keep the Horn outta their hands… I mean paws. No matter what."

"You're the boss, baby queen." Mordred shucks Neo's preppy raincoat and hunkers down to unlace his borrowed boots.

Despite the urgency of the crisis, I take a minute to appreciate the visual of six feet plus of sex demon, naked from the waist up except for the inky tattooed sleeve running from shoulder to wrist on one arm. With every movement, his delts flex and his pecs ripple. The deep pelvic vee of his Adonis belt plunges under the scaly black breeks that cling to his bulging quads and muscled calves. He's totally channeling Jason Momoa, right down to the goatee and the dark tangle of hair spilling down his spine.

"Dayum," I mutter. "Helluva time to sex me up, demon."

"Working though, ain't it?" He dimples and winks at me, then uncoils his powerful body in a long dive that propels him deep into the black water.

With the Horn of Ceres still strapped to his body.

I'm not particularly a sports fan.

Never had time for organized sports in my law-skirting cat burglar life.

But I know enough to recognize that entrusting our magical artifact to a wild card player like Mordred the incubus shifter is what any sports fan would call a Hail Mary pass.

Chapter Fourteen
Mallory

This is the most dangerous spell I've ever tried to cast.

Knowing Draco and my long-lost brother are both outside with the others, hurling themselves into danger to protect me from an AIB kill squad while I invoke this dangerous magic? Knowing my friend and her entire harem trust me, Mallory McSnicker, the carrot-haired running joke of the whole Academy, to save the day? Knowing it's on me and my mediocre witchcraft to defend the rightful queen and keep the torch of rebellion alight?

Not helping.

Now the distant tyrannosaur bellow of Max's dragon (scary as heck) startles me so badly I fumble and drop my amethyst.

Welp, there goes the last chunk of crystal I need to ward the four quadrants of that protective pentacle I've chalked into the rough stone floor.

Propelled by my jittery nerves and that dragon's frustrated roar—or just by my usual clumsiness—the precious crystal skitters across the floor with a *chink-chink-chink* that echoes off the ancient walls.

"Darn it!" I lunge after the stone and trip over my own big feet, clunky in my saddle shoes.

As usual.

I end up sprawled on the floor, palms abraded and knees stinging, nerves jangling in alarm over my near-faceplant.

But the blush scorching across my face?

That's worse. Way worse.

Way to go, McSnicker. I swallow down a sigh of resignation. *It'd be so great if you could save the witching world without tripping over your own feet. Just once.*

You know, for a novelty.

"Whoa, Mal, you okay?" Zara stops pacing to scoop up the fallen amethyst and rushes to help me up.

But Jae reaches my side first.

"Eh, *bébé*, you be more careful, you," my guy murmurs tenderly.

While I scramble to get my feet back under me, Jae wraps an arm around my waist from behind. Which definitely heats me up, both in my face and… other places.

For *reasons.*

My distracted brain rushes straight to the savage way my werewolf shoved me facedown over Draco's dorm room bed this morning, spread my quivering thighs wide, and railed me until my knees turned to jelly and I creamed all over his dick.

Then Draco cleaned us both off.

Really thoroughly.

With his tongue.

I'm still breathless and tingly with *that* memory and wondering how this can even be my life now—hooking up with not one, but two of the hottest, sweetest, most protective warlocks in the whole witching world—when Jae's wiry strength pulls me to my feet.

I suck in a badly needed breath to compose myself. Then I turn into him and nestle into his feverish shifter heat, tucking my flushed face into his neck and breathing in his comforting scent of bayou moss and patchouli.

"I am being careful," I say into the side of his neck.

The feel of my mouth on his skin makes his wolf rumble. His hot hands close on my waist and pull me closer, right into his sinewy hips and thighs.

I nuzzle his neck and sneak my arms around his lean waist for a hug to reassure both of us. The beads and juju dripping from his dreadlocks tickle my forearms.

You worried about our amou? Jae whispers through our bond, because he's part Valyrian and a major telepath. Even if he completely refuses to bite me, due to some paranoid fear about his shifter recessives taking over and turning me into a monster like him.

(Even though he isn't a monster.)

"I believe in Draco," I whisper into his neck. Honestly, I still can't believe this fierce and beautiful man is my lover. He and Draco both. The only lovers I've ever had. Our whole relationship feels like a dream, and I don't know where we're going.

But there's one thing I know for sure.

"I believe in you too, Jean-Emilien Labête," I tell him. "I believe in you both."

Ah, bon. His wolf growls and mutters in his chest. *Take more than a few mangy hyenas to bring down a badass like Draco Mars, eh?*

"I know. He'll be okay. They all will. They have to be." I pull in a shaky breath, loosen my desperate clutch on my boyfriend, and step back.

My gaze shoots straight to Zara's worried eyes and puckered brow.

"They'll all be okay," I repeat, for her sake.

Lucius Aries (who's my History of Witchcraft prof, a faculty member I typically try to impress) and Neo Mercury (who vies with me every semester for that top spot on the Dean's List, but it's a friendly rivalry) hover at her shoulder and look concerned.

Both watching me with doubt written all over their patient faces.

Even that blue-haired Fae with the webbed feet and the wicked grin is watching me from under the reservoir. I know he is, I can sense that stuff, even though I can't see him. It's a survival skill. His kind and mine—the Dark Fae and the Light—we're ancient enemies.

I swear I can feel him lurking down there, coiled against the grate of the rusted portcullis embedded in the back wall, where the rainwater flows to the septic tank.

Crap.

Now everyone's concerned.

I mean, except Vasili.

Vasili Romanov is still the most terrifying bully in the whole Academy. Even though he mostly ignores me, like I'm (thankfully) beneath his notice. Especially since he hooked up with Zara, who kinda curbs the worst of his sadistic excesses (at least, when she's around).

When she isn't, he's still the terror of the student body.

To my intense relief, Vasili's lying in wait, all the way over near the outer door. Spying. To give us as much warning as possible in case those hyenas slip past our perimeter.

Which is more than a hypothetical danger.

Get it together, McSnicker, I tell myself firmly, studying the circle of worried faces around me. *You're not exactly building confidence here.*

More than anyone else, I know how important it is to instill confidence and keep calm in an emergency. I'm not only the First Girl on the Dean's List. I'm also a hall monitor. That makes me the safety warden of our dorm.

I'm trained for this stuff.

"Everything okay here?" Zara asks cautiously, holding my fallen amethyst between two fingers like she's afraid it'll burn her.

"Uh huh." I nod so vigorously a curl springs free from my pigtail and dangles over my eye.

Zara studies the chunk of amethyst she's gripping. "Then I'm guessing you want this back. Right?"

"Um, yeah, thanks. We're almost ready for the incantation." I tuck that wayward spiral of carroty curl behind my slightly pointed ear, pluck the amethyst from my friend's fingers, and position it at the pentacle's north corner, right at the spot I've carefully marked with my compass.

I'm about to ask for the grimoire Neo's been poring over when a shrill, ear-splitting *screech!* lances through the skylight.

Geez Louise, that's awful.

That sound practically makes my ears bleed.

I know what it is. That piercing nails-on-chalkboard scream is the cry of a hunting dragon.

Not Max.

But that acid-breathing green monstrosity who answers to the Dark Fae King.

I swear every hair on my body stands on end.

As the secret heir to the Seelie Queen, I've lived my life in perpetual dread of the Dark Fae King. He's been my personal bogeyman for a really long time. Even though we never actually met (since I've been hiding from him) until today. I know Ash says he's safe and all. But hearing and believing are two really different things.

I've been mourning Ash... and hiding from Zephyr... for years.

"Take it easy. That's only Xhevith," Zara tells me gently, referring to the screeching dragon. Probably because they all just saw me flinch at the sound. "He's just sounding off. He's actually a big softie."

I gape at her. That dragon is a *softie*?

"I happen to know Avalon dragons are carnivorous," I mutter. "The Dark Fae unleashed them to hunt down the Seelie and eat us in the bad old days. It's in the lore. But whatever."

Zara actually giggles, like the thought of a Fae-eating dragon is funny. (This is one of the reasons her enemies call her the Mad Queen. I mean, her inappropriate laughter.)

When everyone else in the room is peeing their pants in terror, Zara Gemini laughs.

"Xhev won't hurt you—and neither will his rider, I promise." My friend's gorgeous face softens and glows. "What went down with Zephyr and Ash after the, uh, abduction… it isn't what you thought, Mallory. Those two are, like, crazy in love. They really are. They're sweet together."

Honestly, it's all I can manage not to roll my eyes.

I'm not letting Ash, at least, wiggle off the hook so easily. Not after all the crap his disappearance put me and our whole family through.

"Your Unseelie, he's a killer, *oui*?" Jae tells Zara. His honey-gold eyes burn with violence. "If he even looks at Mallory any way she doesn't like, he'll answer to my wolf."

Zara's saved from having to reply to *that* when an airborne Vasili zips into our huddled circle, combat boots sparkling with violet glitter. The Academy bully alights in our midst with a vicious glare.

"Dear fuck. Why on earth are you all standing around?" Vasili tidies his windblown mane with an irritable flick of his punk-rock hand. "Team Zara isn't doing particularly well out there, just in case anyone happens to be wondering. That AIB kill squad is *extremely* well trained. They're using the tree cover to particularly inspired effect."

"What does that mean?" I ask timidly.

The Academy bully immobilizes me with his basilisk stare, like he's literally turning me to stone. "It *means* Maxim can't flame in the forest without incinerating half the island. And His *lah-dee-dah* Radiance isn't having any discernible effect from the air either."

"Ah, *merde*," Jae groans.

"I'd give us another three minutes… if I'm being generous. Then that pack of cackling hyenas will be gnawing our bones," Vasili snaps. "So *hurry.*"

My heartbeat leaps and bounds like a terrified rabbit.

This degree of direct attention from the Academy's most notorious bully is exactly the kind of notice I've spent my whole life striving like heck to avoid.

Get a grip, McSnicker, I remind myself. *Zara's counting on you.*

"Okay." Breaking through the protective paralysis that grips me—my ingrained instinct to *hide* so the bullies don't find me—I steady the open grimoire, held open to the correct passage in Neo's helpful hands. The faded ink of the spell writhes over the yellowed page and makes my eyes blur. Nausea twists in the pit of my belly, but I swallow it down and square my shoulders. "Master Aries, can you please hold the flashlight so I can read the incantation?"

"*I* can't even read the incantation," Neo murmurs, blinking at me behind his glasses. "What is that, ancient Latin?"

"Yes. It's the Book of Flame and Breath. From the rare books collection in the library. I signed it out," I explain earnestly, just so no one thinks I stole it. "It's not even overdue."

"Oh, *that's* a relief." Vasili jibes, in a tone that cuts like the hidden cache of knives the whole school knows he carries. "At least, after those hyenas have torn us limb from limb, snapped our bones, and sucked out the marrow, we won't have to contend with late fees."

"Don't be a jerk, V," Neo says to him with a level of fearlessness I find astounding, then gives me a sympathetic look. "Just ignore him, Mallory. He's in the doghouse right now in this harem, and it makes him pissy. I mean, more than usual."

"He *is*?" I sneak an astonished peek at the terrifying Vasili, who purses his lips in a discontented pout.

Of course, that bully doesn't answer.

"The important thing is," Neo says patiently, "can you actually read that spell? I mean, are you sure you know what it says?"

My shoulders hitch in a modest shrug. "Yeah, sure. I studied ancient Latin in prep school."

Neo blinks at me and looks impressed.

"I do seem to recall that commendable detail from your academic transcript, Ms. McSnicker." Master Aries gives me a respectful nod. "Unfortunately, this particular grimoire is normally locked away in the rare books collection for an excellent reason. I fear there's more than ancient Latin in play in some of the less savory spells."

Clearly, if he thinks that would deter me from signing the book out, my History of Witchcraft prof has underestimated the lengths I'll go to in order to earn an A.

"Yeah, I know. This particular spell is hexed. I mean, the text is all jumbled under a major confusion curse. That's what drew my attention in the first place, when I was writing my research paper for your class." I frown over the open page while my prof looms helpfully over me with the flashlight.

"Indeed." He trains his light directly on the page. "It appears you're correct, Ms. McSnicker."

"Five points for class participation," Vasili purrs. "Well done you."

Zara nudges him with an elbow, paired with a look that hovers somewhere between reproach and laughter.

But I don't have time to be bullied right now.

The hexed words of the opening spell dance across the ancient parchment like imps around the fires of hell. I bite my lip and steady the book with a gingerly hand.

"Pardon me for stating the obvious, *do*," Vasili drawls. "But shouldn't we be *inside* that protective pentacle you've just drawn?"

I smack my forehead with my palm. "Um, yes. Obviously. Everyone inside the circle."

"You're making her nervous, Goblin King," Zara murmurs to Vasili as we all grab our gear and crowd into the chalk circle, which is barely big enough to hold us. "Be nice."

"Oh, certainly, that's what I'm known for," Vasili says with poisonous sweetness. "Being *nice*."

Carefully I position Neo with the book before me, my prof at one side with the flashlight, and Jae holding my bespelling candle aloft at the other. Everyone else crowds around me, subtly nudging Zara into the safe spot between her headmaster and her dominant alpha. Beyond the dim circle of their worried faces, the blank wall of the hidden passage looms.

Are the shadows getting thicker? Or is the daylight leaking through the slit in our ceiling getting dimmer? The dragon's increasingly frustrated bellows, bouncing off the walls at erratic intervals, make my ears ring. But I can't hear the hoot and chuckle of those hyenas at all anymore.

Which probably means they're… hunting.

With a bone-deep shiver, I dig out my lighter. But before I light it, I hesitate.

"Um, shouldn't that… Dark Fae aquatic of yours… come inside the circle too?" I ask Zara carefully. Even though the idea of letting any Unseelie into my safe space flies squarely in the face of every survival instinct that's kept me alive. "If the spell backfires, it might get really gnarly in this chamber."

"Gnarly?" Neo blinks at me through his glasses. "Can you be any more specific?"

"Any spell uttered from the Book of Flame and Breath that fails," Master Aries murmurs, "either suffocates the casting witch or sets her afire. Nor is the Book known to discriminate when choosing a victim for its malice. Anyone within range who's breathing is a likely casualty."

"Cheese on toast." Zara clutches her duffel to her chest (for some reason I haven't figured out yet, she's carrying a kitten in there) and looks worried.

"However, I believe Mordred may be shielded from both effects, so long as he remains fully submerged." My prof furrows his brow. "At least in his current form."

"Ah, *oui*?" Jae gives the cistern a narrow look, even as he wraps a possessive arm around my waist. "I thought I smelled shifter on that one, me."

This is all super intriguing, but I can't afford to get distracted.

I flick on my lighter, cup a careful hand around the bespelling candle Jae is holding, shield it from the dank and foul-smelling wind that's just kicked up from nowhere, and touch my tiny flame to the wick.

As the taper begins to glow, I whisper the spell that unravels curses.

I'm a weak witch in general, like really weak. But curse-breaking is similar to healing. Both are meant to restore the natural order.

These are magics any Light Fae can summon.

A pale green flame flares to life and dances on the wick. The dry scent of sage and a fresh green whiff of dill tingle in my nostrils. Then a finger of olive smoke twines from my candle and curls over the spellbook's open pages.

I hold my breath and pray for luck to Saint Raymond, the Catholic saint of secrets. Sure, I'm Seelie, but I'm baptized and educated in Catholic prep schools, another way we hide from the mortals.

And maybe my patron saint is listening.

Because, under all our expectant stares, the words of the spell blur and waver. The handwritten letters squirm and wriggle across the page like worms.

"Bon bagay," Jae whispers, soft as breath.

I sneak a hand down to clutch his warm fingers, still firmly gripping my waist.

The squirming letters settle into stillness.

"Oh, crap," I whisper into the spellbound silence. My eyes fly over the text. "That's… like… a really archaic dialect."

Zara gives a little hop that broadcasts both excitement and impatience. "Well? Can you still read it?"

I blink at the strange accents and sigils that bedizen the letters and nibble my lower lip. "I mean, it's still Latin. I think I can pronounce the words. It's just—I don't totally know what they mean or what they'll do—"

From the smothering shadows, a diabolical chuckle rises.

Every follicle of hair on my head crinkles and lifts. The back of my neck crawls.

In reply, a low hoot echoes. From the clotted darkness near the door, two round eyes glow an eerie electric blue.

Scattered here and there in the darkness (because it's definitely gotten darker in here), matching eyes wink into sight.

Master Aries mutters an oath in Hungarian and slips from the protected circle on silent feet.

"Lucius!" Zara whispers. "Wait!"

But my reliable professor is gone. Vanished. Lost in the dark.

"Shit!" Zara hisses. "Aren't we safe here inside this circle?"

"We're only safe from witchcraft, babe," Neo tells her earnestly (and accurately). "Not flesh-and-blood shifters."

Now every eye in the circle turns to me.

"We're out of time to indulge your insecurities, McSnicker," Vasili snaps. "Cast that spell now if you want to live."

Without even waiting for me to nod, he levitates and zips off into the darkness.

Darn it.

Every gnawing niggle of insecurity I've ever felt, every insidious whisper of doubt I've ever heard (and they've been filling my ears all my life), every haunting fear that I'll never be good enough, never be brave enough, never be worthy enough, roots my feet to the floor in a paralysis of dread.

What are you even doing here, McSnicker? You're a pathetic excuse for a witch. You're a reject. A freak. A failure. You're going to fail *and get everyone killed—*

"Steady, *chere,*" Jae murmurs in my ear, because of course he feels what I feel. He hears what I hear—that din of corrosive voices that's eroding my meager supply of courage. "I believe in you, me. And Draco, he believes in you too. Time to be showing the world what you can do now."

I've never fought for what I love.

Never.

I've always just *hidden*.

So it feels way beyond the realm of the possible to believe a weak witch like me—Mallory McSnicker, the class klutz, the school geek, the laughing joke of the whole Icarus Academy—can even save myself.

Much less all of us.

But Jae believes.

Believes in *me*.

Maybe he believes enough for both of us.

I duck my head over the thicket of impenetrable text, press a shaky hand to my gut to quiet the butterfly nerves doing backflips in my belly, fling myself headlong into the first incomprehensible sentence in a blind leap of faith…

…and speak aloud the words of that awful spell.

Chapter Fifteen
Zara

The first clue I get that something's gone sideways is that hyena.

The thing explodes from the clotted shadows that fill the cavern and bounds straight for our charmed circle. Which, as we've already established, *isn't* charmed against flesh-and-blood shifters.

Over Mallory's turned shoulder, I glimpse a flash of spotted fur, powerful fangs snarling in a grizzly muzzle, an electric flicker of eyes pulsing an eerie blue. Massive shoulders bunch under a matted pelt. Then the monster launches through the air in a leap.

Straight at Mal's defenseless back.

I suck in a breath and roar in the lightning voice, *"STOP!"*

The resonant vibrato of my voice mingles with a deafening peal of thunder. Neo barely snatches the duffel from my shoulder in time before an ultraviolet crackle runs over my scalp and down my body.

That shit lights up the black pit of this basement like St. Elmo's Fire.

For just a blink, my lightning gives us all plenty of light. Hyenas are pouring into the room. My guys playing offense, the ones whose protective perimeter was supposed to keep those hyenas out of the *domus*—Ronin and Max and my two Fae—they're nowhere to be seen.

Which is not a good sign.

My chest clenches like a fist. My tummy twists in a tapeworm of anxiety.

Then the hyena leaping for Mal's exposed back just… ignites. That shaggy spotted fur bursts into green flame.

That's a whole new problem.

That combustible flash of pus-green fire, appearing out of nowhere to engulf the attacking hyena, is *not* my witchcraft.

I'm no pyro. I don't set shit on fire when I summon.

That's Ronin's gig.

Flamethrower.

And, like I said, Ronin's not here.

Warned barely in time by my bellow, Jae snarls, flings himself over a startled Mallory to drive her to the ground, and covers her protectively with his own body. Still clutching my duffel while the kitten yowls in protest, Neo scrambles clear of the flaming hyena.

Right out of the circle.

I fling myself the other way.

Also out of the circle.

My inner dragon bellows in the lightning voice. Summoned by my witchcraft, the narrow slit of sky splits with a crackle of purple lightning.

My control's better than it used to be. So I'm not waiting around for some weird green fire of unknown origin to finish the job and barbecue that hyena. I hurl my reliable bolt straight at the attacking animal, like a vengeful Zeus on Mt. Olympus.

By the time the hyena hits the space where we were all just standing, that shifter is a flaming husk.

I'm still staring, watching our four-legged attacker dissolve in a swirl of ash and cinders, when the darkness ignites with another flash of green fire. I spin toward a second hyena—this one bigger than the last— bounding across the cavern toward our scattered, transfixed, and largely undefended bodies.

That line of pus-green fire streaking down its spine? That fire just helps us see the rabid beast coming.

A wild-eyed Jae drags Mallory to her feet. "*Chere*, what is happening!"

"Oh, no." Mallory looks desperately from my electrified form to the flaming hyena galloping toward us. "The booby trap on the secret door. My spell must've tripped it!"

"Not the trap," Neo yells back (which could be the first time I've ever heard my bookworm yell anything). "Look at the book!"

In unison, our frantic eyes converge on the Book of Flame and Breath. The abandoned grimoire lies open, face down on the flagstones. The crumpled pages glow and pulse with pus-green fire.

"Oh. Fuck. *Me*." I groan from the heart.

The psi fire that's incinerating random hyenas is the exact same shade as that fucking cursed book.

The *book* is attacking.

Not attacking the witch (Mallory) who just channeled its freaky power. Because Mal and Jae are still crouched inside the circle of protection that's chalked on the floor.

Deprived of the casting witch as a target, that spiteful spellbook is going apeshit. Roasting random others. Maybe every sentient being that book can find. Or just the ones it doesn't like.

Possibly including my warlocks.

And me.

"Cheese on toast!" I grab Neo's arm—the only one of my guys I can even see—and drag him back into the pentacle. Who knows if it's even still intact? If all our rushing around has broken the chalk circle, Mal's protective pentacle is now useless.

Just to have a Plan B, I summon my own levitation witchcraft and shoot ten feet straight up in the air, my entire body glowing with purple fire like Storm the sexy mutant in *X-Men*.

I hover directly over sweet Neo, who's clutching our kitten and staring transfixed at the hyena closing in. (That hyena isn't burning fast enough, for real.)

My dragon bugles and bates in the cage of my skin. She's desperate to shift. But there's no fucking room.

Zaraaaaa! she trumpets in a deafening interior roar that makes my eardrums hum. *Save our mates. We rise!*

"Take it easy in there, showgirl," I mutter. "Don't bring the roof down. I got this."

Hoping like hell the borders of Mal's protective circle reach this high, so I don't get fricasseed in pus-colored fire (which is not the way I wanna kick the bucket), I hum in my throat to call my lightning.

The hyena's almost on top of us when my bolt of purple whup-ass forks through the skylight and fries that monster to a crisp.

Halfway across our circle, the beast dissolves in a cloud of ash and smoke.

Neo's still blinking at the mess when a harsh metallic clatter fills the air.

"For fuck's sake," I mutter. "Now what?"

In unison, we all spin toward the rusted medieval portcullis embedded in the rear wall. That's the grate the reservoir flows through. The grate that normally blocks the low, creepy, cobwebby tunnel I assume leads to the septic tank.

Only that portcullis isn't blocking the tunnel anymore.

The whole contraption is rising, bars vibrating, hidden gears whining. Iron teeth coated with centuries of green goop—beslimed and dripping—emerge from the black water.

"Yay, it's the passage!" Mal yells. "We opened it!"

I'm still staring suspiciously at the slasher flick setup of that freaky-looking tunnel when Jae sweeps Mal to her feet, snatches up her bulging backpack, swings the beam of the flashlight around, and drags his girl straight toward the tunnel. Disheveled and unsettled as she clearly is, Mal still has the determination to slip free of her guy, tear out of her uniform blazer, and throw her garment over the glowing spellbook.

"Are you crazy?" I yell down to her. "Don't touch that thing!"

"The curse is already triggered," she calls back. "Its power is finite. And we might still need the book."

"Sweet Jesus, Mal…" I cut myself short with a frustrated headshake. My stubborn friend is already stumbling toward the passage, propelled by Jae's urgent grip, with the wrapped book clutched to her chest.

Very clearly, no one's safe outside the circle.

But it's equally clear we can't stay where we are.

From my elevation, hovering ten feet above the fray, the shit's flying fast and furious. Spotted hyenas from this AIB kill squad are leaping and bounding toward our circle from all directions. Here and there, the virulent green fire of the triggered curse is incinerating a handful of shifters to ash. Which gives me enough light to see the rest.

A chill of foreboding skitters down my spine.

There are way too many bad guys.

"Shit," I whisper. "What happened to the rest of my warlocks?"

And Mal's right about one thing. That curse is a spent force. No new fires are lighting.

That means if we wanna live, we're gonna need to fight.

Before my eyes, Jae shifts into his monstrous two-legged werewolf. His *loup-garou.* Muzzle lengthening and splitting around slavering teeth, black fur bristling down his chest, talons sprouting from gnarled fingers. Fully shifted, he twists with a snarl and lunges at a hyena that's headed straight for Mallory.

The two go down—hyena and werewolf—in a thrashing tangle of limbs and teeth and claws that rips a horrified scream from Mal.

Girl oughta be hauling ass for that passage, for real. She's the weakest witch in the room.

A liability right now, if I'm being honest.

Well, Mallory McSnicker might be the running joke of this Academy.

But she's definitely no coward.

Plus she clearly loves her wolf. The same way I love mine.

Grim and white-faced with resolve, she hovers just beyond the snarl and thrash of fighting shifters till she sees an opening. Then she darts into the fray and smashes her phone book-sized grimoire on the hyena's noggin. She brings that book down like Thor's hammer.

The beast drops without a whimper.

Jae lunges in and rips out the monster's throat in a spray of bright arterial blood, then tips back his wolfish face in an eerie howl.

Chills race over my skin and goosebumps swarm down my arms.

But Mallory just squeezes her werewolf's bristly shoulder—with zero fucking fear—and urges her bloodstained monster gently to his feet.

Under her tender hand, the two stumble toward the tunnel.

Now that the path is (temporarily) clear, it's way past time for me to get Neo to safety.

"Hey, baby," I call down to my fated mate, who's staring in astonishment at the sight of innocent Mallory wrapped fearlessly around her big bad wolf. "You gotta vamoose. Into that tunnel. I'll cover you."

My bookworm gazes up at me, wide-eyed with trepidation. He's no fighter… like, *at all*… even though he's been begging us nonstop to teach him. But his alphas (including me, if I'm honest) have all been kinda dubious.

None of us want him hurt.

Now's the exact moment I realize teaching Neo to defend himself is a common-sense good idea.

You know, assuming we make it outta this mess alive.

I swoop down to land next to my guy and grip his thick biceps, quivering with nervous tension under his Academy blazer. "It's okay, baby. It really is. Go with Jae and Mal. I'm right behind you."

My bookworm sucks in a breath, then gives me an earnest nod, coupled with one of those trusting wide-eyed looks through his glasses that guts me.

Every. Single. Time.

Gently I stroke a comma of soft magenta curls away from his anxious eyes. From the depths of my worried heart, I summon up a smile for him.

His own sweet smile blooms in reply.

My heart does backflips in my chest when he smiles. It always has, and it always will.

"I love you," I tell him quickly, before something else gets in the way. "I don't say it enough, baby—to any of you—but I really do. You're half the reason we all even work as a polycule. Now you gotta haul ass, okay?"

Happiness shines in his big green eyes. More than any of my guys, Neo loves to be praised. He soaks up every syllable like a sponge.

"I love you too, babe. A lot!" He lunges in to kiss me—one of his soft sweet kisses that tastes like mint and bookworm. Then, hoisting his backpack over one shoulder and our makeshift cat carrier over the other, Neo ducks out of the circle and trots obediently toward the tunnel.

Within a few steps, the shadows swallow him up.

Worry for him grips my chest like a heart attack.

Literally. I'm so freaking worried for him and all my guys I can barely breathe.

With my lips still warm and tingling from his kiss, I shoot back into the air like an Avenger and try to get my bearings in the unnatural dark. Yeah, I'm worried about Neo. Worried about the guys who are MIA. But my biggest fear at this exact moment is something else.

I haven't seen Lucius or Vasili since they split.

Plus I don't even hear Xhev's distinctive nails-on-chalkboard scream anymore. I'm praying nothing happened to Zephyr. Way beyond this *domus,* Max's distant bellows are pretty much constant.

Filled with rage.

But somewhere much closer, lost in a shadowy maze of pillars and water, a twist of shredding pain claws at my mating bond and clings like an anxious hand.

Is that a hyena whining in agony… or a wolf?

"Zarina Selene Gemini." Vasili's arctic voice, crackling with a Compulsion spell just to get my attention (the jerk), spins me toward the portcullis with a gasp.

I fucking hate being Compelled and that snake knows it. Even so, hearing his voice, a shot of genuine relief spurts through me.

There's one of my alphas, at least.

Apparently unharmed and not even disheveled, except for the fresh blood spattering his narrow hands and staining the crisp cuffs of his uniform shirt. My Goblin King is levitating over the raised portcullis, casually gripping one of his hidden cache of knives (also dripping with blood) in each hand.

Guess he's gotten stabby with a few of those AIB killers. He likes to kill that way when it's personal. The way it is for him now, with his asshole dad in play, maybe even lurking somewhere in this dungeon with us.

Watching.

No wonder V's guarding the tunnel.

If any of our enemies (like his father) manages to slip into that sewer ahead of us, we'll be trapped like rats.

Under Vasili's floating feet, a narrow walkway emerges, slime-coated and dripping. It hugs the edge of the tunnel. Looks to me like that Open Sesame Mallory conjured has done more than raise the portcullis. It's lowered the actual water level in the reservoir to expose that walkway.

Curse or no curse, that's one helluva spell Mal unleashed.

Barely illuminated by the flashlight's wavering beam, Jae and Mal have already reached the walkway. Now they race right into the tunnel, Jae guarding his girl's back as she runs, awkward and stilty on her long pale legs, with that grisly spellbook—the Book of Flame and Breath—still clutched fervently to her chest.

I bet my apple-polishing bestie is afraid of late fees from the library or something if she loses it.

Me? I've seen enough of that book in action.

A yelp from Neo yanks my attention back to him. Without the flashlight's wavering beam ahead to guide him, he's barely visible in the dark, but still blundering determinedly toward the tunnel. Unfortunately, he's hindered—both by the backpack strapped to his broad shoulders and the duffel he's cradling protectively in his arms.

Sounds like our kitten has definitely had enough of that carrier. Piercing meows, piteous with protest, rise incessantly from inside.

Still airborne and guided more by sound than sight, I weave my way through the forest of shadowy pillars, each one emerging suddenly from the dark, and call down to his shadowy form. "Neo, baby, you gotta haul ass."

"Trying!" he calls back. "I can barely see, babe."

"Just follow me, okay?" I hum to summon a crackle of voltage, then lower myself to float a few feet before Neo like a human glow stick. At this elevation, of course, I'm vulnerable to attack myself.

Well, bring it on, world. I'm fucking *ready*.

I'm sick to death of being hunted.

Forcibly I regulate my spiking adrenaline and ratchet my aggression from an electric crackle to a steady hum. The important thing right now is, the subdued violet light of my electrically charged body is guiding my fated mate.

Directly before us, no more than thirty feet ahead, the tunnel yawns.

A hyena's sinister chuckle rises from the dark.

We're being stalked.

I growl, swerve to put myself between Neo and the sound, and tell him roughly, *"Run."*

Yeah. I'm definitely gonna teach my bookworm some basic self-defense skills, like he's been repeatedly asking for.

As soon as we make it outta this mess.

"I'll hold you to that," Neo whispers, plucking the thought right out of my head. "I mean it."

Then he's running blind, blundering from pillar to pillar for the tunnel. If he falls in the water, I earnestly hope Mordred will catch him.

Mordred.

That's one mating bond that would be useful for me to have right now. I mean, if only to communicate with the guy (just leaving all actual sex with the sex demon out of it). I'm definitely hoping V has that demon on a good tight leash.

But I can't ask, because V himself is suddenly all murky and cloudy in our mating bond.

Which means one of these shifters, prowling and slinking and converging on this tunnel from all directions, must be toting that nullifying object.

I desperately wanna shift. My dragon eyes see infrared in the dark, but my human eyes can't. And my dragon queen wants *out*. She's snarling and thrashing in the prison of my skin. Frantic to defend our mates and protect our dragonets.

(Second time today she's mentioned that, by the way. Dragonets. Like maybe she knows something I don't?)

Stop distracting me, showgirl, I instruct her firmly. *We gotta concentrate.*

If my shift takes out enough of these supporting pillars, I'll bring the roof down.

And Lucius is still out here. Somewhere.

Aided just enough by the dim violet glow of my electrified body, Neo lopes across the cavern and rushes under V's floating body into the tunnel.

Thank fuck for that. At least that's one of my warlocks safe—

A hyena explodes from the darkness, right on Neo's heels. I give a warning yell and streak through the air in pursuit.

But Vasili's much closer.

He's a slim violet glitter in the near-total dark. With the wicked slash of one pale hand, V's telekinesis hurls that hyena, howling and snarling, through the air into the reservoir.

With a mighty splash, that shifter vanishes in the depths—and doesn't resurface.

I think of Mordred lurking down there and shiver.

Yeah, I'm not bonded with the kraken. But I hope like hell V gave marching orders to his demon before that nullifying object kicked in. Because we need Mordred and the Horn of Ceres in that tunnel with us.

Suddenly indecisive, I alight beside the reservoir and peer into the inky depths.

"Mordred?" I whisper. "You still in there, Aquaman?"

But I'm hella distracted. Somewhere in this pit of darkness, the whine and growl of labored breath tugs at my sleeve for attention. Sounds to me like shifters fighting—

Zara!

Sweet Jesus. V's telepathic rasp makes me jump.

I hear you, bad boy. Projecting through the obstruction of that nullifying object—wherever it is—feels like trying to breathe with your face smothered in a pillow.

Zara... My dominant alpha's voice whispers through my head. All faint and staticky, like an old-fashioned car radio broadcast in the mountains that's almost outta range. *Without you, little queen, this entire performance is for nothing. Stop fiddling with that kraken. I'll find Lucius and the others. Kindly get your luscious* derrière *inside this tunnel.*

Yeah, no.

Not happening.

I'm not leaving. Not without Lucius.

Especially when the walls ring with a shrill yip of wolfish pain.

Resolve fires in my diaphragm like a flaming sun.

I fling back my head, open my mouth, and voice a pure high note that summons a sheet of heat lightning beyond the slit of skylight.

In that flash of electric light, I finally find Lucius.

Fully shifted, his wolf is all the way across the cavern. He's single-handedly (but with paws) guarding the outer door like Cerberus guarding the gates of hell. Fighting like a titan to keep a whole ravening pack of hyenas outside. Filling the doorway, my wolf is savaging three of the hugest hyenas I've ever seen. They're like the A Team of hyenas, I seriously didn't know they could get that big.

And Lucius.

God.

He's getting savaged in turn. My mate's shaggy flanks and haunches are streaked with gore and bloody gashes. His chestnut fur is soaked and dripping with blood.

Even as I stare in horror, the biggest of those hyenas—like the pack alpha—lunges in and clamps its jaws around my mate's throat.

Lucius!

My dragon queen roars with fear and outrage.

Her bellow fills my head till my skull rings like a bell. My shift, which I've been barely holding off by my fingernails this whole time, thunders over me in a flash of blinding white.

My spine lengthens. My tail sprouts. My muzzle emerges, my legs thicken, my forearms elongate, my wings unfurl.

The snap of my opening wings unfolds in a mighty downstroke that vaults my body high into the air. All around me, stone pillars snap like matchsticks.

The exact thing I was desperate to avoid.

With a handful of those supporting pillars knocked off kilter, the high ceiling trembles and fissures. A few scattered chunks of debris tumble down and ricochet off my soaring body.

Fuck. Me. Sideways.

The roof is coming down.

I roar in my lightning voice with enough decibels to make any hyena's ears bleed. Then I lengthen my neck, snap my wings tight to minimize more structural damage, and arrow toward Lucius through a hammering hail of falling concrete.

Behind me, I'm desperately hoping Vasili's close enough to the tunnel to swoop inside with Neo.

If we're lucky (for once), both those guys will be safe in there with Mal and Jae, shielded from the skull-crushing danger of falling concrete.

But I can't join them. Not yet. Whatever else goes wrong in this fucked-up day, I've gotta save Lucius.

Before the whole roof comes down.

Chapter Sixteen
Vasili

I'm gleefully sinking one of my knives hilt-deep in the beating heart of another loathsome hyena—one of several I've caught and butchered trying to sneak past me into the tunnel—when Zara's dragon brings the roof down.

Glaring straight into the hateful snarl of my father's minion (and devoutly wishing it were my actual father), I twist my knife with vicious spite. A chuff of hot breath, stinking of blood and carrion, spills from the creature's lungs directly into my face in the most disgusting way.

"Do you mind terribly?" I inquire coldly, over the rend and tear of splitting rock. "That's repulsive. Next time, try a breath mint, *do.*"

Apparently my little verbal jab is the *coup de grace*. The wicked glow of life in the scavenger's eyes goes dark.

Truly, it's about time.

"Oh, *crap.*" Neo's voice, shrill with alarm, spills from the tunnel behind me. "V! Watch out!"

A long shadow falls across my eyes. Fueled by blind instinct, I wrench my knife from the shifter's carcass and leap aside. In fact, I leap barely in time to avoid being crushed to a bloody smear—like my four-legged prey—under a falling pillar.

The stone column hammers into the floor behind me with a deafening *boom!* that makes my ears ring.

The tingling rush of my Mogadon magic triggers my levitation. Seeking safety in the air, I let the violet soles of my favorite combat boots lift from the ground.

Just before a falling rock strikes my brow a glancing blow.

My focus splinters into rubble. My witchcraft sputters out. An eyeblink later, my stunned body collides with the floor. Knees throbbing, palms stinging, I stare blankly at the chunk of concrete lying before me that nearly split my skull.

Something warm spills down my brow and drips in my eyes. My dazed hand drifts to my throbbing forehead, then lowers, dark with blood.

"Ouch," I murmur, faint and breathy, trying to focus my doubled vision on the blur of my bloodstained fingers. "Let's hope… I don't scar."

In the distance, Zara's dragon is roaring—a brassy bellow of challenge that lights up the sky with my queen's electric rage. Oddly, I can barely hear. My ears are ringing like a school bell, a shrill buzz that muffles her deafening roar and the rumble of falling concrete.

Dimly, thoughts forming slowly, like a swimmer backstroking through a soup of mud, it occurs to me the roof hasn't *entirely* fallen.

Yet.

But that open slit of skylight now yawns much wider than is structurally sound. Misty gray daylight, weeping with rain, seeps through the split. After the Stygian darkness of McSnicker's wretched spell, this sudden blaze of light hurts my eyes.

Swaying on hands and knees, I lower my throbbing head and breathe. In. Out.

Concussion.

The word floats to the surface of my dazed mind. Blood drips from my eyebrows, between my splayed palms, to splatter the floor with crimson.

Somewhere in the distance, now strangely muffled, Neo is shouting my name. "V, are you there? *Vasili!*"

I may be damaged, but I'm still his alpha. I'll always come when he calls. So I swing my head toward the dear boy's voice.

Even that modest arc of movement makes my gut heave.

The bleary sight of that fallen pillar lying across the tunnel—blocking the entrance, sealing Neo and the others inside, shutting the rest of us out—rips from my chest a groan of dismay.

Overhead, lightning forks and dances through the skies. No doubt summoned by my vengeful queen, who's raging across the cavern. I'm a bit nearsighted (a flaw in my scrumptious perfection I'll never admit, and don't even *mention* wearing glasses). Still, my head injury makes the condition worse. I struggle to focus my blurred vision, swing my head toward the far entrance, and resolve my splintered eyesight from three Zaras into one.

My little queen's teal dragon alights near a writhing tangle of four-legged shifters, fighting and snarling at the entrance.

A vicious swipe of her taloned foreleg carves a path through the slaughter. Her long neck snakes in, jaws parting to grip a writhing hyena. She slams the creature into the wall with killing force, hurls the carcass aside, then trumpets in the deep bronze rumble of the lightning voice.

Her outraged roar cleaves my throbbing skull like a battle axe.

Yelping with alarm, hyenas scatter before her rage.

Scales gleaming in the dim light, Zara parts her jaws around a fork of lightning that electrifies her next four-legged target to a blackened husk. She's a lightning dragon, a very rare one, and feared for an excellent reason. Snarling a warning at the rest, she plants her magnificent bulk protectively over the still form of a fallen wolf, his familiar chestnut pelt dark with blood.

"Lucius," I say thickly. "Dear God."

A desperate fear for my love (for Lucius is that, I love him, I'm ridiculously in love with him) squeezes my chest and ribs like a bear hug. My gut twists with dread. Surely, surely, my little darling will protect him.

My Zara.

My faith in her is absolute.

After all, I wouldn't bend the knee to just anyone. I'll follow no other queen, love no other queen, *obey* no other queen but this one.

The Gemini queen.

Typically, I find it rather quaint that our luscious sovereign believes it's *her* role to protect *us*. It should rightly be I, as her alpha and Lucius', who protects them both.

But I can't.

I can't.

Not just now. I can't even protect myself.

Thunder crashes and savages my head. With every thud of my pulse, a red stab of pain digs cruelly behind my eyes.

Gradually, while Zara guards Lucius' fallen wolf and hurls gigawatts of lightning at any hyena who dares venture into sight, it occurs to me I'm in considerable trouble. Debris from the compromised roof rains down around me like hail. Tiny nuggets of rock pepper my skin. I'm already bruised. Contused. Concussed. Confused. Now dust chokes my lungs and dries my mouth to cotton.

Very clearly, I must find shelter.

Somewhere.

The problem is, with the tunnel and the door both blocked, I'm not at all certain where to go. Levitation is, rather obviously, out of the question. The mere thought of trying to shift to my serpentine dragon form and fly out makes me so nauseous I nearly hurl.

Not to mention the fact that yet another dragon popping into existence in this battered cavern truly will bring the roof down.

Over the muffled chorus of Neo's insistent and increasingly desperate cries, shouting my name with an urgency that makes my chest ache, the grinding crack of splitting rock drags my aching eyes up.

Another of those pillars—one of several smashed by Zara's dragon—is swaying on its pedestal.

"Move your *derrière*, darling," I murmur. Not to the pillar, but to myself.

Like a drunk, I too sway, braced on hands and knees, witless as a cow. I simply can't seem to gather my legs under me. Instead, as that compromised pillar trembles, teeters, then tips heavily to one side, I observe its majestic descent toward my unprotected body with an odd detachment.

My, my. That's going to make *such* a mess—

A hand closes around the back of my collar, grips a fistful of my uniform shirt and blazer, and drags me backward so forcefully I'm lifted to my feet. Stumbling in my glittery combat boots like I'm strapped into platform heels, I find myself hurled with considerable force into the tiny cavity created by two fallen pillars, one slanted over the other.

Head spinning so hard my eyes cross, I fling out my arms blindly. I collide against the rear wall behind the pillars with bruising force. Thanks to my outflung arms, I barely manage to avoid breaking my precious nose.

Behind me, my unseen rescuer crowds into the modest cavity. Behind *him,* the deafening boom of the falling pillar makes my skull ring like a bell.

The crossed pillars overhead shudder violently. A cloud of dust fills the close air. Unless I'm mistaken (which rarely occurs), that final pillar has just sealed me into this alcove.

Together, in uncomfortably close quarters, with my unknown rescuer.

"For your information… there was no need to toss me… like a dwarf." I lean my aching head into my crossed arms and pray I don't humiliate myself by vomiting all over my favorite boots. "You needn't have been… quite so rough."

"I'm sure I beg to differ, Vasili Nikolayevich Romanov," a cool silver voice says wryly. "You were about to be crushed under that baluster like a beetle under a boot."

Truly, this day just keeps getting better.

Hearing Zephyr's silky tenor stroke my senses, I barely swallow a groan. Of all men living, having this infernal creature witness my moment of weakness is really too dreadful to endure.

He may be my sworn enemy—my rival for Zara's love *and* Ronin's—but I never underestimate him. Not for a moment. To stand toe to toe with a creature of myth and legend like the Dark Fae King demands every atom of wit and strength and cunning I possess. At present, I'm not feeling at all my usual glorious self. Not to mention, I'm positively disheveled.

Now don't laugh, darling. I'm terribly vain. I truly am. Even at such a moment.

Vanity is one of my many sins.

Faced with my miserable silence, the infernal Fae crowds closer. "Cat got your tongue?"

"For fuck's sake. If you have an ounce of decency… *don't* talk to me about cats… at a time like this," I mutter, speaking thickly with my cottony tongue.

Beyond our enclosure, through God knows how many feet of solid rock, the distant bellow of Zara's dragon makes the walls tremble.

I fully intend to remain upright, the better to deal with this entire situation. But my legs have other ideas. My knees buckle without my consent.

Zephyr mutters an Unseelie oath.

I'm sinking to the floor like a swooning Victorian, laced too tightly into her corset, when his hard hands catch me under the arms and lower me gently to the ground.

I'll admit, for a bit my world goes dark.

When my vision clears, my predicament has not demonstrably improved. My battered skull rings with pain, throbbing with the dull monotony of a church bell tolling at midnight. I'm still wounded. Still parched. Still wedged into this miniscule alcove, trapped between three fallen pillars and a wall.

With my mortal enemy.

Barely lit by a dim spill of light slipping through the cracks, Zephyr's sharp-featured Dark Fae face peers down at me. The narrow slash of his eyepatch bisects his olive skin. His moss-green hair, somehow still sleek under a film of silver dust, spills down on either side around the sharp tips of his ears. I'm lying across his sinuous dragonscale-sheathed legs, with my aching head cradled in his lap. His ridiculous codpiece nudges my ear.

But a cloth, gloriously soaked with cool water, soothes my throbbing brow. Gradually, I realize this Dark Fae tyrant is… tending my wound.

With deceptive gentleness.

In fact, the trickle of water over my skin is what woke me.

"Back among the living, I behold." Zephyr sighs. If I didn't know better, I'd almost fancy that Fae sounds… relieved… that I didn't expire in his arms. "This being the case, I suppose you'd better try to drink a little."

By some miracle, he's holding a water bottle to my lips. I grope to steady the bottle, my hand closing over his. Too parched to quibble with the intimacy or the indignity of my circumstances, I guzzle mouthfuls of the delicious liquid without complaint.

Ambrosia.

I can't abide the grit of dust between my teeth.

"Slowly," he cautions—easing the bottle away before I've drunk anything like my fill, the prick.

"Go to hell," I mumble, trying to reclaim the bottle.

But I'm pathetically weak. Easily my rival eludes my clumsy grasp, even while otherwise occupied, bathing my aching forehead with an alarming semblance of care.

"Fucking sadist," I grumble.

His single jade eye narrows in a frown. "I'm not being needlessly cruel, beautiful one. I'm no expert in human anatomy—far from it—but I am mated to a healer who enjoys talking about his trade. You appear to be suffering a possible concussion."

"Tell me something… I don't know." With a sigh, I let my heavy eyes close.

Sounding carefully neutral, as though he wishes to betray nothing of his feelings, Zephyr clears his throat. "In your condition, 'tis likely you shouldn't sleep."

"'Tis likely you shouldn't care." Merciful fuck, I sound petty. But I feel far too wretched to give a shit.

After a moment, his cool fingers graze my cheek. Without bothering to open my eyes, I swat his hand away.

The prick leaves me in blessed peace for approximately five seconds. Then…

"I fear I may have slain your father," Zephyr says casually. "I hope you don't mind?"

Well. *That* wakes me in a hurry.

My violent twitch of reaction drives a white knife of pain through my skull. With a gasp, my eyes fly wide. My nemesis is still peering down on me from above, watching me alertly in the half-light.

I fumble about for something snide to say. Fumble to snatch up the saber for another vicious bout of our verbal fencing.

Alas, my addled wits fail me.

The blade of my spite droops like a wilted daisy.

"How?" I struggle to form the words. "My father… has built an entire career upon… his spectacularly bloody start in life as a trained assassin. He's considered… rather difficult to kill."

"Not for me." Zephyr's feral mouth curves in a secret smile. I swear, that sly smile curls my toes in my boots. "I kill as I please, with none to deny me. I am the Unseelie King."

My tongue darts out to touch my upper lip. His gaze tracks my tongue like a snake tracks a bird.

"How?" I whisper.

Not only *how did you kill him?* But also *how do I feel if it turns out to be true?*

"I loosed Xhevith upon him." Zephyr offers me the bottle. "More water?"

His dragon. Who breathes acid. If Zephyr used Xhev to kill my father, then surely… surely… my father must be dead.

I close my hand over the Fae's and drink. This time, he lets me have the bottle while he dips into a backpack I recognize—it belongs to Maxim, who would have shed it before he shifted—and produces the rudimentary first aid kit Neo insisted we drag along.

Between blissful sips of H2O, I watch closely while Zephyr shakes out a couple of capsules. I'll have to trust his judgment that they're safe for concussion, but frankly I'll take anything that might put a dent in this headache. I accept the meds meekly and swallow them down without protest.

I'm far less sanguine about the pinch of grassy, bittersweet-smelling dried herbs the Fae shakes out next, extracted from a tiny pouch at his belt. He sprinkles this weed delicately over my throbbing brow like a pinch of fairy dust, with the words of a whispered spell.

To my suspiciously raised eyebrow, he explains, "Seelie comfrey. 'Tis an herb with anti-inflammatory qualities. Ash never lets me ride into battle without it."

"Hmmm." I manage to convey my active skepticism of his primitive Fae medicine without even opening my mouth. Because it would never do to imply that I trust him.

Although his Ash is indeed a gifted healer. I'd be a fool to deny that much.

Admittedly, that sickening lightning bolt of pain—the agony that cleaves my brain in relentless nauseating tempo with my pulse—*is* easing.

"That herb should speed your recovery." Zephyr gives my fretful face a grave nod. "But no vodka martinis for at least twenty-four hours, beautiful one."

Dear fuck.

Is that a flicker of *humor* warming that seductive voice of his? Could this Unseelie tyrant actually be trying to make *a joke*?

With difficulty, I recall my wandering wits to the subject at hand. "You were saying… about my father…"

A subtle chord of tension runs through his supple thighs beneath my head. "What of him? I left him for dead."

Left him for dead doesn't mean much, not when you're talking about Nikolai Romanov. I let out a sigh and rub an absent hand over the burning ache in my chest.

Zephyr tilts his head and eyes me with a quizzical gaze, very much like the sparrow Ash calls him.

"If by some miracle you did manage to kill him, I will certainly not mourn him," I say clearly.

Even though I'm *not* entirely certain that's true. But I'm not some archaic pointy-eared Fae. I can and do lie with impunity.

For years, the combustible fuse of my feelings toward the detestable parent who rejected me has been a buried landmine I'm scrupulously careful never to trigger.

"I gathered as much," Zephyr allows. In the ghostly twilight, his face turns cautious.

I turn my own face away, the better to hide my thoughts, and lean my cheek into the sleek dragonscale that sheathes his quads. "But why target him? I mean, him in particular?"

Zephyr's silken voice hardens to steel. "I tracked your sire from the hyena-infested wood—where he was clearly behind the entire attack—and found him lurking just outside this chamber. Your father was setting Zara in his sights with a blowgun."

"What?" Alarmed, I twist my neck to eye my rival.

Rival or no, this revelation carries the ring of truth. When it comes to assassination, poison is often my father's preferred weapon.

Zephyr levels me with a grim look. "I overheard him telling his four-legged hyena minions it was stonefish venom."

"Christ." I recognize the substance (I'm not an assassin's son for nothing) and struggle to sit. His firm hand eases me back. "That's a hellish poison. It causes… excruciating pain. Convulsions. Paralysis. Its victims die in agony."

"Just so." Zephyr's jaw knots and his mouth tightens to a ruthless line. "Cleopatra's courtier babbled about some sort of queen killer, dispatched by that accursed Messalina to eliminate Zara from the Dean's Challenge. Permanently. It appears to me your father may have been Messalina's anointed one. Her chosen killer."

My thoughts swirl and flounder like chum in a shark-filled sea.

"Well… Daddy Dearest is typically beyond bloodying his own hands these days. Although if the queen herself requested it, he might make an exception—but wait." Desperately I struggle to think. Curse this wretched concussion. "When… when did you speak to Cleo's courtier?"

"Oh, I may have tortured one or two." The Unseelie menace lifts one shoulder in a shrug.

"You don't say?" To my surprise, I find my lips curling in a grin. At times like this, I could *almost* bring myself to like the man—if he weren't my mortal enemy. Hastily I rearrange my expression into some semblance of my customary sneer. "When was that, exactly?"

Zephyr waves a hand in regal indifference. "Just now. In the wood. Ronin and I captured two of the wretches. We… repurposed the villa mantraps."

Recalling the vicious steel teeth of those rusty traps, I give way to a vicious smile. Then a more urgent thought shoots to the surface of my addled mind. "Where is Ronin?"

Our gazes meet in a look that acknowledges this awkward truth.

We both love him.

Ronin.

We love the same man. And the same woman.

Once again, an unfathomable idea surfaces. I don't always have to hate Zephyr.

Perhaps, just for the duration of the Dean's Challenge, we can be…

Not friends.

Never friends.

But allies?

Rather like a marriage of convenience. Separate bedrooms, and all that.

"Ronin is safe, never fear," Zephyr says softly, as though he too is loathe to puncture this fragile accord—delicate as a soap bubble—that swells between us. "I saw him aloft, like the dragonrider he was born to be, on your dragon shifter Maxim. A truly magnificent beast, that shifter of yours."

I'm well aware of precisely how magnificent a beast Maxim's dragon is. After all, my own dragon wouldn't let just any flying lizard rail her through her heat. After the superheat we've just endured, Maxim Rasputin owns her genital slit.

Even if I'll never admit it.

The worst of the agony in my skull is definitely receding. Carefully I gather my strength to sit. This time, His *la-dee-dah* Radiance actually deigns to assist.

Once upright, in these close quarters, I'm essentially sitting in his lap.

Just for the moment, I don't bother to remedy the situation.

Just for the moment, he doesn't push me away.

I drape an arm around his sleek dragonscale shoulders. Solely to make myself more comfortable, you understand. Definitely *not* because I want to hold him, or be held in turn by his muscled arm wrapping possessively around my waist. Not because I like his fingers hooking in the belt loop of my uniform trousers. Especially not his thumb sneaking under my shirt to graze the skin of my bare back.

The silence beyond this cavity presses down on me. It's been some time since we've heard a peep from the outside world. I choose to believe that's a good thing. My wits are far too addled by concussion for telepathy. Still, if Lucius were… dead, I'd know it. If Lucius were dead, Zara would raze this island to the ground.

If Lucius were dead, I'd burn the world down to avenge him.

Still, the silence raises many alarming questions.

Striving for my signature imperious tone, I demand like the diva I am, "Where is everyone?"

"We slaughtered as many enemies as we could catch in the wood." Zephyr's gaze slides away, as though he's ashamed to have left any alive. "Once I realized some of the creatures had slipped past us, into the *domus* where none can fly, I ordered the others in my contingent—your dragon shifter, Ronin, Ash, Xhevith—to the wing. They'll keep Cleopatra and her allies distracted and busy—since presumably she can't be certain which of us carries the Horn of Ceres. We'll reunite with our allies at the Academy Vault and attack there at full strength."

"All well and good, Your Transcendence," I say pointedly, unwilling even now to acknowledge this Dark Fae tyrant did the best he could against overwhelming numbers. "Except for our latest little problem. Even if we were to assume Zara has managed to save Lucius…"

"I think we'd know if she hadn't." Zephyr's sober gaze drifts over the contours of the stone prison that holds us, as though that keen eye of his can see through solid rock. "I think the entire witching world would know."

I'll never admit it, but it's a relief to know his cool head agrees with my rather desperate logic.

To conceal my crushing fear for all my mates—the crippling fear that makes me so vulnerable—I salt my words liberally with sarcasm. "Out of curiosity, how do you imagine we'll get out of this tomb and into the tunnel?"

Now Zephyr's arrogant face turns wary. His thumb stops stroking my lower back (which, admittedly, I've rather enjoyed) and his voice becomes grudging.

"If your beautiful head is now clear enough, Vasili Romanov," he says stiffly, "I'd advise you to summon your demon."

Chapter Seventeen
Zara

"There's no need to worry, my dear," Lucius says for at least the third time, "and certainly no need to weep. Not over me, in any event. I'm quite well."

"Bull. *Shit*," I tell my headmaster through a flood of belated tears. Once my dragon queen Hulk-smashed a few of those hyenas, zapped a bunch more with our lightning, then bullied the rest into flight, I swear, it's like someone turned on a faucet.

Since I shifted back to human, I haven't stopped crying.

"Language, Ms. Gemini." As Lucius limps slowly across the ruined cavern, even though he's naked and caked in rock dust with an arm wrapped around my waist for support, the guy manages a wheezy chuckle. "I ought to assign… detention."

Well alrighty then.

If my headmaster feels recovered enough from his horrific injuries to joke (or even impose actual discipline, which is when he's at his most yummy), the least I can do is meet him halfway.

I wipe away my tears, tighten my own arm around his waist (carefully avoiding his injuries) to take as much of his weight as he'll let me carry, and say hopefully, "Detention with you in the crypt?"

"Try not to sound so delighted, you minx. You're supposed to live in terror of your headmaster's displeasure." This time, his chuckle ends in a breathy gasp.

Damn it.

He's putting too much weight on his half-healed leg.

The one a hyena savaged in its powerful jaws while Lucius was down.

Shifter or no, I'm fucking glad I Hulk-smashed that mangy hyena to a bloody pulp, for real. My inner dragon snarls in agreement.

"Slow down a little, Lucius," I urge, shifting more of his weight onto my equally naked body, and trying to keep the growl of my lightning voice out of it. "Your injuries—"

"Are healing rather swiftly. One of the advantages of being a purebred shifter. Not to mention having received a mating bite, laced with fast-healing biochemicals, from another shifter."

Oh, right.

Given all the shit going down in this Dean's Challenge, I've briefly forgotten that Vasili and Lucius once swapped mating bites. Lucius bit Vasili, way back in the first season of our soap opera romance, to trigger his recessives and bring on his first shift, so Vasili could rise to my dragon's first mating flight. V bit Lucius because he's V—and Lucius' alpha. (Without asking, which was a big crisis at the time, but also very V.)

Anyway. I'm extra glad for it now.

Lucius and I might both be naked, barefoot, and covered in rock dust. But my headmaster's voice is getting stronger and his steps more certain by the minute. Those awful gashes in his belly and flanks from multiple hyena bites are already healing.

"One thing to be thankful for, anyway." I let out a sigh, eyeing the wreck around us. "God knows, we need one."

Here's another plus. Since the ceiling's half gone, there's plenty of light to see by.

But there's also a major minus.

Half those pillars I wiped out when I shifted seem to have fallen across the tunnel where Neo and Mal and Jae (and hopefully V) have vanished.

I can't see or hear or smell any of the others, literally none of them. Which is concerning as fuck. The outraged roars of Max's dragon and Xhev's nails-on-chalkboard screech went quiet a while ago, my nerves are so jangled I'm not even sure when.

Plus I'm picking up zilch in the telepathy department, which is not a good sign.

As for the Horn of Ceres and that sex demon we've entrusted with our prize? I eye the still black water of the reservoir with deep disquiet.

"Hold on a sec, Teach, okay? Just catch your breath. Think healing thoughts." Gently I prop Lucius against one of the pillars that's still standing. "I gotta check on something. I mean someone."

"Indeed." Moving carefully so he doesn't reopen a wound, Lucius studies my worried face with his knowing gaze, then sweeps his tumble of curls out of his face into a tidy knot at the back of his neck.

That action is just so *Lucius* that he stops me in my tracks. My eyes devour my alpha—my wonderful, steady, strong, reliable headmaster that we all count on in so many ways.

My wise mentor. My precious mate. My wolf king. The one I just almost lost.

After all, he's the reason I'm doing this, they all are. All my guys. All my loved ones. I've always known I don't give a single shit about being queen for my own sake.

I'm not saving the witching world for me.

I'm saving it for *them.*

Not for power. Or greed. Or ambition.

I'm saving it for love.

Suddenly, my chest burns, my throat swells, and my eyes are overflowing.

Again.

"God, Lucius." I hurl myself across the space between us, burrow into my mate's surprised body, and throw my arms around his neck. My face tucks into his strong shoulder to breathe his familiar wolfish scent in deep.

"We could've lost you," I mumble into his skin. "We can't—*I* can't—ever lose you. Not ever."

He's still barely standing, but he handles my needs the way he always has. My alpha's arms close around me, he nuzzles the scars of my mating bite where my neck meets my shoulder, and he murmurs soothing words like *there, there* and *it's all right* and (my personal favorite) *you've been such a good girl.*

I mean, he isn't my alpha for nothing.

He knows what I need and he gives it to me.

Same as always.

"I love you, Lucius," I whisper into his shoulder and into his mind. "I mean it. You're one of the first I knew I loved. You and Neo. You make the rest of us—all the psychos in this polycule—complete."

"My dear girl, what makes us all *complete* is you. The way you love all of us. The way we love all of you. From your tender heart to your flexible morals, from your voracious sexual appetites to your appalling study habits. But most of all, for the way you take care of others." He pulls in a breath and smooths a firm hand over my hair to settle me. "Speaking of others…"

"Yeah." I pull in my own shuddery breath, lift my head from his tear-damp shoulder, and step back with a sniffle. "We gotta get our shit together. Those hyenas won't stay gone forever."

I'm working to clear my head and suss out what we'll need to reopen that tunnel (which is probably some variation of me Hulking out again plus V's telekinesis, assuming we can find him), while simultaneously eyeing that reservoir and wondering if we still even have the Horn of Ceres, because that demon's been pretty quiet down there…

…when the black water ripples.

The surface ripples in a vee, like a massive arrow or a shark racing under the surface, carving a beeline down the channel, straight toward the jumble of pillars before the tunnel.

"Shit," I whisper, all echoey in the stillness. "I really hope that's Mordred—"

An inky tentacle, glowing a wicked violet with phosphorescence and thicker than a cruise ship anchor chain, shoots from the water and wraps around a fallen chunk of column. Then a tangle of tentacles uncurls from the deep. And the whole damn monster heaves into view.

That's Mordred all right.

In, like, his kraken form.

He's massive when he's shifted, night-black and glistening under that eerie blue-violet glow, just a spaghetti of thick tentacles covered with indigo suckers that's gotta make it easier for him to grip. He's like the monster in *Lord of the Rings* that erupts from the pond to drive Frodo and the gang into the Mines of Moria.

Even knowing that kraken is (theoretically) on our side, I totally understand the elemental sense of terror that sent those hobbits fleeing frantically into the mine.

Cruel beak gaping, the kraken hurls a whole pillar aside. Through clouds of rock dust, I glimpse a fast-moving streak of green dragonscale emerging from the rubble like a cork popping from a bottle.

My heart leaps into my throat and wedges in my gullet. Then a boiling murk of rock dust obscures my view.

Now chunks of pillar are whipping through the air, tentacles coiling and flexing, deafening booms of rockfall making my ears ring. I try to shove forward (you know, to see better). But Lucius grips me firmly, with an impressive show of shifter strength, and drags me behind one of the few remaining pillars into a meager cover.

I strain to peer around the column and see through the churning melee of flying rubble. Is that the violet glitter of V's favorite combat boots, the ones he's fucking wearing?

That does it. The suspense is literally killing me.

I bellow in the lightning voice, "Sweet fuck, Aquaman. Will you please hold up!"

The tangle of tentacles quivers and stills. From the sloshing depths of the reservoir, one dark round eye, burning with amethyst fire, rolls curiously toward me.

"Take it easy with that shit, will you? You're gonna bring the rest of the roof down." Gently I detach from Lucius' protective grip. But I have to steel myself to move into plain sight, away from the safety of my alpha, and inch toward the kraken (flesh-eater, natch, I read about them in Elementary Monsters class last quarter) lying in wait in the black water.

But I'm the queen and I do it.

"You take it easy," I tell that kraken in my queen voice. His beak opens like he's gonna talk back, so I raise my hand to silence him. "I thought I saw—"

"You *did* see…" a familiar voice murmurs "…us."

The silky purr of Vasili's voice is followed by the actual Goblin King. He emerges from a billow of rock dust, atypically disheveled, looking like some 1980s rock star straggling home from the club after an all-night bender. His gilded shag of hair is tousled, his cuffs are stained with dried blood that I devoutly hope isn't his, and he's got a goose egg swelling over one eyebrow like he's been in a bar fight.

Zephyr scrambles through the rubble at his heels, deft and graceful despite being coated with dust like he's been rolled in flour, crossed blades jutting over armored shoulders, eyepatch slashing through sharp Fae features. A worn backpack dangles from his hand.

At the sight of these two, a starburst of relief lights me up like Fourth of July fireworks. My heart explodes in a pinwheel of joy.

"Oh, my fucking God." I launch myself at both of them, both my mates. I'm way too wildly relieved to find them both alive and ambulatory to even wonder what they're doing together (since they hate each other). "Thank fuck you're both okay—I mean, *are* you both okay?"

We meet in a jumble of limbs and bodies, because they're both intent on holding me and kissing me first. So we end up in a three-way hug, their arms around my waist, my arms thrown over their shoulders, with me kissing both of them simultaneously, which means the two of them are also kinda kissing each other.

Mmmm.

Three-way hug. Three-way kiss. Three-way everything.

This I can handle.

The cloves-and-nutmeg spice of Zephyr's kiss mingles with the juniper bite of Vasili's. The hot lick of Zephyr's tongue meets the snakebite prick of Vasili's fangs.

Wow. These two guys together, the two most intense warlocks in my harem? They've never worked together like this before.

They're… a lot. Almost too much to handle.

Even for me.

I pull back to suck in a desperate breath, the leather-and-brimstone reek of dragon mixing with the caramel and musk of V's Mogadon mating scent. Because my dominant alpha is scenting really heavily. My fingers skate over the tips of Zephyr's ears (erogenous zone, always makes him shiver) and sift through V's moussed-up mess of hair. I'm checking for hidden injury beyond that scary-looking lump on his cranium, but not finding any.

Me backing off the kiss lets them turn into each other, eating at each other's mouths with savage intent. Just a lick of fiery kiss that's somewhere between a warning and a promise.

Mmmm, that looks tasty, my dragon queen purrs.

"Doesn't it?" I whisper back, wondering what the hell I missed. Because, until this exact moment, these two warlocks couldn't stand each other.

I mean, not that I'm complaining…

Without looking away, I sense Lucius coming up behind me. I reach back and pull him into the hug. V surfaces from whatever intense thing is happening between him and Zephyr to claim Lucius in a hard devouring kiss. My headmaster rumbles at V to reassure him too, then rubs his jaw against Zephyr's to scent him, which makes Zephyr smile (just for a blink).

"Hey, group hug! Can I join?" Mordred's baritone purr pulls me out of the moment.

The incubus is bipedal again, God help us all, wiry hips and quads encased in those scaly pants that cut across the sinewy flex of his Adonis belt. Those pants seem to be part of the demon dress code, like the sealskin pouch slanting across his naked chest. The substantial lump inside that pouch shouts *Horn of Ceres here, hello!* to my newly triggered clairvoyance.

Thank fuck, we've still got the prize.

But that sex demon's a major distraction.

Water glistens along the bronze plane of his pecs and trickles down the luscious bulge of his biceps. The indigo sleeve of his tattoo sheathes his arm from shoulder to knuckles. The wet tangle of his midnight-blue hair spills over broad shoulders.

His hot purple eyes slide down my naked body like a lick of tongue. That look tightens my nipples and pools honey in my cunny.

God, I'm in trouble.

Just a look from this guy's enough to make me wet.

When he catches me watching, his dimples pop. "So… group hug?"

"Uh, no group hug. Not when half of us are nakey," I manage to say. "Nice try though."

"Can't blame a guy for askin', true?" He grins at me. "I'm a sex demon, baby queen. And you're sexy as fuck. Plus nakey. You and the prof both." He leans to one side a little to check out Lucius. "The way I see it, it'd be rude not to ask."

I don't need to see Lucius to know he's blushing.

My headmaster, raised by his very traditional Hungarian grandpa in an actual castle, is uber-reserved and modest in front of strangers. Hell, the way that incubus is eyeing my exposed ass (since my exposed front is still engulfed in Zephyr and V) is even making *me* blush

"There you are, demon," Vasili sniffs. Even looking kinda the worse for wear, with dust clinging to his mascara, he manages a snaky sneer. "I felt certain you'd abandoned us."

Mordred's easy grin stays in place, but his sly eyes narrow. "Y'all told me to hide, not fight. You're my summoner. When you're silent, I got me some leeway. But when you issue orders, I gotta do what you say. You don't like the result? Gimme more leeway next time, babydoll."

"Duly noted," V murmurs. "And don't call me babydoll. How's that for an order?"

Mordred gives him a pout, then a playful wink. Vasili turns away with a huff and wanders over to investigate the rubble-strewn tunnel— now mostly clear, thanks to the kraken's efforts.

Mordred watches him go with eyes that smolder like purple embers.

One of the things I find most appealing about our temporary sex demon ally is that he's a true pansexual and so damn open about it. As far as I can tell, he has zero sexual hangups of any kind. (Which is kinda refreshing, given the history of our polycule.) He's straightforward about being as much into my guys as he's into me.

And the fact that I'm even thinking about his sexuality instead of the reassuring bulge of the Horn of Ceres in his messenger bag tells me he's doing it again.

Sexing us up.

We don't have time for this shit, for real.

With some difficulty, I avert my gaze from Mordred's sexy smirk to the backpack now resting near Zephyr's booted feet.

"Is that Max's pack?" I ask. "Because if it is, I've got clothes in there. I need 'em." Being a shifter, I've learned to plan ahead for that shit.

"If you must." Zephyr eyes my naked curves with a hungry look, then passes me the pack and pivots to plant his lean body squarely between me and Mordred's lascivious stare.

"Sorry, but I gotta." I'm afraid to ask, but I need to know. "If this is Max's pack, then where's Max?"

Over the crossed swords that rise above his shoulders, the Dark Fae twists to bare his tiny fangs at me in a feral grin. "That dragon of yours is a most fearsome beast. I rather approve of your taste, my bride."

"Glad to hear it, Your Transcendence," I drawl. "So where is he?"

"I've sent him ahead to the Vault, along with Ash and Ronin and Xhevith, to sow terror and dismay among your enemies," Zephyr says with fiendish relish. "As your advance guard, they'll prepare the way admirably for your royal arrival. With any luck, they'll also draw off some of your four-legged pursuers."

"Oh, thank fuck." For at least the third time in the past ten minutes, a surge of debilitating relief for the safety of my guys sends me for a loop like a corkscrew coaster. A breath I didn't even realize I was holding rushes out of my lungs in a whoosh.

The hills and plummets of this adrenaline surge I'm riding are exhausting. I'd like nothing more than to get off this carnival ride.

But first, I gotta get this Horn back into the Vault and Cleo's aerobicized ass outta my throne.

I lock onto Zephyr's keen jade stare and lean in to cup the hard plane of his cheek in a gentle hand. "Thank you for that, Your Radiance. Thanks for taking care of my guys."

"I live to serve my bride," he whispers, just for me.

That just makes me wanna explore other ways the Dark Fae King can be of service.

Feeling all warm and tingly, I pull back from his magnetic pull and hunker down to dig through the pack, with Lucius hovering hopefully at my side, my headmaster clearly praying I'll find him some pants to replace the ones he shredded in his shift. He's way more bothered by his own nakedness than I am by mine, so I make him the first priority. I root through the mess of Max's gear (that dragon's a thorough packer, but not tidy) and pass Lucius a pair of Ronin's leather trows.

They'll be an interesting fashion choice on Lucius, but he accepts the garment with a grateful murmur.

Me, I wiggle into a pair of lime-green lace panties. I'm working my way into the matching underwire bra, tucking my tits into the lace cups and keenly aware of the sex demon watching my every move, when I realize I'm not the only one who's fixated on the incubus.

"You left the matter of your dramatic intervention in this lethal battle rather late, cousin, did you not?" my Dark Fae says pointedly to the demon. "You could have hidden the Horn and joined the fight without violating the essence of your summoner's command. This, thou art clever enough to know."

Always a bad sign when Zephyr goes all ancient Fae formal.

"Dude, you sound Biblical. It's the twenty-first century." Mordred snorts. "Just come out and say it, in modern English."

"Very well." Zephyr's narrow frame bristles with threat. "Were you waiting to see which side prevailed, so you could ally yourself with the winner?"

That's a possibility I never considered, in the heat of the moment. Now I wonder if it's true.

Finally, Mordred's gaze shifts from my tits to my suspicious face, then veers to my Dark Fae consort. "Just playin' it safe, cuz."

"Very safe indeed, kinsman," Zephyr says in that voice like gray silk. "I never knew you for a coward."

Behind me, Lucius pulls in a slow breath.

Shit. Like they say in the cartoons, them's fightin' words.

These two Fae have an ocean of bad blood between them, Zephyr's never really bought into the story that Mordred only tried to dethrone him back on Avalon because the demon was powerless to disobey his summoner. Now seems to be the moment the whole unresolved mess between these two political rivals is coming to a boil.

I rush into the crisp French poplin of my school blouse and start buttoning.

"Yeah, well, the other team's got a shark and a sea dragon, you feel me?" Mordred drawls. "You want me following the prime directive from He Who Shall Not Be Named Babydoll and guarding that Horn? Meant I needed to cover my tentacled ass, true? Found me and the Horn a nice dark grotto down there and sat tight."

"Perhaps 'tis so," Zephyr breathes. "Or perhaps 'tis merely easier for one who is barely half Fae to lie."

Cheese on toast.

By now, it's so quiet in this chamber, I swear you could hear a mosquito hiccup. I drag my plaid schoolgirl skirt (burgundy, for Wednesday) over my hips, pull up the zipper, and leap to my feet.

My words tumble out in a rush. "Well, he's here now, and the Horn's safe, so we're all good—"

"Tell you one thing that's the gods' truth," Mordred says softly, locked on Zephyr like a heat-seeking missile. "You're still so scared I'll end up stealing your crown and warming your throne and fucking your consorts, sweet cuz, that you're pissin' yourself in that pretty green armor. And that's no lie."

In a blur of speed that's almost too fast for the human eye to follow, Zephyr unsheathes his double swords in a hiss of steel on leather. Slicing the deadly blades through the air till they sing, he springs for the demon with an animal snarl of rage.

Chapter Eighteen
Mordred

I don't know why I always gotta jerk my cousin's chain. Always have, ever since we were tykes.

Maybe because he always makes it so gods-damned easy.

Maybe because I always burned to wipe that self-satisfied smirk off his pretty face.

Either way, my royal pain-in-the-patootie cousin is supernaturally quick, that's a Fae thing. Only his rabid snarl gives me a blink of warning to defend myself. I summon my trident into my outstretched hand and swing the shaft sideways, like a staff, to catch both of his descending blades with a *clang!*

The clash of my demon-cursed silver against his moon-blessed steel rings through the joint like a church bell. Cousin Z's strong as fuck, because dragonrider. The force of his blow jars my bones, no lie, he drives me a step back. I pivot on one foot and absorb the impact through my braced shoulders.

I know it's a bad idea to taunt him. But I legit can't resist.

Old habit, you feel me?

I grin into his savage face. "That the best you can do, cuz? Must be gettin' weak in your old age."

He's exactly one year older than me.

He retaliates with a whirlwind of slashing parries that keeps me on my toes. As I parry and retreat, parry and retreat, his upper lip curls in contempt to reveal one tiny fang.

"That's just cute, for real." I give him a wink. He knows I like those fangs of his, always have. Told him so the one and only time I snogged him, back in our Avalon Academy days, at his royal birthday masquerade.

Right before he kneed me in the nuts.

Seeing my wink, Zephyr's eye narrows with wrath. He hisses a vicious incantation. The moon-blessed steel of his swords lights up with cold lilac witchfire.

Shit just got real.

"Whoa there." The queen's worried face hovers on the periphery, but the chick's combat trained herself. She knows better than to get between us. "Zephyr. Mordred is *not* the enemy."

"He is my enemy," Z says through gritted teeth. "My mortal enemy. He is the serpent you allow in our bed!"

"Yeah, one time, and only to *sleep*." This time, I aim my grievance over that sucky compromise at the whole room. "Y'all made me sleep across your feet like a dog."

Cousin Z extends his fiery sword to point at my chest. The blade hums like a lightsaber. "That demon covets my throne—"

"Naw, that you can keep. Told you before, cuz, that whole insurrection thing was all your auntie, with me in a summoning circle. Babydoll broke the old witch's curse when he summoned me outta Avalon to the mortal plane." I shift my grip on my trident and give it a good spin.

Yeah, sure, I'm showing off a smidge. For Cousin Z and his girl. So far, the queen of the witching world seems totally immune to my flirting, which frustrates the hells outta me.

I mean, seriously? Who's immune to an incubus?

"Lies. All detestable, moon-fucked *lies*!" My cousin scowls fiercely at my showy theatrics. "You cannot deny you covet my bride!"

My grin shifts to the bride in question. "Well, he ain't wrong—"

Zephyr growls like a hellhound and leaps for my throat, both blades whirling through the air. I bark out a laugh of fierce delight and slant my trident to meet his blows—*one two three four*—then follow up with a vicious jab at his gut. Just to earn his respect.

I mean to have that much.

His respect.

Even if I can't have everything else from him I want.

He twists aside with a hiss. The tines of my trident graze his dragonscale. Just the way my fingers grazed his abs when we danced at his birthday party. The one and only time he ever let me touch him.

My trident can pierce the hide of a megalodon (and yeah, we got those in the Avalon Sea.) So evading is a prudent move on his part.

Still, I'm pulling my punches. I don't want him dead, for real.

And he's warrior enough to know it.

"Fight me like a man, you squid." He sneers at my polite restraint and rolls out that childhood nickname I always hated. "If you dare."

Finally, a jellyfish sting of annoyance pricks even my thick hide. I scowl and pivot into a vicious sidelong swipe that makes him jump. If he hadn't, my tines woulda opened his quads to the bone. He whirls into a vicious two-bladed riposte I barely catch on my trident.

I spin into another sweeping parry to make him jump higher. Guy jumps like a flea. Oughta look ridiculous doing it (the way I would). But he's the Dark Fae King, so he just looks agile and lithe and hot.

"How's that?" I say on a growl.

"Better. How's this?" Z bares his fangs in a savage grin and lunges directly at me, both blades fully extended, for a killing blow—

"Hey!" The Gemini queen bellows in the resonant rumble of the lightning voice. "Both of you. I said *stop*!"

Her bellow ends in a deafening peal of thunder.

A flash of ultraviolet light eradicates my world in a blinding blaze of white.

When my ears stop ringing and my vision clears, the queen of the witching world's levitating just off the ground between my cuz and me. Through the spots of white floating in my dazzled eyes, her teal curls and schoolgirl skirt whip around her tiny frame like she's standing in a gale-force hurricane. Her violet eyes are pinwheels of purple fire. Her fingers crackle with lavender sparks.

Hells' bells. Chick's hot as fuck when she's witchy.

Behind her, my furious cousin—who just got knocked over by the aftershock—scrambles to his feet. Also hot as fuck behind the slash of his eyepatch, with his olive skin flushed and his green hair all mussed. Even the tips of his pointed ears quiver with wrath.

Guess I'm glad the queen told him to stop. Otherwise I'd have his moon-blessed steel buried hilt-deep in my gut.

"Boys." Zara sighs and locks her witchy eyes on Zephyr's startled face. Her tone's so quiet I gotta lean forward to hear. "I'm either your queen or I'm not. Which is it?"

Well, shit.

Not gonna lie, this cupcake's been on my mind since Avalon. And not just cuz she's sexy as fuck. TBH, this queen's plunged her royal fist straight through my chest to wrap around my beating heart (figure of speech, not literal). All that sexy's the least of her pull. Most anyone can manage to be sexy enough, one way or another, to pique my interest for an hour. I mean, yo, sex demon, you feel me?

This witch is something more.

Sure, Zara Selene Gemini is a certified badass. I've known that much since the day I watched in secret while she went toe-to-toe with Cousin Z's psycho mom, the late unlamented Unseelie Queen Maeve. Since the night Zara Gemini reached through a sheet of witchfire with her bare hands to claim Maeve's crown and become the Unseelie Queen. Girl sealed the deal last night, when I watched her face down a gods-damned sea dragon, fathoms deep, in an aquatic atmosphere where Zara can't even shift.

This Gemini queen is more than strong. More than fierce. More than stubborn when she gets her Irish up.

Underneath all that badassery, she's a softie. Cousin Z melted her heart with a kitten, for fuck's sake. Plus it's obvi she loves this sack of dicks she has for a polycule. Got loads of room in her heart for all of 'em.

I wonder if she's maybe got room for one more.

She just protected my sorry ass. Summoned lightning to protect my hide from getting skewered by my enraged cousin.

I don't get protected.

Even in my world, I'm the freak you need protection *from*. Too much Fae for my rogue demon dad. Too much monster for his Unseelie old lady. Accident of birth, the kid no one planned for or wanted.

My own blood never thought I was anything worth protecting.

Right now, as Zara Gemini levitates in front of my freaky self— three times her size, potent as fuck, and armed with a magic trident— with zero fear or hesitation, protecting me from my cuz and my own shithead ways, sweet-faced as a schoolgirl?

This is the exact moment I fall in love with the Gemini queen.

This whole sitch is so surprising it tangles even my silver tongue.

"Well?" She alights to the floor between us, taps her toes, and crosses her arms over her curvy chest. Which deepens the lush swell of cleavage under her half-buttoned school blouse. "That wasn't a rhetorical question. Am I your queen or not?"

My royal cousin still seems to be struggling to close his mouth and douse the witchfire that's humming through his swords. So I seize my moment and *carpe* me some *diems*.

Ain't no royal who doesn't like a little kowtow, true?

I prop the butt of my trident against the floor, lower myself to one knee, and bow my head.

"You're my queen three times over, baby," I tell her gruffly, keeping my eyes on her impatiently tapping toes. Somehow the fact that she's wearing black-and-white schoolgirl saddle shoes just adds to her overall cuteness.

"You're the Unseelie Queen, and I'm half Unseelie," I say through the curtain of my own blue hair. "You're the dragon shifter queen, and I'm a shifter. Plus, uh, you're the queen of my heart."

At this, I risk a hopeful upward look.

"Queen of your heart, am I?" Her head tilts suspiciously. She taps one opal-painted nail against her chin. "Is that the incubus talking?"

"That dude talks with his dicks, for real." I grin and give her a wink. "I got more rizz than that. Heart's all mine—I mean, all yours."

"Have a care, cousin," Zephyr says coldly, scrambling gracefully to his feet and sheathing his swords on his back. "The hearts this queen collects, she keeps. Mine foremost among them. Besides which, I am her royal consort, forsooth. Swear to her, and you swear to me."

Before I can self-censor, a snort slips out. "Like that's supposed to deter me?"

Cousin Z slips up next to his queen and cocks his head like a curious sparrow to study me. For literally no reason, my heart kicks in my chest and my pulse picks up.

Biblical language aside, here's the truth. My sweet second cuz cut his baby teeth on my heart. By the time I was old enough to do anything about it, he was Ronin's. Then, after he healed up from the horrific injuries Ronin gave him (body and soul), he was Ash's.

Never mine.

I mean, he was always the Dark Fae King. I was just the awkward weirdo no one wanted.

By the time we were both old enough to know what we wanted?

We were enemies.

Maybe here, now, with Zara, I got me another chance. A chance to win both of them. My untouchable royal kinsman and his bewitching mortal queen.

Plus Babydoll.

Him—Vasili—hells, I wanted that guy from the sec he summoned me, all smoldery and hot and powerful as fuck, with insecurities a fathom deep hidden under all that pretty.

I wanted him before he even gave me his mating bite.

Even when V's not visible cuz he's wandered off down the tunnel, probably hunting the rest of our missing crew, that shifty snake of a warlock's lurking in the back of my mind. His bite on my neck pulses with seductive warmth.

But Zara's the queen, and she's waiting.

"You were saying?" She lifts her teal brows. The psi fire in her witchy eyes has dimmed, but she still fucking slays me. "About your heart?"

"Imma be your knight in shining armor, baby queen. Your knight of hearts." I lift my head with a grin to lock onto her wary eyes. "So you can either tap my shoulder with a sword like Queen Guinevere in the Arthur legend, or we can seal this deal with a kiss. Me, if I got a say? I vote for Option Two."

"Hmm." She pops one curvy hip like a runway striking a pose, which is sweet as shit. Her turquoise eyes narrow on my hopeful face. "Tell me something, Aquaman."

"Hit me." I lean into my trident and wait.

"Did you really go after Zephyr's throne because you didn't have a choice?" she says quietly. "And either way, do you still want it?"

My royal cousin hisses in a breath and glares at me over her shoulder like he'd love nothing more than to douse me in oil and toss a match. I shift my gaze from her serious face to meet his burning jade stare.

"Reason number ninety-three why being a demon sucks ass," I tell him. "Gotta do what my summoner says, don't I? Some of the bunch, like your Auntie Blossom, they're real shits. That whole life, liberty, pursuit of happiness thing? They ain't exactly constitutional rights for a demon."

I keep my tone light and my face set in a lazy grin, because these are truths too painful to share. I don't give a shit about anyone's throne. I ain't a free demon, and I never will be.

I gave up on the idea of *belonging* a long time ago. A freak like me? I'll never belong anywhere. With anyone.

I'd settle for my freedom.

But I'll never have that either.

Because, yo, demon.

I'll always be at somebody's demonical beck and call. Benevolent summoner's the most I can hope for. One who's strong enough to keep me. Considering some of the shits who've summoned me and circled me over the years? Let's just say the monster isn't always the guy inside the circle.

Maybe Babydoll and Cousin Z and this sweet-faced Gemini queen are the ones I've been waiting for.

But I've been painfully disappointed so many times I don't even wanna hope.

"Then it wasn't your choice to go after your cousin's throne," Zara murmurs, watching me close. "Do you still want it, Mordred? Tell me the truth."

The lure of her closeness pulls me toward her. Under the chalk of rock dust still floating in the air, her lush scent of cream and roses, spiked with tangerine, makes my kraken purr.

Dayum.

The way she smells, that dragon of hers is ripe for breeding. There's a reason all her shifters are in full rut. If I ain't careful, she'll trigger my own kraken into a mating rut.

Under my pants, right on cue, my junk swells up like a blowfish. Both barrels locked and loaded. I shift my weight subtly to ease the pressure.

"Do you want to rule," Zara says softly, "or serve?"

"I'm on my knees. I look like the ruling type to you?" I glance at Cousin Z for affirmation. "Back me up here, cuz."

He frowns at my plea, but mooches up next to Zara to slip an arm around her waist. "Regarding my unfortunate aunt, I'll allow the demon may speak truly. Still, I remind you, he isn't a proper cousin. We're *second* cousins, once removed. Lest you fear I'll suddenly sprout tentacles in our bed, my bride."

His queen slides me a sidelong look that perks my sulky kraken (who never likes being landlocked like he is now) right up.

Oh, fuck me.

In those dreams I sent her back on Avalon, she liked my tentacles fiiiine.

Meeting my heated look, her soft mouth curls. Then she gives me a headshake of reproach.

"It isn't his tentacles that are the problem," she murmurs. "It's his intentions. Vasili can't hold his leash forever. And I can't read his mind. Fae brains are a black box for a telepath. But I need to know if we can trust him."

"Worked out okay so far, ain't it?" I lean my weight into the butt of my trident, since I'm still kneeling on this hard-ass floor. "I'll swear any oath you like that I'm yours, long as I ain't summoned into someone else's circle and told to fuck you up. I don't have control over that shit. But no one on this particular plane—the mortal plane—except He Who Shall Not Be Named Babydoll—no one else holds my leash. And I ain't free from him till I've completed his task and returned your Horn to the Vault."

"Which means we can trust you… for now." Zara sighs. "Okay. I'll take it. Even though I'll probably regret it."

Elation fizzes through me like champagne bubbles.

Dude. This young mortal queen's definitely got under my skin.

"We gotta seal the deal." I shoot her a hopeful look and give my dimples free rein. "With a kiss?"

She rolls her pretty eyes at me, but her own grin slips out. "A kiss might be on the table, just to say thank you for helping today. But only if you don't sex me up, demon. I mean it."

"I promise not to sex you up… much." I stay on my knees and grin up at her.

Cousin Z looks as though he'd like to protest, but he hasn't been back in his bride's good graces long enough to get cocky. Instead it's the prof, Lucius Aries, who looms suddenly at Zara's shoulder. Looking sexy as fuck-all, bare-chested and rangy, all sinewy thighs and ass, poured into Ronin Pendragon's leather pants. Chest hair like a wolf pelt covering his powerful pecs. Plus the prof's got knotted abs I'd like to lick.

"My dear, we haven't much time," Lucius murmurs in her ear. Which I can hear, no problem, with my shifty senses. "Those hyenas *will* return—"

"Hey now, not cool to cock-block the kraken." I give Lucius a wink that brings color to his pale cheeks. "Gotta wait your turn, professor."

With a muttered oath, Cousin Z pivots sharply on his heel and strides for the tunnel. Like he can't stand to watch me flirting with his mates.

"This won't take long." The Gemini queen, bless her royal bad girl heart, seems to have made up her mind. She crouches before me (which is a treat to watch in that little schoolgirl skirt, believe me) and cups my chin gently in her small hand.

This ain't my first rodeo, I've kissed plenty, but right now you'd never know it.

My heart kicks against my chest like it wants out. My mouth is dry, and my tongue sneaks out to swipe across my lower lip, so I ain't all chapped when she kisses me.

Her thumb strokes the fork of my short beard. None of her guys are bearded, except for that cute goatee on Lucius, so I guess I'm a novelty for her.

"Soft," she breathes.

"Not everywhere," I try to joke, because no lie, my junk is *very* interested in having her this close and hopefully a whole lot closer.

Her sea-colored eyes lock on mine, and I'm aquatic, I can breathe underwater. But I swear to fuck, I'm drowning. The gills tucked behind my ears flutter and flare. My kraken stirs and uncoils in my skin.

"Your eyes are turning black," she whispers. Her fingers rest against the racing pulse in my throat.

"Just my kraken," I tell her, all husky. "He likes you."

"Mmmmm. I think maybe I like him too." Light as breath, her soft warm lips graze mine.

And my whole gods-damned world shifts sideways.

Chapter Nineteen
Zara

I finally give in to the insidious pull I can't seem to resist.

I finally kiss the kraken.

That's when my whole goddamn world shifts sideways.

Mordred's built like a tank, like he's indestructible, he's badass and right now he's running cool to the touch. Just like Vasili, my other cold-blooded shifter. But the midnight-blue beard that grazes my fingers is silky soft. The demon's full lips are a shock of carnal heat. Even when he's holding himself in check, so I can take the lead.

I swear, this guy has a mouth that would tempt a priest to sin.

With a teasing lick of tongue, I nudge his lips open. A shiver works through the powerful body kneeling at my feet. A deep baritone rumble rises from his broad chest like a purr.

That's his kraken, I know it. He's purring a welcome.

My dragon queen croons in reply.

Mordred's tongue meets mine in a lazy swirl of heat. The burn of spiced rum and saltwater taffy explodes on my tongue like candy. Now it's my turn to moan and lean into the kiss, licking his mouth like a sweet gooey treat that's melting in the heat. My free hand drops to his tattooed shoulder to anchor us both.

Under my palm and a canvas of inky skin, his massive deltoids ripple and clench. His big hand lands on my waist to ease me closer.

Incubus. Lucius' protective warning whispers in my head. *This is the very essence of his power. For any mortal, that demon is forbidden fruit. In the Christian era, with a kiss like that, his kind could ensnare your soul. A good Irish Catholic schoolgirl like you would damn your mortal soul to hell for a taste.*

Yeah, well, good thing I'm a lapsed Catholic, Lucius. And I've never been a nun. I grin against the warm suck of Mordred's mouth. *Pretty lucky thing for all of us. Right, Teach?*

My teasing makes Lucius growl.

God, I can feel him lurking at my back, his wolf too close to rising. Then my wolf king pushes right into me. His sinewy leather-clad legs graze my back. The turgid bulge of his swelling dick nudges my head.

Now my dragon croons for both of them. Both my shifters. Except—wait—

Mordred isn't *my* shifter.

The kraken is *ours,* my dragon hums, rich with certainty, like the randy bitch she is. *Claim our mate.*

Fuck me. Fuck my life. Just fuck.

We're claiming *another* mate?

In response, my whole body throbs and vibrates with a drumbeat of yearning.

Guess that's a big fat yes.

Only if Mordred feels the same, obviously. He's an incubus. Not exactly known for committed relationships. And assuming my guys agree. Which, given that minefield of unexploded Mordred-Zephyr ordnance, is a lot to assume.

Lucius' possessive hands grip my shoulders, like he and his rutting wolf are fighting the instinct to drag me away from danger.

Mordred chuckles against my mouth, then nuzzles his bearded face into my throat. He's kissing me and he's scenting me and he's even scenting Lucius, rubbing his jaw into my alpha's wrist just a little.

The soft rasp of Mordred's whiskers against my exposed jugular makes me shiver and sway. I grip his hips for balance. The scaly stretch of fabric over his corded glutes reminds me he's aquatic, he's nothing human. He tastes like a caramel apple on a summertime boardwalk. He smells like rain and lightning, like the sea after a storm. His wet blue hair spills over all of us.

I love being pinned between my guys, always have. (Even if Mordred isn't actually one of my guys.) So this whole setup floods my core with liquid heat. Under my uniform skirt and panties, my vag opens like a flower, dripping with nectar. The sudden scent of cream and roses, spiked with citrus, floods the air.

That's my mating scent. I mean, lately.

Me walking around smelling like a ripe tangerine is still kinda new.

That scent means I'm fertile.

At the scent (or maybe the thought), Lucius' growl deepens.

"Take it easy, professor," the demon rumbles into my neck. "Don't blow a nut. My kraken and me, we ain't alpha, we're cool with sharing. Plus we're pan. And you're bi as shit. S'all good, okay?"

Lucius' hands tighten on my shoulders. I lean into his legs for reassurance. Both giving and receiving.

"If you transpire to be my queen's choice, truly, I'll not be the one to oppose you," Lucius says gruffly. Saying not one word about his own preferences, but that's Lucius for you. "As for Vasili, he claimed you when he bit you, whether that was his intention or not. Since he is this polycule's dominant alpha, his desires carry a certain weight. However, I don't speak for the others. Especially His Radiance."

Mordred growls into my neck.

Which makes Lucius sigh. "Now is hardly the moment to press this matter with the Dark Fae King."

Hearing my alpha invoke Zephyr like a spell, I open my eyes (which I didn't even realize were closed) and try to pull my head together. I haven't explicitly chosen Mordred, even if my dragon thinks we have. That kiss was just a kiss. But Lucius is right—as usual—about the rest of it. Zephyr and Mordred have major shit to settle.

Me? I have finals to pass and a revolution to win.

"Yeah, I hear you," I tell my wolf king with a sigh. "We'll continue this convo later. All of us. Once we're safe."

Whenever that is.

Mordred lifts his head and gives me a smoldery bedroom look with those purple eyes that almost sets my panties on fire. He's still gripping that badass trident with one hand. The other rises to graze my cheek, which is warm and probably flushed. Against my sensitive skin, his fingers are rough and calloused like a fisherman's. With hands like that, I can imagine him hauling a net, straining with the morning's catch.

Right now, the morning's catch is me.

But his touch is gentle. Wondering. Just as gentle and sweet as Neo.

Which is the weirdest thing, considering he's... you know... a demon?

Here's the thing.

Looking deep into those wicked eyes, I don't see a cursed being or a damned soul. What I do see is the powerful pull of... longing.

A longing so intense it makes my chest ache.

"Mordred?" I whisper. "Why are you hurting?"

He opens his mouth to say God knows what. Suddenly my heart is thundering in my ears. My whole body leans toward him, hand rising to his face—

"Are you *ever* coming into this tunnel, or should the rest of us simply go on without you?" Vasili's waspish tone makes us all jump like a bee sting. "This catacomb is a fucking maze, but McSnicker and her rabid werewolf *do* seem to have sniffed out the path."

I blink into Mordred's startled gaze. Our fragile bubble of intimacy shatters like a thrown glass.

"Catacomb?" Sounding startled, Lucius pivots toward V. His protective hands fall away from my shoulders. "The catacombs on this island were condemned and sealed centuries ago. Surely you don't mean to suggest Ms. McSnicker has unsealed *that* hellhole?"

Looking suddenly wary, Mordred plants his trident against the floor and pushes up. Alarmed by Lucius' ominous tone, I scramble to my feet and spin toward the tunnel.

V and Zephyr stand framed in the entrance together, close enough to touch, with Neo's eager face peering over the Dark Fae's shoulder.

"Blood of Christ," Lucius mutters into the fraught silence. "I asked you a question and I fully intend to have an answer. Did Ms. McSnicker unseal that hellhole?"

"She has," Neo says happily, while Zephyr glares at Mordred and the Goblin King looks cross because we've all kept him waiting. "Mal knew the exact spell to unseal the, uh, hellhole."

Lucius groans and covers his face in dismay. "Oh, dear."

Chapter Twenty
Draco

The kick of my sniper rifle bucks into my shoulder on the discharge like a punch. Feels like a kiss, when you're a guy like me, raised on a daily regimen of death and violence.

My silencer muffles the shot, because I don't need to give away any more intel about where I'm hiding than necessary.

But that hyena shifter I've been tracking through the scope?

Bitch is the pack alpha, I'm pretty sure, and she takes my silver-coated anti-shifter bullet (contraband ammo that's illegal as shit in the witching world) right through the meaty hump of her shoulder. Her mangy carcass flies backward with a yelp and tumbles over the edge of the sea cliff that tucks up against our *domus*.

Oopsie.

She's fallen, and she can't get up.

I snicker under my breath. But even while I'm having my jollies, I know she's still in play.

Shifters don't make easy kills. Believe me, I know. I'm as trained and lethal as any professional wet boy in the AIB kill squad.

Once upon a time, I did my own wet work for the Mars clan mafia.

But that was before.

Lying on my belly on a big mossy rock behind the *domus*, guarding the basement door like my girl asked me, I got drizzle going *pitter-patter* against my biker jacket and dripping down the back of my neck. But that's nothing for an *íslendingur* like me.

I'd lie naked in an ice storm to keep Mallory safe.

While rain trickles down my scalp and soaks my buzzcut hair, I scan the sea cliff with my scope. I'm waiting for that alpha bitch or her backup to show up for seconds. This isn't my biathlon rifle and I'm not wearing my skis, but I'm in full competition mode.

Focused as *fokk.*

I always feel better when I'm packing heat. More centered. More grounded. More in control.

That's what makes the voices in my head go quiet.

Not good for nothing, is you, Draco? My father's gruff voice echoes in my ears. *Why can't you be more like you brudder, eh?*

The memory of the staggering blow that typically went with that kinda Q, like a burger with fries, bunches my shoulders around my ears.

But the solid feel of the rifle, all that quiet power gripped in my hands, quiets the chorus of shouts and screams in my noggin.

Under the distant boom of the sea on the rocks way below, the rain-soaked cliff is quiet.

Too quiet.

Been a minute since I've heard the brassy tyrannosaur bellow of Maxim Rasputin's big black dragon or the nails-on-chalkboard scream of that Dark Fae bastard's green monster.

The gray skies are empty.

They're Zara's guys, so no surprise, they did what the Dark Fae King ordered. Right now they're headed for our school on the wing, they're flying decoys, and they drew off a shitload of those AIB wet boys in pursuit.

Me?

I don't take orders from anyone. Except my shithead dad, Magnus Mars, a.k.a. the big boss. Head of the witching world mafia. I definitely *don't* take orders from that royal Dark Fae prick who whacked Mallory's brother.

Even when, it turns out, he didn't. Big brother Ash still hasn't kicked the oxygen habit.

But, *hel,* the Dark Fae King's been giving Mal nightmares the whole time I've known her.

Anyway, my point is, some of those AIB hyenas stayed behind. That's why I'm still here.

Hey, amou? Jae's telepathic whisper, drizzled with a honey of soft Cajun vowels, trickles through my brainbox. *If you're still out there, you, it's time to be coming,* oui?

I'm no telepath, not like he is, so I can't answer shit. Not unless he gives me a mating bite, which he's dead set against doing, for all his bullshit reasons. But my boy picks up emotions when they're strong enough. I shoot a strong pulse of *I gotchu* in his general direction, engage the safety on my rifle, and swing the piece over my rain-soaked shoulder.

Then I grab my gear bag, roll over, and drop from the boulder to the rough terrain behind our *domus*. I land in a crouch, letting my thick quads absorb the impact, shitkicker boots sinking deep in the mud with a *squelch*.

Between the rain and the mud, plus the blood that spattered my jacket when I had to use the hunting knife strapped to my thigh, I'm a mess. Definitely not in line with the dress code in the Academy Codex, you follow?

Mal's gonna be unhappy with my mess, for real.

She tries to keep my sorry ass outta detention whenever she can. Especially lately, since she doesn't trust our new headmaster in House Hadrian.

For *reasons*.

Let's just say I'm not the only killer in our *domus* anymore.

I'm already jogging along the perimeter, senses humming on high alert, my piece back in my hands at the ready, the crooked turrets and sharp angles of Villa Caligula looming over me in all their haunted house glory. With the Dean's Challenge in full swing, the joint's empty. All the kiddos are out trying to win the prize, pass their *fokking* finals, or at least not get whacked.

Me?

I don't waste my few brain cells worrying about my health. Sooner or later, I'll be checking into the Wooden Waldorf myself. When you're a made man, you don't tend to die of old age.

Till my ticket gets punched, I've got my girl and my boy to protect.

I close in on the storm cellar hatch that leads down to the basement. It's latched shut, just like I left it, so I flex a little telekinetic muscle to send the hatch flying up without breaking stride.

I'm already bringing my piece into play, trigger finger at the ready, as I hit the narrow chute of the steeply sloping stairs. Because anything could be lying in wait for me down there in the dark.

Shadows cluster thick at the base. Shadows thick enough to hide the body.

Now I guess you wanna know what body. Right?

I'm talking about the heat.

The fed.

Uncle Sugar.

Oh, come on. You know, head of the goddamn AIB?

The Dark Fae King's nasty green dragon juiced Nikolai Romanov right at the top of our basement stairs. Just sprayed the man down with a bellyful of flesh-eating acid. I watched Romanov's tall skinny frame, encased in top-of-the-line black exfiltration gear like the trained and sanctioned government killer he is, topple backward down those stairs, sizzling as the acid ate through his high-end gear.

Between the dragon and the fall?

Dude's no longer eligible for the census, if you know what I mean.

Still, you never underestimate a Romanov. (That goes for Vasili *and* his piece of shit dad.)

Not if you wanna live.

So I creep down those steps like the killer I am, hugging the wall where the shadows are thickest, placing my big boots with care so I don't make a sound. Going slow enough to let my eyes adjust.

By the time I reach the bottom, I can see fine. Good enough to make out the faded Art Deco speakeasy decor down here, the cobwebby bar where we hold our keggers, the dark bulk of the oil drums we use for light and heat. Underneath the musty smell of mildew and stale beer, my sharp Mogadon nose picks up the tang of old blood.

Used to be a dungeon down here in medieval times, where they'd punish unruly students. Taking detention to a whole new level. Our new headmaster, same guy who just spruced up the forest around our perimeter with lethal mantraps, likes to joke that he wants to return us to our roots. That's what he means.

Despite the clammy air down here, I'm starting to sweat.

"Helvitis," I mutter, scowling at the spot.

The spot where I fully expected to find the acid-eaten body of Nikolai Romanov. Russian oligarch, master spy, all-powerful director of the Arcane Investigative Bureau. Maybe with a little *rigor mortis* setting in around the face.

Instead, he's *fokking* gone.

Which means—somehow—that viper's still on the slither. He's down here somewhere, breathing and armed and deadly.

Somewhere very close to Mallory and Jae and the Gemini queen.

Chapter Twenty-One
Zara

"I might be queen of the witching world," I tell the small group of friends and lovers clustered close around me in the musty-smelling darkness of the tunnel's creepy confines. "And yeah, me wrapping my head around this whole royal destiny gig took a minute. I'm queen. But I'm not, like, a god."

"We don't need divine intervention to find our way through these catacombs," Mallory says patiently, her freckled face lit up from underneath by the comforting beam of her flashlight. "Just a really good location spell. I have one all teed up."

Vasili, who's still looking pale and kinda rough around the edges but who totally rejects any hovering over his head injury, gives Mal a suspicious look. "When precisely did you become such a powerful witch, McSnicker? You've certainly shown no aptitude for witchcraft in the classroom."

Somewhere behind me, Mal's Cajun werewolf lets out a warning snarl—a warning clearly aimed at V—that makes my scalp crawl.

Jae Labête's prowling at the rear of our Scooby gang, guarding our backs and seemingly not needing any light for that assignment beyond the wicked green glow of his own eyes. TBH, he creeps me out. Both Mal's guys are kinda freaky, especially the absent Draco. But I'm not the one fucking them.

These days, I'll gratefully accept any political allies I can get.

Plus I'll need those powerful bloodlines, like the exotic *loup-garou* werewolves of the Louisiana bayous and the brutal protection of the telekinetic Mars clan mafia, standing at my side when I ascend.

Queen or no queen, that's one truth I've internalized. My free agent cat burglar days are history.

And I can't queen it alone.

"I can do common magics." Mal clutches the Book of Flame and Breath defensively to her skinny chest and sidles away from Vasili. He used to bully her and the rest of the student body, same way he bullied me, so I can't blame her for being nervous about being trapped in this tunnel with his malignant self. "That's all a location spell is. Common magic. I left my sweater in the Academy library—you know, accidentally but on purpose?—after class to anchor the spell."

"Oh, wow." Neo pushes his glasses up his nose and looks impressed. "The library is directly above the Vault. That was so clever, Mallory."

Mallory looks a little awkward at the praise, which she doesn't tend to hear much around this Academy, given her class geek status. She ducks her carroty head to hide a blush. "Uh, thanks. Anyway, a simple location spell will lead me—and all of us—right to the Vault."

"I agree with Mr. Mercury. That's a very resourceful strategy. I'll ensure you receive full marks for ingenuity per the exam rubric, Ms. McSnicker." Lucius gives her an approving nod that makes my Goblin King sneer. Lucius tends to fall back on formality when we're around other students.

But V only gives him a hard time when Lucius goes all Old World formal with *us*.

My headmaster's grisly thigh injury is thankfully healing, like Neo would say, shifty-swifty. So fast that Lucius has not only stopped limping, but slipped back into the role of exam proctor. (I honestly don't think he can help himself.) He's started recording marks for our individual contributions to solving the Dean's Challenge with a neatly sharpened pencil and the leather-bound grade book he's produced from our backpack.

I mean, at least he isn't toting his oxblood leather briefcase around these catacombs.

Honestly speaking, I need to exert all my willpower not to ogle my wolf, all shirtless and furry-chested, with his thick thighs and muscled butt filling out Ronin's leather pants. Maybe that's the tail end of my heat talking.

Or maybe that's just Lucius.

"So… catacombs. Who knew?" Reining in my runaway libido, I force myself to turn away from Lucius' yumminess (for now) and play my own flashlight over Exhibit A.

A truly grisly row of human skulls.

All yellow-toothed and hollow-eyed and gnarly with age, the cranium collection grins at me from a cobwebby ledge set high in the tunnel wall. Directly beneath on either side, a lattice of ancient femurs and tibias and ribs—all the major bones in the human body, I guess—frames a narrow arch.

A funky-smelling breeze drifts from the dark passage to tickle my face like a ghostly finger.

By sheer force of will, I manage not to shiver.

Step up, showgirl, you're the queen here, I tell myself sternly. *No shivering.*

Lucius stops scribbling notes in his gradebook long enough to give me a serious look with his lovely sherry eyes. "As a matter of fact, *I* knew. These catacombs loom rather large in the history of this academic institution. This place is where the witching races secretly interred their dead in Roman times, while we were persecuted by the Empire, much like the early Christians. Frankly speaking, I would have preferred to avoid the place entirely. But it seems that is not to be our fate."

Zephyr prowls up like the feral predator he is and runs a professional eye over the row of gaping sockets and grinning teeth. With a hiss, he peers into the low passage with his keen Fae eyesight. He's the smallest of my guys, but even he has to stoop.

The crossed swords jutting over his armored shoulders keep him outside that scary hole, which I totally don't mind.

"I've never understood this morbid mortal custom," my Dark Fae murmurs, "of encasing your dead in rock to molder. In the natural order, a rotting corpse returns nourishment to the soil and the wild creatures who inhabit it."

"Oh darling, that visual. So picturesque. Rather like the way you buried your cousin's head in our rose garden." Vasili smirks, but the comment lacks the barbed wire sting of his usual malice. Either my Goblin King is still struggling with that alarming head injury he claims doesn't bother him, despite the numbing potion and Seelie herbs we've doctored him up with…

Or there's been a fucking miracle in this harem, and my dominant alpha truly has softened toward Zephyr.

At least temporarily.

I mean, a girl can hope. Can't I?

"Tight fit in there," I mutter, bending to aim my own beam over Zephyr's dragonscale-armored shoulder, and already missing my catsuit. "We'll have to squeeze in single file and all hunched over. That's assuming we're all going."

My voice echoes and re-echoes weirdly inside, like the walls are murmuring. I can't see shit beyond a crumbly stone stair that slopes down around a sharp curve. My dragon stirs and grumbles unhappily in my skin. She doesn't like being underground and encased in a sleeve of rock too tight for her to shift.

That makes two of us.

Neo slips an arm around my waist and cuddles the white kitten to his chest. He's just fed her, with Mordred's interested assistance, so she's all sleepy and limp and purring against my bookworm's brawny shoulder. "We can always turn back, babe. Try another way."

I suck in a lungful of the dank-smelling air. "No, we can't. This tunnel led straight here. The only other way to go is back. And since we gotta find the Vault before the AIB finds *us*—"

"Back is not an option." Draco Mars emerges from the darkness behind us with a suddenness that makes me gasp.

Zephyr spins and unsheathes both his swords with a snarl that bares his tiny fangs.

Draco wraps a casual hand around the butt of the big-ass rifle propped over his hulking shoulder and gives my menacing Dark Fae King his own unfriendly look.

"Something you gonna do with those swords, Unseelie?" Mal's guy growls in his guttural accent, sounding like Schwarzenegger in his *Terminator* days.

Now I'm just waiting to hear him say, *Hasta la vista, baby.*

Lucius and Vasili—both my currently available alphas—step protectively in front of me. That protective shit used to bother me, but I'm working like fuck to let my alphas do what their instincts demand. Protecting me is a genetic need for them, so I gotta learn to accept it.

At least sometimes.

I'm more surprised to see a reaction from Mordred (who's no alpha and is barely even an ally, but OMG, that kiss! Even in our current crisis, I can barely stop thinking about it.) He muscles up behind my alphas in backup, his broad shoulders filling the narrow tunnel, silver trident magically appearing in his hand. Still toting the Horn of Ceres in that sealskin bag slanting across his bare bronze back.

"I'm commonly addressed as Your Radiance," Zephyr says coolly to Draco. But at least he sheathes his swords over his shoulders. That move defuses the worst of the tension.

Though definitely not all of it.

"I don't give a *fokk* how you're addressed, Unseelie." Draco eyes him warily. "You're not Mallory's king. And you're definitely not mine."

This is the first I've seen of Mal's Icelandic mafia warlock since he loped off with the others to deal with those hyenas. Draco Mars is alarming enough in normal circumstances. Seeing him now, with dried blood spattering his spiked biker jacket and the side of his rugged face, cold eyes glittering like arctic ice under his pale buzzcut, and a rifle slung over his shoulder?

He looks like a total psycho.

I mean, even more than usual.

"Hey, *amou*, we missed you, *oui?*" Jae slips up behind Draco and rubs his face familiarly into the side of the guy's neck to scent him. Totally undeterred by the blood and the rifle and the crazy, natch. The Cajun werewolf's black-rimmed eyes gleam liquid gold at me in the dim light.

Mallory rushes over with a cry and cuddles up against both of them, exclaiming over the blood. Draco assures her it's not his, slings his thick arms around both of them, and generally lets his two mates love on him with a lot more patience than I expect.

That reaction makes me temper my original diagnosis about him being cray cray.

I mean, he's definitely crazy. But his mates make him sane.

These three haven't been together long, but they're already pregnant (a fact not generally known at the Academy, but Mal shared it with me.) They've clearly settled into their menage. I squash down a twinge of envy that Mal has both her guys safe beside her, while half of mine are missing and in danger.

Instead, I focus on how good it feels to see Mallory happy. She's my friend and she deserves it. Even if her guys aren't anything I'd have chosen for myself.

Once I'm queen—if I'm queen—I intend to encourage a lot more relationships like theirs.

What the witching world needs most, to reverse our slow slide to extinction, is more witches.

Of all genders.

Fucking.

"Well, Mars, don't leave us in suspense." V eyes the menage and their lovefest with poorly veiled impatience. "Precisely what—or *whom*—have you left alive and ambulatory behind us?"

Draco lifts his head from nuzzling the side of Mallory's neck and rubs a rough hand over Jae's beaded dreads to soothe him. His pale Nordic eyes drill into Vasili's. "We got Uncle Sugar and the feds breathing down our necks. Matter of fact, Romanov—"

"For fuck's sake. You were given one job." V cuts him short with a slash of his slender hand. "So much for the formidable reputation of the Mars clan mafia. Evidently you're all bark and no bite."

I can tell V's head is hurting, which makes him irritable (you know, more than usual).

But the real issue is he's worried.

About me and all of us.

The sharp edge of his fear for my safety knifes through our mating bond.

Draco, who seemed like he was about to say something significant and who doesn't have access to my snake's secret worries, shuts down like a clam and scowls. "*Hel,* I got a higher kill count than you, Romanov. But there's always room for another notch on my knife."

"Whoa." Looking concerned—which is justifiable—Mal plants her fragile beanpole body between her guys and mine. Her huge gray eyes plead silently for my help. "Draco, we're Zara's allies, we're even in her harem, uh, temporarily, you can't go around killing her warlocks. And Vasili, you stop baiting him."

I'm honestly impressed that Mal's standing up to her bully. (I mean Vasili, not Draco.) Before my snake can do something truly awful, like close his telekinetic fist and crush her throat for sassing him, I leap into the fray.

"That's right, guys. We're all on the same side here, remember? And we gotta keep moving. You're with me, Goblin King." Without waiting for a verbal consent I know I won't get, I loop my arm through V's and tug him along with me. I swing my beam grimly toward the tunnel. "In we all go, I guess."

Vasili pouts at me, an effect somewhat lessened by the gauze bandage wound rakishly over his forehead and his smudgy morning-after mascara. But he takes my flashlight with a sigh and bends his tall frame to peer skeptically into the tunnel.

With a final squeeze, Draco releases his two lovers and gives me a level look. "No guessing. You need to motor. You're being hunted, Gemini."

"So what else is new?" I touch the stiletto strapped to my thigh for reassurance, twist my hair into a high ponytail to keep it outta my eyes, and hum in my throat to summon a crackle of static. "No one else technically has to come with—except Mordred with the Horn if you're still game, demon—but I'm definitely going in."

"Yo. I'm down, baby queen." Mordred banishes his trident with a blink (still a startling magic, but I'm getting used to it) and swanks up to the grisly catacomb entrance with a grin. "This'll be dope, for real. Gimme that flashlight. Imma go first."

"Needless to say, we're all going," Lucius says firmly (to no one's surprise). "You can entrust the flashlight to me."

Everyone's already committed, but I need to know it's their choice. Even though I'm not surprised, I'm still hella grateful.

To all of them.

I give my wolf an appreciative grin, then squeeze in beside my demon—I mean, *the* demon. I breathe in a hit of the mouthwatering saltwater taffy scent that rises from all his exposed skin, then reach to aim V's beam purposefully down the tunnel. "I figured I'd go first. With my lightning."

"Oh dear fuck. Here we go again," Vasili murmurs.

Mordred exchanges a level look with V, which reminds me those two share a telepathic bond since that mating bite.

Then the demon winks at me. "You're the ruling royal, for real, and your rival wants you dead. You gotta stop thinking like a cat burglar and start thinking like a queen. Let the rest of us protect you. You know, for a change."

I gaze up (way up) into the kraken's clever purple eyes.

Well, great.

Now I'm literally getting trust lessons from a summoned demon.

A demon so hot he steals my breath. Behind that forked blue beard and that tangle of wet blue curls and the dusky skin stretched over those strong bones and shining like copper in the spooky light, there's someone a lot less confident, less cocky, less *I don't give a fuck* than the swaggering sex demon he lets the rest of the world see.

But I saw him… the *real* him… the guy he hides away… when we kissed.

Under all that sexy, the kraken is lonely.

My inner dragon croons in sympathy. One of those bird trills I vocalize since I started shifting. In reply, a baritone purr rumbles from the kraken's chest.

"For once, the sex demon isn't thinking with his delectable dinky." Vasili gives the incubus a cool nod of approval that brings out Mordred's dimples. That demon loves to be praised, a useful fact I file carefully away for later. "Let McSnicker lead, with Jae and Lucius. Their wolfish noses are what's needed, along with that location spell."

Jae Labête snarls in agreement and moves to the front, where Mallory's already standing with her broad-beam flashlight ready. Lucius tucks away his gradebook and moves alertly out in front.

V's sharp stare shifts to me. "Little queen, you and Neo and Mordred—with the Horn—you're in the middle. With me."

"'Tis my place then to guard your back, my bride," Zephyr says with satisfaction, moving right into place like he and V have shared sentry duty a million times. "Along with this one. Dracomir Guðmundur Mars, is it not?"

I'm not even a little surprised that my Dark Fae King has sussed out Draco's full name. That's how Unseelie witchcraft works. In Dark Fae culture (as I'm learning, since I'm now the Dark Fae Queen), just speaking someone's full name out loud is a threat. And the only reason I can fathom for Zephyr to threaten Draco is because, just a few minutes ago, Draco threatened V.

What is even happening between those two warlocks of mine?

The Goblin King and the Dark Fae King.

Are they now... allies?

"Marriage of convenience," Vasili whispers in my ear, with a wicked swipe of tongue that makes me shiver. The Fae aren't the only ones whose ears are erogenous. "With separate beds."

While Mordred gently helps Neo tuck our drowsy kitten safely in her carrier and everyone else queues up for the catacombs, I give my dominant alpha a disappointed look.

"Separate beds? Where's the fun in that?"

"He means I'll need to seduce him like a skittish medieval virgin on her bridal night." Zephyr's cool silver voice slides along my other ear like a caress. His fist knots in my ponytail and tightens to drag my head back. "With your collaboration, my queen, 'tis a challenge I fully mean to master."

Vasili wraps one arm around my waist and reaches past my tummy with the other to trail his languid black-nailed hand over Zephyr's dragonscale codpiece.

Even through his armor, the light contact makes the Dark Fae groan.

"Good luck with that, Your Tumescence," V whispers against my throat with a wicked chuckle.

Sandwiched between two of the deadliest guys in the tunnel, I breathe in Zephyr's scent of burnt amber and sunbaked dragonhide, mingled with the musk and caramel of V's Mogadon mating scent. While my Dark Fae exposes my throat with that fist wrapped around my ponytail, my snake hums with pleasure and bends to drag his hot tongue down my jugular. His wicked fangs graze my skin with the silent threat (or promise) of yet another mating bite.

Yowsa.

The potent hit of Vasili's pheromones and mine, swirling through these close confines, almost takes the top of my head off.

Honestly speaking, this shit's enough to make us all horny.

Too bad now isn't the time or the place.

"Once we win this Dean's Challenge?" I breathe in reply, all sexed-up and throaty. "Sign me the hell up for that."

Chapter Twenty-Two
Mordred

"Do you smell something funky?"

The Gemini queen's whisper barely stirs the heavy silence as the chick and her warlock court wind down the tight coil of the catacomb stairs in single file, with me and my Horn in the middle, like a conga line on a cruise ship.

Only without the booze.

That's a real shame.

From the front, where the redheaded witch's broad-beam flashlight sweeps the dark like a lighthouse beacon, the professor's whisper drifts back. "Indeed, I do. The odor is redolent of manure, rather like… livestock. Wouldn't you say, Mr. Labête?"

"Ah, smells like a barn to me, *oui?*" the werewolf says in his thick bayou growl. "And under the stink of animal shit… I smell death."

"Go figure." Zara snorts and edges away from the grisly banister of human bones that mooches along inside the spiral stairs, guarding the deep black drop into infinity in the middle. We already shined our flashlights down there, but that pit's hella deep.

Too deep to see the bottom.

"Animal, huh?" I take a good sniff myself, but my cranium's already swimming with the creamy rose and citrus haze of Zara's heat. Laced with the rich musk of Babydoll—my new lord and master—the drippy punk rock warlock with the cold hands and the hot eyes who's breathing down my neck.

Just a whiff of Vasili's Mogadon pheromones makes heat pulse through the double puncture of his bite on my neck. Despite the dank breeze wafting up from the abyss, that heat ripples over my bare skin and makes me sweat.

I already got one hand planted on Zara's tiny waist, kinda guarding her from that scary drop. Now my free hand rises to find the inflamed punctures at the side of my neck.

From behind, the warlock's cool fingers brush my heavy mane of hair outta the way. "Is my bite troubling you, demon?"

"Feels kinda achy," I admit. "Might need you to kiss it better, bae."

Because isn't that what these alpha shifters are supposed to do? That's what Lucius the prof said. Babydoll—Vasili—he's supposed to take care of me.

It's all I can manage not to laugh out loud. Like the mortals say, LOL. If he does take care of me, that'll be a change. He'd literally be the first.

Babydoll's hot whisper slithers into my pointed ear.

"It's a mating bite. You need to be fucked."

The heat pulsing through my body gathers in my junk. This time I give in to a low chuckle. "I am *so* totally down with that plan."

Zara's little hand snakes back to thread her fingers through mine. "Can I watch?"

"Me too?" The bookworm's hopeful voice rises behind Vasili.

I'm kinda flattered at the attention, no lie, since I'm not even working right now to rizz anyone up.

Neo's schlepping that kitten and a loaded backpack, but the guy doesn't sound winded. He's an appealing kid, for real, with those soft curls falling around his earnest face and those big eyes blinking behind his schoolboy specs. Definitely a royal favorite, the way Zara cuddles and loves on him. Plus I've seen Cousin Z give him that predatory once-over that tells me Neo Mercury's got a hot date coming with the St. Andrew's Cross fuck-me furniture suspended over the Dark Fae King's royal bed back in Avalon.

"Ain't got no problem with that," I say from the heart. "Truth. Hells, you can all join right in if you—"

"I'll be the judge of that," Babydoll says coolly, like the pissy little bitch he can sometimes be. "I'm your alpha."

"Well, whatever you decide, *alpha*," Zara says wryly, "you better decide *soon*. I guess maybe you don't know this, Mordred, but alpha shifter spunk is laced with biochemicals to break a mating fever."

"Yeah, and that's a major thing," Neo pipes up. "Ronin got mating fever after Lucius first bit him. Only Ronin was sulking and wouldn't let Lucius take care of him. He almost *died*—I mean Ronin—before Lucius kinda took matters into his own hands, I mean paws. They're both totally in love now, but that's how Lucius and Ronin first hooked up—"

"Hush." That's Lucius—the prof—and his chiding whisper sounds all embarrassed. "Mr. Labête and I are trying to listen for any pursuit."

"You may be certain there is none behind us." Cousin Z's silver voice cascades down the stairs from behind. "If anyone dares to follow, Dracomir Guðmundur Mars and I will address the matter."

Hardy-har. *Address the matter.*

I just bet they will.

Cousin Z's never minded a little murder. I wasn't even surprised when he capped my late unlamented brother—a real piece of work—and buried the dude's head in Zara's garden to help her roses grow.

And even though Zephyr just threatened Draco again by trotting out his full monicker, the Icelander's grim chuckle in reply sounds psychotic.

Those two are a good choice for guard duty. I mean it. An axe-murder psycho and a feral Fae tyrant.

We all fall silent for a while. My webbed feet are clumsy in Babydoll's borrowed combat boots, so I gotta take care groping down these stairs in the dark. If I miss a step and go down, imma take Zara and her skinny redheaded friend and all those guys in front down with me like dominoes.

Lucky if we don't all break our necks.

But Zara's warm little hand stays soft and trusting in mine, tugging me along after her like she and that dragon queen of hers are actually glad I'm here. My kraken slithers around in my skin and gives a happy rumble at the thought.

I rest my fingers over the double punctures on my neck. When I'm not all sexed up (which is rarely), no lie, that bite does ache. Might even be starting to seep a little.

Babydoll hisses in my ear, "Stop fussing with the bite, *do*, or you'll make it worse. I'll take care of you when we stop, shall I?"

His hot tongue flickers over the tip of my ear, there and gone in a blink. Hells' bells. He might as well have shoved his pretty hand down my pants and squeezed my junk.

An audible groan slips outta me. "Don't be a fucking tease. If you're gonna jump my bones to break my fever, you better mean that shit."

Zara glances over her shoulder, ponytail swinging pertly, her sweet face alive with mischief. "You *do* have options, you know, Mordred. If the Goblin King isn't playing nice, you can always ask Max or Lucius for a fuck."

"Or you," I say gruffly, speaking over the prof's startled exclamation up front and Vasili's huff of annoyance behind. "You're an alpha too, baby queen. You and that cute teal dragon."

A chirp of interest, like a bird sound, slips between her sweet lips. That's her dragon sounding off, I bet, adding her two cents to the convo.

Zara's glowing turquoise eyes slide over my naked chest and pause on the Horn in my messenger bag in a way that makes the ancient fertility relic hum with interest against my hip. Then her smoldering eyes drop to my crotch.

I swear to fuck, it's all I can manage not to press her sweet hand to my dicks. All that holds me back (barely, in my current horndog state) is the knowledge that I'm a lot to handle down there when you ain't prepared.

For real.

"Sweet Jesus. I'll tend your bite, I promise," she whispers, gaze roaming slowly back over my abs and pecs till she finds my face. "As soon as we stop for a breather. All the alphas in this polycule like to share. But no sexing me up like you are right now. Do we have a deal, Aquaman?"

A broad grin breaks over my face. "Shit, I ain't sexing you up. That's my natural rizz, not my hocus-pocus. You're into me, baby queen. You're *so* into me."

Behind me, Babydoll voices kinda this snort of disdain. But the butterscotch scent of his Mogadon pheromones kicks up a notch. Succinct as shit, he says clearly, "Darling girl, we'll work on him together. You lick and I'll fuck. The last thing we need is this demon distracted by mating fever when we're trying to break into the Vault and win the Challenge."

"He's *so* altruistic, our Goblin King." Zara's turquoise eyes dance with mischief as she glances between us. "Who knew?"

"Yeah, he hides it, like, really well." From behind Babydoll, Neo gives a happy-sounding chuckle that's almost a giggle. The kid's enjoying their banter even when he's not directly part of it.

Me? I'm grinning ear to ear like a kid at Christmas.

Feeling the energy dance between this baby queen and her court, these warlocks she's all gonna crown and turn into kings, I get why they all orbit around the chick like planets around a sun.

I do, I get it.

Even grumpy Cousin Z in the rear whose suspicious frown drills into the back of my noggin.

They're all freaks and misfits, each in their own way, they're all different from the normals.

Just like me.

Yet somehow, their love for each other has stitched this crazy quilt of shifters and witches and Fae into the thing I've never had and always wanted.

A family.

All that love wraps around them like a blanket. They all belong here. They've all found their place. They've all created this safe space that lets them be who they are, without fear of ridicule or rejection.

Fuck me, I want that. I want that for myself. I want it so bad I can taste it.

The ache of longing for that shit—a sense of belonging, acceptance, a real family like the one they've stitched together—burns in my chest like heartbreak. I can taste my own yearning clogging the back of my throat like tears. All those tears I never let myself shed.

Instead, I learned to laugh.

When you laugh hard enough and you laugh long enough, people stop trying to make you cry.

Hells. At this point, imma cry like a baby.

Lucky for me, this is the exact moment Zara bumps up against Lucius' back. I bump up against her, and Babydoll crowds into me from behind.

"What's happening?" Neo demands as we all bunch together on the stairs. The gaping abyss in the middle has vanished behind a wall of rock. We're all packed into a narrow stone chute, with a low ceiling and tons of solid rock above us.

"We're at the bottom," Mallory calls back, the pale beam of her flashlight swinging around. "There's a really tight squeeze here. Everyone stop pushing, okay?"

"*Chere*, I go first for you, *oui*?" the werewolf growls. "And I don't need a flashlight, me."

"Hold up," Draco calls from the back in a tone that does not invite argument. "No one goes anywhere without me. *Fokk*, Unseelie, move your skinny ass and your *fokking* swords so I can shimmy past—"

"Stop pushing me, brute," Cousin Z says irritably. "There's no place for me to go."

Chaos ensues in the tight chute of the stairs. The guys in back are pushing, the ones up front trying to make room. Zara loses her footing on the steep stairs with a cry, but I catch her under the arms and hold her up. She feels hella good in my arms, depending on me, all warm softness and womanly curves, her silky ponytail brushing my face, the creamy citrus tang of her mating scent calling to my kraken like a fucking Siren—

"Oh, crap," Neo yelps. "I've lost my glasses."

The sharp crunch of breaking glass behind me—coupled with Cousin Z's short curse—isn't good.

But none of us have time to focus on that, for real.

That's when we hear the werewolf howl. A long, mournful, soul-rending dirge of grief and pain.

Then all nine hells break loose.

Chapter Twenty-Three
Zara

"I honestly think I'm going to hurl," Neo mumbles, pretty much saying what we're all thinking.

Standing with my arms wrapped tight around my fated mate who's quivering with suppressed emotion, feeling the fear and horror in his brawny arms wrapped tight around me, I wanna say it's gonna be okay. I really do.

Except I never wanna lie to him.

I'm afraid none of us will truly be okay ever again. Not after this.

After the shit we're staring at? We're all gonna need therapy.

Specifically: the unfamiliar werewolf, clearly very dead even if he hasn't been for long, nailed to the ancient cross in this underground mausoleum.

Mallory's own werewolf, Jae Labête, hasn't stopped howling since he found the guy. Now, with Mal and Draco both wrapped tight around him, holding Jae together with the desperate strength of the love those three share, Jae sinks slowly to his knees before the cross, like his legs are giving out.

(If they are, I don't blame him.)

Wretched, he bows his head so his beaded dreads hide his half-shifted face.

"Roy," he growls, all hoarse and wolfish. Blindly he gropes to lay a hand-slash-paw on the corpse's gnarled leg. *"Roy."*

Then he's howling with grief again.

"Oh, shit. Guess he knew the guy," I whisper to Neo under the howling. Which makes the whole thing even more awful. I barely know our resident *loup-garou,* so I give Jae's own mates the space to comfort him and wrap myself harder around Neo, who also needs comfort.

Vasili tucks in behind us and hugs us both tight, Neo and me, simultaneously lending us his alpha strength and guarding our backs. Our Goblin King has seen worse—hell, he's probably *done* worse, even if he's never actually crucified his enemies (that I know about).

But he doesn't like when we're upset.

And he definitely doesn't like when we're in danger.

"I knew the wolf as well," Lucius says quietly, making the whole thing even more awful. "We all did, all the wolf shifters. *Roy* simply means 'king' in Cajun. This man is… *was*… Jean-Baptiste Boudreaux. King of the Cajun werewolves."

"Roy, man." Jae shakes his head and covers his face with his hands. I get the uneasy sense he's fighting to stop howling and hold off his shift. His voice is thick with his wolf's guttural growl. "Why are you even here, you?"

"May he rest in peace." Lucius lays a steadying hand on Jae's bowed head. Which Jae tolerates from him, since Lucius' own wolf is, like, uber alpha. "All your king's troubles are now ended."

Our headmaster doesn't need to say it, but we're all thinking it. *Too bad the same thing isn't true for the living.*

Some shifters aren't totally sentient when they shift. They go feral, like Malky the great white from House Tiberius, who bit a chunk out of Mordred's tentacle during our dive and gulped it down right in front of him.

Now I'm getting the uneasy sense Jae might be the same kind.

While the *loup-garou* visibly shudders under his mates' protective clutch, Zephyr summons a flare of pale witchlight with a hiss. His witchcraft sets his Unseelie swords glowing like lightsabers. Then he prowls the shadowy confines of the tomb, blades held at the ready.

He's checking the place out.

Securing our perimeter.

Hunting through the dark for our enemies like the wild animal he is.

Without a word of discussion, like he's been guarding us his whole life, Mordred summons his trident into an outstretched hand and strides off in the opposite direction to do the same.

Right now, a little extra vigilance definitely feels like a good idea.

"Silver nails." Lucius is, respectfully but thoroughly, examining the dead wolf's body. His calm demeanor steadies me too, despite the deep disquiet that seeps through our mating bond. Deferentially, he peers at the grisly wounds that mark the clawed feet and outstretched hands of the dead werewolf.

Jean-Baptiste, I remind myself. *That werewolf had a name. Probably a family. This is fucked up.*

"If it's any comfort," Lucius murmurs, "I do believe the wolf king expired by other means."

My Irish Catholic upbringing rises irreverently to the fore. "You mean a spear through the side, like Jesus?"

"No, Ms. Gemini." Lucius, who's a devout Christian himself, spares me a look of mild reproach from his whiskey eyes. "And before you ask, he isn't wearing a crown of thorns either."

"You mean he was killed *before* he was crucified?" Vasili stops rubbing Neo's unhappy back and gives Lucius a sharp look. "Then why the silver nails?"

"The silver nails were likely… an insurance policy of sorts," Lucius says, "against the legendary resilience of the *loup-garou*. To ensure the dead king would not… rise."

Through his curtain of fallen dreads, Jae gives the corpse a haunted look. "Yaya, like a *zonbi*. This he could do, him. If not for the nails."

"Oh, fuck me," I whisper. The concept of that poor werewolf *rising* from the dead like a damn zombie gives me a cold shiver, like a ghost walking over my grave.

Respectfully, Lucius examines with his flashlight the gory row of puncture wounds that stipple the dead wolf's chest. Including the puncture that drove through the wolf's furry throat, which was surely the killing blow. Under all the grizzled fur and dried blood and the tatters of the wolf's ripped shirt, plus my instinctive reluctance to look at the grisly carnage too close, I'm only now noticing what Lucius apparently saw right away.

"What could have—done that to him?" Mallory says in a shaky voice, all the while pressing Jae's half-shifted face fearlessly into her exposed neck.

"At a guess? It appears Jean-Baptiste stumbled headfirst into one of your new headmaster's mantraps. With injuries this severe, even this formidable creature's passing would have been swift." Lucius' flashlight plays over the deep row of punctures. "Then he was brought here and crucified—after the fact. To what end, I cannot surmise. As an outsider, the werewolf king should never have been on this island, especially during the Dean's Challenge."

"By the moon, we should not linger."

Zephyr materializes from the shadows, blades gone dark, with a suddenness that almost makes me scream. Neo yelps in surprise. V levitates six inches and hisses like a stepped-on rattlesnake.

"Sweet Jesus." Between the horror show ambience of these catacombs and the crucified werewolf, even a thoroughly lapsed Catholic like me has to fight the reflex to cross myself. "Zephyr. This is *not* the time to sneak up on someone. I coulda hurled lightning."

Thankfully, since I'm still hugging Neo and Vasili both for comfort, my control's gotten way better than the early days. I don't actually electrocute anyone, even if my ponytail and uniform crackle with static.

V lowers himself to the ground, rubs my back and Neo's to settle us down, and pouts at Zephyr. "For fuck's sake, wear a bell. Must you creep around this tomb like a cat? You're lucky I didn't throw your radiant self through a wall."

Zephyr sheathes his swords over his back, gives V a contrite look (which is definitely new), and touches my cheek with a gauntleted hand. That's his version of an apology, because they don't teach you to say *I'm sorry* when you're the Dark Fae King.

I lean into his touch to convey forgiveness.

"Don't keep us in suspense, Your Quintessence," V says, more tolerantly (for him). "Did you find something to cause any particular alarm—aside from a crucified werewolf—while you were skulking about?"

I'm really expecting Zephyr to take offense at this point. But my Dark Fae King is totally focused elsewhere.

On me.

"I sense no other breathing creature in this particular tomb," Behind the slash of his eyepatch, Zephyr's face hardens and his jade eye narrows in warning. "For the moment. 'Tis an uncanny place, in truth. Neither alive nor fully dead. My bride, we should make haste."

My shoulders straighten and my chin comes up.

He's the king of his own realm, but he's appealing to me as the queen of this one. I'm the Fred Jones in charge of our Scooby gang, I'm the HBIC, not some bubble-headed bimbo of a Daphne. And Zephyr's right, we do need to vamoose. But, very clearly, Jae Labête needs a minute to recover from the shock.

TBH, we all need a minute.

Besides, it doesn't feel right to leave that poor crucified wolf just hanging there.

"*Helvitis.* We can't leave him like that." Accurately reading the room (probably because he's been watching Zephyr and all his interactions with open suspicion this whole time), Draco rises to loom protectively over his huddled mates. "Let's get the wolf king down, *já*? Make the man decent for now and bury him later. After the Challenge."

"He needs to be buried on consecrated ground, him," Jae mutters, still looking gray and shocky, but clearly working hard to pull his shit together. "Otherwise, with juju like his? He'll rise and walk, he'll be *zonbi*."

Mallory blinks at him in concern. "Yeah, you said that before. I was hoping it was a figure of speech. You mean an actual zombie? Like a literal werewolf zombie?"

Jae snarls in agreement through his fangs.

"Oh, great." Neo clutches our makeshift cat carrier (sparking a meow of complaint from the kitten) and looks anxious.

Sweet fuck, what next in this place?

I lean into my fated mate for mutual comfort. "Uh, yeah, let's try to avoid anyone rising if we can."

"We can inter him in one of these crypts temporarily," Vasili murmurs. "Just for a few hours. Until we win the Challenge."

But V's distracted, not even looking toward where Lucius and Draco are gently lowering the crucifix with its gruesome burden so they can at least lay the dead wolf flat.

Which is hopefully not a prelude to some kinda *Walking Dead* situation, only with werewolves.

Vasili isn't thinking about zombies at all right now.

He's frowning at Mordred, who's propped his trident against the looming bulk of a cobwebby sarcophagus. The sex demon himself is huddled at the base, blue head bowed, tattooed arms wrapped tight around his knees. Even from a distance, at a time when he's clearly trying not to draw attention, I can see the demon shivering. In the wavery light cast by our scattered flashlights, his bronze skin gleams with a sheen of sweat.

"Mating fever." Looking uncharacteristically perplexed, V rubs a hand over his face. "Shit."

This catacomb's turned into a shitshow, but one thing is very clear. My priority—now and always—is the people who need me.

Right now, that includes Mordred.

"Yeah." I sigh. "That poor demon isn't doing too well. We gotta take care of that ASAP."

Torn between the competing demands of the various guys who need me, I glance from Mordred to Neo.

"I'm okay," Neo mumbles, still snuggled in my arms, face naked and defenseless without his glasses, whose broken frames are now tucked into his blazer pocket. "Need to let the kitten out anyway while we're, um, stopped. She probably needs to pee. The two of you should definitely help Mordred. You can take my flashlight."

There it is right there.

Like the nine hundredth reason why we all love Neo.

Our bookworm is just the sweetest, kindest, most generous guy in our whole polycule.

"Yes, he is," V whispers, because that's a thought I haven't shielded. He drops a kiss on Neo's worried forehead and exchanges a look with Zephyr that silently conveys the role of bookworm bodyguard to our resident Unseelie.

Zephyr's chest swells under his dragonscale armor. He dips his chin in a lordly nod.

Neo's already crouching at our feet, working on the zipper of his duffel. Zephyr sifts a proprietary hand through Neo's soft curls and definitely does not look displeased to have our bookworm kneeling at his feet.

Before I can properly appreciate that dynamic, the Goblin King wraps his cool fingers around mine and draws me away from both the pet relief process Neo's starting and the werewolf interment sitch that's dominating everyone else's attention.

Together we cross the mausoleum—me at a brisk trot because I'm worried about Mordred, V sauntering with a definite sway in his sexy hips. Sadly, his overall effect is kinda wasted. Mordred's powerful body is all hunched up, hugging his knees and trying not to shiver.

When the beam of my flashlight plays over the kraken, Mordred flinches, then looks up through a curtain of sweat-damp blue hair. Behind his forked beard, his face turns savage with need. His purple eyes devour us with a naked hunger that makes my core clench.

"Yo, baby queen. Time to mosey, right?" That demon bluffs it out and tries to stand, but the guy has to sit down again in a hurry.

Fuck me.

Not good.

He's so dizzy with mating fever he can't even stand.

"Yeah, no. We're just gonna hang here a little longer." I hunker down next to him (the closer the better) and make my voice as gentle as possible, because anything V says is not likely to be sympathetic. "It's okay, Mordred. Vasili and me, we're both alphas. We know what to do for mating fever."

"Lucky you." V unbuttons his uniform blazer in a slow tease and smirks down at the demon. "This is about to become one of those days you write about in your sex diary, darling."

Chapter Twenty-Four
Vasili

I don't bother saying it, but that sex demon isn't the only one who's about to get lucky.

I'm placing myself at the top of that list.

Clearly, Zara's still ovulating. By now, she might actually be pregnant. Lord knows, Max and Lucius and I—all her alphas—have barely had our dicks out of her succulent cunt in days. Now, with the luscious additional prospect of incubus sex looming, even if only for medicinal purposes (obviously)?

Under that pert schoolgirl skirt, my little queen is dripping with last night's warlock spunk and a fresh river of her own slick. How do I know?

I know because she's Zara.

Also, because my darling girl's scrumptious peaches-and-cream mating scent is drenching this entire catacomb with the most delicious *mélange* of pheromones.

Truly, she's never been riper and more fertile than she is at this moment. My inner dragon snarls in hungry anticipation.

Speaking of dragons.

I'm nearly certain Maxim, at least, has managed to plant a pea in our girl's pod. For him, getting Zara pregnant is literally the pinnacle of a lifelong ambition.

But a dragon shifter queen, like a cat, can carry fertilized eggs from multiple mates. God knows, I don't intend to stop fucking Zara until her womb is stuffed to bursting with little Vasilis and Vasilisas (the female version of my name).

If I play this right, we might even slip a sweet little Vasilisa Lucia Gemini bun into Zara's thoroughly preheated oven right here and now.

"Yeah, you should tap that, if she's down for it," Mordred says to me gruffly, still huddled at my feet in a manner that's both promising and worrisome. "You and Lucius both. Me, I can wait."

With a start, I realize that demon is reading my mind. He's no natural telepath and neither am I. But we're linked through our mating bond.

Exactly as I *meant* us to be linked when I bit him.

Even though my secret motive for summoning and biting him—to rid this harem of our odious common rival, the Dark Fae King—no longer seems quite so pressing.

"Lucius is otherwise occupied at the moment. But fear not, sweet demon. I'm entirely capable of fucking both of you." I grace Mordred with my sultry smirk. "Since you're both in need. Zara, darling, why don't you go first?"

Zara gives me her own sidelong grin, because of course she loves it when I let my alpha out. But her immediate priority, very clearly, is Mordred.

She drops to sit beside him on the ledge, back propped against the gloomy Roman-era sarcophagus that presumably holds the bones of some tedious witching world ancestor. Above her long stockings, her skirt rides high to expose her tanned thighs.

While Mordred and I both leer at all that deliciously exposed leg, she strokes his hair back gently to inspect his bite. Even from six feet away in a shadowy tomb, my twin punctures, inflamed and angry, stand out against his corded throat.

When the demon flinches at her gentle touch, my heart gives a highly unsnakelike lurch.

Dear fuck.

Clearly, Mordred isn't the only one sensing the insidious tug of a mating bond snapping into place.

I just hope I'm not catching, well, *feelings*.

Being irrevocably in love with one witch and our multiple warlocks is dangerous enough. Literally the last thing I need is to add this incubus to my enemies' hit list of not-so-secret Goblin King vulnerabilities.

"Easy there, Aquaman," Zara croons at the demon to soothe him while she inspects his bite. "I'm just looking."

"'S'okay," Mordred mumbles, head hanging. "You should fuck your alpha. I can wait."

He says it like someone who's resigned to waiting. Like someone who's used to it. Like someone who's been waiting his whole life to be someone's—*anyone's*—first choice.

Well, he isn't wrong. Even I didn't bite him for his own sake.

I bit him to help Zara, but also (secretly) to help *me*.

To help me get rid of Zephyr.

Now, *most* inconveniently, an unexpected shoot of… sympathy… for this infernal creature unfurls in the depths of my black and twisted heart.

Yes, sympathy. Even kinship.

Because, until Ronin and Zara and the others came along, I was never anyone's first choice either.

I'm still looming over them, startled by my extremely rare moment of selfless understanding, when Zara says gently, "Yeah, no, we're not waiting, Mordred. You need this right now."

As delicate and deadly as that terrifying feline concealed like a weapon in Neo's duffel, Zara leans in to sweep her tongue up the sex demon's throat.

Right over his inflamed bite.

A low baritone groan rumbles from his bare chest. It's a resonant sound, laced with profound relief and aching hunger.

"That's it," she whispers, licking his bite in long slow swipes like melting ice cream on a scorching summer day. "Feels good, doesn't it?"

"You have *no* idea," the demon moans.

He's leaning into her touch, aided by the hand she's resting on his shoulder and the other she has wrapped in his hair. His hands clutch the stone ledge between his knees as though he—the notorious incubus—is afraid to touch her in return.

"Mmmm, I do though. I know how you feel." Zara nuzzles her face into his neck and really starts working on those punctures I've given him, bathing them in the healing biochemicals of her shifter saliva. "I have mating bites from all my alphas."

"Some more than others," I remind her with a diabolical chuckle. I've bitten Zara multiple times and have no intention of stopping.

I prop my combat boot on the ledge, angle my flashlight so the lovebirds aren't directly spotlit for the whole catacomb, and lounge comfortably against the sarcophagus to enjoy the show.

"Yeah, V's always a little extra." Zara lifts her head long enough to stick out her tongue at me, which makes me gasp in outrage. But her attention returns at once to the demon. "Long story short? We know how to make you feel better."

This time, when she leans into Mordred's bite, her wicked hand trails down his bare chest, over the washboard ripple of his abs, to settle on his muscled thigh.

Mordred groans again, knees falling open in blatant invitation. My, my. He's packing *quite* the boner under those indecent crotch-hugging trousers. In fact, that trouser snake he's packing is so massive it's practically an anaconda.

My mouth literally waters in anticipation.

Zara's teasing him, the little flirt, prolonging the anticipation for all of us while she ministers to his mating bite. The furrow of pain between his brows has smoothed, his eyes have fallen shut, and one tiny fang presses into his full lower lip.

But he clutches the ledge as though he'll drown if he loses his grip.

"For fuck's sake, demon," I point out to him, "you're allowed to touch her."

"Yeah, what he said." Zara snuggles her hot little body into his side. "In fact, it's encouraged."

She punctuates this suggestion by caressing the tip of his pointed half-Fae ear.

That's all it takes, really.

The demon explodes into motion. His hands close around her waist, swing her into the air, and drag her into his lap so she's straddling his hips.

Zara yelps in surprise, then purrs in approval. Her knees close around his hips. Her arms wind around his neck. Their mouths meet in a searing kiss.

I've already been enjoying this little performance. Now even I'm caught off guard by the deep throb of arousal that wraps around my dick and squeezes.

To use Zara's turn of phrase, either that demon is sexing us up...

Or the ancient fertility artifact strapped to his delicious beefcake body is having a moment.

Still tucked into his messenger bag, the Horn of Ceres is pressed between their bodies. Mordred's brawny arms engulf Zara's waist, tattooed scales ink-black in the near dark, and pull her into his broad chest.

The saucy minx moans and undulates into him, grinding her cunt into his dick. Her plaid skirt rides up her hips to reveal the lime-green lace of her boy-cut briefs, hugging the ripe globes of her *derrière*. The sweet tang of peaches and cream floods the air, mingled with the buttery aroused incubus aroma of saltwater taffy.

Under my uniform trousers, my dick swells and rises like a fucking blimp. I barely retain enough of my Goblin King mind to switch off the damn flashlight.

The catacomb's thick darkness drops around us like a curtain, concealing us from the distant others, all gathered and murmuring around the yawning black mouth of an open vault on burial duty in a wavering bubble of electric light.

Not that we'd mind the rest of our polycule watching. But McSnicker and her men (especially her traumatized werewolf) should be spared the soon-to-be-naked-and-wildly-fucking sight of us.

The distant beams of the others' flashlights offer just enough light for my keen shifter senses to follow the action unfolding at my feet. Zara has her sweet face tucked right into the demon's neck, sucking on his bite with an avid determination that ought to earn her brownie points for community service in Lucius' gradebook (if he were watching).

Mordred is groaning with relief and rising need, dry-humping her through his trousers and her panties. Over her shoulder, his wild purple eyes lock on mine and smolder into my riveted stare.

"She feels so fucking good," he says thickly, "imma come in my pants."

"Well, I certainly know the feeling." I smirk down at him. "But what a waste that would be."

"You just gonna watch? Or…" His gaze roams down the length of my tall body, taking his time, and fixes on my interested dick "…join?"

My own need is indeed straining. My inner dragon (very male at the moment) is coiling under my skin like a cobra. Of course, sometimes I *do* like to watch.

But that won't be nearly enough to satisfy.

Not this time.

I slip out of my uniform blazer and let it drop. While the demon drinks in every move, I pop my Academy cufflinks, one by one. Leisurely, button by button, I open my crisp French shirt to expose my slim torso, pale in the shadows, and watch his eyes ignite.

"Hells' bells," he scrapes out. "You're a tease. I fucking knew it."

"Well, naturally." I saunter up behind Zara and slip into place between the demon's spread knees to purr in her ear. "Zara, darling, you're wearing far too many clothes. Take everything off, *do*. Quickly. Or I'll do it for you… my way."

I punctuate my polite request by sliding the pocketknife from my trousers and thumbing it open with a *snick!*

My girl's teal head snaps up from the demon's neck. Her startled face turns toward me. "Oh, no you don't, Goblin King. No knives! I'm down to my last pair of panties. No knives till we get back to the *domus*."

I admire the wicked edge of my blade. "I'll be the judge of that."

Zara's half-laughing and sultry with arousal, eyes glowing periwinkle like pinwheels, mouth swollen and breathless with kisses. I can't resist the urge to swoop down and claim one for myself. Not one of my swift snakebites that leaves her gasping, but a deep claiming kiss that plunders her hot silky depths to make her moan. She even tastes like peaches, her entire fertile body priming her for mating, overlaid with a burnt taffy taste that's new.

"Hmmm," I breathe into her mouth. "Is that the taste of sex demon?"

"Mmm-hmm." The minx's tongue dances around mine. "You like?"

"Oh, I like." Finally, I turn from my girl's succulent mouth to find *his*.

This demon I've more or less added to her harem.

I kiss him before he can "rizz me up," to use his line, with all that infernal incubus charisma. I snake out a hand to circle his beefy throat, tighten my grip to choke him, and kiss him when he opens his mouth to protest.

His sleek blue beard is smooth as silk. His full lips are soft and sweet as Zara's. He tastes like her too, like peaches drizzled with taffy. But the raw hunger that surges from his kiss is all potent male. His tongue meets mine in a slick lick that sends fire streaking through every synapse I possess.

I hiss in approval, tighten my grip on his throat, and deepen the kiss.

Just so he'll know who's directing this little production.

His hard hands, callused as a construction worker's, push inside my open shirt and slide roughly over my ribs. Pressed against my front, Zara wiggles desperately to unbutton her blouse and slip out of it before I can slice it open with the knife I'm still holding, quite deliberately, where she can see the blade.

Of course, the threat of my knife would be far more effective if she didn't already know, to the marrow of her bones, that I'm psychotically in love with her. As a result, Zara hasn't been properly terrified of despicable me—her horrible alpha—in quite some time.

The price we pay for love.

Trapped between the three of us, buffeted by our writhing bodies, the Horn of Ceres pulses like a beating heart. It's a pulse I can feel with every one of my warlock senses, a heartbeat I can hear thudding through my skin. Under my trousers, my engorged cock weeps with need.

All the while Mordred, the naughty boy, sucks on my tongue like it's my dick. Still throttling his throat, I hum to encourage him and shift my knife to tease the waistband of Zara's skirt.

"Don't you dare. I mean it, you snake!" Indignant but still laughing, Zara pushes Mordred flat on his back (which breaks our kiss), nudges my menacing knife aside, and gives us all a moment to adjust.

With my strangling grip finally dislodged from his throat, Mordred seizes his moment to suck in a shaky breath.

Zara seizes her moment to reach under her skirt and slip demurely out of her panties.

I seize mine by unclasping her bra from behind with a casual flick.

Even though I really *do* want to use my knife.

That lacy scrap of lime-green lingerie flutters to the floor.

Mordred sprawls on his back, a moveable feast of bulging pecs and deltoids and abdominal six-pack sheened with sweat, wild blue hair flung over the stone beneath him. When his gaze devours our queen's exposed breasts, his wicked eyes turn savage with hunger.

Still wearing her saucy schoolgirl skirt and stockings, Zara kneels between his legs and slides her hands up his thighs.

The demon blinks rapidly and looks like he's struggling to find his words. "Uh… before you go there… I should prolly tell you…"

"No more talking." I slip out of my own shirt, let it fall where it will, and press myself against the graceful line of my darling girl's spine. My arms slither around her tiny waist and my hands close around the lush fullness of her breasts.

Zara moans in my arms, her head falling back against my shoulder. Her tits fill my palms and spill over my cupped fingers in the most delectable way, a glorious abundance of soft curves and satiny skin. Her pierced nipples, ripe as cherries, are particularly sensitive during her superheats. Especially when I twist her little silver rings the way I know she adores.

"Oh, fuck me, that's hot," the demon rasps. "Like skibbidi hot."

"So pleased you approve. Shall I show you what she truly likes?" I grin down at him and let my fangs show, in a way that's new for me. I've spent my entire life thinking my snakelike incisors are freakish. A carnival sideshow of the grotesque. At the very least, an unfortunate flaw to be hidden.

But for some reason, my fangs make Zara wet and all our warlocks hard.

"Yeah. That's what I want." The demon arches his spine and writhes in the most delicious abandon. Especially when Zara's hands reach the juncture of his thighs. "But, hells, baby queen—"

"Whoa." This comes from Zara, who's just cupped a hand over the demon's considerable bulge. "Um, Mordred…"

"That's what I'm trying to tell you," he groans from the heart. "Fuuuuck…"

When she bends intently over him and starts simultaneously groping and kneading, like she's absorbing the contours of his anatomy and can't believe what she's finding, his head falls back and his eyes fall shut.

Well, I've had more than enough of this.

With a huff of impatience, I stop tormenting my girl's exquisitely sensitive nipples (temporarily), grip the demon's trousers in my ruthless hands, and drag them down his hips.

In the near darkness, his bush blazes blue, a thick forest of indigo (not exactly a shocker, after Zephyr's green pubes).

What is a shocker, absolutely, is the thick curving dick that rises from his blue lagoon like a long-necked brontosaurus rising from the swamp. Or more precisely, the second dick immediately beneath, nearly as large as the first, rearing taut and proud above his swollen ball sack.

"Dear fuck," I say blankly, stripped of all my wiles. "You're diphallic."

Because you don't live for twenty-three years as a gay boy, darling—at least, *I* didn't—without harboring a few secret fantasies about someday stumbling across a double-header. Or knowing what to call the phenomenon, if you should ever be so lucky.

"Cheese on toast," Zara breathes. My little darling sounds positively awestruck. "Mordred. Either I'm suddenly seeing double or… you literally have two dicks."

"Been trying to tell you, no cop," Mordred says meekly. "It's a kraken thing. Bottom one hides in a coital slit when I don't need him. But, uh, when I'm horny…"

"They both come out to play," I finish for him.

In unison, Zara and I lean forward in shared fascination. I rest my chin on her silky bare shoulder, cradle her luscious tits in my palms, and simply enjoy the view.

One kraken.

Two dicks.

Both fully erect and rising from that thicket of wiry blue curls, both nearly too girthy to wrap my hand around. Copper skin flushed violet with need, thick shafts threaded with swollen veins I ache to trace with my tongue. Precum beading both velvety crowns.

I leave it to Zara to voice the question we're both burning to ask.

She sucks in a breath and gamely takes the plunge. "Do they both work, like, independently?"

"This ain't a show-and-tell." The demon winks and grins at both of us in a way that makes his dimples pop. "One way to find out, bae."

Belatedly, with a jolt of comprehension, I recognize this creature's constant banter for precisely what it is.

A defense mechanism.

He's horribly afraid we're going to reject him—or, at the very least, fetishize him like a sex toy—for his apparent *deformity*. Which is probably the reaction he's been confronting his whole life.

Secretly, I experience another unexpected twinge of… sympathy… perhaps even compassion… for this freakish half-shifter that I find deeply unsettling.

Fortunately, my darling Zara knows just what to do. She takes this bomb-shell (or should I say sex bomb? I snicker) of revelation fully in stride.

Without missing a beat, she says easily, "Okay, Aquaman. You have mating fever, I'm in heat, and V's raging hard-on is poking me in the butt. Fair to say we're up for the challenge."

"Yeet." The demon leers at both of us. "Imma try not to disappoint, for real."

But I'm watching him too closely to be deceived by his juvenile Gen Alpha swagger.

Now that I'm alert to this creature's little deceptions, I can read like newsprint, from the way his jaw unknots and the lines of strain ease around his eyes, his profound relief that we're neither freaked out nor repulsed.

In fact, we're the opposite.

Although, truly, he's holding his breath to see if that changes.

Nimbly Zara scrambles to straddle the demon's hips. Then she reaches beneath her, with both hands, for his dicks.

Chapter Twenty-Five
Zara

"Sweet Jesus," I whisper. "If I'm dreaming, do *not* wake me up."

Straddling Mordred's hips under my naked crotch, I've got both hands wrapped around his thick dicks, currently jutting between my spread thighs like he's the yoke of a 747 twisting into a turn and I'm his pilot. Both his cocks are cola-can thick—especially the bigger one on top that doesn't retract into the coital slit tucked above the plump fullness of his scrotum. I'm gripping a solid ten inches up top and a very respectable eight down below. Under all that velvety skin, his dicks pulse and swell against my fingers.

In fact, his entire body radiates heat like a burning ember. The copper skin stretched over slabs of pectoral muscle and the taut flex of six-pack abs is glistening with sweat.

That's mating fever. He's unwell. He needs this.

Just call me Florence fucking Nightingale.

I fist both dicks until the demon groans and writhes between my legs.

"Don't be greedy, little queen," V purrs in my ear. "I want some too."

My snake's cool fingers slip between my thighs from behind and close over what I'm already thinking of as Mordred's back-door dick. Because the placement's gonna be perfect for that, like the genital spur on one of Ruby Dixon's yummy aliens in *Ice Planet Barbarians*.

Only bigger.

Mordred grins lazily (but also kinda shyly, which is totally adorable) at me and at V, who's peering over my shoulder. "No fighting, you two, for real. I got me enough baloney pony for both you cowboys to ride."

I bite my lower lip around a grin.

"Well, darling," V whispers in my ear, "are you ready to saddle up?"

Yee haw, my dragon queen purrs. Apparently, she's highly into the concept of kraken sex. And God knows, I am here for it.

Our shared enthusiasm startles a fizz of laughter from Vasili and *his* dragon through our mating bond. Aside from his trademark evil snicker, V rarely laughs.

When he does and it's real, it means he's happy.

Oh, hell to the yeah.

This sex demon with his hidden insecurities and double dicks might literally be the best thing that's happened to all of us since we flew back from Avalon and landed in the fucking shitstorm of this Dean's Challenge.

Literally. The best thing.

We're adding this guy to the harem.

I mean, assuming he wants that, and assuming the others (especially Zephyr) all agree.

My mind's made up to try, and it's not the double pleasure lurking in Mordred's Aquaman pants that did it.

It's the look in his eyes when I kissed him.

The same look I'm seeing now.

Under all that John Wayne swagger and saucy banter, this tattooed, hot-as-hellfire sex demon is just a guy trying to find a place he can call home. A home and maybe a family that loves him. A family he can finally love back.

These are all things we can give him.

Our polycule has an agreement that we can add to my harem, it's a queen thing, and it's healthy for the witching world. Still, I feel like I can't make any promises, not without the others consulted and fully on board.

Especially Zephyr.

But there's definitely one thing I can give that kraken right now.

I relinquish Mordred's back-door dick to V's tender mercies and wrap both my hands around the kraken's dominant joystick. Burning with need and fever, his shaft fills my palms to overflowing, like my fingers can barely close around his girth. His fat cockhead is flushed violet with craving.

When I rub my thumb over his slit, precum spurts against my skin.

"Hells, baby queen. Just like that." Breath rough and uneven, Mordred engulfs my thighs in his big hands to steady both of us as I work him over.

Between my legs, under my uniform skirt, I'm fucking drenched. He's huge, but my titanium pussy can take him.

I try to clear my head and think. "Uh, so, incubus. Are you the kind that practices safe sex? Because the guys and me, we're exclusive, so we don't—"

"I'm half Unseelie. I don't catch mortal diseases or carry 'em." The demon's clever eyes drift over my tits to the weeping pussy that's barely covered by my skirt. "And you're already knocked up, true?"

"Uh, that's a maybe. We gotta take the test to know." I study him, all sexed up and ready to rumble. Most guys'll say anything to get in my pants at this point, especially with me having extra and totally involuntary "powers of attraction" since I claimed the Unseelie Queen's crown.

But hasn't Mordred already proven we can trust him?

"Soooo…" I decide to make the implicit explicit. "What you're saying is, no condom required?"

"We'd all better be quite certain," V observes, sharp fangs nuzzling into my neck in a way that makes me shiver. "You're very fertile."

"Kinda a long shot that *I'm* fertile. A lotta krakens ain't. Endangered species for that exact reason, true?" By now, Mordred's blatantly undressing me with his eyes. "But my boy would be into your dragon—both your dragons. My kraken, he's pan too."

My nipples are still swollen and tingling from V's cruel attentions. Having Mordred watch me with that smoldery look in his swarthy face makes my dragon purr and my body hum.

When my snake nudges me forward from behind, my skirt flips up to expose my bare ass.

"My, my." V's attention veers abruptly from Mordred's two dicks to my own back door. The reason I know is because V nips the curve of my ass in a way that makes me yelp. Then he drags his snaky tongue up my crack, from my perineum to my tingling pucker, in a long slow tease.

My eyes drift closed, my cunt clenches, and an aching moan slips out.

If my hole could blush, it definitely would.

"Suddenly," the Goblin King purrs into my rosebud of sensitive, nerve-packed skin, "we have an absolute smorgasbord of options. I do believe I'd like to see our demon double-dicking you, darling. Since I'm not diphallic myself."

Through the sex-drenched haze that's hijacked my brain, I need a sec to work out what he's saying.

"You're gonna break Mordred's fever with your alpha shifter

spunk," I say finally, for all of us. "While he simultaneously fills both my holes and fucks me."

"Oh, fucking hells." Mordred's hands tighten on my thighs. His hungry face ignites with need. "I'm *so* down."

"Sounds like that's good then, Goblin King. That's real good." I glance over my shoulder at V. "So, uh, while you're back there…"

"I'll get you ready to ride, cowgirl. Never fear." My dominant alpha is more than the Goblin King. He's also the rim job king. His tongue circles and teases and pokes my quivering pucker and generally works me open with a thoroughness that makes me come apart.

Under V's teasing tongue, my rosebud softens and my bones dissolve in a way that has me writhing against the swollen length of Mordred's front dick. The slick folds of my cunt engulf the kraken's pulsing shaft. I rock my hips and frot along Mordred's length, audible moisture sucking with every stroke. Every time the kraken's cockhead nudges my clit, fireworks pulse in my core and my pussy ripples.

With a growled curse, Mordred unzips my skirt, pulls it over my head, and tosses it aside. That way, he gets an unimpeded view of my naked thighs bracketed in his possessive grip. Of my plump pink love petals, flushed and glistening with hunger, sliding along the stem of his ruddy cock.

All without interrupting what V's doing to me back there.

"She's ready for you, demon," V finally hisses against my thoroughly soaked back door. His saliva drizzles down the backs of my thighs. "And so am I."

When V pulls away, I whine with disappointment. But the buzz of his zipper placates me. My snake is stripping down behind me, which is never a bad thing.

Mordred's hands coast up my inner thighs so he can spread me open like a peach. My engorged clit pulses under his stare. He arches his back in a way that makes the vee of his Adonis belt flex. He's trying to shift our angle so his cock can get inside me. I angle my hips too, simultaneously teasing him and craving more clitoral stim.

Because he'll get off harder if I make him work for it.

And me?

Just color me desperate to get off.

Period.

The crinkle and tear of foil from V's vicinity makes my dragon chirp and the kraken snarl in recognition—a raw, hungry sound of pure animal need.

Leave it to Vasili to bring lube to our class finals.

Restless and edgy, Mordred shifts under me, trying simultaneously to fuck me and get his knees up so V can fully access the kraken's love canal.

By this point, things are moving really fast.

As I squirm against Mordred's thick dick, I try to clear my head long enough to check on the rest of our Scooby gang. A wild glance across the cavern tells me they've got the werewolf down from that awful cross. They're interring the dead king in one of these big sarcophagi lining the walls, in some way I'm trusting Lucius to make sure is sufficient to keep the werewolf king from *rising*.

I've got zero doubt my guys over there on interment duty—Neo, Lucius, and Zephyr—know exactly what we're doing over here in the dark.

But as long as we're quiet, Mallory and her guys can pretend not to know.

Anyway, those three (Mal and her warlocks) literally hooked up the first time during an orgy in their *domus* basement last semester. An orgy I instigated by accident with my first-ever mating heat. So it's not like anyone in this catacomb is gonna join the prude patrol at this late hour.

I just don't wanna disrespect Jae's grieving process.

Satisfied that we've got the basic level of privacy required to check the decency box, I turn back to Mordred and bend forward to lick my way up the demon's sculpted chest. Under waves of burning heat, his skin tastes salty like the sea, laced with that hint of spiced rum and burnt taffy.

I tongue his nipple and nuzzle him with my shifty incisors to make him gasp. Not all guys like that, because even vestigial nipples can be sensitive. But I'm really glad this guy does.

"Hells, Zara," he grunts, chest heaving. "Have a little mercy. Either fuck me or kill me."

I'm nothing if not a merciful queen. So, finally, I give in.

I wiggle my greedy pussy over the broad head of his cock. Slowly, because he's a lot to take in, I sink down his shaft, inch by throbbing inch, cunt stretching and pulsing around his thickness. I sink down and down, head tipped back and moaning with effort, till his crown bumps my cervix.

Still swimming in the sea of my own mating heat, I can practically feel my uterus opening like a flower to welcome a nice fresh cum shower from the neighborhood kraken to seed my fertile womb.

"Oh, fuuuuuck," Mordred groans from the heart.

His cock pulses against my slick walls like a heartbeat. Inside the shell of my skin, my inner dragon spreads her wings in a scream of triumph.

Cheese on toast. She's claiming another king.

"Ssshhh," I whisper to everyone. "We gotta be quiet."

Even though I'm feeling pretty shivery and like I wanna give a good yell myself.

"Mmph," Mordred says into the palm I've pressed over his noisy mouth.

Still encased in the kraken's sealskin pouch, the Horn of Ceres juts into my hip like another dick. I swear the thing radiates its own heat. By now, every sensation in my body seems uber-heightened.

Mordred's feverish heat searing down my front.

The desperate clench of my cunt rippling around his cock.

The cool slick of lube drizzling over my pucker.

The deft glide of V's finger dipping inside to prep me.

Then the hard hot press of dick—Mordred's extra—knocking on my back door. My lubed-up channel tightens in resistance, but V's cool hands work all that girth past the constriction. Mordred's back-door dick slips through the tight ring of my sphincter with a pop that triggers a giddy endorphin rush.

Given the potent pheromone cocktail of V's Mogadon mating scent mingled with mine that we've all been quaffing since we started, that extra kick of adrenaline almost takes the top of my head off.

Fuck. Me. Sideways.

The surge of demon dick… both dicks… fills me sooooo full. Especially when those two dicks start pumping me in unison.

"Sweet… fucking… *hell*," I gasp, hand falling away from his mouth. "Mordred."

"All yours, baby queen." His eyes burn into mine like purple coals. "Yours and his."

"Hmmm. Duly noted." V's slim hands knead my ass as I ride Mordred's pony. Vasili is clearly enjoying the rear view of my double reaming, his own arousal coiling and twisting through our mating bond like a den of vipers.

Heat or no heat, Horn or no Horn, this perfectly choreographed double fuck feels so good my eyes cross.

So good I can't see straight.

So good I can barely talk.

So good I can barely even think.

God knows, in our polycule, I'm used to multiple dicks. But not from the same guy.

Thankfully, this demon knows how to follow a beat.

Mordred doesn't falter. He gives me exactly what I need, hands pulling me forward into his chest, my ass in the air, rocking me into his pistoning cocks in a relentless rhythm that grazes the engorged nub of my clit on every thrust. He doesn't even falter when V uses the rest of that lube on his own pretty cock, presses Mordred's knees right up against my ass, and gets the kraken's back door ready for a visit from the Goblin King.

This kinda care from both of us is exactly what Mordred needs.

Under our combined attentions, that sex demon falls apart. He's a sweating, swearing, moaning, thrusting, writhing hot mess of a man. That beefcake body of his flexing and bunching and thrusting like a piledriver between my legs. Our dominant alpha lurking behind me as he pins Mordred's knees against my ass and methodically and ruthlessly fucks Mordred into a sex coma.

Multiple orgasms stutter through us like seismic tremors. The first big O wrenched out of Mordred by the strangling clutch of my ass around his rear cock. His second one moments later, when his monster dick spurts and floods my cunt with oceans of kraken seed. Running through the whole show like an undertow is V's relentless reaming of the kraken from behind...

Let's just say: we get the job done.

Really thoroughly.

I break into a million pieces in a climax that spins through me like a tornado, with my teeth locked around Mordred's beefy shoulder, moaning into the wedge of his trapezius muscle, the teal cloud of my hair swirling around us and purple sparks crackling from my fingers.

V dissolves into his own gasping climax and droops over my back like a swooning Victorian, wrapping Mordred and me both in his arms, purring with satisfaction and nuzzling breathless goblin kisses into the side of my neck.

Mordred breaks his mating fever shuddering and groaning my name, buried deep in my body, rooted deeper in my soul.

With his shoulder sporting the bloody half-moon crescent of a fresh mating bite.

My bite.

The bite I never meant to give him.

We're keeping him, okay? I whisper sheepishly through our mating bond to V and all my guys, eyes closed and head cradled on the kraken's heaving chest. *I guess V had the right idea, biting him in the first place. Sorry I made such a fuss.*

Under my cheek, the kraken's finally cool to the touch.

Thank fuck.

Across the catacomb, I vaguely realize, Jae's chanting what sounds like a prayer in Cajun French over the sealed vault that holds the werewolf king, while the others attend in respectful silence. Under that singsong murmur, Lucius' careful reply whispers through our bond.

Zara, my dear, concerning the kraken... we'll have to see. Let's revisit the matter after we complete the Dean's Challenge.

I heave a sigh but don't press it. Because I know my headmaster is right.

Hidden in the shadows except for a glitter of emerald dragonscale and the gleam of a cold jade eye, Zephyr is watching.

And brooding.

As I struggle to pull my spinning head together and fumble around to find my discarded clothes in the dark, I do my best to convince myself that silent scrutiny from the Dark Fae King is anything but ominous.

Chapter Twenty-Six
Maxim

"They are very late," I mutter to Ronin in the dark. "Zara and all our mates. We expected them hours ago."

"Tell me about it," Ronin mutters back.

It is now past midnight. Something has very clearly gone wrong.

We are huddled in the dark—Ronin, Ash, and myself—in the open tower of the belfry in the gothic cathedral that houses the Icarus Academy. My skull is still ringing from the sonorous *bong!* of the vast church bell at my back, tolling the witching hour with its deafening peels.

From here, we watched helplessly as a clueless contingent of students from House Hadrian—the ones Vasili calls Hufflepuffs—were caught and captured by Cleo's house. Those Hufflepuffs are still searching the seas for the Horn, because they do not know Zara has it. They were sneaking off in a borrowed boat from Racetrack's dive shop in the harbor when they were found and captured.

Cleo's crew did not even need to bother. These Hufflepuffs are so far behind, they will never win.

But those bullies from our rival house—House Tiberius, Cleo's bootlickers—they did it for spiteful pleasure.

Simply to shatter the others' hopes.

And to cause them pain.

Now the victims are in the school infirmary, being treated for second degree burns. All injuries incurred when a Tiberius warlock used his witchcraft to set the dive boat on fire.

This much, Racetrack told us herself, when she and Dez met us at our *rendezvous* spot. Then our two housemates hastened to the *domus* for spell ingredients and privacy, where Dez is cobbling together various magics, including a counter curse to block an immolation hex.

I know it is pointless to ask, but my dragon is restless, and I must. "Ronin. Our mates. Can you still not sense them?"

Sprawled on the ledge over a bone-breaking drop to the cobblestone piazza far below, sleek and deadly in his catsuit, with one long leg swinging over the abyss, Ronin levels me with a tawny-eyed look that simmers with impatience.

"Not with that bloody nullifying object in play." He grimaces. "At this point, I can barely sense *you*, love. Tells me either that wanker Xiao or Vasili's old man—maybe both—must be close. They're the only ones we know who use that shit."

Hopefully I emerge from the stairwell where I am lurking.

The choir loft directly below us, which holds the school library with its collection of rare and arcane books, is our blind spot. I am guarding these stairs to keep Ronin safe (and also Ash, because I know Zara loves him and has chosen him for our harem).

"Then our sovereign and our mates must be close now, yes?" I venture, tingling with adrenaline and aggression. "Since Cleo's men are hunting them, and *they* are close."

"That's what I figure, yeah." This quiet contribution comes from Ash.

The Seelie Prince is standing on the ledge, as far from Ronin as he can manage (which is typical), with his magnificent pewter wings fully manifested and shimmering with rain. They spread from his muscled shoulders to billow gently in the night breeze. He stands like an archangel, sculpted and vast, with the circlet of thorns tattooed around his biceps weeping crimson ink like blood, ready to drive all the devils back to hell.

To my keen dragonish senses, his spiky hair gleams pewter—like a halo—in the rain-washed night.

Ash has just returned from scouting on the wing. This was a fruitless maneuver since our mates are still absent and he has learned nothing. But he too is restless. At least, he is well concealed from hostile eyes by the misty drizzle that shrouds the island tonight. His return has tangibly heightened the tension in this belfry, because he has never liked Ronin.

It is a sentiment of which Ronin, who is no fool even if his telepathy cannot penetrate Fae minds, is well aware.

"Saint Sergius guard us." I abandon my post in the stairwell to pace, growling and circling the vast bulk of the hanging bell. My accent thickens when I am agitated, so I must concentrate on my English. "They have taken too long. There is trouble. Who threatens our mates!"

Ash stirs and retracts his wings with a sigh. He is currently shirtless and dripping with rain, so the wings fold visibly into his corded back, where they melt to form the impressive angel wing tattoo that spreads across his shoulders. "Let's not get twitchy on that trigger finger, Max. Just checked on Xhevith, didn't I?"

"And so?" My dragon lurks in my voice, fully roused and alarmed by any hint of danger to our queen.

"Big green guy's right where we left him," Ash says patiently. "Waiting to do his thing just like we planned, all snoozy and fed and quiet. If anything went sideways with Sparrow, he wouldn't be. That dragon would be taking the roof off."

Ronin pushes up to sit, careless of the steep drop beside him. He sweeps back his banner of inky hair, loose and swirling magnificently in the wind, with a scowl. "Hate to say it, but the winged wonder's got a point. Besides, if anything happened to *any* of them—any of our mates— I'd bloody well know it. Null or no null."

"No offense, but I trust Xhevith's bond with Sparrow more than I trust your *feelings*." The Seelie Prince sounds very measured, but he looks as though he is seriously considering pushing Ronin and his feelings off the roof.

"Bothers you, doesn't it?" Ronin swings one shitkicker boot over the abyss and skewers Ash with a piercing stare. "You being the only bloke in this belfry without a mating bite? The only one who can't sense her. Even Zeph's dragon has an empathic link to his rider."

I tense to intervene if I must, but there is no need. Ash stands his ground and says calmly, "Yeah, well, I'm Fae, not shifter. We don't do mating bites. No offense, Max."

"None is taken," I reply.

His quarrel has never been with me, nor mine with him.

He is new to our queen's harem, he is Zephyr's official consort, but Ash is not yet fully part of our polycule. He is easy company, easy to live with, easy on the eyes, yet I do not... desire him. Not the way I desire Zara and Vasili and Ronin and Neo and Lucius. Ours is a desire whose intensity grows and deepens steadily with time.

But I am interested and pleased to see that Neo has claimed this Seelie. I suppose that, if Ash fully joins our family, I too will bed him. Especially if my bedding him pleases Zara.

But only if he causes no trouble for Ronin.

If he tries to hurt Ronin, I will slay Ash myself.

Still, this Seelie Prince seems an honorable man, and he has promised Zephyr to make his peace with Ronin. Ash does not need to love Ronin, so long as he keeps his distance. Instead, Ash eyes my restless pacing, around and around the bell.

The Seelie's next remark is meant for me. "Look, this whole setup sucks, don't I know it. But we gotta wait this thing out. When it comes to getting that Horn back in the Vault, we're only gonna get one shot."

My dragon snarls and rages, but I hold my beast in check. I prowl to the ledge and peer over the steeply sloped roofs of the darkened village, shining silver with rain through the mist. Over the midnight sea that laps our shores, the dark spear of the abandoned harbor lighthouse gleams like a bony finger.

I grip the ledge and scowl. "Where is the enemy queen? Cleopatra. Where? When we find her, she will be the first one I kill."

"Zara won't fancy that, love," Ronin says softly. "Yeah, Cleo betrayed her, but they were family once. Our girl has a soft heart. She still loves the bitch. If Cleo gives way on the whole queen bit, if she accepts her loss and walks away? Zara will want us to let her live. Let bygones be bygones. Turn the other cheek, and all that rot."

While I growl ferociously at this foolish and dangerous notion, Ronin crawls along the ledge until he is directly before me. Then he sits up, puts his back to the drop, and swings a leg around so his legs bracket mine. His hot Leo hands come to rest on my waist.

This entire placement is one I do not mind.

"You and me, Max, we'll keep our girl safe." The dark familiar spice of his ambergris fragrance mingles with the scorched brimstone of my dragon and his mating scent. "If Cleo doesn't toe the line and bend the knee, she's dog's meat."

I growl in agreement, wrap my arms around my mate's waist to keep him safe from the drop, and bury my face in his neck to nuzzle his mating scars. Lucius was the first to bite him, and kissing the scars Lucius gave him—while Ronin shudders with pleasure in my arms—makes me feel closer to both of them.

If Lucius wishes it, when this revolution is over and we have won and our precious sovereign is safe, I too will welcome Lucius' bite—

"Ever met anyone you can't seduce, Pendragon?" Ash's dry tone makes us both twitch. "Must be nice to be you."

I tighten my arms around Ronin in warning, because my mate can be savage when threatened, and Zara has asked them not to quarrel.

Ronin merely perches his chin on my shoulder to gaze at Ash and says lazily, "Well, mate, there's you. Haven't popped your cherry yet, have I?"

Ash's laugh sounds startled.

Clearly Ronin's reply has caught him off guard.

After a moment, Ash answers in a casual tone. "Yeah, you're a couple decades too late to be my first anything. I'm twice your age easy, kid. And then some."

"Old man then." Ronin muses. "And you're a bottom, even for Neo. Could almost like you for that, by the way. Bit of fun to see our boy Red on top for once."

"Nothing you can't give him yourself. You're real versatile." Even while he downplays what might well be the first decent words Ronin has ever said to him, Ash ambles to stand at my side.

Though he is new to the harem, Ash knows me well enough not to stand behind me, where I am always twitchy and protective of my scarred back.

I am still standing with my arms around Ronin's waist, his knees bracketing my hips, my face buried in his neck. Now I try to straighten, but Ronin curls a hand around my head and tucks my face back into his neck.

My dragon voices a pleased and possessive rumble, deep in my chest. My palate tingles and my incisors descend. But Ronin already wears my mating scars, so I content myself with palming my mate's tight ass and nipping his neck in warning.

If he will tease me, then he must be prepared to please me.

"Mmmm, fuck." Ronin sighs into my touch, but I can sense him watching Ash. "Like a bit of 'tie me up, tie me down' too, don't you, Ash? You're a right proper sub."

"And you're a switch. You swing both ways." Ash's tone is growing more guarded. "What kinda convo are we having right now?"

Ronin hitches one shoulder in a careless shrug. "That depends on you, doesn't it?" He pauses. "Zeph's birthday's coming up. Night of the summer solstice, innit?"

"Yeah. That's right." Now I can sense Ash's gaze upon us. He is watching Ronin's legs hook around mine, pushing Ronin's pelvis into mine in a way that sends hot blood rushing straight from my brain to my cock.

"Well, then," Ronin says, low and husky, because he knows the effect he is having upon all of us. "Think of it as a birthday gift for the bloke we both love. Maybe even a coronation gift for Zara."

Even with my face buried in Ronin's neck and my senses swimming with Ronin's scent, I can hear Ash's breath hitch.

"You got anything to say about that, Max?" Ash says warily. "Your guy hooking up with someone new? Dragon shifters are a pretty possessive bunch. Sure, Zara won't mind. Lucius is reasonable and we rub along. Even Beautiful and me…" He is speaking of Vasili "…I figure we can work something out."

Ronin snickers, because Vasili is our dominant alpha, and he has been gloating all semester about the night he Compelled Ash with his witchcraft and put him in a collar and leash.

I lift my face from Ronin's sexy neck and look soberly at Ash. "I do not own Ronin. It is his choice whom he fucks. But he will only fuck within the polycule. So that is a choice *you* must make, Asher, Eagle of the Air. Whether you will join us fully. Or whether you will always remain apart, on the edge of us and what we share, loving Zephyr and Zara only, and breaking our Neo's tender heart."

Ash studies me in return, with Ronin wrapped around me, my mate smoldering and heavy-lidded with arousal.

"How old are ya, dragon king?" the Seelie Prince says at last.

"I am twenty-one." I hesitate, but I am always honest, so I finish with a mutter. "Almost."

"And Pendragon not even twenty. Geez." Ash rubs a hard hand over his craggy face and sighs. "What any of you wanna do with an old guy like me… it's beyond me. But I'm in this thing ass-deep now, ain't I?"

"You are," I agree. "But it is still your choice."

"Okay then." He nods, but I am not certain whether this is his agreement to bed Ronin, or his acceptance of something less. "One thing at a time. Just gotta survive this hootenanny and get Zara's sweet ass planted on the throne, don't we? Then we'll see about the rest."

As though he has summoned them, the familiar thunk of Racetrack's combat boots sounds on the belfry stairs.

She is running.

I release Ronin and pivot with a growl rising in my throat.

Ronin leaps down from the ledge to stand at my shoulder. His hand cocks back like an American pitcher at the mound, golden psi fire already gathering in his palm. Ash plants himself at my other shoulder, solid as a tree, booted legs spread and ready.

For this moment, the three of us stand together.

Racetrack bursts into the belfry at a dead run, wiry legs churning under her plaid uniform skirt, worn leather jacket slung over one shoulder. Under the careless thatch of her short blond hair, her gray eyes burn with urgency.

"They're here," she announces. "Zara and the guys. And they got trouble. C'mon, we gotta motor."

Chapter Twenty-Seven
Zara

"Looks like trouble," Draco Mars says shortly. *"Fokk."*

"Tell me about it." I bunch together with my guys—Lucius on one side, Neo on the other—and peer into the spooky, cobwebby hole that yawns in the tunnel floor.

The echoing coil of the catacombs lurks behind us, twisting like intestines in a human gut. We navigated that shit with our flashlights, our shifty noses, and Mal's location spell leading us through the labyrinth like the thread in that Greek myth about Theseus and the Minotaur.

But these catacombs are vast, and winding our way through them took longer than I liked.

Way longer.

Last time we checked, the hands on Mal's wristwatch were both pointing straight up.

Midnight.

The witching hour.

Thanks to the handy stash of granola bars and bottled water in Mallory's well-stocked hall monitor backpack, we're still functional. But this whole time, I really haven't liked the idea of a zombie werewolf sealed in a sarcophagus back there, a werewolf whose whole presence on the island we still can't explain, maybe rising and pushing the heavy stone lid aside—

"Yeesh." Picking up the gruesome thought I must be broadcasting on all frequencies, Neo cuddles the kitten against his chest and tightens his arm around my waist. "We're gonna lay that poor werewolf properly to rest, babe, like with holy water and an actual priest. We just need to ace our finals first."

Not only pass them. But ace them.

That's so Neo.

"We will, First Boy." I nuzzle his warm cheek, all raspy with stubble. Then I stroke the kitten's sleek white head—we gotta name her, but we've been a little busy—and drop a kiss between her tiny tufted ears for luck.

The kitten blinks up at me with earnest green eyes. Very much like Neo's.

Finally, I entrust our new pet to our bookworm's gentle hands and step forward with a sigh. "Gimme that flashlight, will you, Lucius?"

My headmaster passes it over without comment. With all our beams converging on that hole like a police spotlight, his sherry-gold eyes are fixed there too with a pensive look I have no problem deciphering. This tunnel led us straight to it, like this is where we're meant to go. And there's a solid wall behind it, so we aren't going any farther.

But there's a narrow staircase beside us (also very dark and cobwebby) burrowed into the wall leading up.

Zephyr is already standing with one boot on the bottom stair, leaning into the pitch-black passage in a way that makes me uneasy.

He hasn't said a word since Mordred double-dicked me. Since I fucked his second cousin (once removed) without asking. My guys and I have an understanding that I can grow the harem, because that's a queen thing, and it's good for the witching world when I do. Still, Zephyr could have objected to me fucking his cousin—I wasn't hiding it, and I would've listened—but he didn't.

However, it's the historical scheming-to-usurp-Zephyr's-throne baggage, and not the tenuous blood tie between them, that's the real issue.

Zephyr hasn't spoken to V since the fuckfest either. Now I'm really hoping our medically necessary but mind-blowing threesome with the demon hasn't totally shattered the fragile new alliance between the Dark Fae King and the Goblin King.

"Xhevith," Zephyr breathes, in a voice deep with longing. "By the moon, my dragon is near. I can sense him. Surely this means Ash and Ronin and Maxim are also near, where I bade them to be."

"Well, the library's that way for sure." Mallory frowns dubiously at the stairs. "I can, you know, feel my sweater up there. And yeah, it's really close. But I think the Vault might be…"

"Down here," I agree with a sigh, hunkering down beside the shaft. "I think so too."

Mallory's feeling the pull of her personal item, but I'm feeling the pull of the Vault. Ever since Mordred and V and I hooked up, I've sensed the Horn of Ceres in that messenger bag brooding like a sentient presence, its power humming in my blood like a beehive.

The Horn wants to go *down*.

Wary, I aim my flashlight into the shaft. A few feet below, the beam dances over an expanse of dark water, black as ink.

Yay.

"Well, as you'll recall, I've been in the Vault before. I went in the front door, from the cathedral crypt near the faculty offices." Vasili levitates over the shaft and alights on the far side, then leans warily to peer in. "I can confirm there *is* a sort of underground spring in the Vault. Once you disarm the ossification spell on the front door, of course."

"As you well know, my dear, I typically prefer not to be reminded of your hair-raising, Codex-skirting indiscretions," Lucius murmurs, giving V a reproachful look. "But in this case, the fact that you've been in the Vault—albeit without my permission—is useful. Even I've never been allowed inside by the Dean."

Vasili glances up at him with a smirk. "I do have my uses, darling. I'm so pleased to hear you admit it."

Under his goatee, Lucius' face turns ruddy. He clears his throat and glances self-consciously at the students he's *not* fucking—Mal and her guys.

I'd normally enjoy the spectacle of V teasing our headmaster to make him blush. But right now? I'm kinda distracted.

I really don't like what I'm thinking—like, *at all*—but the Horn is humming so loud in my head I can barely hear anything else. So I know what I need to do.

Now I just need to convince the others.

My gaze shifts past Lucius' embarrassed face and Neo's—blinking and myopic without his glasses, but still one hundred percent beside me—to assess the others.

Zephyr is clearly yearning for his dragon and our absent mates. So I can work with that, as long as he thinks I'm safe.

Seemingly recovered from his recent bout of mating fever, Mordred is sitting right on the edge of the shaft, heedless of the cobwebs and any creepy-crawly inhabitants, leaning way forward to peer into the hole with interest.

"Pretty deep in there, for real," he comments, looking like he wants to hop right in. "And it's seawater."

He'll do what V tells him, since he won't have a choice, due to that whole summoning bond. Even if I'm not comfortable with the idea of compelling the guy.

A safe distance back from the edge, Mal is crouched and burrowing through the grimoires in her book-stuffed backpack, while Draco and Jae loom over her like gargoyles, both fiercely protective. They'll go where she tells them, so she's one of those I need to convince.

Along with my alphas.

They'll be the ones who cause problems.

I clear my throat and summon my queen voice. "The front door of the Academy Vault is where Cleo and her Villa Tiberius goon squad gotta be lying in wait. They know we have the Horn, and they know we need to get in. But if we slip in the back, with the Horn, then this challenge is in the bag. We win, they lose, and Cleo's whole '*I'm the superior witch*' claim is totally discredited."

"I'm not at all certain I like where this is going," Lucius mutters.

"C'mon, Teach. This is what you trained me for, remember?" I wink and pass the flashlight back to my worried headmaster, then circle around behind Neo to unzip his backpack.

This morning on the yacht, I thought it was overkill to pack a portable dive lung and mini scuba tank with our gear, and I said so. But our bookworm pointed out that Ronin and I already needed to dive once, and Cleo's a sea dragon, and did we really want to give her the whole ocean uncontested.

When I pull out the skinny neon cylinder of the mini scuba tank, no longer than my forearm, Vasili's eyes narrow dangerously. "I suppose you imagine you're going into that shaft alone, little queen."

"Ronin isn't here to dive with me." I know arguing with him is rarely a good idea, but this is one of those times when I gotta. "No one else here is a certified diver, so—"

"I'm one," Draco volunteers unexpectedly, with a scowl. "But I will not leave Mallory."

Mallory abandons her industrious beavering through her backpack and rises to her feet, with a spellbook clasped in her skinny arms and a determined expression stamped on her freckled face.

"I'm not carrying the Horn," Mal says reasonably, "so I'm not the one in danger. Draco, if she has extra gear, I really think you should go with Zara. I mean, we are members of her harem, even if only temporarily, so—"

"I'm a member of *your* harem," Draco growls at her, deep in his powerful chest, in a way that tells me he does *not* consider himself to be also in my harem, no matter what Mal and I hastily agreed so we won't get disqualified from the contest for working together.

Well, that makes two of us. I don't consider Draco to be a member of my harem either.

I eye the Icelandic warlock—reportedly a made man in the Mars clan mafia and definitely psychotic, whatever else he might be. I imagine swimming through the dark tight confines of an underground tunnel with that sociopath lurking behind me. Then I try to think of a diplomatic excuse for saying *gosh thanks but no thanks* to Mallory's well-meant offer.

Before I can muster the words, the vast darkness of the catacombs behind me echoes with a low sinister chuckle.

Every hair on my body rises to stand straight on end. My horrified brain shoots straight to the zombie werewolf rising scenario.

But wait. No. That's a hyena chuckle.

Still distant.

But not distant enough.

Lucius twists toward the noise. He growls and his eyes glow red. Since he's still shirtless and wearing Ronin's leather pants, his powerful body looks fucking savage, like the wolf king he is. Jae echoes his growl and drops to a crouch. Jae's hands get all gnarly and curling black talons—sharp as box cutters—sprout from his twisted fingers.

I'm honestly impressed. Mal's werewolf is like a cross between Edward Scissorhands and Freddy Krueger.

But what matters most right now is that he's following Lucius' lead. I mean, for now. If Jae goes full shifter and lets his monster out, he's non-sentient.

Then all bets are off.

"Oh, crap." Neo cuddles our kitten to his protective chest. "The AIB kill squad. I thought we got rid of them? Those hyenas must be tracking our scent."

V rises like a rearing cobra and zips across the dark shaft to my side. He doesn't alight, but hovers just above the ground, his combat boots glittering violet in the electric twilight of our flashlights.

"They're functioning as hunting hounds," V hisses, face vicious. "Driving their prey—*us*—straight to the hunters."

"Quickly." Zephyr unsheathes his double swords, already humming with blue witchfire. "Everyone up the stairs. I'll summon Xhevith. His rising will alert our mates. Then shall *we* become the hunters."

Neo's decanting our kitten gently into her carrier (she's protesting, two little white paws shooting out to grip the duffel, but he patiently persists) while Mordred scrambles to his feet and summons his trident.

Mal's guys look to her for guidance, but she's looking at me.

More whoops and cackles rise from the darkness behind us. Still distant, but those hyenas are closing in. Clearly, they know we're close. My brain is racing like a hamster on a wheel. The pulse of the Horn fills my ears with a second heartbeat.

At this point, I can sense that artifact like an extra limb. The Horn of Ceres wants down the shaft, down that deep dark cobwebby hole in the ground (because of course it does).

And the artifact's draw is pulling me in.

Uneasy and resistant, my inner dragon squirms under my sternum. She doesn't like when I dive, especially not a tunnel dive like this one, where there's not even room to shift in a crisis.

To be honest, I'm not wildly crazy about the whole idea myself.

But I don't see any alternative. The only other certified diver in our polycule is Ronin, and he's not here. Besides, as we've already established, it needs to be me specifically who returns the Horn to the Vault.

C'mon, showgirl, I tell my reluctant dragon. *We gotta woman up and do this.*

Ignoring her grumbles and moving as fast as I can, I toe out of my saddle shoes, peel off my knee socks, and start giving orders. "You guys take the stairs. Follow Zephyr, he'll lead you to Xhev and the others. I'll, uh, go this other way. With the Horn."

While I finish stripping down to my skivvies, I simultaneously deal with the expected protests from Neo and Zephyr and an alarmed Lucius. But Mal, after a single piercing look, helps me make the case and gets our Scooby gang organized in an impressive display of hall monitor efficiency.

Vasili, atypically, is silent.

But silence—for him, right now—is a behavior I interpret as support. He's never hovered over me like a traditional alpha (because he doesn't have a single traditional bone in his long, lean, sexy-pretty-dangerous punk-rock warlock body). He's never tried to shelter me from the big bad world. He trusts me, in a unique way most of the others try to emulate but can't, to take care of myself.

It's obvi to me that he's worried. But he's trusting me to handle my shit.

That's what I'm doing right now.

While I strip down to my boy-cut briefs and bra, V commandeers my discarded clothing (which I'm gonna need again after), rigs the slim one-liter pony bottle of precious oxygen into the harness, and straps the lightweight gear over my shoulders. Unlike a standard tank which goes behind, the mini scuba tank sits in front between my boobs.

While Jae and Lucius backtrack down the tunnel to scout for the bad guys, I delegate Zephyr and Draco to take Mallory and Neo (and the kitten) upstairs. For the bookworms—our First Boy and First Girl—combat isn't their strong suit, and I want them both safe.

Besides, Zephyr needs to be fully linked up with Xhevith to trigger the next piece of our plan.

I expect Zephyr to kiss me before he goes, one of his fierce feral Dark Fae King kisses—smelling like burnt amber and dragonhide—a farewell kiss to make my toes curl. Especially with me standing there, practically naked, in my lime-green lingerie.

Instead, the Dark Fae King rakes me with a single piercing look that drinks in every detail of my entire being, from my determined expression to the stiffened nipples that press against my lace (because it's chilly down here in the catacombs without my clothes).

Then his gaze swerves to Mordred.

Behind the eyepatch, Zephyr's face hardens. His jade eye darkens to stormy green. His upper lip curls to reveal a tiny flash of fang.

The sex demon grins back, teeth flashing in his dusky face, and lets his dimples show. "Yo, cuz. How 'bout a kiss for luck?"

My breath catches in my throat. Because I'm honestly not sure whether Mordred is asking for a Dark Fae kiss for me or for himself.

Zephyr's burning stare sears through me. "My queen is mighty. She crafts her own luck."

His hand rises to touch his armored chest and his green head inclines in a bow—to me. Zephyr's never done that before. The quaint gesture is like a cross between an old-fashioned love token and a royal salute.

We still haven't talked since I fucked his cousin (second cousin, once removed) and basically asked to add Mordred to the harem.

I still don't know if we're okay, Zephyr and me.

But I take heart from that gesture, that oddly formal but somehow warming gesture, that breathes affection and soul-deep respect. You know, in an Unseelie kinda way.

So I grin and blow Zephyr a cheeky kiss. "Right back atcha, king of my heart."

Neo gets a real kiss, all sweet and solid and bookwormy with many whispers of love, before he hurries after the others up the stairs.

I root through the pack to find my diving goggles and underwater flashlight, but we had to leave my fins behind on the yacht for space reasons. By the time I buckle the dive knife to my thigh, open the little tank's breathing valve, and run through my safety check, my jitters are gone—channeled into action—and my head's in the game.

Which is totally a good thing, because my sharp shifty hearing is picking up scattered snarls and yowls from the catacombs that tell me Lucius and Jae have found the first of our hunters.

"Okay, so, we gotta vamoose." I fling myself into V's arms for a short but intense and yummy goblin kiss that tastes like butterscotch. All V's kisses are yummy, he's like the world champion kisser in our polycule, and we all fight to get them. "You going after Neo or Lucius?"

"Lucius. I won't leave him behind. Zephyr will take care of Neo." V isn't the demonstrative type (to put it really mildly) but his ice-blue eyes glitter down at me with the broody protective fire I love in our dominant alpha. "I'll go as soon as you're submerged in that hideous shaft."

My whole chest swells like a helium balloon with an emotion I don't have any trouble naming. I gaze up at my snake, my Goblin King, the most complicated and horrible and terrifying and yet simultaneously damaged and fragile and precious of all my warlocks.

"I love you," I tell him, from the heart.

"Hmmmm." His pretty mouth curls in his sly smile. A hot light kindles in his glacial gaze. "I know. How dreadful for you. I'll try to make it worth your while."

Even now, he manages to make me laugh.

Shaking my head at him, I bite my lip, force myself to relinquish his eternally alluring body, and turn toward the burly blue-haired demon lounging against the wall, that sealskin pouch swinging against his hip.

Now the moment for levity has definitely passed.

Because, fuck or no fuck, this is the moment we'll finally know if we were right to trust the demon.

I lock onto that sex demon's smoldery purple stare, extend a royal hand like the badass queen of the witching world I fucking am, and tell him, "Moment of truth, Aquaman. Hand over that artifact and you'll break V's summoning spell. Then you'll be free to stay or go. It'll be your choice. Either way you choose… I'm grateful."

Vasili's breath hisses softly in my ear.

Even though we've both fucked the guy, Mordred's a demon, we can't read his mind, and we really can't know for sure what he'll do once he's loose.

And I'm not sure I really *am* ready for him to hand over the Horn and poof outta here like a genie.

I mean, he can apparate. It's a demon thing. So he can literally vanish from this plane and our lives as abruptly as he originally appeared.

But the sounds of combat are rising. I'm twitchy with the ruthless psychic hunger of Lucius letting his wolf out. We're flat out of time.

"Zang, baby queen, you got real rizz," Mordred says softly, in that teasing drawl he hides his real feelings behind. "Not gonna lie, I'm a sex demon. I've been with a lotta baes, all genders, true? Mostly, they're easy come, easy go." He pauses and his blue head tilts. "Mostly. But the two of you… and this whole found family you cobbled together… you hit different."

I'm still working through his slang to what I think he means when Mordred unloops the messenger bag from his shoulder and tosses it, all casual, to me.

I catch the football in both arms with a gasp.

Under the suede-soft pouch, the solid weight of the Horn of Ceres sings in my head like a fucking choir.

Literally. It's a fertility artifact.

Suddenly, with the thing clutched to my chest, *all* I can think about is fucking. All the blood rushes to my clit. My nipples tingle, my breath quickens, and my cunt floods with slick.

"Sweet—bleeding—*Jesus*," I moan, thick and husky with sex.

"My, my," Vasili breathes, dark and low and delicious. "The way you *smell*, little queen."

Oh yeah. My alpha is *definitely* feeling this shit.

It's all I can manage to stagger away from both of them—both my guys and their delectable cocks—and drop the messenger bag crosswise over my own tingling body. Singing in my head like Pavarotti, the Horn of Ceres nestles against my hip as if it's meant to be there.

It helps that the Horn wants in the shaft. Even while my pussy aches and clenches with the need to be stuffed with dick until my eyes cross, the artifact drags me toward that hole in the tunnel floor.

"Stop pushing," I mutter at the damn thing singing an aria against my hip. "I'm going."

The shaft opens at my feet, a still expanse of black water gleaming in silent threat. I switch on my flashlight and shine it around the depths. Mordred already told me it's deep. But the only way to really know what's down there is to jump.

With a sigh, I drop to sit on the edge and swing my bare legs over. Cold water closes around my feet, so cold I almost yelp and pull them out.

But that would be unqueenly.

I'm supposed to be a badass, aren't I? I'm *mighty*. Even the King of the Dark Fae says so.

I'm fitting my goggles over my eyes when Mordred swings down to sit beside me, toting the spare scuba tank, and tugs off his boots to reveal his webbed feet. "Imma go with. I'll carry your spare. Guard your back."

The breath rushes out of my lungs in a ragged sound that's practically a sob of relief.

He didn't apparate.

He's still here.

Here with me.

Only now, he's here with me by choice.

I'd rather fuck him than fight Cleo, for real. That Horn hums and trills against my hip like an opera at the Met.

Fighting like hell to concentrate on something, *anything* beyond the Horn's pull and the rhythmic pulse of heat in my hoochie, I tug my ponytail free of my goggles and tighten my head strap.

"Hey, thanks for that, Mordred," I tell him softly. "I mean it. Thanks for still being here. But I've seen you shifted, remember? This hole's way too tight for your big-ass kraken. I'll carry my own spare."

He shakes back his long hair and tilts his head to show me the parallel slits tucked behind his pointed ear. "I got gills, baby queen. I can breathe underwater in this form just fine."

Wow.

Apparently I really am adding Aquaman (like, literally) to this harem. I mean, assuming Zephyr ever gets over the idea of adding his nemesis (and cousin, but the blood tie is so nebulous) to our polycule.

"Take him with you, for fuck's sake," V says shortly, from a good way down the tunnel. The Goblin King is already levitating a good two feet above the ground, and I definitely wouldn't want to be the first AIB guy he encounters. "The demon's still here, isn't he? Without being bound by my summoning spell."

I've noticed, I tell V through our mating bond, just for the comfort of the contact.

"And Lucius needs you, bad boy," I finish out loud to V, so Mordred too can hear. "Okay, guys. Let's go kick some sea dragon ass."

Heart pounding against my sternum like orc drums in a Tolkien film, I press the mouthpiece of the mini scuba tank between my lips, fold my arms over the cylinder strapped to my chest, and drop over the edge into the shaft.

Chapter Twenty-Eight
Mordred

Zara Gemini is more than a queen.

Hells' bells, my girl's a damn goddess.

I eel along at her heels through the cool flow of the underground river the shaft dropped us into. Her flashlight plays along the rough stone walls, slick with algae, as her sweet curvy body wiggles through the water like a mermaid.

I mean, if they had mermaids on this mortal plane.

Even in my human form, I got shifty senses, thanks to my kraken. Means I can sense the steady, tireless thud of Zara's heartbeat pinging through my skin like sonar. I can taste the creamy peach of her mating scent in the back of my throat.

Like I said, that girl's got rizz, for real. Her magnetic pull, that tidal force that's been dragging me toward her since the first night I got a sniff of her unique personal magic back on Avalon? Shit's way beyond the magical power of attraction she picked up when she became the Unseelie Queen. I'm not glamoured by her Unseelie crown. That's not why I want her.

I want her because she's Zara.

I want her because she's mine.

I want everything she is and everything she stands for. Her and that found family of Lost Boy warlocks she's knitted together like a quilt stitched in love.

Her and Babydoll and Cousin Z (the guy I've been crushing on since I was twelve)?

They're the hill I'll die on.

By now, the raw power of Zara Gemini's pull sucks me after her like an undertow.

Girl's a strong swimmer, even without fins or gear, and she's handling the unexpectedly strong current and total lack of direction and disorienting underground darkness like a fucking Navy S.E.A.L. (They're a thing on this plane, not some kinda seal shifter either, I read a story about these guys on the yacht.) The Horn of Ceres bobs at Zara's hip, safely swathed in my pouch.

Still, I'm worried about the temp of this water.

Real worried.

Not that the cold bothers me, my kraken digs it, but Zara isn't wearing neoprene. She's naked except for a few scraps of lace. Her teal ponytail swirls behind her and her cute opal-painted toenails glitter in my enhanced eyesight.

I got a protective membrane that drops over my peepers when I dive. The gills behind my ears flutter open to filter in the oxygenated water I need to breathe and siphon out the spillage I don't need. The saltwater tide buoys my big body and hugs me like a lover. My webbed feet propel me along behind my girl without effort.

I'm built for this.

But we've been down here a while, no lie.

And Zara's little neon scuba tank only holds a few minutes' worth of air.

When my girl curls around at a bend in the passage to anchor herself against a protruding rock—slick with seaweed—and shines her beam toward me, I'm ready to help. I lock onto her wide turquoise eyes, intent and worried behind her goggles. I know she needs her spare.

I anchor myself nice and steady next to her, sheltering her tiny body from the current's pull, and help her swap tanks. A lotta divers would be freaking out, that's the gods' honest, this deep in a cave dive without proper gear, with only this meager stash of oxygen.

But Zara Gemini, badass queen of my heart, she be bussin'.

We finish the tank swap and she takes the lead again, kicking strongly with the current, the pale beam of her flashlight bobbing before us. Her strokes are sharp with urgency, because now we're on her last tank.

And we've gone way too far down the shaft to turn back. Especially against this ebb tide.

She's committed now.

And so am I, because I won't fucking leave her here to die.

The tunnel narrows and the current picks up. Dead ahead, Zara's flashlight plays over the dark hatching of a metal grate, bars wrapped in tendrils of streaming seaweed.

That grate lets the water swirl through, but totally blocks our way forward.

Zara anchors herself against the grate, flashlight searching, and starts feeling her way along the bars for weakness or a latch. I anchor next to her and do the job more efficiently, using my mass and muscle to give the grate a few hard pulls.

No joy.

This shit's solidly soldered in the rock. I can't find a weak spot.

Or a latch.

Zara's anxious eyes turn toward me. I've been counting down the minutes in my head. I know her last tank is running low, even though she's visibly working to keep her breath slow and steady so she doesn't make the problem worse.

I close my hand over her flashlight and direct her beam through the bars.

Beyond the grate, the tunnel widens. Golden light glimmers through the water overhead. That's the Academy Vault, gotta be, right on the other side of this grate.

We just need to get through these bars. ASAP. Before Zara runs outta air.

Lucky for her, I know what I gotta do.

I twist around to meet my queen's wide-eyed stare and give her a cocky grin for reassurance. Suddenly her mating bite pulses on my neck. The building coil of our shiny new mating bond hums between us like an electric cable.

I ain't a natural telepath, my Fae DNA isn't built for it.

But fuck me. These shifters and their mating bites?

They're hella potent.

Yeah, I know… it's a lot. Sorry… The first whisper of our bond crackles to life in my noggin like electric static, same way it did with Babydoll after he nipped me. That's my girl, that's her voice, and she's clearly fighting to keep her cool.

Through the growing bond between us, I can feel the pressure building in her chest. The parched dryness of fear in the back of her throat. The ache in her empty lungs as she sips carefully on her last wisp of air through the mouthpiece her lush lips are wrapped around.

Gently her hand floats up to settle against my cheek. My heart gives an anxious ping. I run cool, it's a kraken thing, but her soft fingers are fucking icy.

Mordred, she whispers in my skull. *I'm running out of air.*

I grip her bare shoulders in my big hands to steady her and lock right onto her. *I gotchu, baby queen. But this thing I do, it's tricky when I ain't alone, and we only got time for one shot. You gotta trust me and not fight me, you feel me?*

Her smooth brow furrows above her goggles. Then her lids drop in a slow blink.

Do what you gotta do, Aquaman... Trust you. I trust you. But you gotta hurry, okay?

Under her lime lace bra, her gorgeous tits heave. She's fighting for air and finding zip.

Zilch.

Nada.

I don't waste time. I'm down with this. I'm sigma.

I wrap my arms and legs around my girl's precious self. I pull her shivering body tight against my torso, with her empty tank and the Horn of Ceres pressed between us.

Then I apparate.

I'm only half demon, I can't summon fire or steal souls. But this is one infernal magic I've fucking perfected. Cuz this shit's useful.

My bones soften. My blood thins. The molecules of my body spin apart and dissolve into vapor. And everything I'm holding dissolves with me.

In a silent commotion of energy and magic, the subatomic particles of our joined souls—Zara's and mine—swirl through the grate into the expanse of open water beyond. The blurred golden glimmer of torchlight pulls me toward the surface.

I gather our mingled essence like a net and sling us toward the light. Fiercely, I *will* our cells and atoms and molecules to separate and reform. I *will* us to take shape. To return to the natural order of our corporeal forms. I *will* myself to be Mordred, the pulsing heart of ancient witchcraft to be the Horn of Ceres, and Zara to be Zara.

That's when we trip the spell.

The spell that wards the Academy Vault.

That's when my soul rips apart.

The last thing I hear before my eardrums rupture under the crushing vise of a pressure curse is my girl.

Zara.

Screaming.

Chapter Twenty-Nine
Zara

I shoot for the surface using every spark of levitation witchcraft I possess. All thrusters firing like I've got a fucking jet engine strapped to my ass. Towing Mordred's thrashing body behind me by the hand I have wrapped around his thick ankle. The crushing force of the pressure curse drops away beneath me as we ascend. But the pressure still threatens to pulverize my legs.

Feels like a deep-sea submarine dive... without the submarine.

I don't even wanna *think* about what all these extra atmospheres of magical pressure are doing to Mordred. He's under me, where it's worse, and he's upside down. His poor head. Beneath my grip, his ankle softens and flexes into a thick rubbery tentacle.

That's his kraken, manifesting under stress.

As my face breaks the surface into open air, I suck in a starving lungful of precious oxygen. Chest burning, throat raw, I barely remember to scream the word that deflects the *other* spell, the one we knew about in advance, the one Vasili taught me to counter.

The ossification curse.

My hoarse yell triggers the protective counterspell that guards me against the Vault's bad juju—that curse that locks down the whole Vault and calcifies any intruder's flesh into bone. Like an instant Medusa effect.

But V's potent counterspell snaps into place around me. I stay nice and fleshy. I don't ossify.

How. Ever.

Mordred doesn't have a mouth right now, just a beak. He knows the magic word, but he can't say it. The tensile flex of his tentacle slips from my desperate grip. The vast weight of his body falls away beneath me into the deep.

Still levitating for all I'm worth, my body explodes from the water like I've been fired from a cannon.

Alone.

I don't have a lotta control right now. Plus levitation's still new for me, I'm not Vasili, I haven't been flying like Peter Pan since my tweens.

I catch a wild glimpse of a bare stone altar rushing toward me, set between two tall torches, with some kind of massive statue rearing behind. I shoot between the flaming torches, skid across the altar's surface, and land on hands and knees.

Hard.

My palms abrade and my knees scrape against stone.

Ouch.

A pained yelp slips out of me. But I'm still too winded from oxygen deprivation to give the good yell I need to express my feelings. My empty scuba tank and mouthpiece are gone, along with my flashlight, but I'm still wearing my bra and panties. The Horn swings forward in its pouch around my torso and hangs suspended under my tummy.

The Horn.

That fucking Horn.

I'm in the Vault. With the Horn.

All I gotta do now is deposit that artifact where it belongs. *Exactly* where it belongs. Wherever that is. But my attention's really divided, because Mordred...

Oh, God, no.

Mordred.

Swaying on hands and knees, drinking in gulps of sweet air, crouched on the altar like a human sacrifice, I whip my head around to peer behind me, slinging my dripping ponytail out of my face.

The blazing expanse of the Academy Vault spreads before me, massive as a concert hall. The whole room gleams like the walls are sheathed in gold. The ceiling slops sharply to a pyramid point high overhead. Lit by burning torches, set at intervals in the sloping walls, the underground spring that disgorged me gleams in taunting beauty.

It's a round pool rimmed in blocks of sandstone, rocks glittering with mica, the water's still surface painted gold with torchlight.

A tangle of solid stone tentacles, eyes round and staring, beak gaping wide in agony, lies draped over the pool's rim like an artist's sculpture titled *Kraken in Distress.*

I scramble around to view this nightmare squarely, then suck in a lungful of air that reeks of incense and shock.

"Oh, fucking *hell*." Horror rips through me and shreds my heart to bloody ribbons. *"Mordred."*

My brain whirls into a tailspin.

I don't know how to break an ossification curse. I'm not sure anyone does. The whole idea was not to trigger the thing in the first place. I'm surrounded by a vast and deadly cache of enchanted artifacts, piles of brassbound chests, dusty crates and sarcophagi and coffins, stacks of ancient books in a cobwebby jumble against the sloping golden walls.

Too bad I don't know what any of these objects are or how to use them.

Trapped in my chest like a bird in a cage, my dragon bates and roars with anguish and rage.

Save him, Zara, we must. Save our mate!

Even through the shrieking clamor of my dragon's mental meltdown, the Horn pulses like a heartbeat against my pelvis.

Right over my uterus.

Sweet bleeding Jesus, that artifact has power.

Raw, primal, untapped power.

I mean, my newly acquired and still erratic clairvoyance has been transmitting the message on all frequencies from Day One. This artifact is strong enough to save the witching world. I just need to suss out how to use it.

Maybe it's powerful enough to save Mordred too.

Still crouching on the altar, directly under the peaked roof of this vast solid gold pyramid I'm trapped inside, I scuttle back around and tip my head back—way back—to eye the statue looming over me.

This colossus is a pregnant chick, busty and ripe with child under flowing Roman robes, crowned with a wreath of fresh fruit and flowering vines, with a sheaf of wheat draped gracefully over one arm.

Pregnant. Fruit. Flowers. Wheat. All symbols of fertility.

I'm staring at Ceres, the fertility goddess. Her outstretched hand descends toward me, fingers curled around empty space.

A space just big enough to hold the Horn.

Well, I was hoping it would be obvi where to return the thing once I got here.

Clairvoyance or coincidence, I catapulted blindly out of that death trap of a pond and flew straight here.

Gasping, I fumble the pouch open and spill the Horn into my desperate hands. The jeweled sigils of the twelve great witching houses, interspersed with arcane glyphs for fertility and abundance, spiral around the Horn in a dazzling procession. In the flickering light, the symbols seem to move, twining around and around the curving cylinder in a way that makes me dizzy.

"Cheese on toast," I whisper, loud in the humming silence. "This is the literal definition of a Hail Mary pass. Too bad I'm a lapsed Catholic, huh?"

Warm and pulsing with life, the artifact settles more deeply into my palms. My fingers curl tight around it. Heat streaks up my arms and down my torso to pool between my legs. The sudden tang of ripe peaches floods the air, cutting the suffocating sweetness of frankincense I'm already breathing in the heavy stillness.

Oh, fuck me. Literally. That ripe fruity tang is my mating scent.

The scent I exude when I'm fertile.

Under the soaked lime lace of my bra, my boobs feel heavy and tender. My nipples tighten and tingle. My chest gets tight and my breath gets quick. Yeah, I'm still wet from my swim, but the sudden hot flood of slick between my thighs is something else.

Instant superheat.

Like, the most intense superheat I've ever had.

A quantum superheat.

Whatever you wanna call it, now is *not* the time. But as soon as I save Mordred from the curse and hook up with the rest of my guys, I want all nine cocks (including Mordred's two) at my immediate service.

Statue, showgirl, I remind myself sternly. *Focus on the statue. Not your needy cunt.*

Cradling the Horn carefully in my hands, I swing my legs around and hop down from the altar to the floor. The stone Ceres looms over me, hand outstretched in expectation, blind eyes turned down to meet mine. She's almost close enough for me to touch the hem of her robes or her sandaled feet.

If I dare.

I take a step forward—

From behind the statue, a tall slim girl slips into view, impeccably dressed in a pristine Academy skirt and blazer, hair swept into a sleek merlot twist. Effortlessly glamorous as a runway model on a glossy magazine cover.

"Ciao, bella," Cleo purrs, eyes wide and guileless behind her super-model lashes. "And *grazie.* Thank you for bringing to me my artifact."

Chapter Thirty
Vasili

"Well, darling, we're certainly fortunate your wolf's a strong alpha," I say fondly to Lucius.

Because it's important to praise your lover when he's done something useful. And, no, this *isn't* the first compliment I've ever bothered to pay him.

Honestly. What sort of man do you take me for?

Trotting purposefully before us through the catacombs, barely lit by the beam of my flashlight as I bring up the rear, Lucius' wolf gives a yip as if to say, *Don't answer that.*

Slinking along submissively at Lucius' furry heels, Jae Labête is still flying his freak flag in fully shifted form. His coarse black fur is splattered with blood and his talons are dripping with gore. But most of it isn't his.

That blood was shed by our enemies.

We spilled their blood on the ground for Zara.

As for myself, I barely bothered using my knives. Instead, I gleefully gave my telekinetic casting hand free rein and ground their bones to rubble.

How dare those little pissants fuck with *my* queen?

Fortunately for all of us, Jae's non-sentient werewolf seems to accept Lucius as his pack alpha. Together, the three of us have dealt with that pack of hyena shifters we sniffed out, slinking along at our rear.

Permanently.

Of course, those mangy mammals stalking us through the catacombs were so few, they must have been little more than an insurance policy for Cleo. Dispatched in case Zara sniffed out the ambush undoubtedly waiting for all of us outside the Vault. In case Zara turned back before the Aquarius bitch could spring her trap.

Fortunately, we've planned a surprise of our own for Cleo.

Lost in the darkness ahead, Lucius' wolf growls deep in his chest.

Instantly I shoot upward, the soles of my combat boots lifting from the floor, and pan my light ahead like a damn lighthouse. Before me, the ceiling rises and the tunnel widens. Instantly, I recognize the ominous dead-end shaft my little queen and the kraken jumped into. Lucius' wolf is sniffing along the rim and whining with worry.

My chest tightens quite unpleasantly. My tummy twists with actual fear.

Clinging grimly to my wits, I alight beside the shaft and shine my light down the hole, while my heart thunders as though the unruly organ is trying to burst through my skin.

But there's nothing to see.

No dead kraken or drowned queen floating heels-up in the well.

My breath rushes out in a hiss of relief.

"It's quite all right, darling," I tell Lucius with a show of confidence I'm far from feeling, though I'm never quite certain how well my co-alpha understands spoken words in his shifted form. "Zara and Mordred have surely reached the Vault by now. They'll have slipped in through the back. She's a cat burglar, after all. She's trained for this. She'll be *fine*."

I tack that declaration onto the end as reassurance for both of us. Still unconvinced, Lucius' wolf leans over the edge and crouches, clearly tempted to jump.

Hastily I swoop down next to him and wrap my arms tight around his furry chest. Beneath my hands, his powerful body rumbles with continuous growls.

"Have you forgotten our plan?" I whisper in his tufted ear, which swivels to listen. "You and I and the rest of our mates will swan through the front door, straight into the Vault to crown Zara queen, like the Gemini kings we are."

Of course, that's assuming Max and Ronin and Ash and that green menace Xhevith have done their part upstairs.

But there's no need to stand here in the dark spilling *all* our secrets.

The wolf peers down the shaft and whines, but at least he doesn't bite my hand off. I hug his shaggy body, press my face into his ruff, and breathe in the comfort of his familiar wolfish scent.

Not that I need comfort.

My faith in Zara is unshakable and absolute.

And I don't indulge in wishful thinking. That's pointless. I'm Zara's alpha. If she were injured… or worse… I'd know.

Christ, I've even bonded with the damn kraken. My bond with him is weaker, it's still forming. I certainly never meant to give him a mating bite, and that's a hill I'll die on.

But surely I'd sense him too… if…

Crouched at the foot of the stairs, the Cajun werewolf rumbles his own guttural growl. I twist around to give the creature a narrow look.

Clearly, while Lucius and I were cuddling, Mallory's pet monster has sniffed out the path to his own lovers, Draco and McSnicker, who went up those stairs with Neo and Zephyr.

Now the Cajun tilts back his long muzzle in a mournful howl.

That godforsaken lament sends shivers cascading down my spine. The ungodly howl wakes my inner dragon, coiled gravid and sleeping behind my sternum. She stirs and rears like a cobra, hissing with alarm.

Vasili, let us fly! Let us kill. We must protect our eggs!

Our *eggs*? Merciful fuck.

I do trust those are *Zara's* eggs we're protecting. (Which makes them also mine.) But there's no sense to be gotten from my genderqueer dragon when they're in such a state.

Wings mantle and spread inside my skin. A serpent's hiss climbs up my throat. Suddenly I'm clinging to my human form by my fingernails.

It's literally all I can manage not to shift in the tunnel like a damn earthworm.

Lucius joins his voice with the werewolf, both baying at the moon we shifters can sense but not see, through tons of solid rock. Their mingled howl fills the tunnel and rings off the rock. I press my hands to my ears against the din.

My brain is my most potent weapon, and I need all my well-honed wits in the midst of this racket to *think*.

By now, we must be under the massive gothic cathedral that houses the Academy classrooms, perhaps directly beneath the faculty offices in the crypt. That's where we'll enter the Vault.

Still, the thought of all that weight and mass of rock suspended over my head is oppressive. And unsettling.

"For fuck's sake." I glare repressively at the howling wolves. "*Must* we announce our approach to the entire Academy? Be quiet, darlings, *do*."

Lucius' wolf stops howling and gives me a hangdog look. His chestnut ruff bristles as he ducks his head and vigorously scratches one shaggy flank.

Christ.

If those mangy hyenas have given Lucius fleas, truly, I'll be vexed. But not nearly as vexed as I'd be to find fleas on myself or Zara.

I *must* remember to insist Lucius de-louse before the next time we all share a bed.

Sparing me an evil glare with those glowing green eyes that would curdle anyone's blood, Jae Labête too falls sullenly silent. Surely no flea would ever dare trouble that beast.

Suddenly, with a ferocious snarl, Jae bounds up the dark stairs in great springing leaps that carry him swiftly from sight.

"Shit." I slide a knife from the cache hidden under my Academy uniform, cuffs dappled with hyena blood and rather the worse for wear, and swing my flashlight up the stairs. "Run along, Lucius, and see if you can catch that Cajun. The fool's running blind. We need to *rendezvous* with Ronin and the others straightaway."

The wolf chuffs out a breath in agreement and trots up the stairs.

Left alone in the tunnel with my flashlight, I spare a moment to reach telepathically for Ronin, to search the twisty channels of my diabolical mind for the electric hum of our bond. My boyfriend's psychic presence is wickedly strong. I can typically feel him coming a mile away.

Tonight, however, that special space our bond occupies— that Ronin-shaped niche in my head and my heart—stays dark and empty.

My chest plinks with a sharp ping of worry. The distant echo of a howling werewolf, almost too faint to discern even with my acute shifter senses, makes my scalp crinkle.

I swear, that howl sounds positivity deranged.

Surely, that ungodly sound isn't rising from the catacombs behind me?

Truly.

Are we to be spared nothing? The mere thought of the slain werewolf king, zombified and raging in his sarcophagus, gives me the yuck.

Swiftly I cross the pitch-black tunnel to follow the two wolves up the stairs, guarding Lucius' back, same as always—

"Vasya."

The low murmur of a Russian voice, speaking my boyhood nickname, slithers from the dark stairwell.

I jolt to a halt.

A tall slim form slips into view, dressed to slay (literally) in the sleek black exfiltration gear of the professional spy and killer he is. His body armor is singed and corroded from Xhevith's acid. Still, clearly, the gear saved his life.

So much for Zephyr's claim of having killed him.

A claim I knew, in the depths of my twisted heart, was too good to be true. Even though, clearly, Zephyr believed it.

Every cell in my body hums and sparks with an electric charge of alarm. If I were Zara, I'd be hurling lightning.

I don't need to see the pale face, framed in a sleek fringe of espresso-dark hair, emerging from the shadows to know him. I don't need to breathe in his scent, so painfully familiar to me from childhood, of expensive red cedar laced with the acrid perfume of Russian cigarettes. Those cancer sticks are a cultural weakness—and the only personal vice he tolerates.

"Oh, it's *you*." I dial up my pissy gay boy attitude to ten and give my father a disappointed moue, merely to discomfit him. "I wondered when you'd turn up, like a bad *kopeck*."

My father's discerning eyes, chocolate flecked with gold, slide over my disheveled uniform and blood-splattered sleeves. "I could say the same of you."

That look makes me feel diminished, like an erring schoolboy, same as always. But that was always my father's default mode when it came to managing me.

To diminish me.

Too bad for him, I've outgrown that charming tactic. I've outgrown his ability to hurt me.

At least emotionally.

Too bad for me, he's always had *other* ways to hurt me.

I keep a wary distance, because I know how brutally swift he is with a knife. (Who do you suppose taught me to use mine?) He's Nikolai Romanov, head of the Arcane Investigative Bureau, and he clawed his way up that lethal ladder the deadly way. So I very carefully don't eye the stairs behind him.

Still, he knows perfectly well where I'm going.

I deploy the Romanov eyebrow. "You can't stop me, *papochka,* so you might as well save your breath."

His own Romanov eyebrow lifts in response. "Oh, but I'm not trying to stop you."

"Truly? Do tell." Seeing my own familiar mannerism reflected in his face makes my chest ache. To hide it, I flash him the smug smirk he's always hated. "You and your AIB hyenas. Your little kill squad may have given Lucius fleas, by the way. You'd best do a louse check on yourse—"

"*Vasya.*" My father's quiet voice hardens. Now he eyes me with grim resignation. "It may interest you to learn that, in response to certain… unforeseen developments, I've chosen to alter my strategy."

Something twists in my tender heart that feels a bit too uncomfortably close to pain.

But it can't be that.

Because I learned to stop loving him, stop longing for his love in return, so very long ago.

"I suppose now you intend to kill me." Try though I might, I can't quite leach the bitterness from my voice. "It was always going to end this way, wasn't it? I'm the queer son. I'm *defective*. I'm the shameful secret you tried to hide away. But as one of Zara's kings, I've now become a public disgrace."

"*Malchik.*" Now it's his turn for emotion, his smooth tenor vibrates with it, and I blink in surprise. Because one, he never allows himself to feel, and two, he hasn't called me *my boy* in years. "Whatever else you are—you're my only son. You're the scion of the Scorpio clan. You were always meant to rule, that was my plan for you from the cradle."

His slender body shifts, brow pinching with a hint of discomfort. If he were anyone else, he'd be wringing his hands and pacing. "For a long while, during your rather unfortunate adolescence, I believed your… sexual eccentricities… rendered you unsuitable for the crown. Over time, I've come to realize, my perception was in error."

Belatedly I realize I'm gaping at him like a dead fish. I close my mouth with a snap. "What exactly are you saying to me? And if you do intend to kill me, you'd better make it snappy, *do,* because Zara needs me in the Vault."

"*Bozhe moi.* You are the most aggravating son any man could possibly have." Under my taunting, the steely Nikolai Romanov finally gives way to a small sigh. "I'm not threatening to kill you. I'm proposing that I join you."

Chapter Thirty-One
Zara

"Apparently now they just let anyone in the joint," I tell my ex-bestie, adding an eye roll for attitude. "There goes the fucking neighborhood."

I'm leaning in on the snark to cover up everything else I'm feeling, and I'm probably overdoing it. I'm choking on that bitter cocktail of anger and betrayal, garnished with residual loss and heartbreak, that I can't seem to stop sipping.

So, for a chaser, I sling back a shot of resolve.

I mean, it's not like I'm surprised to run into her. I didn't even need my erratic dash of Valyrian foresight to know she'd be here.

Waiting for me.

So she can kill me. That's the most likely scenario.

Though I am kinda surprised that she seems to be here alone.

"Evidently so." Cleo's shimmering stare slides over me, next to naked in my soaked lingerie, then shifts to Mordred's ossified kraken, zapped while climbing from the pool. That's when her head tilts and her tone turns curious. "That one is a friend of yours, yes?"

Her flicker of interest triggers my possessive side. This quantum superheat I'm suddenly rocking makes my hairpin emotional trigger ten times touchier.

Oh, fuck me.

Fuck me *hard.*

Now I'm overwhelmed by a sudden vicious impulse to tattoo that kraken's gorgeous copper skin with a warning label that reads *Property of Zara: Hands Off.* Complete with lightning bolt.

Oh, don't get me wrong. I'll gladly—*so* gladly—share Mordred with V and all the warlocks in our polycule. But *not* with the celebrity supermodel ex-girlfriend, ex-BFF, ex-accomplice, ex-everything who betrayed me.

My inner dragon snarls and claws at my chest like the alpha bitch she is. She wants *out*, so she can protect her kraken mate from this rival queen, like *now*.

Clearly sensing my raging dragon with her own shifty senses, Cleo's eyes widen. Her human pupils elongate to vertical slits.

Settle down, showgirl, I tell my dragon sternly. *I got this.*

My dragon trumpets a protest that thunders in my ears.

Over all this internal racket, it's really hard to strategize. Still, I know how to stake a claim. I know how to keep what's mine.

I tuck the Horn of Ceres securely against my side, prop a hand on my hip, and announce to Cleo, "You can stop thinking what you're thinking. That kraken's way more than a friend. He'll be one of my kings."

I mean, assuming my warlocks agree.

But that's a complication Cleo Ferrari, who's never met a guy she can't have, doesn't need to know.

"*Alora.* You always did have… exotic tastes." My ex's gaze roams my face, the teal ponytail almost long enough now to graze my ass, the no-doubt defiant line of my mouth, the row of silver studs rimming my ear. Then the jut of my pierced nipples, pressing against the soaked lime lace of my French brassiere.

She's taking inventory.

Sure, I might be the only girl she's ever been with. We had a "bi for you" relationship happening, one reason she got inside my defenses so easy (unless she was lying about that too). Still, she doesn't look like she minds what she's seeing.

But her choice of phrase gets my hackles up.

Exotic tastes.

"You used to like that about me," I say tartly, because isn't that how we both hooked up with each other and Xiao in the first place? Literal solstice orgy on the beach in Bali. "Speaking of which… where's Xiao?"

Since I still can't believe Cleo has the moxie to face me alone.

Much less kill me.

Her perfect face tightens in a tiny frown. "I sent Xiao home to Hong Kong. He's a relationship we have both outgrown, no?"

Stoked by this bullshit, a fiery coal of anger flares in my gut. She acts like she's not even responsible for her own ally. Too bad for her I'm not buying it.

Will she still blame Xiao once I'm lying dead at her feet?

Yeah, no, that's not happening. The witching world needs me alive and queening it. *I* need me alive and queening it. So I can enjoy my HEA with my warlocks and our babies.

Testing her resolve, I take a menacing step forward. Cleo falls a wary step back, then totally stands her ground. Her dragon pupils telescope wide in warning.

Is she that afraid of me? Or is this one more disguise from her bag of tricks? A trap she's baiting just to lure me in?

Cleo Ferrari, alone and vulnerable.

My idiot heart gives a ping at the thought. At least my gambit got me one step closer to the Ceres statue. But Cleo still stands squarely in my way.

Which is a metaphor for our whole fucking relationship since the night of her big reveal.

Since then, I've learned to respect both her half-Fae speed and her vicious streak.

"Nope." I pop the P for emphasis. "Way to downplay all that shit Xiao pulled. I'm not buying it. Your boy toy literally tried to slit Ronin's throat on your mom's royal yacht—not to mention put a bullet in me—at my own twenty-first birthday bash."

"But he did these things without my consent." Her slitted eyes narrow and she purses her lips in a pout. "That night is precisely when I realized we have—both of us—outgrown him."

I give way to a skeptical snort.

My self-control isn't the greatest right now, with the Horn singing in my head like a choir, my dragon screaming to challenge her sea dragon rival, and my body on quantum superheat fire for a fuck.

Plus I still expect Xiao or Nikolai or those House Tiberius bullies to come slinking out from behind a crate. Even when my shifty senses tell me we're alone in here.

"Yeah. While we're on the subject of *that night*," I cradle the Horn protectively to my chest like a football and make air quotes with one hand "thanks for broadcasting that private warlock sex tape—you know, the one my guys and I never consented to you filming?—all over WNN. Thanks for humiliating Neo, trying to steal my crown, stabbing me in the back, and basically ruining my life on live TV."

I tick off her offenses on my glittery fingers till I don't have any fingers left, then tap my bare toes and scowl at my ex-bestie. "You gonna say *that* was done without your consent too?"

Shit.

I'm getting worked up despite myself, exactly when I need to keep a cool head.

She tilts her sculpted chin with a tiny wince. I'm distracted all over again by the wide silk ribbon tied around her elegant neck above the prim collar of her schoolgirl blouse, knotted in a jaunty bow. That ribbon isn't part of the Academy uni, and neck ribbons aren't trending on the runways, so I can't figure out why she's wearing it—

Until I recall, with a stab of remembered dread, the way Ronin discharged his speargun into her throat at seven fathoms.

Clearly, my ex-GF heals fast. Shifty-swifty. Faster than I do—just one more thing to hold against her. But Ronin's aim was ruthless, and that injury was almost mortal. Shifter or no shifter, you don't bounce back easy from a hit like that.

A pang of concern tightens my chest and hitches my breath.

Then I'm pissed all over again, this time at myself, for being so ridiculous and so soft-hearted and just so goddamn gullible.

For *caring*.

How many times does my bitchy ex-bestie need to betray me before my stupid heart gets the memo?

She doesn't love me. And she fucking never did. She lied to me from Day One.

Just like you lied to her, my inconvenient conscience pipes up. *You didn't tell her who you really were either. Your whole relationship was built on lies.*

"Your humiliation was Nikolai's plan." Something fractures in Cleo's voice when she says the dude's name, but you'd never notice if you didn't know her like I do. "It was never mine. And it was Xiao and not I who filmed you with your lovers."

Like she's totally not responsible.

For any of it.

When it was all—every bit of it—done in *her* name.

If the bullshit in here gets any thicker, I'm gonna need galoshes and a raincoat. Plus the burn and ache of this quantum superheat between my legs is really straining my patience.

Despite the fact that I'm practically nakey and it's uncomfortably cool down here in the Vault, I'm burning up. Not to mention the lingering tomb scent of myrrh and frankincense in this pyramid is clashing with Cleo's *ylang ylang* perfume in a major way.

I shake my head till my ponytail flies, just to clear my brain. "Are you really gonna play Little Miss Innocent? With me of all people? Because trust me, Sunshine, it's not a good look on a future fucking *queen*—"

"*Cavolo, bella,* I told him his plan sucked." Finally, Cleo too sounds impatient. I wonder if she can hear the Horn the way I can, if it's eroding her control the way it's eroding mine. "Leave it to Nikolai Romanov to order a sex tape starring his only son to be broadcast on live TV—exposing his hidden queerness to the world—merely to serve a political purpose."

In startled silence, I absorb the sucky impact of that pending revelation on Vasili. The only guy in my harem who's ever broken into this Vault on his own. The one I'm hoping will come swanking through the front door with the rest of my warlocks in tow any minute now.

Assuming that part of our plan isn't toast.

A fresh stab of worry for V and all my guys, including the ossified Mordred, needles my tone with spite. "Yeah, well, you shoulda tried harder to exert some influence, *bella*. You know, since you aim to be the next queen, and your bitch-witch mom is the actual sitting queen? Like, maybe you could exert some agency over your own fucking minions?"

"My *minions*? Is that what you think Nikolai…" Under the flawless facade of cosmetics she's wearing, an intriguing hint of color climbs in her cheeks. "This entire damned situation is far more… complicated… than you seem to think. Unlike yourself, *amore mio*, I was never given a choice. Remember?"

"Don't call me that," I fire back. "I'm not your love and I never was."

Her gaze drops to the Horn I'm cradling to my chest (also possible she could be checking out my tits, since I'm so close to naked in my soaked lingerie I'm practically indecent.) Slowly, her face changes. Her lavender eyes darken to amethyst. Her pearly whites sink into the wild berry matte of her pouty lower lip.

I know that look.

It's her conniving look.

The look I used to love calling her out for.

Tingling with adrenaline and instinct, I sidle out from between her and the altar. Just to give myself fighting room. My dragon bates her wings in my chest and tries to rise till my skin stretches tight around the shift I can barely stave off.

Dial it back, showgirl. I say when we shift. If we shift. Remember? Still, my ponytail starts floating. Sparks crackle at my fingertips.

Too bad I can't summon real lightning in an underground vault with no windows.

What if I just bolt for the statue—?

"*Merda.* I don't suppose you will simply give me the artifact." Cleo sighs like my stubbornness is a real fucking nuisance. "This would save us both a great deal of trouble, *si?* It's the practical step, the safe step, which is why you will never do it. If you would only acknowledge my claim, Zara! I could protect you—and your mates—from my mother's insecurity and her jealousy. I could even protect you from Nikolai and his ruthless political schemes."

"Protect us? How?" I force out a laugh, though this whole sitch is so far from funny it's tragic. Static crackles in my ponytail. "Cleo, they both want me *dead.* You couldn't even stop Nikolai from filming us."

I watch her face carefully when I say his name—and there it is again. Her silky lids flutter in a blink. The smooth skin between her waxed brows tightens in a pinch of pain.

There's something there.

Something between those two, between Cleo and Nikolai, beyond all the prickly assassin-spy-*protégée*-mentor baggage my glamorous ex-BFF and V's homicidal dad are toting around and juggling between them like knives.

Something.

I just need to suss out what it is. And how to use it.

My gaze sneaks past Cleo to the statue of Ceres looming over her. I'm so fucking close to victory I can taste it—

"Leave Nikolai to me," Cleo says tightly. A fresh current of cunning arcs through her like voltage. "And if you wish to distract me while you return that artifact to the goddess and claim my rightful throne, this I cannot allow."

Here it is at last.

The moment my ex-GF finally tries to kill me.

My pulse hammers in my ears.

"Too bad you don't have a say over what I do, Sunshine," I breathe. "Not anymore."

Her eyes pulse gold like dragon orbs. "If you will not give me the Horn freely, *bella,* then I must take it."

Humming with adrenaline, voice thick with witchcraft, my gaze locks on hers. "Come and get it."

Faster than thought, she's on me, in a blur of Fae swiftness way too quick for the human eye to follow. But I'm not human. I levitate and zip to one side, barely evading her deadly takedown. When I land, I stamp my foot to summon the little lightning. A ripple of electricity crackles across the floor, a swiftly spreading circle with my body forming the epicenter.

The golden pyramid of the Vault rings above us like a church bell.

But Cleo's already airborne, vaulting upward with that inhuman Unseelie speed to land on the altar. She somersaults across the surface, springs to the floor a breath after the electric ripple passes, and plucks a shining shaft—taller than she is—from the jumble of magical artifacts piled against the walls.

I catch a single glimpse of the thing—a spear tipped with long-edged blades at both ends. In a flash, I recognize the weapon from a spellbook drawing Ronin (the weapons expert in our polycule) showed me once.

He called it a double-headed glaive.

Standing just beyond range of my still-electrified body, Cleo grips the edged weapon in both hands and starts spinning. "Say hello to the Glaive of Wind."

Whipped into being by the Glaive, a slim column of air twists into a tornado between us. In a breath, the wind builds to a howl. It sucks at me with killing force.

Clutching the Horn to my chest with both arms, I sprint for the Ceres statue. The stone goddess waits for me, hand extended in expectation for her treasure.

I can almost touch her fingers when the wind whips under me and plucks me from the ground.

Now I'm the one who's airborne.

And not under my own steam.

I can't levitate in this shit.

While my limbs windmill for purchase, the Horn of Ceres flies from my arms and spins away on the wind. I yell in protest and dismay, but the twister roars in my ears like a locomotive to deafen me. The stinging scourge of my ponytail lashes my face. The golden walls blur around me. I've got maybe a heartbeat to register that I'm about to be Hulk-smashed and smeared across all that gold like a bug on a windshield.

Then my inner dragon roars and her wings snap open. The shift sears through me, my world goes white, and all fucking hell breaks loose.

Chapter Thirty-Two
Ash

I'm pelting through the witch academy choir loft library, pounding after Pendragon and Maxim and those two gal pal housemates from Zara's *domus* as hard as I can push these old bones of mine.

That's when Xhevith's nails-on-chalkboard scream rips through the church walls and just about shreds every eardrum in the joint.

Oh, Geezus.

A combustible rocket fuel of anticipation and dread launches my ticker right into my throat.

Because there's only one reason Xhev would bust out screaming from the ruins of the old Roman warehouse down by the harbor where we've had him holed up hiding.

Sparrow.

If that dragon heard his rider calling through the empathic dragonrider bond they share.

Or if Xhev felt his rider in pain.

Or dying.

Good old-fashioned terror dumps a bucket of adrenaline through my system. Mainlining cortisol like a goddamn drug, I veer off from the group and power for the gable window.

Unlike the fancy-shmancy stained glass art in the nave downstairs, most of the library windows up here are plain leaded glass.

I don't waste time. I hit the nearest latch and swing the pane wide.

Under a drizzly night sky, barely visible through a curtain of rain and fog, Zephyr's big green dragon is winging up, climbing steeply from the rain-washed cobblestones of the village piazza right underneath me. A lithe rider in green dragonscale clings to the saddle, fierce with intensity behind the slash of his eyepatch, moss-green hair streaming in the wind like a banner.

That's my Sparrowhawk.

All the fear for him I didn't realize I was carrying loosens its clamp on my neck and rushes outta my shoulders.

"Sparrow!" I shove my head out and bellow, heart thundering in my veins.

Shooting past me in a windstorm of powerful wings and buffeting gusts, the dragon screams like a chick in a horror flick. As the two flash past, my retinas fill with a single blazing glimpse of Sparrow's slim body, braced in the dragon saddle with muscles straining, leaning all his weight back against the reins to urge his dragon higher.

Okie-dokie. Guess we're done being subtle.

I wonder like hell where Zara is. Geez Louise, could she be in the Vault already? Is my princess already throwing down with Cleo?

I shove my big shoulders through the jambs right into the rain and give a good holler.

"Sparrow! Over here—"

Ah, crap. I'm too late.

Under the powerful pull of his rider's will, Xhev wheels in a flash of pale underbelly and soars outta sight over the church.

"Bollocks! I've got them," Pendragon cries behind me.

Attention good and divided, I mutter a curse and twist around to stare. Pendragon's already diving into the twisty corkscrew stair that plunges down to the student commons in the church.

"They're in the crypt," he calls back. "Neo and Lucius. That's Lucius ringing me up."

He's speaking metaphorically, on account of no cell phone coverage behind the Academy wards. For a telepath like Pendragon, rocking a mating bite from Lucius Aries, those two don't need Ma Bell to connect.

That's the signal we've been twiddling our thumbs up here waiting for. We're all converging on the Vault like we planned, which is a hopeful sign, no lie. Plus Neo's no fighter and he's definitely been on my mind.

But shoot.

Guess Pendragon and his fancy Jedi mind tricks ain't sensing our princess.

Or he definitely woulda said so.

"Where is our sovereign?" Max growls at his heels, right on cue. "Where is our mate!"

Pendragon's voice echoes up the stairs. "Could be in the Vault already. Leg it, Max!"

"Hold on a tick, will ya?" I shout after them. "Sparrow and Xhev—"

Aw, heck. It's no use. I'm wasting my breath. Those two hotheads and their gal pals are rushing straight into whatever malarkey Cleo and company got planned downstairs.

Somebody around here needs to keep a cool head.

Guess that'll have to be me.

I clamber onto the window ledge, shove my big body under the lintel, then leap into the open air. A drizzle of cool rain hits my face and shoulders. Then my wings spread wide with a snap, sprouting from the tattoo inked across my shoulders.

Beating my wings in a downstroke, I soar over the piazza. A gust of rain-drenched wind rushes over my body. My lungs fill with the mineral scent of wet stone. Cool mist condenses on my face.

In a blink, the soaring structure of the gothic church vanishes behind a rolling bank of fog.

Despite every damn thing that's riding me—my gnawing worry for Zara and our gang, not to mention those big brother protective instincts firing on all six cylinders for Mallory, the kid sis I just barely reunited with—I need a sec to exult in the headrush of flight.

I'm a Seelie royal, even though I'll never rule, that'll be Mallory's gig someday. But I'm meant to soar. I'm Asher Apollo Aurelius, Eagle of the Air, Prince of the Light Born Fae.

And I'm done dicking around.

Time to unload a can of whup-ass on that usurper witch Cleo and her bootlicking, shit-kicking, ass-kissing pissant cronies.

A gust of rain-drenched air rushes through my wings. My primary flight feathers extend for thrust, while the tertials along my shoulders fluff and spread for warmth. A few powerful beats lift me high enough to scan the dark belfry we just vacated. The sloping roof and turrets, the scowling rainspout gargoyles puking water from the gutters, the arched rows of the church's flying buttresses flash before my eyes.

Right before another fogbank rolls in.

I ride a downdraft to get a closer look. In front of the church, the shimmering cobblestone expanse of the piazza is empty. The Roman-era ruins of the village loom dark and broody over the square. What with the overcast and the moonless night and the rain and the fog rolling in from the sea, even my eagle eyes are straining to ferret out what's what.

Bottom line?

I can't see Xhev and Sparrow. They're hidden in the low-hanging clouds.

All of a sudden, the tall stained-glass windows of the church flare with a pulse of fiery light. One, two, three pulses of light. That's psi fire. Right on cue, a thin chorus of terrified cries seeps through the thick stone walls.

Fire in the hole down there, for real.

Sure looks and sounds like Pendragon's work to me. He's the Leo scion—flamethrower—and he's in there raising hell. Hopefully with Max and the girls to cover his six.

Once upon a time, I woulda been okay leaving the dickwad to fend for himself. Ronin Pendragon's been on my shit list for years.

Ever since he took Sparrow's eye.

Even after we figured out what happened was a tragic goddamn accident, I've had a hard time letting that shit go.

But I did just kinda promise to give the guy a chance. Looks like we even got an actual date the night of Sparrow's birthday.

Besides, we're all Team Zara now. She's gonna need all of us working together tonight.

Through a blurry mizzle of rain, my restless eye roams the impenetrable church walls to find the one breach in that Christian fortress. The round oculus window, shattered during some kinda scuffle that went down between Zara and Cleo while I was back in Avalon keeping the Unseelie throne warm for Sparrow's royal butt. The school hasn't had time to replace the glass, so the hole's covered with a billowing tarp to keep the rain out.

I tilt my wings and soar into a spiral so I can sneak a peek.

I'm halfway there when the curtain of fog parts. The vast green bulk of Xhevith's big-ass body soars into view, fully extended like a javelin, with Sparrow crouched over his shoulders and vicious with intent.

The dragon coughs. A shower of steaming acid sprays from his jaws. The tarp over the window dissolves in tattered shreds.

Xhevith screams with triumph, tucks his wings against his outstretched body, and sails through the oculus into the church. I tuck in behind his forked tail, riding his slipstream, and soar in right after him.

Inside, it's a nuthouse.

Around a scatter of study nooks and carrels, the student commons is seething with junior witches and warlocks in Academy garb, hurling spells and ducking hexes, all mixed up with a snarling scrum of hyena shifters.

Geez, it's like the climax of a Harry Potter flick down there. All that's missing is Voldemort and a goddamn game of Quidditch.

The hootenanny's centered at the head of the stairs leading down to the crypt—and the Academy Vault.

Right where we need to get.

That's where we gotta hook up with Zara.

Because I can already see she's not in the church. Neither are Neo or Mal or the others who went with her.

While Xhev overflies all this crazy, with his nails-on-chalkboard scream bouncing off the walls and his monstrous form spreading screaming pandemonium through Cleo's rank-and-file (because dragons ain't too common here, the way they are in Avalon), I sweep in a low circle to scout and get my bearings.

Like I figured, Pendragon's raising hell down there, spraying psi fire like flaming gasoline from his outstretched hands, golden eyes all fiery, teeth bared in a snarl in his swarthy face, black hair swirling around his lethal frame in an inky cloud.

While every Aquarius stooge in the witch academy tries to take him out.

I ain't a big fan of random slaughter, what with being a Light Fae healer. Plus I don't much care for killing a bunch of kids who are less than half my age that I'm supposed to be teaching next term under the Academy exchange program. All that's enough to make me hang back a tick.

But I'll do what I gotta.

Right now, Max and our gal pals, they got Pendragon's back. That butch blond Racetrack is hell on wheels, using fists and feet and wicked teleportation skills to keep Cleo's cronies off Ronin's ass. What Max lacks in finesse, he makes up for in vicious, no-holds-barred butchery, aided by a couple of good-sized knives that are already bloody. Little Dez mainly stays on the sidelines, but she's stealthily creeping closer than anyone else to the stairs.

Clearly, that little witch has a plan.

Even as I watch, the gal dips a hand in her backpack, then hurls a fistful of what looks like silver glitter right at the clique of Aquarius witches in schoolgirl unis guarding the crypt stairs.

Dez yells a casting word, the glitter pops and flashes pink and lavender. When the sparkles settle, three witches are slumped on the floor.

Huh.

That's a common magic sleep spell, used to good effect.

The remaining witches converge on Dez, who suddenly looks nervous. I dive into a spiral to lend her a hand. Abruptly Racetrack winks into view beside her, throws her arms around her gal, then whisks them both outta sight.

Right about now, teleportation's a nifty trick to have up our collective sleeve.

With a snarled curse, Max goes down under the weight of a big alpha hyena, wiry arms straining to keep those gnashing jaws away from his throat. Xhevith banks and soars right over the melee, plucks the hyena off Max with his outstretched forelegs, and wings off with the snapping shifter dangling in his claws.

While Max struggles to reorient himself and scramble back to his feet, Pendragon's temporarily isolated.

Exposed.

His psi fire's burned out or something, guess he needs a tick to recharge. Meanwhile, he's fighting hand to hand, snapping an impressive sidekick into a rival warlock's diaphragm that hammers his target into next week. The next guy who comes at him goes down and stays down under a punishing back kick that definitely cracks a few ribs.

Uh-oh.

Pendragon's got incoming.

A hail of flying spellbooks whizzes at him, wielded by some telekinetic witch who's attacking from the cover of a study carrel. Under the bombardment of this airborne library, Pendragon ducks and blocks and curses.

Meanwhile, three hyenas are converging on his thoroughly distracted ass.

Xhevith hurls the hyena he snatched right at a wall, which looks ouchy. Then the big green guy twists into a turn, weaving and tilting to keep clear of pillars and walls—tight squeeze in here for a full-grown dragon. Wending his way back to Pendragon's gonna eat up precious seconds.

Seconds that warlock who's been the bane of Sparrow's life and mine just doesn't have.

I got maybe a breath to decide.

I don't ponder my options. I just act.

As the lead hyena crouches and springs, I swoop down behind Ronin, wrap my arms around his waist, and sweep my bane and nemesis into the air.

He stiffens up, natch, and whips out a serious knife from a hidden sheath. "Bloody fucking hell—"

"Appreciate if you'll take it easy on my hide, Pendragon," I drawl in his ear. "Considering I just saved your ass."

"Blimey," he grouses. But at least he doesn't knife me. "*Ash.* Warn a bloke next time, there's a love."

"You're welcome." For some damn reason, don't ask me why, I'm grinning.

He's a bulkier guy than Sparrow, with wider shoulders and a lot more height—but I'm bigger. I can handle him. I can even appreciate all that Leo body heat he's radiating and the dark spice of ambergris rising from his skin and the silky mass of his long hair trapped between us.

Well, hell. I hate to admit it.

But I'm starting to maybe get why Sparrow's gone apeshit crazy and lost his Dark Fae mind over Ronin Pendragon.

I get my butt in gear and beeline our flight for the stairs and the crypt. Dez made us a hole with that sleep spell. Ronin's done a lotta damage with his psi fire. Now, with Sparrow calling the shots from above, Xhev is spraying the remaining hyenas with gouts of his acid breath. The critters yelp and hoot and scatter in all directions.

Racetrack is already urging Dez down the stairs. Max is pelting in that direction, dragon eyes flaming and Slavic face all savage with intent—because the crypt is where we're supposed to hook up with Zara—with all the single-minded fixation of a rutting dragon.

As I swoop toward them, the warlock in my arms voices a whoop, then lets loose with a riff of maniacal laughter, like he always does on dragonback.

Clearly, Ronin Pendragon loves to fly.

Guess that's something else we got in common.

Along with loving the same guy and worshipping the same gal and sharing the same darn polycule.

I deposit Ronin gently near the stairs and land a few feet past, running a few steps to bleed off momentum. Wings still flared and mantling, I lean over the dark stairs to get a gander.

Halfway down, Dez leads the way with a flicker of pink light dancing in her open palm. Racetrack and Ronin and Max power down the steps on her heels.

"Hey, guys and gals," I call down after them. "Do we even know for sure if Zara—?"

"She is," Sparrow's gray silk voice murmurs in my ear. "With any luck, our queen has already entered the Vault, along with that moon-cursed kraken."

My wings snap shut and melt into the tat inked into my back. Heady relief flooding through me, I turn toward my consort with a grin. "Howdy, Sparrowhawk."

He gives me a fierce smile that shows off his tiny fangs, throws a forceful arm around my neck, and pulls me down for a short savage kiss that makes my bones melt. Xhevith swings his big head over us and chuffs out a snort to say howdy.

That dragon'll stay put up here, guarding our backs like we planned. No one—and I do mean *no one*— gets past Xhevith.

Through the haze of yielding warmth that always seeps through me under my guy's commanding hands, a clamor of excited cries floats up the stairs. That's Neo's eager voice greeting the new arrivals, then my kid sis Mal calmly taking charge like the future Seelie Queen she is, punctuated with what sounds like an urgent yip from Lucius' wolf.

I'm so relieved to hear my sister's voice, I'm wrecked.

Now we just gotta get to Zara.

ASAP.

I surface from Sparrow's kiss and run an affectionate hand over my guy's windblown hair. "Our princess is already in the Vault, huh?" When he jerks his chin in a tight nod, I nod back. "Guess that's where we gotta get—pretty darn quick. C'mon."

Chapter Thirty-Three
Zara

My dragon queen is finally free.

Free to fight.

Free to rage.

Free to reign.

And man, is that girl *juiced.*

My wings snap open, which would be a really bad move for a bigger dragon in this confined interior space. But my dragon is still a juvenile, like a bratty teen, which means she's more than mouthy. She's also on the smaller side and super agile. We pivot on a wingtip toward the Ceres statue and the gleaming golden crescent lying at the statue's feet.

In the flickering torchlight, jeweled glyphs spiral around the Horn. Those symbols that represent the twelve witching world houses—they're glowing and pulsing purple with psi fire. Literally dancing around the Horn's curving length like worshippers in a ritual.

The artifact sings in my ear like an opera diva, an aria soaring with range and power. A coda powerful enough to bring the house down.

ZARINA SELENE, GEMINI QUEEN.

CLAIM.

YOUR.

THRONE.

Oh, hell to the yeah. After years of dodging and running and fighting my fate, I am *so* totally down with that plan.

Problem is, I'm clearly not the only witch who's hearing this shit.

Cleo's already sprinting for the artifact, tossing the Glaive of Wind aside like a crushed beer can at a kegger while she lunges for the big prize.

My jaws part and I roar like blazes, because that is *my* fucking Horn.

My lightning voice guns my engine and brings kilojoules of voltage crackling up my throat. I dive for my rival with forelegs extended and a bolt of purple lightning forking through my fangs.

The bolt slams into the pyramid floor at Cleo's heels, hard enough to shatter stone. I'm revving up for the kill shot—even though I still (frustratingly) don't really wanna kill her—when Cleo cries out and whirls an arm overhead.

A thick column of bespelled water rises from the pool and pours through the air. Funneling straight at me like a firehose.

Because my ex-bestie, like Zephyr, commands elemental Dark Fae witchcraft. And while Zephyr commands the wind…

The element Cleo commands is water.

I've seen up close and personal the damage being bitch-slapped by one of her rogue waterspouts can do to a flying dragon. The last one she summoned knocked Vasili's flying serpent right out of the skies and almost drowned him.

But I'm not having any.

Leaning into my teenage dragon agility, I veer and dive under the water cannon. Bellowing with rage, I sweep down on Cleo from behind. She's diving for the Horn, long legs churning under her short plaid skirt, a silky swath of merlot hair streaming in her wake, when I plow into her like a locomotive. My forelegs close around Cleo and pluck her from the floor while she howls in protest.

She's slippery as an eel in my talons, twisting and writhing to free herself from my grip. But I don't wait to find out what other deadly spells she's hiding in her bag of tricks. I wing across the Vault, the golden walls blurring around me, overfly my ossified kraken's tortured shape, and drop Cleo's struggling body directly in the pool.

Cleo's bloodcurdling scream of terror cuts short with a gurgle as she goes under.

Bugling with satisfaction till the walls ring with my triumph, I pivot in midair and arrow for the Horn.

My dragon just broke free from the cage of my human body. So she's nowhere near ready to give up her freedom.

But I'm the one running this show.

I'm the fucking queen.

I dive straight for the floor and fiercely will myself bipedal.

I land hard on my own two feet. Running, naked, and human. With a snarling cry that bursts from my throat, I snatch up the glowing Horn—

blazing hot enough to burn my fingers. Gasping with pain, I drop the artifact into Ceres' waiting hand.

A blinding flash of white light dazzles my eyes. Punctuated by a camera shutter's crisp click.

That shit's nothing magical. Just the pop of an old-fashioned flashbulb.

Through the silver spots dancing across my vision while I blow on my burned fingers to cool them, I spot a vintage automatic camera, rigged to the wall with a selfie stick and magically triggered to memorialize this moment—the climax of the Dean's Challenge—on film for the witching world masses. Like the bloody *Hunger Games* finale, but with witchcraft.

That's the flash that just got seen round the world on WNN. Like, we interrupt this broadcast to bring you a special message.

And, of course, I'm nakey.

You know, same as usual whenever I show up on TV.

From the pool behind me, a resonant howl builds. The piercing shriek of a soul in torment. That unholy sound makes my scalp crawl and my eardrums scream.

Sweet bleeding Jesus.

That shriek is literally not human.

Every cell in my body tingles with electric charge. I whip around with my whole heart jammed up against my esophagus.

My eye rivets right on the long snake neck of Cleo's sea dragon, rising from the pool like a cobra rising from a basket. Her brilliant crimson ruff writhes in Medusa snakes around her wicked head. Her fangy jaws leak steam around her scimitar teeth. Her golden orbs are slitted and glaring with intent.

That powerful column of neck, glittering garnet with dragonscale, spirals from the water and just keeps coming.

Fuck, she's arrowing straight at me.

I have a split second to wonder whether I'm about to be eaten on live TV, and if that will make Cleo queen, even though she just lost the Dean's Challenge—

Then her deadly advance falters… slows… as dull gray stone creeps up the ruby scales that sheathe her neck. My ex-BFF roars out a single deafening trumpet that makes the walls ring with despair. Swiftly the crawling gray spreads through her ruff and down her fangy muzzle.

Her eyes are the last thing to ossify, fixed wide and imploring, locked onto my horrified face.

"Cheese on toast," I whisper into the sudden blistering silence.

I don't even know how to feel, except grateful to be still breathing. This isn't the ending I ever wanted for Cleo.

As for Mordred, it's definitely not the ending I'm gonna settle for.

I'm still staring at my ex-lover's sea dragon statue, now horribly matching the anguished kraken statue beside her, when that awful silence is shattered by the quiet snick of a lock releasing.

A panel in the wall I didn't even know was a door swings open.

"That's one way to disarm an ossification curse," Nikolai Romanov says calmly, stepping through the gap.

To my complete fucking shock, he's not even looking at me. He's turned away to speak over his shoulder to Vasili, my Goblin King, who saunters calmly into the room on his heels.

V's sharp pale eyes, blazing like the northern lights, lock onto my riveted body. In a single penetrating sweep, he assesses every inch of me for damage—an assessment made easier since I'm, you know, naked.

Having reassured himself that I'm ambulatory, his gaze shoots straight to the Horn and statue behind me.

His sexy-pretty face kindles with a fierce possessive pride.

Then my dominant alpha does something he's never done before.

For anyone.

V drops gracefully to one knee and says, in a voice that makes the walls sing with triumph, "All hail the Gemini queen."

Swiftly Nikolai pivots toward me. When he catches sight of Cleo, his coolly controlled face turns white as chalk.

At this exact moment, I don't give a single shit that I'm standing mother-naked in front of V's dad and the whole witching world on live TV.

I bolt across the floor with a cry and hurl myself into my Goblin King's arms.

V's tall body folds around me and wraps me tightly in his supple strength. My alpha's delicious scent of caramel and vetiver swamps my senses, laced with that rich note of birchwood that I associate with his mating rut.

I bury my face in his cool slim neck, grip his uniform blazer in both fists, and swallow a whimper against his skin

"Well done you," V purrs into my hair. "Although rather less fortunate, I see, for the kraken."

I know right away he doesn't wanna give anything away that his shithead dad could use against us. Still, his concern for our kraken pours through our mating bond.

Somewhere in the middle of this revolution we've been leading, my horrible snake of an alpha seems to have grown an actual heart.

For fuck's sake, he hisses in my head. *Don't tell anyone.*

"Yeah, no." I struggle to get my shit together in front of his sharp-eyed dad and twist around to shoot our kraken's ossified form an anxious look. "Mordred couldn't control his shift. Then he couldn't speak the counterspell with his, uh, beak."

"I see," V says coolly. "How unfortunate."

Behind his facade of indifference, his face is bleak and desolate.

I tilt back my head, lock onto his baby blues, and whisper, *Don't despair, bad boy. I got a hunch how to fix him.*

How? His sharp eyes narrow to search mine.

I'd like to share the deets with him, I really would. But I don't wanna lay all my cards on the table with V's asshole dad right there, somewhere behind me, and hopefully not staring at my bare ass. If Nikolai has mad telepath skillz in his warlock assassin toolkit, I don't wanna find out the hard way.

Instead I settle for saying vaguely, "I've kinda got an idea what to do about Mordred and his, uh, situation. But I'm gonna need you… and all the guys… with me to make it work."

"Color me intrigued, Your Majesty," V murmurs. Driving home his point and reinforcing my claim to the throne with every snaky breath.

Gazing past him at the open door and the empty crypt hallway beyond, I frown. A fresh spurt of alarm kicks my heartbeat into overdrive. "Speaking of which, where is everyone? Ronin and Max and Ash and the whole gang. Is everyone… okay?"

Oh, sweet Mary, Mother of God. What will I do if they're not?

"Well, they were when I left them." Deftly V shrugs out of his uniform blazer. "Don't fret, darling. I daresay they'll be along. Lucius is bringing them."

Gently (for him), he wraps his jacket around my naked shoulders. When I shove my arms through the sleeves and button it, I look like a high-class stripper (all I need are platform heels and a briefcase). But at least my boobs and butt and crotch are covered.

I seem to be struggling to string words together, but I manage a few more. "So, um, your father?"

"Indeed." V's voice is an absolute study, suspended somewhere between irony and suspicion. "As highly unlikely as it seems, he now appears to be on our side. Or so he claims. Just wait until you hear his proposal."

In unison, we pivot suspiciously to study the subject of this hurried convo.

Nikolai Romanov stands perfectly still, directly before the sea dragon's outstretched head, his straight back turned toward us, dark head tilted back to gaze up at her in silence. Even from behind, he gives Mads Mikkelsen vibes from *Casino Royale* in a major way. All that's missing is an asthma inhaler and an eye that weeps blood.

Like he feels the weight of our stare, Nikolai says into the brittle silence, "Once it's been triggered, there's no known counterspell to break an ossification curse."

At his words, my formerly unpredictable dash of Valyrian foresight starts singing like a glee club. I've had my dark suspicions about that gene—foresight—being one of my recessives, along with clairvoyance, that got switched on, back when I claimed the Unseelie Queen's crown in Avalon.

But now is the moment I finally know for sure.

I fold my arms across my chest for extra decency (since I'm not wearing a bra) and tell Nikolai Romanov, "That's where you're wrong, Le Chiffre—wrong about Mordred and Cleo both. I'm queen of the witching world for a goddamn reason. Ceres is a fertility goddess. The Horn is a fertility artifact. I'm fertile as fuck and all my alphas are in rut. There's literally one thing, and one thing *only,* my warlocks and I need to do right now."

And my dominant alpha, bless his horrible snaky black heart, picks up what I'm putting down like it's an Olympic relay and we've trained four years with a coach for this shit.

"And I'll be fucked if I'll do it with you watching, *papochka,*" Vasili says coolly. "Because there *are* limits, even for despicable me. Clearly—for whatever intriguing reason—you want Cleo back, ambulatory and breathing, even knowing she'll never be queen."

"She's a highly trained agent and a valuable AIB asset," Nikolai says, dark eyes inscrutable. "Of course I want her back."

I'm not sure I trust the guy's reasons, but whatever. Between my foresight and my deep belief in what I need to do to save the witching races from slow extinction, not to mention this quantum superheat I'm still rocking, my mind's made up.

Vasili hums (that's him being unpersuaded by his untrustworthy dad, like I am) but keeps right on going. "As for Zara and myself, we want Mordred. So you'll need to go somewhere else, along with McSnicker and her menage and anyone else who isn't in the royal harem who comes blundering along—and let the rest of us start fucking."

Chapter Thirty-Four
Neo

"Wow," I say when I can finally breathe again, after finding the Vault door wide open, my cherished one finally safe and queen of the witching world inside, Mordred and Cleo both shifted and turned horribly to stone, and all the rest of our polycule (except Vasili) wrapped in each other's arms and clustered together, glaring daggers of suspicion at V's awful dad.

V's clearly taken the lead on dealing with his dad, and he seems to feel he can't be smothered in a group hug while he's doing it.

However, V does keep a very possessive arm wrapped around Zara's waist at all times, even while she's shimmying back into the plaid schoolgirl skirt I've brought along for her.

"It's a perfectly reasonable explanation," Nikolai Romanov says calmly. "I'll explain my rationale to the rest of you the way I've already explained it to my son."

"Be sure to speak slowly, Le Chiffre, so those of us who aren't in the spy business can understand." Zara buttons her skirt and props a hand on her hip. My precious fated mate is completely naked under that skirt and V's uniform jacket, which makes her eye-popping cleavage look amazing.

To his credit, I guess, Nikolai Romanov keeps his unreadable chocolate eyes on her face without peeking.

Somehow, he's not even tempted by my fated mate's incredible hotness. Despite the fact that he's apparently straight.

It's unnatural.

Honestly, I swear, the father is as bad as the son used to be. Nikolai Romanov must have an ice cube in his chest instead of a heart.

Maybe that's a job requirement for being the AIB director.

"They were lovers before," Nikolai says now, in a tone that sounds completely controlled, despite seeing all his twisty political machinations defeated and having his *protégée* turned to stone behind him. "They can be lovers again."

"Vasili and Cleopatra were lovers?" Draco Mars tucks Mallory more tightly under his protective arm and stares at Vasili. "What the *hel*, Romanov? I thought you were supposed to be *fokking* gay."

"Oh, please." Vasili raises his eloquent eyes toward the peaked roof of the golden pyramid we're standing in. "Get with the program, darling, *do*. I happen to be bisexual. But that's beside the point. Zara is literally the only woman I've ever loved. What's more to the point is, she's the only woman I ever *will* love. Rest assured Cleo Ferrari appears nowhere on my sexual Christmas list. I'd rather get coal in my stocking."

"I wasn't referring to my son." Despite being a total enigma, Nikolai Romanov's tone gives some things away. Right now, he's straining for patience. "I'm referring to Cleopatra and Zarina. The two queens of the witching world."

Now fully bipedal, still bare chested but buttoned back into Ronin's leather pants (which make him look unbelievably hot), Lucius finishes tying back his hair and gives V's dad one of his stern headmaster looks. "In point of fact, Director Romanov, Zara Gemini is now the sole occupant of the witching world throne. Based on the weight of recent events, I fully expect Theo Mercury and the Arcane Senate to vote for Messalina's immediate abdication."

"That's right," I chime in stoutly. "I just called Dad from the landline in Lucius' office, that's the whole reason I was late. The entire Senate, even the anti-monarchists, ratified Zara's claim as soon as they saw the Dean's Challenge newsfeed. No one's doubting anymore that she's the strongest witch and the best possible queen we can have."

Lucius gives me a nod of approval for my initiative that makes me warm all over. Especially my face.

Because, of course, I'm blushing.

"As for Ms. Ferrari," Lucius tells Mr. Romanov, "there can be no such construct as *two queens*. There's simply no precedent in witching world law or history."

"Rest assured I'm well aware of the relevant provisions of witching world law and history, Master Aries," V's dad says, all crisp and crackly with annoyance. I guess he doesn't get contradicted very often. "I'm referring to the fact that, just as a queen's male consort acquires the title of king, a queen's female consort—should she claim one—acquires the title of queen."

When I realize what he's implying, I practically swallow my tongue. I literally have to cough before I can speak.

But there's no airspace for me to even protest, because Max and Ronin and Zephyr are all objecting simultaneously in their various emphatic ways. While Vasili, who's apparently heard this idea before, gives his awful dad the Romanov eyebrow and a smug *I told you so* smirk.

Racetrack and Dez both look appalled (even though they aren't in the polycule and obviously don't have any philosophical objection to the idea of Zara being with another girl).

Even Mallory's mouth falls open as she stands, protectively bookended, between Jae and Draco.

Ash helpfully rubs my back to stop me from coughing, which is so comforting and nice. But his distaste for the proposed addition of Cleo to our polycule is stamped all over his craggy face.

"Oh, hell to the no." Zara plants both hands on her curvy hips and stares Mr. Romanov down like the badass she is. "That's a hard no. Not only because I can never trust Cleo again after the way she betrayed me and lied to me and all the other shit she pulled, and then didn't even have the integrity to take responsibility for. But also—I don't share my guys with other chicks. They're *my* kings, not hers."

Mr. Romanov frowns down his aristocratic nose (which is very like Vasili's) at Zara. "That is a highly unreasonable attitude for a polyamorous queen to assume. Why should your males be confined to a single woman while you, despite being allegedly bisexual—"

"She is bisexual. But we do not want any other woman." Max looms right over Mr. Romanov (who is not a large man) and scowls ferociously. "We only want Zara and each other. Stop interfering in matters you do not understand."

"None of your bloody business who we fuck, is it, mate?" Ronin says heatedly.

Steely with resolve, Mr. Romanov says, "I beg to differ. Whom our queen chooses to mate is the entire witching world's business and therefore mine—"

"Moment of truth, darlings. Behold the hidden motive for my father's sudden swerve of heart," V proclaims, all sharp and snaky with malice. "As Zara continued to evade his clutches and close in on the prize in this Vault, he simply recalculated the odds—and realized those odds now favored Zara rather than Cleo for the throne. So he turned his coat."

Every word Vasili utters drips with the venom of scorn. "Obviously, he grasps that he'll never hold the same leverage over Zara that he wields over Messalina. So he's hoping to retain his political influence by adding his naughty celebrity assassin-spy *protégée*—Cleo—to our harem."

We all look accusingly at Mr. Romanov, who's actually starting to perspire a little, even though it's cool in the Vault. Now he definitely looks like Le Chiffre sweating through a poker game against James Bond.

I have to admit, I'm starting to see Zara's point about the resemblance.

However, Mr. Romanov still looks more irritated at his son than worried about his own fate.

"Are you deliberately overlooking the obvious, Vasya, or can you truly be that obtuse? Because I would genuinely hate to believe the latter regarding any son of mine," V's dad raps out. "My only heir is now the new queen's dominant alpha and will shortly be crowned one of her kings. With any luck, during that mating rut you're obviously experiencing, you'll sire the next queen—assuming you haven't already. Like it or not, the primary vehicle for my continued political influence is *you*."

V's lips part on a gasp so his fangs peep out. Then his pretty eyes narrow dangerously. "If you actually believe I'll lift a finger for your sake, *papochka,* you've clearly lost your mind. Have you forgotten I'm *queer*?"

Mr. Romanov's slender frame stiffens and his own eyes narrow right back.

"Whatever else you are, Vasya, you're still my son." His slippery voice goes rough. "The only son I have. Just as I'm your only father."

Hearing those words of quasi-acceptance (or at least tolerance) we all thought he'd never hear from his homophobic father, V hisses in audible shock. Under the patina of crypt dust we're all wearing, Vasili's already pale face turns several shades paler.

If he was anyone other than Vasili, I'd be worried he might faint.

Mr. Romanov's brow folds in a frown. He glides a step forward, but V's casting hand flashes out in warning. Our alpha's telekinesis sweeps his father violently a good six feet back.

So much for family reconciliation.

I guess the Romanovs don't do that.

Before that snake Vasili can do anything worse to his awful parent, my cherished one steps decisively between them. She looks so completely fuckable in her little skirt and V's blazer, with her teal curls swinging to her saucy ass, that I'm totally distracted.

Not to mention the way she's flushed and scenting and sexed up in our mating bond.

"I feel like we're getting off track here," Zara announces in her queen voice. Her glittery finger rises to emphasize. "The first priority is busting Mordred free from that ossification curse. Period. That's Number One."

While Vasili regains his composure and Mr. Romanov straightens his clothing with an irritated tug, I give my wonderful fated mate my full attention.

Eyeing Mr. Romanov, Zara sighs and unfolds a second finger. "We gotta save Cleo too, I guess. That's Number Two. Even though she definitely *isn't* joining this harem, and that's final. Besides, I think she's got Milan Fashion Week coming up or something."

"It's Paris. She does Milan in September," V's dad mutters, showing a level of familiarity with Cleo's celebrity supermodel schedule that I find interesting.

"Oh, right. But let's not forget the biggie." Zara's third finger shoots up. "The sooner we start saving the witching world, the better. That shit can't wait, like, *at all*. The witching population literally gets smaller every day. Every witch and warlock who dies needs to be replaced just to stop the decline. But what we really need to do is reverse it."

Now her queen voice becomes her sex voice and drops two octaves. "By fucking. All of us. Now that I'm really queen."

My precious one's sex voice squeezes my dick like a hand. All the blood in my body gathers in my shaft. Every guy in our polycule shifts and discreetly adjusts his fly.

"Sign me the fuck up for that, love," Ronin says huskily. "Sign us all up."

"Should we go back to the *domus* then?" I ask hopefully, with visions of Zara's big medieval bed dancing in my head.

Zara turns thoughtfully to eye the WNN news cam overlooking the scene from its selfie stick. Slowly she says, in her breathy Marilyn Monroe voice, "No, baby. I think we'll do it here."

Instantly the temperature in this room spikes at least ten degrees hotter.

Ash stops rubbing my back and sucks in an audible breath. Zephyr stops prowling the confines of the room and pivots sharply to face Zara, swords bristling over his shoulders, face intense behind his eyepatch.

Lucius' brow furrows and, even though we don't share a mating bond since he hasn't bitten me (yet), I know he's worried about his professorial dignity.

But only until Zara locks onto our headmaster's pensive face. Then her lush lips curl in a grin that's pure mischief. "You up for that, Teach?"

"I…" Lucius clears his throat and glances uncomfortably at Mr. Romanov, who happens to be a trustee on the school board.

"They can't fire you," I point out to Lucius helpfully. "You're about to be crowned king. We'll all have honorary seats on the school board. We'd outvote the opposition if they tried."

Lucius' fierce gaze shifts to Zara and turns wolfish. He's just so intensely aware of her right now, the way we all are. All her mates. Her scent of creamy peaches, the intoxicating scent of her fertility, perfumes the air like incense.

Her pink tongue sneaks out to moisten the full bow of her upper lip. At the sight, Lucius' fangs drop and his eyes pulse red.

Zara saunters across the floor to wrap her arms around his neck. That move makes her skirt ride up until the pert swell of her ass peeks out.

At the sight, Maxim snarls and closes in behind her. He and Lucius have a thing building between them too, it's been really sweet to watch. When Max wraps his possessive arms around Zara's hips, he's also holding Lucius. His golden dragon eyes look imploring, like he's begging Lucius to love both of them. I don't think it's a look Lucius can resist for long.

A low continuous growl rises from Lucius' chest.

To me, that sounds like a growl of anticipation.

Vasili smirks at the scorching scene that's igniting right in front of us, then crooks a playful finger at Zephyr. "In that case, I do believe I'll call in that little favor you owe me now, Your Radiance. Dark Fae King to Goblin King."

It takes me a minute to remember Zephyr owes V a blow job. In exchange for the one V gave Zephyr on my dad's yacht.

Oh my gosh.

"Oh, fuck yeah," Ronin mutters, sharing a heated look with me. "About bloody time for those two, innit?"

"Uh-huh." I nod vigorously and definitely wish my world wasn't so blurry without my glasses, whose cracked lenses are still tucked in my blazer pocket. I'll need to find an optometrist on the mainland later.

For now? I need to get closer to the action.

Much closer.

You know, just so I can see.

Unlike me, Ronin has no modesty, so he drags his shirt over his head with one hand, without even waiting for all of us to finish talking about it. Thankfully, he's close enough to my nearsighted eyes that I have two whole seconds to appreciate the heart-stopping visual of my boyfriend's sculpted body with his raven hair pouring down his back and the black dragon inked across his golden chest and winding around one shoulder.

Then Ronin reaches unselfconsciously for his fly.

"Oookay then," Racetrack announces to the room. "Everyone who isn't hers, we're outtie. Even if they are all gonna boink on live TV, they don't need a physical audience in here breathing down their necks."

"Maybe leave the kitten though, cobber," Dez suggests gently. Someone (probably Dez) has let the kitten out of her duffel and apparently fed her some kibble while I was on the phone. Now our sweet pet is curled up on the altar in a pool of creamy sweetness, contentedly washing her face.

"Thank you, Racetrack. Thank you, Dez," I tell them earnestly, because it's really obvious no one else is going to. "And yeah, you can absolutely leave the kitten with us. I mean, she's part of this too. Part of our family."

Zephyr is already stalking toward V. That Dark Fae is taking his time, easing open the zipper of his dragonscale armor—literally one centimeter at a time—while V devours every move with lips parted and eyes glittering. Ash is kneading the nape of my neck with his big callused hand, letting me know without words that he's totally ready for a repeat of that one unforgettable night I railed his incredibly tight ass, and I can hardly even breathe just thinking about it. Zara and Lucius are drowning in each other's eyes. While Max is already nuzzling Zara's neck and unbuttoning her blazer from behind.

"C'mon, Teach," Zara whispers to Lucius, low and husky. "Let's make some puppies."

Racetrack and Dez and Mal and her guys hastily clear the room—thankfully ushering out V's stiffly unwilling dad, who still seems fixated on somehow getting back into Vasili's good graces and unwilling to drop the subject.

"Have fun in here, guys. You've definitely earned it." Mallory blushes a little when she says it, but her soft smile says it all. She's happy for Zara. Happy for all of us.

"Guess we've already aced the final." Zara grins back at her friend. "If this is what ends up saving the witching world, we'll call it extra credit."

"You'll probably be the next First Girl, Zara." Still smiling, Mal has barely closed the door behind herself when Lucius' control completely shatters and he pounces.

Chapter Thirty-Five
Zara

I've got maybe thirty second tops to prep my titanium pussy before I take Lucius' knot.

Fortunately, Max's dragonfire-hot hands are already under my skirt and between my legs. Now he spreads my bare folds wide, ignoring for the moment the quantum superheat building and swelling in my clit, to work a finger into my slick cunt.

Sweet baby Jesus in the manger.

Max has barely gotten started. But I'm already so soaked I'm hearing an audible wet sucking sound with every pump.

I have a breath to wonder if that camera's rigged for audio. And, if so, exactly how sensitive the mic might be.

"Your delectable pussy is proof of your fertility," Max growls in my ear. Because of course my dragon king alpha is reading my mind through our mating bond. He nuzzles into the mating bite scars on my neck. "They should all see and hear how well we please you when we fuck you."

Between the suck of his mouth on my sensitive scars and the thrust of his finger in my wet cunt, I'm already breathless.

Now, hearing his words, all I can do is whimper.

Without even waiting for my response, Max works a second finger into my greedy hole. My cunt pulses and clenches around the delicious fullness, which makes me moan and widen my stance.

Again, my gaze drifts to the camera's winking light.

My modesty is still preserved (barely, I guess) as long as Vasili's blazer covers my tits and my skirt covers my crotch.

But that modesty only lasts until Lucius pushes the blazer roughly off my shoulders. The fabric falls away behind me to bare my tits to the world.

Good thing I've never been the shy type.

With a groan, my headmaster cups and cradles my boobs in his possessive hands, then pushes them together and mouths his way across the swells. They're extra tender and full due to my heat, like I'm gonna need a bigger bra. Lucius loses his mind during my heats, so his wolf talons are already sprouting. Every prick of claw and fang makes my nipples tingle and tighten.

The torchlight flickering over the pyramid walls casts a shimmering golden light over my skin and Lucius' Renaissance mane of chestnut curls. That light makes my nipple rings shine and turns Lucius' sherry gaze to cognac.

When my headmaster's fangy mouth closes over the tight bud of one nipple to tongue my piercing, my head falls back against Max's shoulder on a whine.

"So good," I gasp. "Fuck, Lucius, that's so good."

"Get her ready for my knot," Lucius mutters, all wolfish and guttural, to Max. His rough voice echoes from the walls.

My heavy eyelids, which have fallen shut, struggle to lift. I have a sec to worry if Max is gonna tolerate being bossed around like that by another alpha.

But it turns out, when it's Lucius, it's all good.

Loosing a gruff dragonish growl in reply, Max works in a third finger that stretches my hole deliciously. My girl cream lubes me up and eases his way. At the same time, his thumb finds my swollen clit and rubs. My back is pinned against his front, so I can feel the tumescent bulge of his complicated dragon cock jutting against my ass.

The building tension coils, hot and low, in my belly. My pussy pulses around his fingers and my clit aches with need.

I whimper and ride my alpha's hand in a way that's impossible for my little skirt to hide.

Cheese on toast.

This artifact-fueled quantum superheat I'm rocking for all my guys?

This shit is *intense*.

The first peak hits me hard and tosses me high. That starter O rips a sharp spiraling cry from my throat that's impossible to mistake for anything but what it is. The sound of me coming all over Max's hand, like the unrepentant slut I am. If anyone in the witching world still harbored any question about what kind of queen they're getting, I've just removed all doubt.

In my peripheral vision, the Horn pulses in Ceres' stone grip like a theme park light show.

I'd really love to see what the rest of my warlocks are doing. Because I can definitely hear with my shifty senses the low male moans and curses whispering from these echoey golden walls. But Lucius is looming over me in a way that blocks out other visuals. He wants my full focus on him.

The wolf king alpha who's ramping up to rail me.

"Take off your skirt, Ms. Gemini," Lucius growls, fangs pricking my full and tender tits like maybe he's revving up to give me another mating bite. "Show me how eager you are for my knot."

Limp and shaky with aftershocks in the wake of my first big O, my hands are trembling so hard I can barely undo my button.

But I'm really well motivated.

So I manage.

Max pulls his fingers out of me—a loss that makes my empty hole clench in protest—barely long enough to toss my clothes aside.

Now I'm naked and exposed.

Trapped like prey between my two carnivorous alphas.

Without my skirt in the way, the whole witching world can see my bare pussy, flushed and swollen and glistening with my juices. With all our warnings, I figure we've delayed the moment long enough for WNN to get an advisory up and responsible adults to clear any minors from the TV room.

With only an age-appropriate audience remaining, the whole world can watch while Max reaches back between my thighs, swipes his fingers through my mess, slicks moisture up my crack, then starts lubing my rear pucker with my own pussy juice.

Right in front of everyone.

"It is an ancient ritual, this, is it not?" Max rasps in my ear, breathing heavily, but still tracking my thoughts through our mating bond. "A fertility rite we practice. Tonight, you are the sacrifice."

My inner dragon bellows with excitement and tries to rise. For her, fucking means a mating flight. But we're not in control here. Neither she nor I.

I've ceded control to Max and Lucius.

Lucius retains enough self-possession and innate headmaster modesty to keep his back to the camera when he drops trou. His shaft juts before him, swollen purple with need and cola-can thick. Nestled in a thatch of wiry chestnut curls, the ruddy bulge of his swelling knot makes my cunt weep with need.

Lucius fists his shaft and squeezes his knot in a way that makes all three of us (including the closely watching Max) push out a thick groan.

"Are you wet enough, my queen?" Lucius' red eyes burn into me. "Wet enough to take my knot?"

"Yeah, think so," I gasp. *Obviously, Teach. Can't you tell?*

Hearing me sass him through our mating bond, he bares his wolfish fangs on a snarl. "Show me."

Like… really?

That command is enough to bring heat racing to my cheeks. My gaze flashes to the camera and the blinking red eye above the lens that means it's still filming.

"Eyes on me, Ms. Gemini," Lucius snaps.

All righty then. Guess this is really happening.

"Oh, fuck me," I moan.

Even for a polyamorous queen like me, this feels like a lot. A lot of exposure and a lot of submission to the first alpha who ever claimed me and bit me. A lot of exposure and submission in public.

But he isn't asking me.

He's telling me.

Good thing that I trust him and love him. The way I trust and love all my guys. I don't always need to be in control. I can safely surrender to his strength.

So I do.

I wave the white flag in surrender.

Biting my lower lip, I reach between my quivering thighs and spread my pussy wide.

The musk of my own arousal mingles with Lucius' gamy wolf scent and the sulfurous bite of brimstone from Max's dragon. Lurking like a stalker behind me, my dragon king probes the sensitive rim of my pucker with a finger. Tremors of sensation cascade over my skin and gather at the base of my spine. I'm still sighing and shivering when he stops teasing and works his digit into the tight clutch of my passage.

Sharply I gasp at the intrusion. The burn and stretch of resistance and pressure.

But I like ass play—I like it a lot—and the building ache of another looming climax is swelling in my clit and making my thighs shake.

The relentless pressure of Max's finger penetrates the strangling ring of my sphincter with a *pop!* that floods my system with a heady rush of endorphins.

"Ah, hell, Max!" Weak with desire, my fingers slip away from my wet vulva.

"No, my queen. Spread yourself wide for me," Lucius says, thick and guttural with his wolf. "Beg me to swive that needy quim of yours."

When he uses that old-fashioned language he learned growing up, reading vintage porn pilfered from the library of his Hungarian grandsire's castle, he always sends me over the edge.

"Fuuuuuck," I groan like a door hinge that needs oil.

But I've been asking for this.

Asking for it every time I tease him.

I swallow and close my eyes against the watching camera. Maybe it isn't miked after all.

"I'm waiting, Ms. Gemini," Lucius grates in his gravelly wolf voice. "Don't make me ask again. Or I swear you'll regret it."

With an elemental thrill of mingled arousal and fear, my eyes flash open to find my headmaster towering over me. Chestnut fur sprouts from his chest and ripples down his shoulders. Muscle flexes in his shoulder as he fists his thick dick in rough impatient pulls.

He and that knot of his are monsters.

But they're *my* monster.

"Please, Master Aries," I whimper, wide-eyed and imploring as I gaze up at him. I freaking love when we play this game. "Fuck my hole with your big cock."

Saliva drips from his massive fangs. He's literally slavering for me. "Now beg for my knot. And make it good."

Oh, I can definitely make it good. Good for him and good for me. Good for the whole witching world, in fact.

I lower my voice to a soft little whisper. "Please. Pretty please. Let me take your knot."

"Good girl," he growls on a long exhale, like the monstrous beast he is.

Barely able to vocalize when he's this close to shifting, Lucius closes in on my trembling body. He swipes his swollen cock back and forth through my copious slick till his length is glistening with my juices. Then he probes my weeping hole and—finally!—works his rod into my splayed pussy.

He's massive, but he's fucking ruthless.

One taloned hand locks under my thigh to hitch my knee high. Then he drives his full length into my hungry channel till he bumps my cervix.

He usually fucks me open a good long while before he knots me.

But not tonight.

(Or do I mean, *knot* tonight? At this point, I'm practically starring in one of the omegaverse romance novels Neo and I like to read together in bed.)

But the press of Lucius' prodigious knot against my vulva isn't taking *no wait suddenly not so sure about this* for an answer.

I dig my heel into my wolf king's flexing ass, wrap my arms around his sweating neck, and hold on tight. Desperately I cling to him, barely balanced on one foot, while Lucius Aries stuffs me full with his bulbous knot. Behind me, Maxim Rasputin strips down, then works his own forked dragon king junk into my ass.

Max's dick is shaped like the Devil's forked tail. The better to stuff me with.

For the sinful pleasure he delivers, I'd gladly burn in hell.

When Max is seated deep, all the way in my rear channel, the plink of his barbed dick engages to lock him in place. Now I'm plugged and spitted in both holes between my two alphas.

Couldn't escape if I tried.

Good thing I'm all in. Escape is the last thing I want from these two. Ever.

I never wanna leave any of my guys. And now I'll never have to.

Pinned tight between my alphas' fiercely thrusting bodies, vision filled with the furry expanse of Lucius' rangy chest, my tits bounce with every pump. Every strike and recoil of cock in hole wrings a cry from my heaving lungs.

Sweet hell, they're working together so good. Max and Lucius. Both dicks rubbing together inside me through the thin membrane that barely separates them, so they're fucking each other as well as me.

This moment has been *such* a long time coming.

"Lucius, I am yours," Max whispers, low and raw, cheek pressed hard against my temple. "Yours and hers. Only swear… you will never leave us."

That's the lonely boy, fatherless and abused in the lair by his dragon bitch mother (now dead, killed by Lucius, and good riddance), longing for the father he never knew.

"Dear boy," Lucius gasps through his fangs. "I swear I will never leave you. *Any* of you."

When my wolf king grips Max's head and pulls my dragon king into a fangy kiss, their intimacy pushes me right over the edge, oh God, into another wailing public orgasm.

The death-grip clench of my cunt floods with jet after jet of Lucius' potent seed. His knot bottles me up tight, so all that copious jizz has nowhere else to go. His spunk floods my fertile uterus. Simultaneously, the kick and spurt of Max's dick in my ass inundates my back door, while his barb traps his potent dragon seed inside me.

Not a drop is spilled or wasted.

Max roars out his climax through clenched teeth. My inner dragon trumpets till my soul rings like a bell.

But neither of my alphas are finished. And neither am I.

God, neither am I.

Even though I squish from both ends with every stroke.

I can't even look at the camera's blinking light. But I hope my subjects are enjoying this royal porn show we're broadcasting, you know, for the good of the realm.

At the thought, my sagging head snaps up.

"First command, queen to subjects," I gasp, staring straight into the lens. "Everyone fuck. Pedigree doesn't matter. Purity of bloodline doesn't matter. You can cross racial lines." Because that misguided belief has been a crippling constraint for the four arcane races for way too long.

Now, my Valyrian foresight is whispering in my ear, that's one of the main reasons we're not multiplying.

"Just fuck," I finish on a moan, pussy flexing around Lucius' knot. "Fuck who you love. Whoever that is. Just fuck."

By now, the Horn of Ceres is projecting a literal laser light show over the sloping golden walls. The entire pyramid blazes with colored lights. The flickering light bathes the tangle of stone kraken poised on the pool's rim and the long sea dragon neck snaking from the surface.

Are those statues *breathing*?

Or is that only an optical illusion from the play of light against stone?

Closer at hand, our kitty is sitting up straight on the altar, whiskers twitching and alert, swiping at the dancing beams of light with a tiny white paw.

Over Lucius' straining shoulder, while his hips piston into me nonstop like a battery-powered bunny, I finally catch my first searing glimpse of Neo and Ash. Both my bookworm and my Seelie Prince are nakey and following my lead so perfectly.

Same as always.

That's one of the things I love about these two.

My bookworm is flushed and excited and bleary-eyed without his glasses, but still so careful as he works his way gently into Ash from behind. As for my Seelie Prince, Ash is braced on hands and knees at the perfect angle so he can watch Max and Lucius ruin me. His silver eyes burn like lamps, his brow is all scrunched up, and the expression on his weathered face is blissful.

Nothing makes Ash happier than submitting. To any of us.

I figured that out on Day One.

When Neo finally seats his shaft balls-deep in our soon-to-be Potions prof, then clamps a hand around Ash's neck to shove his head down (because Neo too is learning what his new lover needs), Ash's big beefcake body sways and trembles all over.

"Oh, Geezus, kid," Ash groans from the heart, reaching between his thick thighs to pump his own rigid length. Between his fingers, his Jacob's Ladder piercings gleam pink and purple in the light show that Horn is projecting.

"It's okay. You're doing really well, Ash," Neo tells him sweetly, all breathless. "You're really tight. Especially when you squeeze like that, wow! You're going to make me come really hard."

Safe to say our First Boy is excelling at this extra credit assignment.

Which comes as a surprise to no one.

Now my gaze swerves to Exhibit B. The other act in this three-ring circus we're staging for the benefit of our viewing audience.

Over Lucius' other shoulder, I can finally see, a naked Ronin has been teasing V and Zephyr. Evading them. Making them hunt him. Really making them work for it.

But, fuck me, those two kings are hunting as a team. They've finally learned to work together.

Now they have Ronin pinned between them in a corner. The guy they've both fought over and practically killed over.

Oh, hell to the yeah.

This is gonna be good. So good it'll definitely trigger my next orgasm.

If the sheer pleasure of watching doesn't kill me first.

Chapter Thirty-Six
Zephyr

"I have not entirely forgiven thee for the kraken, Vasili Romanov," I warn my nemesis in this harem, falling back on formal dialect for maximum effect. "Thy treacherous plan to recruit my enemy as thine ally in this harem. All thy sly and snakish schemes have now fallen to ruin."

"Oh, bloody hell, will you two get over this blooming rivalry?" my Ronin demands. He's naked and furious, in part because we've finally trapped him in a corner, and his ego doesn't care for being bested at his own game. "Vasili knows he bollocksed it all up. Don't you, love? But it's all worked out in the end, yeah?"

"For most of us." Vasili spares a pensive glance for my ossified cousin in the pool, still a tangle of stone tentacles and gaping beak—a sight I've been careful to pretend I find entirely untroubling. "I'll admit this wasn't entirely the outcome I intended."

"Not bloody done yet, though, are we?" Despite his annoyance at being cornered, Ronin is violently erect. The heavy silver ring of his Prince Albert piercing, like the dragon tattoo that twines around his torso, is an adornment he added during our years apart.

I can't get enough of it. Or of him.

"Stop mouthing off to your king and come here, you rascal." I wrap a hand around Ronin's wrist and reel him in while he grumbles and resists, which merely serves to inflame me further.

Vasili smirks at me over his shoulder and closes in behind him. We've both been stripping while we hunted. All of us driven, I dare say, by the electrifying impact of my scrumptious bride being double-dicked and ridden hard by the wolf and the dragon.

Zara's moans and sobs and cries of pleasure, coupled with her shifters' guttural growls, are still making the walls hum.

By now, Vasili Romanov is nearly naked, his Academy uniform scattered across the floor, mingled with my swords and boots and dragonscale. Vasili has retained only a pair of mouthwatering black lace panties stretched over his pretty cock. That tease of a garment cups his perky ass the way my hands will shortly do.

Together, he and Ronin are striking.

These two have loved long and true, all those years while I skulked behind the Avalon portal licking my wounds and stoking my rage.

I swear they are perfect. Perfect for each other, yes. But also perfect for me.

Ronin is flame-eyed and tawny-skinned and powerful, black mane slithering around the potent flex of a warrior's muscle. Aloft, he commands any saddle like the dragonrider he was born to be.

Like the wily fuck he is, Ronin wields every atom of his sexual appeal to taunt and torment.

Whereas Vasili is deceitful and vicious and fiendishly clever. Slim and pale as cream poured from a pitcher, all balletic grace and supple strength, crowned by a shag of gilded hair that frames sharp cheekbones, delicate jaw, and cruel mouth. His ice-blue eyes flash warning beacons as I pounce on Ronin like a hunting dragon and drag him into my arms.

"Come on, love." Ronin reaches behind him to reel Vasili in too. "I'd really fancy seeing the two of you share a proper snog."

Over Ronin's shoulder, our gazes lock.

Mine and Vasili's.

An electric current of raw desire, laced with aggression and domination, arcs between me and my horrid nemesis.

Then one corner of Vasili's mouth curls in a wicked grin. "Oh, but we've already kissed and made up. I'm terribly afraid you've missed it."

Ronin's expectant face falls with disappointment.

This, I cannot endure.

"Vasili Nikolayevich Romanov, by the Goddess, you are the most provoking creature." I pin Ronin against my violently erect cock with one arm, wrap my free hand in Vasili's silver hair, and drag the Goblin King into a claiming kiss.

Zara calls this one her dominant alpha, a title that invariably makes me fulminate, while the insufferable creature himself preens like a peacock. Still, this vicious rival yields to me. Vasili tucks up against Ronin's fine ass and sighs a note of tolerance (if not submission) into my mouth. His serpent's tongue slips between my lips to lick my tiny fangs. Simultaneously, his silken fingers graze my exquisitely sensitive ear tip.

That searing moment of foreplay, intensely sexual for any Fae, nearly launches me into orbit.

"That's it," Ronin says, thick and husky, nuzzling my neck and kneading my ass with his scorching flamethrower hands. "Be nice to each other. For Zara's sake, if not for mine."

"'Tis done for both your sakes," I mutter between feverish kisses that set my soul alight. "Always. And for Ash, who also desires this snake for some godforsaken reason."

Slippery as an eel, that imp of a Ronin chuckles and wiggles out from between me and my nemesis.

All too suddenly, I am holding Vasili in my arms.

With Ronin wrapped around both of us.

I don't entirely protest. Not when Ronin's mischievous hands are busily easing those inflammatory panties down Vasili's long legs. I fist Vasili's hair, soft as cobwebs in my grip, and slot his wicked mouth more deeply into mine.

Once we've disposed of Vasili's alluring lingerie, Ronin nudges into the kiss too, his hot tongue slicking against mine and Vasili's.

This shared kiss is messy and chaotic and wonderful.

I'm still accustoming myself to this maelstrom of sensation—Vasili's sleek cool body twining around me like a python, Ronin's hot mouth and fingers dancing along our joined limbs like tongues of flame—when Ronin sneaks a hand between us. His bold grip wraps around my aching shaft and fits me up against the curving length of Vasili's pretty cock.

I'm obliterated.

Ruined.

Immolated by this first incendiary flash of intimate contact, cock to cock, with my rival king. This terrible creature I have envied and distrusted and hated. This lover who replaced me, who claimed all the decadent delights of Ronin's wicked body and tempestuous soul during those endless years when Ronin thought me dead.

The one Zara has placed first above all others—even me, a male born to rule, with a kingdom at my feet—in her harem.

My eye locks on Vasili's startled face.

His pretty lips part to expose the tips of his fangs. His cock twitches and pulses against mine. His smooth brow furrows. The point of one razor-sharp fang presses into his lower lip.

"Thou art mine now, beautiful one," I whisper, under the rhythmic rising whimper of the relentless reaming Neo is giving Ash nearby.

Hearing me assert my claim, Ronin sucks in a sharp breath.

"Hmmmm." Vasili tilts his head to study me. The eyepatch that hides my deformity. The pointed ears that proclaim me *other*. The dragon-honed strength of my naked shoulders and biceps.

At last, his gaze falls to the turgid shaft jutting from the lick of green between my legs.

Then, like the demon he is, Vasili smirks. One lid lowers in a playful wink. "I beg to differ, Your Tumescence. I'm not yours. You're *mine*."

"Bloody hell. The two of you. Not boring with you lot in the harem, I'll give you that." With a chuff of laughter, Ronin wraps his fist around both of us—my aching shaft and Vasili's—and jacks our dicks together. Base to crown and back again.

The intensity of feeling both of them, both my lovers, old and new, rolls my eye back in my head under a tidal wave of obliterating pleasure.

When my vision clears, I'm kissing both of them together, frotting both of them together, slinging my pelvis into the punishing rhythm of Ronin's ruthless fist. I work a hand between us to find the jut of Ronin's pierced dick, because he too deserves pleasure, and pump him until he moans and writhes.

"Darlings," Vasili gasps into our heated kiss. "You'll come when I tell you… both of you… and not a moment sooner."

"Thou art an arrogant creature, boastful and vain," I gasp. "But damn the moon if you haven't stolen my soul."

I have observed how strongly Vasili Romanov is affected when his mates tell him they love him.

I'm not quite using the word *love* myself with this dangerous and deceitful creature.

Not yet.

But my admission strays perilously close. And, after all, he knows I cannot lie.

Vasili arches into Ronin's fist, throws his head back, and cries out to heaven as his climax boils through him.

The first splash of my rival king's hot seed against my dick sets me off like a witchfire explosion.

Blinding pleasure gathers at the base of my spine, coils in my balls, and boils down my shaft. I erupt with a shout into Ronin's pistoning fist, my cock spasming wildly in his grip, and anoint all three of us with a generous libation of royal Unseelie semen.

The ruthless rhythm of my fist around Ronin's cock ignites him too. The heavy ring of his piercing bounces against my fingers. The hot splatter of his cum drenches my hand and drips obscenely down my torso.

From the Horn of Ceres, a kaleidoscope of colored light shatters against the walls.

The wild display bathes the golden ceiling and paints the writhing tangle of our naked bodies in flickers of pink and violet and cobalt fire. The howl of Lucius' wolf, the bellow of my beloved Ash finding his own release with our sweet Neo, and my bride's triumphant scream of climax make my ears ring.

Even the kitten voices a startled mew.

The empathic bond I share with my dragon, standing sentinel over the crypt stairs to protect us during this precious sacred interlude, hums with Xhevith's excitement and satisfaction and love.

Completely spent and sated in every conceivable way, I slump limp and boneless into my lovers' embrace. In a moment of weakness, I even deign to allow my forehead to rest on the convenient shelf of Vasili's shoulder.

I breathe in deep his powerful mating scent. Caramel and musk and birchwood.

"Now… by the moon… I forgive you…" I pant into the pounding pulse under my lips "…for the kraken."

"Hells' bells, cuz. Will you *please* get over yourself?" The familiar drawl of Mordred's voice snaps my head up with a cry.

My eye locks on the familiar annoyance of a flamboyant cousin who's taller, more muscled, more liked, more sought-after in our youth than a sullen, bookish, introverted slim-boned Fae like myself could ever hope to be.

Mordred is fully himself again, more's the pity. I am exposed to the full effect of his midnight-blue hair and copper skin and the twin dimples bracketing his goatee in a mocking grin.

"Mordred," Vasili murmurs, still spent but visibly pleased to see the sex demon bane of my entire existence lurking at our side. "Thank fuck. It seems our public orgy has achieved the intended effect."

At the moment, I cannot see past him to the sea dragon. Cleopatra. She is my cousin, her Dark Fae sire was my uncle, and I would not wish her ill—if not for her monumental offenses against Zara.

But my rivalry with Mordred has always been personal.

"Sure did, babydoll. Y'all saved me from a long and boring life as a water ornament." My cousin's white teeth flash in his dark face. But his keen purple eyes never veer from mine. "Listen up, Cousin Z. Cuz I'm only gonna say this once."

"Go ahead," I say, with as much lordly dignity as I can muster in my current disheveled state, filthy and dripping with three men's semen. "Since it seems I cannot prevent thee."

Gently Mordred engulfs my chin in his big hand—greatly to my shock, since we haven't touched in years.

"Growing up," he says, low and earnest, "I never wanted your throne. That was always yours. I ain't my asshole brother. *He* wanted your throne, and I ain't sorry he's dead. All I ever wanted was *you*."

"Er…" Utterly befuddled in a most unroyal way, I blink up at him, not at all certain I trust the evidence of my own keen Fae senses. "But you… me…"

"It's appalling, really," Vasili intervenes, amusement dancing in his pretty eyes. "It's practically incestuous. The two of you are literally cousins."

"Second cousins, once removed." Still cupping my chin in his big hand, Mordred gives Vasili a playful wink. "That shit's even legal in the mortal realm."

"Got a point, he does," Ronin murmurs, nuzzling my shoulder. "What d'you think, love?"

In truth, I hardly know what to think. I require a moment to ponder my options. All too clearly, my bride has accepted this insurrectionist sex demon Unseelie kraken into her bed and her heart. That much became apparent when she fucked him and bit him in the crypt. As for Mordred, he chose to remain with her—with all of us—willingly. Even after we broke his summoning bond.

These others in our harem—especially Vasili—seem prepared to give the demon the benefit of the doubt.

Well, I am king now. Crowned and throned. Safely wedded to my royal bride. Even if he wished, Mordred can no longer supplant me as the Dark Fae King.

Also, there is the matter of that incendiary closet kiss we shared at my Avalon Academy birthday party all those years ago.

The kiss I've never quite forgotten, if I'm being honest (as I must be, for a Dark Fae cannot lie).

Mordred's fingers tighten infinitesimally on my jaw. He doesn't like to show it, but he's afraid of what I'll say.

Afraid of being hurt.

Afraid of being rejected.

Again.

His fate lies in my hands.

"I suppose," I say slowly to the circle of expectant faces around me, lovers old and new, "I can learn to live with a sex demon in our harem."

I wrap my hand in the wet spill of Mordred's midnight blue hair and draw his mouth to mine in a deep, claiming, not-so-cousinly kiss.

Chapter Thirty-Seven
Zara

"Cavolo, bella." Cleo exhales one of her long drama queen sighs. "Believe it or not, I don't actually want your crown. The truth is, I never wanted it. But my wishes have always been irrelevant. I never believed I had a choice."

I'm curled up in the depths of the Renaissance sofa in our *domus* great room with the kitten (who really needs a name when we have a minute) sleeping peacefully in my lap. Both of us are engulfed in the fragrant steam of the enormous mug of Neo's peppermint cocoa I'm cupping in my hands.

Beyond the sliding-glass doors, dawn is lightening the confines of our Roman-style courtyard, shimmering purple along the surface of our in-ground pool where Mordred is taking a quick dip, and painting the sky pink with Mediterranean sunrise.

I can already hear the drone of helicopter rotors as the first WNN news crews circle our villa. They're all hoping for an exclusive with the new queen and her eight warlocks.

As if the X-rated spectacle of all nine of us fucking on live TV was somehow not enough to satiate even the most avid subscriber in their viewing audience.

But I'm not gonna get sidetracked by the paparazzi.

"Sorry, Sunshine, but I'm not buying it," I tell my ex-BFF. Cleo's curled up alone on the ottoman, dewy-eyed and flushed from the shower we begrudgingly let her take in our *thermae*. Long limbs engulfed in a borrowed Academy bathrobe, she's pensively sipping a mug of black coffee (no calories).

My many grievances against my ex have lost the worst of their sting since I won the throne and she lost, but they're still facts. I tick them off with my fingers. "Let's see. You lied to me, betrayed me, literally tried to kill me—"

"Oh, please." Cleo shoots me a look of sheer exasperation. "If I wanted you dead, *amore mio*, I would not have resorted to my fists or pushed you—a levitating Mogadon, of all witches!—off a study carrel roof. Believe me, I know better ways to kill."

"Yeah, see, that right there's another problem," Ash points out. His big body is sprawled across the sofa beside me, with one arm slung around my shoulders and one around Zephyr, who's finally stopped pacing long enough to accept a mug of herbal tea from Lucius.

Now Lucius is tied up on the landline. But the comforting murmur of his voice floats from the doorway where he's stationed himself, phone cord stretched to the max, so his wolf can keep a protective eye fixed on me.

His freshly knotted mate.

Lucius' steady voice and Ash's solid strength, mingled with Zephyr's burnt amber and nutmeg scent, are all grounding as fuck. God knows, right now we all need that. Gratefully I lean into Ash and rub my cheek against his hand to scent him.

Good for Cleo to remember he's mine.

They're all mine.

My ex-bestie's violet eyes flicker wistfully over me and my guys on the couch, drift past Neo cuddled happily on the carpet at our feet, then lift to find Max, who's prowling and lurking behind the couch like the alpha dragon shifter he is.

"Be more specific, Asher," Cleo murmurs. "What problem precisely do you mean?"

"You being a trained killer," Ash tells her flatly. "And being one for years, apparently. How the heck does that even happen?"

"Don't blame Ms. Ferrari. Those were the terms of my arrangement with Messalina, agreed when Cleopatra was still very young." Nikolai Romanov has been standing so still before the glass doors (an escape route in case our come-to-Jesus convo goes to shit) that half the room's forgotten he's standing there.

Vasili and my other alphas and Cleo and me, we haven't forgotten.

Not for a sec.

Nikolai Romanov is the deadliest man in this room, even now when he's trying to play nice.

Especially now.

After their long and agonizing father-son estrangement, I really worry about the effect of his prolonged presence on Vasili.

Now, in the face of Romanov Senior's enigmatic comment which hasn't actually explained anything, V heaves a put-upon sigh from the dining room table where he's ensconced in his kimono, dabbing on high-end facial serum with the aid of an elegant hand-held mirror.

After our various ordeals and their aftermath, we've all showered (except Nikolai, who seems way too tense for that). And shortly we're all supposed to be eating Belgian waffles, judging by the homey sounds and yeasty smells emanating from the kitchen where Dez and Racetrack are cooking.

"He imagines he's answered your question, so that's all the information you're likely to get from him." Vasili waves his serum dropper in his father's general direction. "But I can tell you what you want to know. Cleopatra's been sneaking visits to *papochka*'s Crimean *dacha* and his Seychelles yacht since she was in diapers… practically."

Silhouetted against the sunrise, V's dad stirs. "Vasya, you were never intended to—"

"What?" V gives him the Romanov eyebrow. "*Know?* I have eyes and ears, don't I? She was your perfect little *protégée*, trained up in the AIB red room to spy and steal and kill. That's how you hid her from the world. Which is what Messalina asked you to do—hide her secret, half-Fae daughter from a world that had forgotten the Fae existed. She left all the pesky minor details of how to care for the brat to you."

Having unburdened himself of all this, Vasili takes up his rose quartz facial roller and starts smoothing serum over his cheekbones.

By giving himself a complete facial at the dining room table and rubbing his homophobic father's nose in it, V is more than making his point.

He's flipping his father the bird.

"But that's what I don't get. Why hide her at all?" Mallory is curled up on the other couch with her Cajun shifter, sipping orange juice and looking all First Girl attentive, while Draco mixes another round of incredibly potent-looking Screwdrivers for himself and Jae at the liquor cabinet.

"I mean," Mal ventures, "Cleo was the royal heir, so…"

"I was never the heir." Cleo frowns into her coffee, long lashes hiding her violet eyes. "I was merely the spare. My mother's legitimate heir was her pureblooded Aquarius daughter Cybelle—my half-sister. Until Cybelle was murdered by the queen killer." Her low tone turns brittle. "Only then did I become useful."

From his vantage at the window, Nikolai's slim body twitches. "You were always useful. To me."

"Ah, *si*, for the AIB, I have always had my uses." Cleo darts her mentor an inscrutable look. "For you and for them, I'm an expensive investment. Too expensive to waste."

Nikolai's dark head snaps toward her. "You will not be *wasted*. As the new queen's consort—"

"No!" Cleo exclaims (thankfully) before I can swallow my mouthful of cocoa and nope out myself on boarding that crazy train Le Chiffre over there is still riding. "If you and the AIB are finally willing to accept Zara on the throne, then I too can concede. And finally dare to dream of what *I* want."

Her voice sinks nearly to a whisper. "If I'm even capable of dreaming for myself after all these years."

Okay, I gotta admit it.

Even though I'll never trust her again after all the shit she's pulled, I'm feeling a tiny (very tiny) tug of sympathy for my ex-GF. Far as I can tell, her mom tucked her away like a guilty secret to protect Cybelle's shaky claim to the throne, even though Cleo was actually the elder *and* obviously the stronger witch. It doesn't take much imagination to grasp that Cleo's upbringing as a trained killer in the AIB red room wasn't exactly a seaside holiday.

Plus there's the obvious fact that Cleo's AIB mentor has some kinda emotional hold on her that neither one of them seems very comfy with. (Though it doesn't seem to stop Nikolai from using her, he's definitely a Romanov in that regard.)

Now Nikolai pivots to face her directly. "If you refuse to obey my orders, Cleopatra, I can hardly protect you—"

"Somehow," I lean forward to point out, "I don't think she needs your protection anymore, Le Chiffre. Or anyone's. She's already renounced her claim and acknowledged mine on WNN." That impromptu press gaggle was a stroke of brilliance arranged by Senator Mercury, for which I intend to thank Neo's dad when I see him. "Who else is gonna hunt her?"

Now, for some reason, both Nikolai and Cleo give me inscrutable looks.

Then Cleo lowers her cup to the coffee table, gathers her robe at her throat in a graceful hand, and rises smoothly to her feet.

"I'm fully booked for Paris Fashion Week. This is the next place I will go. Then, eh?" One shoulder lifts in an artless shrug. "We'll see."

Maybe my brain is playing tricks on me, because it's been two days since I slept. But it seems to me that, given our collective fatigue, my ex-bestie's Italian accent might be slipping.

One more piece of her disguise falling away.

How many more layers does she still have left to lose?

A mini commotion ensues while Cleo glides elegantly upstairs to dress. Nikolai excuses himself abruptly and leaves without her. A flurry of goodbyes and thank you's need to be said as Jae and Draco usher a tired-looking Mallory (whom I suddenly recall is pregnant, a fact not generally known) out the door for their *domus* and some badly needed sleep.

Ronin coaxes Vasili to shift his extensive beauty ritual from the dining room to the bathroom, then persuades Max to stop lurking and hovering over me long enough to help Ronin set the table for breakfast.

Mordred tromps in grinning from the courtyard pool, dripping from his sunrise swim.

Neo wheedles fresh coffee from our temperamental espresso machine while Ash helps Dez and RT plate the waffles. Zephyr slips out quietly to check on Xhevith, who needs a proper dragonlair established somewhere around here once the dust settles.

Add that task to the already rapidly expanding list of my queenly duties, right after naming our kitten, getting some shuteye, addressing my new subjects in a real press conference and officially announcing my engagement to all eight of my kings, then shopping for wedding rings on the Italian mainland with my warlocks.

Meanwhile, Lucius wraps up a murmured phone call in Hungarian with his aristocratic grandsire on the landline, then hurries over to shift our limp and sleeping kitten from my lap to his nice comfy shoulder and squire me to the table for breakfast.

Pretty drowsy and sluggish (but also hungry) now that the excitement's behind us—I mean, you know, for now—I'm more than happy to reach for Lucius' outstretched hand, relying on his strength to pull me to my feet.

I'm barely standing when Lucius utters an exclamation of shock and falls back.

"What?" Naturally, I jump like a cat and twist around to look behind me, with my heart pounding and my inner dragon (who was snoozing) chirping with annoyance. "I mean, literally, what now? You're white as milk, Lucius."

My headmaster doesn't answer right away. He's staring at me like he's riveted. Or more specifically, he's staring at my hands, poking from the oversized sleeves of Neo's Academy hoodie which I've bundled into for comfort.

I follow his gaze, push back my sleeves, and discover something adorning my own body that's totally new. A stipple of quicksilver pigmentation along the back of my hands and twining around my wrists. The markings look sort of like a henna tattoo, only silver. They're really pretty.

But not something I put there.

"What the actual fuck, Lucius?" I extend both arms so we can all stare.

"Forgive me, my dear," my headmaster says swiftly, while the rest of my guys rush over to cluster protectively around me. Even a startled Vasili zips from the bathroom (levitating) and darts to my side, giving his alpha free rein.

"There's no cause for alarm," Lucius tells the room, clearly chagrined for scaring us.

"I will be the judge of that." Max's nostrils flare and his voice drops to a dragonish rumble. "What threatens my mate!"

"Nothing threatens her." Lucius' own voice trembles with barely suppressed emotion. His face is flushed and his eyes glitter with powerful sentiment. "Those markings on her hands are a well-known sign, a very early one, among wolf shifters. It's just that… with so many mates in the polycule, I simply never dared to hope…"

"Well, don't keep us in suspense, Teach." Alarm replaced by a growing prickle of curiosity, I tilt my head and give my headmaster a wry look. "We're all definitely listening."

"Zara—my dear girl—I can scarcely believe—" Lucius' voice splinters and breaks. He clasps my hands in his string warm grip. His incredulous gaze, shining with joy, clings to mine. "You're pregnant. And at least one of the offspring you carry is mine."

Epilogue
Mallory

Zara's wedding is the celebrity event of the year.

Although I'm always uncomfortable attracting attention to myself, I'm thrilled to be a bridesmaid. And I'm so incredibly happy for my best friend, who's definitely earned her happily ever after.

It just sucks that both my guys have to miss it.

Jae's home in New Orleans, interring the zombie wolf king properly in consecrated ground in St. Louis Cemetery. Draco very emphatically didn't want to leave me. But right now, very clearly, Jae needs him more, so I convinced Draco to go with.

Besides, I'm safe here at Icarus.

Especially with my big brother Ash now living here full-time, getting settled in at Icarus as Potions prof for the fall semester under the new faculty exchange program Zephyr and the Dean set up with the Avalon Academy.

Also, my awful new headmaster at Villa Hadrian has packed his gloomy vintage portmanteau and decamped for summer break. So my *domus* has reverted, if not to the status quo, at least to someplace I can tolerate while I take summer school classes in the Honors track with Mistress Aggie. We've disarmed the mantraps while our headmaster's away, and resumed our time-honored house tradition of hosting unsanctioned keggers in the dungeon.

The royal palace for the witching world is a gloomy centuries-old palazzo that's slowly sinking into the Venetian Sea. No surprise Zara and her guys have chosen to get married in their own *domus* right here on Icarus Island.

Despite the intimate small group setting in the Roman-style courtyard under the blaze of Mediterranean sun in a cloudless summer sky, it's the wedding of the century in the witching world. Every invite is hotly coveted. Today, as the whole world knows, we're celebrating more than Zara's wedding to all eight of her Gemini kings.

Zara and her polycule are not only crowned and mated.

They're pregnant.

"Congratulations again, big brother. For everything." Mindful of the fragile crystal given my notorious clumsiness, I lift my champagne flute to touch Ash's in a careful toast.

We're watching Mordred and Neo delve under the filmy layers of Zara's wedding skirts to slip off her garter, with Neo managing the voluminous layers of silky tulle while Mordred hunts for the garter. Max hovers protectively over all three of them and glares ferociously with his flaming dragon eyes at any guest who dares venture too close, either to Zara's exposed thigh or to Neo's rear while the First Boy's innocently bent over in what I guess some might consider a provocative way.

I notice in passing that Neo is sporting a half-healed mating bite, a thick double puncture just above his starched collar, that looks like it came from Lucius and his wolf.

Watching Ash watch his mates with that soft tender look making his silver eyes glow like stars, I feel my heart getting all floaty and soft and euphoric in my chest.

I'm still getting used to having a brother again. Especially a super protective one like Ash.

"I appreciate it, Freckles," Ash says easily in response to my toast. His eyes never leave his mates, but he slings an arm around my shoulders and gives me a side hug.

I loop an arm around his waist in return. We're both abnormally tall (which is a Seelie tell, if you know it), so hugging him is easy.

"Are you hoping for a boy or a girl?" I ask.

"At least one of each, if I get my druthers. It's too early to know much, but Zara's foresight's getting stronger every day. That's how we know she's carrying triplets, and which of us did the honors."

I nod and smile, because Zara's already confided in me, even though the fathers' identities have yet to be made public. One from Lucius, who's quietly proud and extra tender toward Zara all the time these days. One from Max, who's visibly bursting with alpha dragon satisfaction that's really cute to watch. And one from Vasili, who's gotten incredibly protective and completely spoils Zara with a conveyor belt of gift-wrapped box after gift-wrapped box of ultra-luxe expectant mama presents from Paris.

Ash and I aren't telepaths, because that's not Seelie magic. But Ash doesn't need witchcraft to follow this particular train of thought.

"Yeah, Beautiful's been a real surprise in the baby daddy department." My brother's eyes crease in a whimsical grin. "He's already converted his own bedroom to a nursery, even though we're barely pregnant. And now he's furnishing those digs down to the last pacifier and baby mobile, like, personally. To be honest, I won't be surprised if he starts changing diapers."

"That *is* surprising," I agree, but I can't suppress a little shiver. To me, Vasili Romanov isn't a doting expectant dad, and he definitely isn't my brother-in-law (even if now, legally, he is). He's the terrifying bully who gave every witch and warlock in this Academy nightmares for years until Zara came along and, you know, got him to be a little less terrifying.

Ash takes a swig of his champagne, then shakes his head ruefully. "Funny thing is, he's got six bassinets set up in there. Even though Zara's one hundred percent sure her stork is only bringing one set of triplets."

"Three does seem like plenty," I say cautiously. "Are you disappointed that one isn't yours?"

He scrubs a hand through his spiky pewter hair. "Nah, they'll all be mine anyway. Neo and Ronin and me, we're not shifters, so we don't have breeding kink and mating ruts and all that jazz. And Mordred figures he's sterile, like a lot of krakens. So we can just love 'em all up, no matter who gets our princess pregnant."

My gaze slips past Zara, who's laughing at Mordred's teasing as he works the teal garter down her thigh, to the green-haired rider wearing dragonscale and the Dark Fae crown who's intently watching the proceedings near the bar with a possessive arm wrapped around Ronin's waist. Those two guys look kinda rumpled, and Zephyr looks dangerously lazy with satisfaction, while Ronin has that heavy-lidded, sleepy-eyed look that everyone at this Academy calls his "just fucked" look.

I wonder if those two had a quickie after they tied the knot. But I'm definitely not going to ask.

"What about Zephyr?" I prod, because Ash omitting the name of his first consort *is* kinda glaring. "Doesn't he want a baby?"

"Sure, Sparrow wants one. A biological kid, I mean. Guy needs a genetic heir to be named the next Dark Fae King—or Queen." Ash shrugs his big shoulders. "I figure we'll all just keep fucking."

I blush over the visual (the curse of my ghostly pale redhead complexion) but can't hold back a giggle. "Well, you're obviously doing something right. *The Witching Inquisitor*'s reporting a sharp spike in pregnancies across all the arcane races… as I'm sure you're tracking. So, you know, thanks for saving the witching world."

"Gotta thank Zara for that." Ash gives me his easy grin. "I'm just your average joe who got lucky."

Seeing Ash so happy makes me happy too.

Maybe now we can all be happy.

Maybe.

I watch my brother's broad-shouldered frame, so impressive in the slate tux with violet accents Zara's guys are wearing today. He wends his way through the cheerful throng toward the head table, where Vasili is deigning to accept nibbles of lavender wedding cake from Lucius' patient fingers.

They each welcome Ash in their own way. Lucius casually rises to greet him as an equal and rubs his cheek against my brother's to scent him. I don't think those two are, you know, *doing it*. (Although I'd literally rather die than ask. They're my brother and my teacher.) Anyway, they seem more like faculty colleagues than lovers right now, although that can always change.

Especially in Zara's harem.

Vasili, though… he's a whole other thing.

That serpent looks at my brother with a territorial smolder so intense it makes me blush all over again. His slim hand snakes out to drag Ash into the chair beside him. Then Vasili leans close to murmur something in Ash's ear that turns my brother's face a dull brick-red.

My big brother actually squirms in his chair, which is definitely a first. But he doesn't seem unhappy. I mean, he literally seems the opposite. He shakes his head, then leans his forehead against Vasili's shoulder and laughs softly. Vasili plants a hand high on Ash's thigh in casual possession, then delicately accepts another bite of cake from Lucius.

Ash is happy.

He's really happy.

And, bizarrely, his new relationship with the Academy bully is one of the reasons for his happiness, along with Zara and Zephyr and Neo. Ash is even getting flirty with Ronin.

But then, everyone gets flirty with Ronin.

I sip a little more of my sparkling grape juice, savor the sweet bubbles foaming over my palate, and scan the well-dressed crowd dancing in the courtyard next to the turquoise oval of the pool. Mordred's already wandered over barefoot to stick his webbed feet in the water, dimples flashing as he coaxes a few of the more adventurous guests into the shallow end.

He really does look like Jason Momoa in a tux (only pan), which makes him hard for most of the guests to resist.

The band is set up on a stage above the waterfall. The tunes are getting louder as the afternoon winds toward twilight. For some reason, Zephyr has instructed them to play only K-pop. (Plus he continually refers to them as minstrels.) In the pool beneath, bright green flashes across the shimmery surface as Zephyr's dragon Xhevith overflies the party in a lazy spiral.

Xhev is providing security for the wedding. You know, just in case.

But there haven't been any incidents, except for all the hordes of paparazzi he's scared away.

Needless to say, Messalina isn't here. The former Aquarius queen has abdicated with the Arcane Senate's encouragement, vacated the royal palazzo in Venice, and used her pension to buy another yacht.

Nikolai Romanov is here on sufferance, as father of the groom, lurking around the periphery where he can watch and listen without really being noticed.

Theo Mercury was welcomed more warmly, since he's officially one of Zara's allies. Now the senator is gladhanding and working the crowd like the master politician he is.

Even Mick Gemini, Zara's casino boss dad, has managed to suck up enough to Zara to score an invite. But Zara said a hard no when he offered to give her away at the altar.

To no one's surprise, Cleo Ferrari is missing in action.

Ever since Paris Fashion Week (when she was literally on the cover of every couture magazine, looking annoyingly perfect), Cleo's gone deep.

No one's heard from her, not even a rumor, ever since. Even the considerable resources of the Mars clan mafia, Draco's guys, can't find her.

Draco says she's off somewhere licking her wounds and we haven't seen the last of her.

With the garter ritual successfully complete, Zara eventually hurries over to find me. My best friend (now sister-in-law) is absolutely radiant. Glowing with happiness in a sparkly strapless wedding dress that shows off her suntan and the pretty silver pigmentation on her forearms, skirts frothing around her feet in a purple so pale it's nearly cream, accessorized with a sash in her signature teal tied around her still-tiny waist to emphasize her curves. Instead of a traditional tiara, she has the witching world crown (returned by Nikolai when Cleo conceded) perched on the teal curls swept high on her head. Her platinum lightning bolt earrings flash in her ears.

"Come on, Mal! I'm gonna do the bouquet toss before we vamoose for the wedding night. You don't wanna miss it, believe me." Flushed and gorgeous in the soft pastel cosmetics she's chosen for today, Zara flashes me a playful grin and beckons me to follow.

The sparkly blue topaz ring her guys gave her, surrounded by a rainbow of eight colorful stones, glitters and winks in the sunlight. She loves that ring and told me each guy picked his own stone. Ash's pick for her was moonstone.

Anyway.

Zara's being *so* playful right now that I really wonder if her Valyrian foresight is acting up again.

While my best friend rushes off to take her assigned place, I hurry to join Dez and Racetrack, my fellow bridesmaids, clustered in the courtyard under the second-floor balcony. Even though RT is rocking a deep purple tux and combat boots with her buzzcut instead of the lavender frocks and updos that Dez and I are wearing, and even though my fiery copper curls are frizzing and flying everywhere in the summer heat as usual, I think the three of us look pretty okay.

Zara appears on her second-floor bedroom balcony, whirls around dramatically so she's facing away from us, then tosses the massive bouquet of cream and violet roses energetically over her shoulder. Streaming teal ribbons and bedizened with swan feathers (an embellishment chosen by Vasili), the bouquet sails majestically through the air.

Very clearly, it's headed nowhere near me.

For no logical reason, because I'm not planning to get married anytime soon while I'm still a student, my chest tightens with a stab of disappointment.

Then the bouquet veers into a sharp ninety-degree turn, like it just cornered on rails—and lands right in my startled arms.

Clutching the fragrant bouquet to my chest and breathing in the scent of roses while the feathers tickle my cheeks, I blink around me at the circle of smiling faces and join in the fun with a surprised laugh of my own.

But I know telekinesis when I see it. I just don't know who—

"Enjoy your flowers, McSnicker," someone murmurs in my ear. "They suit you."

I spin around in shock to find Vasili looming over me. I'm the tallest girl in my class, but somehow he manages to be taller.

Even when, like today, he's not wearing heels.

Unlike the rest of the guys, V's narrow tux is a pale mauve, accessorized with a sparkly bow tie in Zara's teal. Also unlike the rest of the guys, he's wearing as much makeup as Zara, and wearing it really well.

I happen to know he and Zara shared a spa day before the main event.

The Academy's worst bully, to my complete amazement, is smiling. He isn't even sneering. It's an actual smile. I can see the tips of the wicked fangs he can't retract, but almost never shows, pressing into his glossy lower lip. I figure he's having the wedding day he probably never dreamed he'd get. That horrible snake, who hurt everyone around him (as Zara gently explained to me) because he was secretly hurting inside so much himself…

He actually looks…

Happy.

In fact, he's acting so nice and so normal (for once) that I screw up my courage to ask him an actual question. Because, as everyone knows, Vasili Romanov is the strongest telekinetic on this island.

I gesture awkwardly with the flowers. "So, Vasili, um, did you by any chance…?"

"Well, whoever else would have done it, darling?" One perfectly painted eyelid dips in a sly wink. "Zara seems certain you're the perfect choice."

You wanna read more about Zara's loyal bestie Mallory McSnicker and her hot bi warlock menage?

Read their spicy story now in *Virgo Queen: A Dark Witch Academy Paranormal Romance Standalone*

(Keep scrolling down for a spicy sneak peek at the first chapter of Virgo Queen.)

THANK YOU, BOOK WITCH!

OMG, witches! This series has been one helluva wild ride to write. I can't even believe I've finished it. I hope you loved Zara & her hot bi harem of sword-crossing warlocks as much as I do. To help other readers like you discover this intimate, inclusive, enchanted secret world where every sword crosses and love is love (because we all really need that right now), pretty please post a review below. You don't have to write a lot! Even a few words makes a big difference. TYIA!

Review *Gemini Hunted* on Amazon here.
Review *Gemini Hunted* on Goodreads here.
Review *Gemini Hunted* on BookBub here.

* * *

To read the epic bonus wedding night epilogue with Zara and her sword-crossing warlocks that's not in the published book, sign up for my newsletter at http://www.LauraNavarreSciFi.com.

For more X-rated bonus content you can't find anywhere else (including the scoop on those extra bassinets, your questions about Max and V's genderqueer dragon answered, and more!) follow me in the Witching World—my enchanted secret circle online reader community—https://reamstories.com/witchingworld.

Virgo Queen:

A Dark Witch Academy Paranormal Romance Standalone
by Laura Navarre

Chapter One
Mallory

I must literally be the last remaining virgin in the whole Icarus Academy.

The reason I say this is because I've already blundered into two couples—and now a throuple—feverishly making out in the shadows of the dormitory stairs in my residential college.

Wow.

That's… actually happening. Two guys and a girl.

Like an actual menage.

They're blocking the stairs and they're distracting. But I just keep going and mosey right on past. I've got someplace I need to be tonight.

"Sorry, guys. Don't mind me," I mumble as I edge around the amorous throuple.

"Sod off, McSnicker. We're busy here." One guy surfaces from that triple sex sandwich barely long enough to lob a discarded bra (regulation Academy uniform, meaning virginal white lace) in my general direction.

When I duck to avoid getting hit in the face by flying lingerie, I almost take a nosedive down the stairs.

"Geez Louise," I grumble, teetering on the edge of disaster on my too-long legs in my borrowed platform heels. "Already own plenty of those, thanks. I have a whole drawer full upstairs."

Not that anyone notices what I'm wearing.

Not even for my special night.

My classmates have already returned to their three-way.

Invisibility is an extinct magical trait in all four arcane races (plus the two hidden species the others don't know about) that comprise the witching world. Magical traits are genetic, and therefore inherited, like we learn in Science of Witchcraft class our freshman year here at the witch academy.

But I don't need any special DNA to slip past unnoticed in this Academy.

Totally unacknowledged in any way after the whole bra incident, I steady my wobbly steps, avert my eyes politely—like the good girl I am—and tiptoe past the half-naked threesome who are now panting and groping (they're a girl from my dorm and two guys from our rival college I barely know). There's barely room to squeeze past on the twisty haunted house staircase that plunges from the student dorm in Villa Hadrian— that's the name of our residential college—down to the spooky basement.

Somehow, I make it work. I have to.

In typical Mallory McSnicker fashion, I'm already late.

Late to my own birthday bash.

Given my general McSnicker clumsiness (which is one inherited trait I could've done without), it's definitely not a smart idea to hurry down these corkscrew stairs in the dark. The ancient treads are worn with age and barely lit by the occasional rusted branch of candelabra sticking out from the shredded ruin of the blood red Victorian-era *True Blood* Fangtasia wallpaper.

But I hurry anyway.

It's easier to camouflage the fact that I'm the tallest, skinniest girl in the whole school when I'm wearing the plaid skirt and blazer and saddle shoes stipulated in the Academy Codex. Tonight I'm a lot more conspicuous (at least in theory) teetering along in these glittery platform heels and a sparkly silver party dress that barely hits mid-thigh on my giraffe-like legs.

In this getup, I'll be lucky if I don't break a leg before I even manage to show for my own birthday bash. Despite the fact that I'm tempting fate, I rest a hand on the wall for stability—because everything in this Academy is ancient, and the banister rotted away decades ago—and pick up my pace till I'm trotting (unsteadily) down the stairs.

The metallic grind of axe-murder metal, mingled with a snarl of youthful voices and an occasional girly squeal, floats up from the dark cavern of the dorm basement.

Firelight flickers from the battered oil drums we use for illumination down there. Facets of light dance against the ruined wallpaper and make my dress sparkle like fairy dust in the darkness.

I pause to let myself savor the magic of this moment.

Just for a sec.

I'm no wicked telepath like my classmate Ronin Pendragon, I'm pretty much a nonentity in the magical superpowers department. But the whole school's excitement pulses from the basement like a beating heart. We're not supposed to be partying down there, in the unsafe and basically condemned medieval dungeon basement—which is also rumored to be haunted.

Not on a school night.

Especially right before midterms.

But my dorm mates will seize any excuse for a party, and I'm First Girl on the Dean's List. The resident, apple-polishing good girl.

In other words, a faculty favorite.

That's why my classmates figured Mistress Agrippina (our rule-enforcing headmistress) would turn a blind eye.

I've never had a real birthday party before. My kind doesn't celebrate them. So it feels really magical to be getting one now. Even if my birthday's just an excuse for an unsanctioned party, I'm allowed to let myself enjoy it.

I'll soak up every magical second of this once-in-a-lifetime experience.

Caught up in the floaty euphoria of sex pheromones and anticipation wafting up the stairs, I descend like I'm dreaming.

As I wobble my way down in my borrowed heels, the unruly cloud of carroty curls I can never seem to tame rises from my bare shoulders and starts to frizz and float in the psychic charge I'm generating.

Tonight's the night, McSnicker, I tell myself like a mantra, trying in vain to tame my rebellious curls. *It's your twentieth birthday. It's a real party. You're at least gonna get a real kiss.*

Because I refuse to count as real kisses those sloppy, totally underwhelming fumbles in the broom closet with Cletus, my equally awkward third cousin, when we were both a pimply fourteen.

All that distraction and commotion below, plus the reek of cheap beer and salsa, *and* the need to concentrate on my rickety footing on these stairs, are all reasons why my typically acute secret senses fail me tonight.

Right when I need them most.

That's when I blunder around the bend like the same complete social disaster I always am—

And walk straight into the two guys I've been crushing on for literally my *entire* sophomore year. Who are, themselves, making out on the stairs.

With each other.

I practically run into Draco Mars' broad back before I pull up short with a thunderous gasp. My heart jams up against my lungs and hammers so hard it practically makes the whole house vibrate. Dizzy with the dark spice of Mogadon pheromones flooding the air and the adrenaline rush of my own endorphins, I grope blindly toward the wall for balance.

Draco's Icelandic and he's a big guy, like the tallest guy at Icarus (but his colossal build is only one of the reasons I'm crushing). However, I'm currently standing above him on the stairs. That vantage gives me a total view, past his pale blond head and those muscled shoulders encased in a worn black tee that looks soft as suede, of my *other* crush.

Jean-Emilien Labête, the Cajun, who goes by Jae.

The werewolf.

(Which I mean literally, because shifter.)

Ohmygosh.

I can't even believe what I'm seeing.

Jae's, like, going down on Draco. Right here on the school stairs!

No one else in the whole Academy even knows those two are together. Clearly, they've been keeping their whole thing secret.

But I've been watching these two particular guys like a creeper all semester, and it's hard to hide stuff from someone like me, so I kinda guessed.

Due to the angle, I can't see much past Draco's powerful frame, beyond his big hands threaded through the mass of dreadlocks and beads and juju Jae likes to twist into his long black hair. I do have a direct view of Jae's hungry hands, which are cupping Draco's always impressive ass (an ass that's even more impressive now, encased in black leather, than when he's wearing his Academy uni). Jae's fingers are kneading and his curvy black claws are out, sharp and deadly as box cutters. Which totally gives me a shiver that runs all the way down my spine to my tailbone.

Underneath my sparkly dress and virginal panties, a sudden flood of tingly heat almost makes me moan.

I suck in a lungful of air and reel under a head-spinning hit of juniper and bergamot—that's Draco, he's part of the Mogadon race, so it's a genetic trait that he scents. Underneath that truckload of come-get-me biochemicals he's pumping out, my enhanced senses pick up the dark green aroma of patchouli and moss and fertile New Orleans soil. The shifters scent too, and that verdant spice is drifting from Jae's sleek braids and amber skin.

Normal humans—even normal witches—wouldn't hear a thing under the staccato grind of death metal rising from the basement.

But I'm not normal.

So I can hear Jae's wolf whining, feral with need, all low in his throat, as he… wow… literally gives Draco a blow job. Right here on our dormitory stairs.

Now this, I gotta see.

I mean, it *is* my birthday, remember? I don't expect any actual presents, but this is the exact gift I want.

I'm standing on tiptoe and teetering in my platform heels, breathless with wonder and straining like anything to see over Draco Mars' shoulder, when the Icelander's raspy voice rubs against my heightened senses like sandpaper.

"You just watching, First Girl, or you wanna join?"

Heat races into my cheeks on a horrified gasp. I practically burst into flames on the spot. I literally wish I could melt and just sink through the stairs.

I'm, like, a peeping Tom. A peeping Thomasina.

I'm busted.

Geez Louise. Draco hasn't even turned his sexy head. But he's a really strong warlock, so clearly he senses I'm here.

With a soft curse, Jae's head thrusts into view next to Draco's leather-clad hip. The Cajun's languid eyes, rimmed in black liner, flame like pools of golden honey.

"Happy birthday, *chere*." Jae pauses—for me to react, I guess—but that's not happening. His lush mouth curls in a lazy grin. "Ah, cat got your tongue, *oui*?"

Come on, McSnicker. Say something. You can do this. I swallow hard, suck in my breath, and open my mouth.

But now Draco is turning. He's *turning*, which (ohmygosh!) brings his fully erect dick—all flushed and shiny with Jae's saliva—right into my line of sight.

That's the first dick I've ever seen—as in, literally the first one—except the full frontal in that vintage art flick *A Room With A View*, which wasn't even sexual.

And Draco Mars… he's… wow.

Just wow.

His thick shaft, jutting straight out between corded thighs in a pale thatch of pubic hair, under the ripply flex of six-pack abs and the slashing vee of his Adonis belt, he's, like, *monumental*.

He's so girthy and so long I can't even imagine how Jae's managing to fit that much of Draco in his mouth.

Yep. Speech is officially beyond me.

My face flames hotter, all the way to my hairline, which paired with my flaming hair probably makes me look like a tomato on stilts.

Great.

So I literally do the only thing I can think of. I drag my fascinated stare away from the combustible vision of Draco's massive boner that's guaranteed to be blazoned on my brain forever. Then I bolt past those two, with their sexy smirks and their knowing eyes, for the public refuge of the party in the basement.

Which—between my borrowed footwear, my flustered mortification, and my general lack of coordination—really isn't a smart move. Even for a smarty-pants like me.

Because of course I miss my footing on these twisty ancient stairs.

My arms windmill for balance, but there's nothing to grab. The jagged tunnel of the staircase, sharp with stony angles that can shatter skulls and break bones, opens under my desperate feet.

With a startled yelp and a spurt of terror, I fall.

Read the rest of this spicy story now in *Virgo Queen: A Dark Witch Academy Paranormal Romance Standalone*

From casual outsider to exclusive insider, enter the intimate and immersive world of my magical reader community by joining my inner circle (my newsletter!) here.

http://www.lauranavarrescifi.com/

For instant access to exclusive bonus content from this series too spicy to publish anywhere else, plus early access to the latest spicy *Dark Witch Academy* why choose story months before the rest of the world, **follow me free or join the Common Magics 101 cohort in the Witching World, my bewitching secret reader world, on Ream** below.

https://reamstories.com/witchingworld

Acknowledgments

This series would never have seen the light of day without the invaluable insights and constant support of my wise editor and brilliant career coach *Angela James* and my fellow authors in the *Success Alliance*; my one-and-only alpha reader, proofreader, co-owner of Ascendant Press, and devoted cosmic mate *Steven*; my exceptional formatter, uploader, and hand-holder *Judi Fennell* of Formatting4U; as well as my ever-diligent and faithful PA *Clare Harrison*, talented cover artist *Kim Killion*, ever-patient webmistress *Rochelle Parry* at Megabite, encouraging ad coach *Scarlett Moss* at Best Page Forward, my enthusiastic beta readers *Kara* and *Taylor*—and all you lovely readers in the Witching World and everywhere who have read and loved this series and these characters! Thanks also to *Traci Lovelot* for inspiring me to write PNR academy why-choose in the first place. If not for her, I would never have written *Gemini Queen*.

Here's a special shoutout to my secret circle of elite insiders in **the Witching World**, my magical secret online reader community on Ream, where I offer original warlock artwork, character secrets you won't find in the books, exclusive bonus content too spicy to publish anywhere else, first access to upcoming Witching World audiobooks and ebooks before anyone else so you never have to wait for the next book, and a curated online book club for readers who love spicy paranormal and omegaverse why-choose with sword-crossing in the harem, but who struggle to find the books and the reading time:

Juicy Juniors (Lucius' Crypt Inaugural Cohort)

Nikki	Lilly	Angie	Karen	Lyssa	Amanda
George	Renate	Christine	Christy	Keri	Melissa
Serena	Rachel	Jenna	Brittany	Cheryl	Neo

Spicy Sophomores (Summer '25 Zara's Belfry Secret Book Club/Avalon Portal Cohort)

Stephanie	Amanda	Red Tigergirl	Primmy	Teresa	Natalie
Barbara	Rachel	Kristy	Katrin	Serafina	Lisa
Melly	Mali	Ronin	Mallory	Mary Elizabeth	

Flirty Freshmen (Summer '25 Common Magics 101 Cohort)

Laura	Aurora	CelticKnotty	Gnome	RSS	Christy
Emily	Alex	Anita	Kay Sarah	Mystique	Ellen
Jenn	EP	MendyLady	Maekayelee	Christina	Juliet
Sheila	Rachel	Jessie	Amarie	Nadia	Katelyn
Maxim	Zara				

About the Author

Bestselling author Laura Navarre (she/her) whisks you away from your unmagical day with extra spicy, extra shifty, wild & witchy why-choose romance starring hot bi heroes and the badass witches who love them. A long time ago in a galaxy far away, Laura wrote dark MF romantasy for Harlequin. Now, with twenty spicy stories released worldwide, this Washington, DC-based nomad writes queer-friendly paranormal adult academy why-choose romance that'll set your schoolgirl skirt on fire.

Laura's a cat lover, globetrotter, wine addict, and president of Ascendant Press. When she isn't conjuring witchy worlds, she's a professional diplomat with a background in weapons of mass destruction. On Ream, Laura creates the Witching World—an intimate, immersive, inclusive reader community that whisks you through the magical wards that hide the Icarus Academy from the average reader to inhabit the sexy secret world of Zara Gemini and her sword-crossing warlocks. Get swept away from your day-to-day and follow Laura free on Ream (just hit the purple follow button!) at https://reamstories.com/witchingworld.

Read more from Laura Navarre here!

http://www.lauranavarrescifi.com/